Julie Cohen wrote her first novel aged eleven. As a teenager growing up in Maine, she spent all her spare time in her local library, so it seemed natural that she would study English at university. After earning a summa cum laude degree with honours from Brown University, where she also drew a weekly cartoon for the *Brown Daily Herald*, Julie spent a year abroad and fell in love with the UK. She stayed on, and a postgraduate degree in English Literature, at the University of Reading, was followed by a career teaching English at secondary level. She now writes full time and lives with her husband, a guitar tech for rock bands, and their son in Berkshire.

THE SUMMER OF LIVING DANGEROUSLY

Alice Woodstock has been running away. Well, not literally. She spends most of her time glued to her desk, writing about grommets and model aeroplanes. Alice is avoiding the real world because she's desperate to forget someone from her past. So when she's commissioned to write about life in stately home Eversley Hall, she jumps at the chance to escape into Regency England — even if she must swap her comfy T-shirt for an itchy corset. Perhaps she'll meet her own Mr Darcy . . . But when her past resurfaces in the shape of Leo Allingham, Alice is brought down to earth with a bump. Reckless, unpredictable Leo reminds Alice of the painful price of following her heart. And the new Alice doesn't live dangerously. Or does she?

Books by Julie Cohen
Published by The House of Ulverscroft:

SPIRIT WILLING, FLESH WEAK

JULIE COHEN

THE SUMMER
OF LIVING
DANGEROUSLY

Complete and Unabridged

CHARNWOOD
Leicester

First published in Great Britain in 2011 by
Headline Review
an imprint of
Headline Publishing Group
London

First Charnwood Edition
published 2012
by arrangement with
Headline Publishing Group
An Hachette UK Company
London

British Library CIP Data

Cohen, Julie, *1970 –*
  The summer of living dangerously.
  1. Love stories.
  2. Large type books.
  I. Title
  823.9′2–dc23

  ISBN 978–1–4448–1261–9

Published by
F. A. Thorpe (Publishing)
Anstey, Leicestershire

Set by Words & Graphics Ltd.
Anstey, Leicestershire
Printed and bound in Great Britain by
T. J. International Ltd., Padstow, Cornwall

This book is printed on acid-free paper

For my son.

Incredible Advances

Incredible advances have been made in composite grommet technology in the past six months; for example, chemists in Luton's Moreosa Institute have formulated something incredibly, mind-shatteringly boring.

I frowned at the words I'd typed on the computer screen. Oh no. I was doing it again. I thought I'd got past that stage.

Delete, delete, delete. I stretched back in my worn office chair and a lock of hair fell into my eyes. Without taking my eyes from the screen, I reached for a pencil, wrapped my hair around it, and pushed it into the hair at the back of my head with all the other pencils.

This was not an efficient way of working. I was deleting more words than I was writing, and the sodding article was due tomorrow. I put my sock-clad feet on the desk next to my keyboard and gave myself The Lecture. Again.

'This is not boring, Alice Woodstock. Rubber grommet construction is an exciting and fast-moving field, and your readers are absolutely gagging for the latest information on it. Also, you are getting paid to write about it. So get to work, woman.'

My eyes wandered to the brand-new paperback on my bedside table. It was glossy and untouched. Maybe I needed a break. Just for five minutes. Honestly for five minutes this time, not like the break I'd taken yesterday, when I'd picked up the other brand-new paperback I'd bought at the weekend and read straight through it all afternoon until I'd finished it at two o'clock this morning.

I shook my head and refocused on the computer. No breaks. I could do this. I was a professional technical journalist. I was good at my job, or at least I was good enough to make a semi-living at it, in between giving myself lectures about how I really was excited about it.

* * *

. . . *chemists in Luton's Moreosa Institute have formulated a new way of bonding thermoplastic elastomers, creating a super-strong compound that can withstand temperatures up to 200 degrees Celsius. 'It's the culmination of months of research,' said Professor Julius Angleby, 'and can you imagine what I'd be like to sit next to at a dinner party? Blah, blah, blah about elastomers all night long while you tried to resist falling asleep into your soup and getting cream of asparagus all over the side of your face.'*

* * *

Dammit.

I jumped out of my chair, which creaked in relief. I wasn't going to touch that paperback yet, not till I finished this article, but I could stretch to a cup of tea. Good old-fashioned tannin and caffeine would focus my mind properly on grommets.

I worked up in the attic of the house, in one of two rooms that my best friend Liv had converted especially. She'd even lined the walls with bookcases for me, in direct contravention of her own minimalist taste. It was an ideal place to work: quiet and private, linked to the first-floor landing by a narrow flight of steps. Halfway down the main staircase, I spotted the small pile of post inside the front door, and my heart leaped.

Not that I was expecting anything much: copies of newsletters and magazines I'd written for, maybe a cheque if I was lucky. But when you work from home by yourself, the daily post is a major event. As is the trip outside to the recycling bin to get rid of most of it. I rushed down the rest of the stairs and scooped it up.

Bah. It wasn't even the post. It was two pizza fliers, one takeaway curry menu, and an advert for a local carpet cleaner. And another glossy leaflet, this one with a photograph at the top of a large house made of gold-coloured stone.

The house looked familiar; it carried instant memories of sunshine and ice cream, the scent of fresh grass. *The Regency Summer at Eversley Hall,* said the headline. I dropped the ads on the floor by the door, and turned over the leaflet as I walked to the kitchen to turn on the kettle.

I was reading it for the third time when Liv came in. She was wearing a sleeveless cream linen shift, as immaculate as her glossy dark hair, and smelled of blossoms. She had a stack of magazines under her arm.

'Is it six o'clock already?' I said.

'Six thirty. It's gorgeous outside. It's feeling like summer already. I hope the weather holds till the weekend. You should get some fresh air.'

'Maybe in a bit,' I said vaguely. 'Did you see this? They're opening Eversley Hall to the public.'

'The Palladian mansion outside of town?' She dumped the magazines on the glass kitchen table.

'They're having a Regency summer,' I said. 'They've restored the house to be just like it was in 1814 and they've got people dressed up in historical costume pretending to live there.'

'That's fascinating.' Liv took down a glass and filled it with water. 'Have you got a lot of work done today?'

'Ugh, I'm bored up to here with thermoplastic elastomers.'

'Take a walk, it'll get your thoughts going. Or do you want to come for a drink? I'm meeting Yann.'

I shook my head. 'I've got to get back to work — I'm just having a tea break. Don't you think that's cool though, the whole 1814 thing? It would be like stepping into a novel. Do you remember all those Regency romances we used to read when we were in school?'

'*You* used to read them, you mean. I think I managed about half of one.'

'All those gorgeous dresses. And the whole day, talking like something out of Jane Austen.'

'You should go. It'll be good for you to get out

4

more, especially once I'm gone.'

'Mm.' I sat on a kitchen chair and picked up the top magazine from the stack she'd put on the table. 'I thought you only read architecture journals?'

'The girls at work gave me some gossip mags for the plane.'

I flipped through the other magazines. '*Bride Monthly* — isn't it a bit late for that? Your wedding's next week.'

'Actually, it's this week.'

'What? This Saturday, really?'

'This *Sunday*, Alice.'

'Oh yeah, this Sunday, I knew that. I'm sorry. It's this working from home thing. One day tends to blend into another — full of grommets and glue.' I opened *Hot! Hot!* and flipped past the pages of gossip to the fashion feature. 'Are ankle socks really in? For June?'

'If you're fed up with grommets and glue, maybe you should look at writing something else.'

'Like what?'

'Well — that, for example.' She nodded at the magazine.

'You're joking. I don't know the first thing about fashion. Look at me.' I pushed back my chair from the table so she could see my non-outfit: baggy leggings, faded T-shirt and slippers that had seen better days.

'You've got good taste. You helped me pick out my wedding dress, and your bridesmaid dress.'

'I think you'll find that what I actually did, Liv, was stand there while you picked them out, and told you that *you* had good taste, which you do.'

'You used to wear a lot of fashionable things, when you were . . . before.'

I grunted. 'Used to.'

'Well — it's not like you don't have an interest.'

'And look at my hair. It's a bird's nest. How many pencils have I got in it today?'

There was a pause as she counted. 'Seven.'

'See? I'm not fit to write for a trendy magazine. I'm so out of trend they would probably self-combust if I even sent them a proposal. Now, if a glossy magazine wanted a piece about *Regency* fashion — that I could get into.' I picked up the leaflet again. There was a photo of a woman on the back, her blonde hair piled up on top of her head with ringlets falling around her face. She wore a white and gold gown and she looked as if she was in the middle of arranging a vase of flowers. 'Wouldn't it be cool to dress up like that for a whole summer? And pretend you were in a book? Just look at her waist.'

I had to give Liv some credit; the sigh she heaved was so slight as to be nearly undetectable. She said patiently, 'Why don't you pitch an article about Eversley Hall, then? To one of the women's glossies?'

'I couldn't do that.'

'Why not? You spend all your time slumping around the house, Alice, and if you're not enjoying what you're writing about, there's no point to it. I'm leaving after next week, and you'll be here all alone, and I — '

I looked up sharply. *Don't say it.*

6

'And I'm worried.'

I didn't have to ask why she was worried. Next week — no, *this* week — my best friend in the world was going to get married to a Kiwi and then immediately move to New Zealand with him to start work on an ecologically sound, aesthetically perfect massive housing project, leaving me to rattle around in the house we'd shared for two years. I was chuffed to bits for her, of course. On the other hand, I was going to be here alone in the house, and it wasn't even mine. It was hers, inherited from her father.

I'd offered to move when she left, but she'd refused, saying the house was as much mine as hers, and that since she wasn't planning on selling it, she'd much rather I stayed than some random tenant. 'And besides,' she'd said, 'I practically lived in your family's house growing up, so it's my turn to pay you back.'

No, she wasn't worried about the house. She was worried about me.

If you're worried, don't go! Get married and stay here! But I couldn't ask her to do that.

'There's no need,' I said quickly. 'I'm fine. I'm always fine. I'll be fine. Also, I'll get myself a pair of ankle socks and I'll be instantly trendy. You won't even recognise me when you come back for a visit.'

'That's not what I meant,' she started, but I had already picked up the *Hot! Hot!* magazine and was flipping through the pages again.

'Actually, Liv,' I said. 'You might be on to something. Look, there's an article here about how people are spending the summer in the UK to save money. Maybe I should send in a proposal about Eversley Hall.'

'You definitely should.'

'I mean, what have I got to lose? Except for more time writing about bits that make up photocopiers and aeroplane engines.'

'Exactly.'

'It'll be a great leap forward for me. A whole new career.'

'You know I'm always right.'

I smiled. It was a catchphrase from our childhood, when Liv was the sensible one and I was the dreamer. I realised I hadn't made myself that cup of tea, so I got up, put a bag into a mug and poured water from the kettle over it. The rest of the kitchen, like most of the house, was shiny and modern, but my mug was old, chipped, and stained with tannin. 'Tea?' I asked Liv.

'No thanks,' Liv said from behind me. 'Anyway, you haven't answered my question.'

'What question? You haven't asked me one.'

'Didn't I? All right, I'll ask it now. Are you okay with my getting married, Alice?'

'What? Of course I am. Why wouldn't I be?'

'It's only that whenever I mention it, you either avoid the subject or make a flippant remark.'

'Do I?' I began mashing my tea bag against the side of the mug to squeeze every little bit of brown out of it.

'I know you're going to be lonely after we've gone. But maybe it'll be good for you. You'll have to get out more.'

'I don't know about that,' I said, mashing. 'If I'm going to have a great new career writing for

8

the glossies I'll probably be up in the attic work-ing more than ever.' I looked over at her. My best friend, who was going to leave me. I loved that look of concern in her eyes, but I hated it, too.

'I'm okay with your getting married,' I told her. 'I'm more than okay. You and Yann are perfect together. And I think it's great that you're going to be so happy.'

She nodded, her hair swinging.

'So you're going to send a query to *Hot! Hot!* magazine?' she asked.

'Yes. I definitely am.'

'And Eversley Hall?'

'Yes,' I said. 'Incredible advances will be made.'

★ ★ ★

There's something about a man in tight breeches and a neckcloth tied up to his chin.

He stood before me and above me, gazing off into the distance. His left hand rested lightly on the gleaming desk beside him and his right hand held a book, as if he had been interrupted whilst reading. His boots shone and not a single golden hair on his head was out of place. The expression on his handsome face was haughty and yet kind, the blue eyes warm and the mouth slightly smiling. A spaniel panted at his feet.

'Wish me luck,' I said to him.

He didn't reply, because he was a painting, eight feet high and made up of glossy oils, framed in gilt and hanging on the silk wallpaper at Eversley Hall.

I still wasn't exactly sure what I was doing

9

here, wearing one of Liv's skirts and a pair of long-neglected heels, with my heart beating like crazy. But I knew who the man in the painting was. I'd read too many novels not to know. He was a hero. He was well-bred and in possession of a handsome fortune. He could ride any horse you gave him, he could dance any dance in fashion, he was kind to servants and dependants. He was honourable and marriageable, and though Jane Austen and Georgette Heyer didn't mention this part I knew that if he got you into bed, he'd shag you senseless.

I could write about that, maybe. It seemed like *Hot! Hot!* would like a sexy reference or two, and that was probably the closest I was going to come to it in a house where they were all pretending it was the early nineteenth century. I was still reeling from the fact that the magazine had been interested, to tell the truth. I'd had an email back from Edie, the Features Editor, within half an hour of sending mine; and then I hadn't had any choice but to get on the phone and arrange a meeting at Eversley Hall.

'Miss Woodstock?'

I started and turned. And my mouth dropped open, because standing in front of me, there on the other side of a velvet rope, was the man from the painting.

He had golden hair, and blue eyes, and broad shoulders and half a smile. He wasn't eight feet tall and made of oils, and he was wearing a dark modern suit with a striped shirt and a deep blue tie. But it was him. He was real. I looked at the painting, and then I looked back at the man. The only thing that was missing was the spaniel.

'I was . . . er . . . sorry. I was talking to the painting,' I said.

His smile widened, and he stepped over the rope and extended his hand. 'James Fitzwilliam,' he said. His voice was hearty and deep. 'You're Alice Woodstock?'

'Yes, I am.' I gave up my hand to his, which was large and warm and firm. 'Sorry, I'm a little bit startled. You look a lot like that painting.'

He nodded. 'Yes, so I'm told. That's my ancestor, who was also called James Fitzwilliam. He was the first member of my family to own the house.'

'Do you own the house?'

'Yes. I'm also in charge of the re-enactment project, which is why although you made an appointment with Quentin, our Visitor Services Manager, you're getting me instead.'

'That's — that's perfectly fine.' More than fine. I tried to remember the last time I had met such a good-looking man, and I couldn't. It wasn't the sort of thing that happened to you in my job. Keith the postman was pleasant enough, but he wasn't in James Fitzwilliam's league.

'Have you been to Eversley Hall before?'

'I've been in the garden once. There was a fête here when I was a little girl.'

'My grandmother's fêtes. I remember them. She was very involved with charities, until she became unwell. What do you think of the house?'

I looked around again. The room was vast, with trompe l'oeil columns set at intervals on the stone-coloured walls. A crystal chandelier sparkled from a ceiling gilded with plasterwork scrolls and flowers, reflecting the light from enormous velvet-curtained windows. The original James Fitzwilliam gazed from the east wall, in the company of other painted figures, gods and goddesses and biblical heroes. The air smelled of flowers and polish, dust and time. 'It's like stepping back two hundred years,' I said.

James Fitzwilliam's full smile was nearly blinding. It was as if I'd given him a personal compliment. 'That's exactly the effect we're trying for,' he said. 'Everything you see here is a restored original, or it's been recreated to match precisely what would have been here in 1814. Fortunately, the house was pretty well documented at the time, and my family never throw anything away. But the level of detail is incredible. This paint on the walls, for example, is made by a specialist manufacturer in Chelsea who did a chemical analysis of the original.' He caught himself. 'Sorry. I can get quite boring about it, and you're not here about paint. Please, come through to my office.'

He stepped back over the velvet rope, and I did too, feeling somehow illicit. I followed him to a small door set flush in the wall, to blend in. 'It's for the servants,' he explained, and pushed it open. It led to a whitewashed corridor ending in a tightly twisting staircase, going up. James Fitzwilliam seemed very large in the narrow space, his head nearly brushing the ceiling as we walked. Together we emerged onto another corridor, where he opened a plain wooden door and ushered me into a small room with bare white walls and the floor carpeted in grey polyester. A laptop and a desktop computer perched amongst stacks of paper on the beech-effect desk; a large framed photograph faced away from me. 'Have a seat, Miss Woodstock,' he said, gesturing to a standard-issue chair as he went behind the desk.

'Call me Alice,' I said as I sat. 'This is quite a culture shock.'

'Yes, well, we had to stash the computers somewhere. So, Alice, you're interested in writing about Eversley Hall for *Hot! Hot!* magazine.'

Somehow, the cheap furniture and the piles of paperwork didn't make James Fitzwilliam look any less attractive. He sat at his desk completely at ease, with the air of someone who owned all he surveyed. I swallowed, and tried to remember exactly what I'd said to Edie at the magazine.

'It's not the house itself so much as what you're doing here,' I explained. 'The readership for *Hot! Hot!* is mostly young women, and with the economy as it is, they're looking for things to do this summer that won't break the bank. Visiting stately homes isn't exactly their normal idea of fun, but that's why this article will be so interesting. I think we can make the Regency cool. I want to concentrate on the fashion, the details, how you're recreating what life was actually like back then, as opposed to the modern world. And also what it's like to be the people who step back in time two hundred years every day. It's an escape, and people want escape.'

It had sounded pretty good in my email to Edie. But it sounded stupid here, in this room, with this man. He wasn't escaping; it was his family home. His life.

'You're right,' James said; 'it's not our normal visitor demographic at all, which is exactly why I'm keen to have you write it. I want Eversley Hall to be a success, and I think it would be wonderful PR for us.'

I let out my breath in a shaky stream. 'Great. That's — that's really great.'

'So,' he said, with that smile again, 'let's get started. What do you want to know?'

I pulled out my notebook and a pen from my handbag. 'Well, I was hoping to be able to shadow a few of the people working here, the ones dressing up — what do you call them?'

'Historical interpreters. What else?'

'I'd also like to talk to you, if that's all right, about the whole project. How you got into it, what you're doing exactly.'

'I'd love to talk with you about that. Cup of tea?'

'Um . . . yes, please.'

James got up out of his chair and went to a side-table I hadn't noticed earlier, which held a tray of tea things. He lifted a knitted cosy off a pot and poured steaming tea into two delicate, flowered porcelain cups. He added milk and I shook my head when he held up sugar tongs.

'Here you are.' The cups were exquisite, with curved handles and violets painted on the side. His looked very small in his hand as he settled back into his chair. 'The tea set was my great-grandmother's,' he explained to me. 'Though my great-aunt knitted the cosy when she lived here during the war. The Fitzwilliam family have lived in Eversley Hall since 1814. Nearly everything you'll see in the house was brought here by my ancestors. It's a place that means a great deal to me personally, for obvious reasons. So when we decided to do an historical re-enactment to help attract visitors to the house in our first season, it seemed natural to start with the beginning.'

I was scribbling with one hand whilst holding my cup and saucer in the other. 'Why did you decide to do an historical re-enactment?'

'It literally brings a property to life. We wanted something special for our opening season; maybe something that would bring in visitors who wouldn't normally come to a stately home. Readers of your magazine, for example. Also, as I said, it's personal to me. I've enjoyed discovering more about my ancestors and how they lived here day to day.'

'It's completely fascinating.'

He leaned forward. 'Do you know much about the Regency period?'

'Well, I — um, I read a lot.'

'Of history?'

'Novels, mostly. And I watch a lot of costume dramas.'

He nodded. He actually appeared to be taking me seriously. Maybe I wasn't so bad at this 'being a writer for the glossies' sort of thing.

'This project is one hundred per cent based on documented fact,' he began. 'Every single person who puts on Regency costume is taking on the persona of an individual who actually lived in this house in the summer of 1814. They've been given a dossier about that individual. Every weekend, from the moment they put on their costume in the morning to the moment they take it off at night, they are that individual.'

'So everyone's a real person,' I said, writing. 'That's interesting. Do they have a script or something?'

'They know the relevant facts about their persona, and of course they're fully informed about the house, but they don't follow a set script. We want everyone to be going about their daily business just as they would in a real house.'

'It sounds like fun. And what about the clothes?'

'Each costume is custom-made for the person who's wearing it, based on fashion records of the time. We have a variety of costume experts producing the clothing for us.' He took a card from a drawer and slid it over to me. 'This is one company we use, if you'd like to contact them.'

'That's great. I'd love to talk with some of the interpreters when they aren't working, too; find out what kind of people they are and what attracted them to the job.'

James Fitzwilliam put his cup down on its saucer. He folded his hands next to it and looked at me. Properly, up and down, from the scuffs on my shoes to the somewhat-tamed ends of my hair. I felt warmth creeping up my body as he leaned forward, a fraction closer to me.

'Alice,' he said, 'tell me something. Are you really interested in Eversley Hall, or is this just a story to you?'

I swallowed. My mouth suddenly felt dry.

Those blue eyes of his were — well, they were quite intense.

'I'm really interested,' I said.

He nodded. 'What size shoe do you wear?'

'What?'

'Are you a five, by any chance?'

'Er . . . yes.' I glanced down at my shoes, and back at him. He didn't appear to be crazy, but . . .

'About five foot four? Dress size eight?'

'I'm not exactly sure what my dress size is.'

'It's not as vital as the shoe size, to tell the truth. Everything is fairly adjustable, with ties and so forth.'

'Ties?' I was feeling a little breathless.

'You're perfect. I knew it as soon as I saw you. And it would be doing me a good turn too. You'd have a lot of work to do before Saturday though.'

'I'm sure I should probably understand what you're talking about, with me being perfect and everything, but could you please tell me anyway?'

He grinned. 'One of our interpreters has a family emergency and can't be here on Saturday. We need someone to stand in for the role of Ann Horton. You'd fit the costume, if you'd like to do it.'

'You want me to dress up? In Regency clothes? Really?' I put down my notebook. 'That would be incredible.'

'Would it help you write your article?'

'Would it ever.'

'I was going to have to spend this afternoon ringing round for a replacement. It's very short notice, and the clothes are handmade to fit each person. But it's about more than the clothes, you know, Alice. You'll have to learn your part and the history of the house. And you'd only have two days to do it.'

'But it would be perfect for the article. It would be no problem at all.'

He reached his arm over to the bookshelf and put his fingertips on a folder, then paused. 'It's not as easy as it sounds. You've got to have a certain flexibility; you need to get on with your duties, and answer questions from visitors, and interact with other interpreters. There isn't a script, remember. The more you know, the better you'll be.'

'I'm really good at reading.' I held out my hand for the folder.

'It's not a novel.'

'I can read practically anything.' Most of my work-reading had consisted of scientific and trade documents. This was about a million times more interesting.

'Have you ever done any historical interpretation before? Any acting?'

'No.' He wasn't going to decide I couldn't do it now, was he? After tempting me?

'I shouldn't be doing this, quite honestly,' he said, still not giving me the folder. 'I might get some grief over it. I've been a real stickler for historical accuracy up till now, and you don't have any experience.'

'I can be a stickler. I won't let you down.'

He considered me again. 'No, I don't think you will. Anyway, it's not a difficult role to play.

As long as you absorb the information and follow the other interpreters' leads, you should be fine.' At last, he handed over the folder and I grasped it. The label on the front said *Eversley Hall, 1814: Ann Horton*. 'These are all the facts about your character: her background, her family, her age, her daily activities. There's a history of the house and some information about the wider historical context — politics, technology, class structure, etiquette, issues of the day.'

It was a thick folder. I was itching to open it, but I preserved a slight bit of dignity by merely resting it in my lap. 'When do I get to try on my dress?'

'If you arrive on Saturday morning about seven o'clock, you'll have time to get dressed and look around the house. Mrs Smudge will help you find your way around. The regular Ann Horton will be back on Sunday.'

'This is going to be so exciting for the article. I had no idea I could get an insider's view like this. My editor will be thrilled.' Well, maybe. *I* was thrilled, anyway. What a difference from wearing leggings and baggy T-shirts and writing about grommets. 'I'm so pleased to be working with you, Mr Fitzwilliam.'

'Call me James,' he said, and he held out his hand for me again. This time, I was slightly less overwhelmed and I appreciated the way his fingers fitted around mine, how he shook firmly but not so much that it was uncomfortable. 'I'm very pleased to be working with you too, Alice Woodstock.'

* * *

I skipped to my car in the tourist car park. The gravel in the wide drive made it rather difficult, especially in my high heels, but I managed it. I clutched Ann Horton's folder to my chest and before I unlocked the door to my battered Citroën 2CV I leaned back against it and took another moment to look at Eversley Hall.

God, it was gorgeous. Its golden sandstone and its high, wide windows gleamed in the late-afternoon summer sun. Two sweeping staircases ran up from the drive to the grand entrance, flanked with pillars and covered with a sort of Greek-style porch. A wing stretched out on either side, to the east and west, like embracing arms. There were probably proper names for the architectural features. They would no doubt be in my folder, along with the dates and stages of their construction. All I knew right now was that Eversley Hall looked like the stuff of costume dramas, the ones where it was always lush and green even when it was raining, the ones where every good character, every spirited heroine, found her own happily-ever-after.

And I'd done it. I'd sold an article — well, in theory at least. I'd got out of the house. And I'd met a very handsome man and had an enjoyable conversation. Aside from nearly fainting when he'd started talking about my shoe and dress size.

And I was going to be dressing up. I opened the door of my car and spotted the leaflet lying on the passenger seat. There was the elegant Regency lady in her gold and white gown, arranging flowers. Was that Ann Horton? Was that going to be me?

I put Ann Horton's folder carefully on the seat, next to the leaflet, and started up the 2CV. As usual, it took three attempts before it sputtered into life. Gravel crinkled underneath my tyres as I drove down to the gates and back into the twenty-first century.

Eversley Hall was only a few miles from Brickham down the A329; the original Mr Fitzwilliam and his family would have found it an easy carriage or horseback ride from their house. These days, however, the roads were choked with traffic, especially at this time of the evening. I puttered along, stopping frequently for tailbacks or red lights, glancing at the folder that lay on the passenger seat and the photograph beside it. It was almost as if I were taking Ann Horton for a drive in the present, to show her the changes that had been wrought in 200 years.

'Here's a petrol station, Ann, and here's a McDonald's,' I said to her, smiling at myself. Everyone driving around me probably thought I was talking to myself, or else on a hands-free mobile. Not to a long-dead person in my imagination. 'Over that way is Broad Street. Not a draper's nor a milliner's in sight. Workhouse Coffee does a great latte, though I don't suppose you've ever heard of one of those. A latte, I mean. I'm sure you've heard of workhouses. The university's up the hill; it was probably a meadow in your day. And here's my house, which was built when you would have been about a hundred years old.'

I parked my scruffy 2CV and hurried up the steps to our house, the folder clutched to my chest.

From the outside, the Allingham house was a big red-and-yellow brick detached Victorian pile, with arched windows and a steeply peaked roof. Inside, most of the walls on the ground floor had been knocked through to provide an open-plan living space, painted white, with gleaming pale wooden floors and white furniture. If the drive from Eversley Hall to Brickham had been like going forward 200 years in a few minutes, walking through the door to the house I shared with Liv was like zooming from Gothic Revival to ultra-modern Minimalism in half a second.

As soon as I opened the glossy front door, I saw the suitcases. Three of them, lined up neatly by the jute doormat. Liv and Yann were cuddled up on one of the big couches in front of the wall-mounted television.

'Hey,' Liv called. 'How did it go at Eversley Hall?'

'Great. Amazing. Incredible.'

'Really?' She untangled herself from Yann and sat up. 'They want you to do the article?'

'More than that, they want me to dress up in costume for a day!'

'Wow, really?'

Yann pushed back his neat dreadlocks. 'Eversley Hall? Is that the Adams house outside of town?'

'John Carr,' Liv told him. 'It's Palladian.'

'Oh yeah, that's right. I always get those neo-Classical dudes mixed up.' He and Liv exchanged a smile at what I could only assume was some sort of architect in-joke.

'Have you told *Hot! Hot!* yet?' Liv asked me.

'Not yet.' I held up the folder. 'This is all the information about the character I'll be playing. The man who owns the house seems really nice.'

'When are you going to do it?'

'This Saturday, can you believe it.'

'Saturday.' Liv frowned. 'It's just Saturday, not Sunday — right? You're not going to miss the wedding?'

'No, it's definitely Saturday. Only Saturday. I wouldn't miss your wedding.' Though belatedly it occurred to me that I hadn't even thought of Liv's wedding when I was agreeing to dress up at Eversley Hall. Phew.

'Or the dinner on Saturday night with all your family and me and Yann?'

'No, I won't miss the dinner either. I promise.'

'We're just going through our vows again,' Yann said. 'We could do with a writer's eye.'

'Oh,' I said, 'I'm sure they're wonderful. Plus I don't want to spoil the surprise on Sunday. I'm going to make a cup of tea. Want one?'

'I'll come with you,' Liv said, and got up. We headed for the kitchen, which was separated from the rest of the living area by a frosted glass screen. I switched on the kettle and got down my chipped mug, while she set out two glass tea cups and found a box of herbal tea.

'Can you believe we got three more RSVPs today — for this Sunday? I've been on the phone all afternoon at work trying to sort out extra plates.'

'Hm.' I fished a tea bag out of the canister.

She squinted at me. 'Is that a cocktail stirrer in your hair?'

I reached up and searched through my curls with both hands until I encountered something hard. I pulled it out. It was yellow and had BEN'S TIKI TAVERN emblazoned on the top.

Shit. I must have shoved it in there this morning to keep my hair back and forgotten about it while I was getting ready to go to Eversley Hall. I wondered if James Fitzwilliam had noticed it. He hadn't said anything, or fallen about laughing, but he seemed to be a well-mannered chap. 'Was it really obvious?' I asked.

'Not unless you were looking hard,' Liv said, but I could tell she was being polite. If you've known someone since you were eleven, you tend to be able to read them.

'Damn.' Without the stirrer to anchor it, my hair fell down around my face, annoyingly.

'I hope you'll keep your hair loose on Sunday,' Liv said. 'It'll look spectacular with the dress.'

'Aren't you worried it'll get in the cake, or in the vicar's face?' I twisted it up and shoved the stirrer back in.

Liv gave me one of her looks, the kind only she could give. That kind of straight, analytical, understanding look that made me feel a bit like a set of blueprints she was studying.

'I've got some news,' she said.

'Have you? I'm starving, do we have any more

24

of that pizza?' I opened up the freezer and reached inside.

'I heard from Leo this morning. He's definitely coming on Sunday.'

My hand stopped. 'Oh.'

'It's my *wedding*, Alice. My brother should be there. He's my only real family.'

'I'm — ' I swallowed. 'I'm surprised he has time in between being famous to look in on Brickham.'

'I know it's hard for you, and I'm sorry about that. I really am, Alice.'

'Of course it won't be hard. It's been two years. I've moved on. I'm fine.'

'Are you sure?'

'Yes. Yes, of course. Besides, there are going to be so many people there we'll hardly notice each other. There's no reason we can't be civilised and amicable.'

I shut the freezer. Suddenly I didn't feel all that hungry.

'I think we should talk about it,' Liv said.

'Don't worry, I won't make a scene. It's your day, right?'

'Maybe — maybe it will be good for you to see him again. You'll get it over with, the first meeting, after . . . '

I swept up Ann Horton's folder from the table where I'd set it. 'It's all fine, everything is great, don't worry about me. Anyway, I've got a lot of work to do. Do you believe I have to read this whole folder before Saturday morning and memorise it? And I've got to get in touch with Edie at *Hot! Hot!* and tell her that the article's focus has slightly changed. I might end up pulling an all-nighter, so I'd better get busy.'

'Aren't you hungry? Don't you want your tea?'

'No, no — no need. I'll grab something later maybe.' I scurried out of the kitchen and up the stairs before Liv could call me back, past the first floor with Liv's bedroom and the guest room and the big bathroom, up to my domain at the top of the house, in what had once been the attic.

Books lined the walls and teetered in piles on the floor. I negotiated round them with the dexterity of much practice and flopped down on my bed, covered with one of my mother's handmade quilts, and opened Ann Horton's folder. Back to a world where frozen pizza hadn't been invented and women wore silk and muslin and ostrich feathers and clocked stockings, where men actually followed a code of honour and I wouldn't have to think about Liv's wedding or her brother Leo or anything other than what was going on in 1814.

This article was more than a good career move. It was going to make the next few days distinctly more bearable.

'Hello, Ann,' I said to the printed pages. 'It's nice to meet you.' And I settled down to read.

The folder was split into several sections, the first about Eversley Hall and its history, the second, thickest section, about the restoration and the various items in each room, and the third, slimmest section, about the woman I would be impersonating. I flipped through the first two sections rapidly, knowing I would go over them in detail later, and turned to the last to read about Ann.

Ann was nineteen years old, having been born in 1795 in Brickham, the second of six children and the first girl. Her elder brother went into the Navy, and Ann went into service at thirteen as —

I sat bolt upright on the bed. Ann Horton wasn't a gentlewoman with silk and muslin and a hero waiting to hand her out of carriages. I wasn't going to be that lady in the white and gold dress.

I was going to be a scullery maid.

Scrubbing Up

'Oh, for goodness' sake, girl. I knew it was going to be bad, but I didn't know it was going to be as bad as *this*.'

The woman looking me over was middle-aged and plump. She wore a brown calico dress under a snow-white apron, a ruffled cap, and a vicious frown. I looked down at myself to see what she was so displeased about, but didn't see anything except for faded jeans, black boots and a light corduroy coat. I'd reported to Eversley Hall bright and early, according to instructions, and been sent round the back of one of the wings, which was called the west pavilion. As soon as I'd set foot into the courtyard I'd been met by a woman who looked like she belonged 200 years ago, and resented every minute of the years between then and now.

'I know this isn't what I'm meant to be wearing,' I said, 'but I haven't got my costume yet.'

'Oh, I know that. I've got it in the staff room for you, waiting. And you'll fit into it, that's a stroke of luck anyway — you're as scrawny as that useless Fiona. What she thinks she's doing swanning off to York when she's needed here, I do not know.'

'James Fitzwilliam said it was a family emergency,' I ventured.

She made a sound halfway between a snort

and a grunt, which I interpreted as meaning something like *Family? What kind of person thinks that family is more important than Eversley Hall? That Fiona needs to grow up sharpish and learn a little bit of responsibility.*

'Are you the housekeeper?' I asked her.

She made another sound, this one more purely gruntish. 'I'm Mrs Smudge.'

I held out my hand for her to shake, but she just frowned more viciously, so I bobbed slightly, in a semblance of a curtsey. This seemed to appease her somewhat, because the lines on either side of her mouth relaxed a bit. 'I'm also in charge of all the personnel below stairs.'

'And is Mrs Smudge your real name, or is it — '

'That is the only name you will ever need to use for me. From the moment the house opens to the public for the day, our everyday personalities cease to exist. We are, wholly and without exception, living in 1814.'

'Yes, James said that — '

'You are not to swear, or to use a mobile telephone, or to smoke a cigarette. You are not to wear a watch or trainers or any jewellery beyond what your character would wear, which would in your case be none. You are not to wear modern make-up or modern perfume, discuss the news of this millennium, or carry any money. You will leave your car in the staff car park and change in the staff room and at all times while in public view you will behave in character.'

'Of course. I'm very much looking forward to it.'

'It only takes one person in Regency dress to be seen eating a Mars Bar to ruin the entire effect.'

'Mrs Smudge, I can assure you that I'll do no such thing. I've been up most of the past couple of nights swotting up on Eversley Hall and Ann Horton, and I think you'll find that I'm one hundred per cent up for the job.'

'Scrubbing pots and pans?'

I repressed a grimace. It was not what I'd hoped, obviously. And I wasn't quite as confident as I was pretending to be. I'd been so flushed with my own success in landing the article and the temporary job, that I'd barely stopped to consider whether I'd be any good at either of them. And though Edie at *Hot! Hot!* had been enthusiastic, the more I thought about the whole thing, the more uncertain I'd become. I spent my days in an attic by myself, transcribing technical language. What made me think I could act convincingly like a person from the early nineteenth century, and then write about it?

But I wasn't about to show my doubts to this woman. 'I can scrub pots and pans,' I said.

Mrs Smudge kept on frowning.

'Just because I'm dressed like this doesn't mean I can't use the Internet, missy,' she said. 'When Mr Fitzwilliam told me you were coming I looked up that magazine you write for. It's one of those trashy glossies. Articles about reality television stars and orgasms.'

'A lot of your potential visitors read that magazine.'

'Well, you won't be talking about orgasms in *my* kitchen.'

I couldn't help it. I laughed, and Mrs Smudge looked even more disapproving.

'I promise not to,' I said, pulling myself together.

'Humph.' She looked me up and down again. 'Well, Mr Fitzwilliam told me it was all right, which means it's all right. But I'm not happy about it, I can tell you. I run a tight kitchen and I don't have room for moonlighters. And I wish he hadn't had the nerve to send me a redhead.' She turned on her heel and bustled her ample self towards a small unmarked door at the far end of the pavilion. I followed her.

'Surely there were red-haired people in 1814,' I said to her back.

'Most likely there were,' she replied, not turning to face me. 'But Fiona is mouse-coloured, and anyone who's visited before will notice the difference. Besides which, red hair stands out, and it isn't the place of a scullery maid to stand out.'

'Surely there were even red-haired scullery maids in 1814.'

'If there were, we don't know about them, and I doubt they lasted long.' She pulled open the small door and went in ahead of me. The windowless room had been fitted with some metal lockers and a whiteboard and noticeboard. There was a kettle and a refrigerator, a table in the corner, and several folding chairs. A large rail stood against the far wall, and on it hung a wide array of costumes.

31

I walked past Mrs Smudge as she stood disapproving and went straight to the clothes. Oh, my God they were beautiful. Straight out of a film. I touched apple-green silk and white muslin, soft as a cloud. A burgundy velvet jacket with black frogging. Kid slippers lay in a neat row on the floor, next to a pair of men's boots. I ran my finger lightly over a puffed pink sleeve.

'Those aren't for the likes of you,' Mrs Smudge said from behind me. 'Those are clothes for the family. Servants' clothing is way over on the left.' She strode past me and pulled a hanger off the rack with a rattle. Sighing, I abandoned the dresses and turned my attention to my future outfit.

Although it was undoubtedly historically accurate, it wasn't that much of an improvement in the glamour stakes over leggings and a T-shirt. It was definitely, unarguably brown. Brown with a pattern of more brown, and a white apron which was a slenderer version of Mrs Smudge's. At least it was stain-free, though with my track record for neatness, I didn't think it likely that condition would persist for the entire day.

'We'll have to stuff your hair under the cap and hope for the best,' said Mrs Smudge grimly.

I took the dress, and the battered leather boots she offered along with it. It did all look like my size, though I wasn't crazy about Mrs Smudge's assessment of me as 'scrawny'. I hoped that wasn't what James Fitzwilliam had thought when he'd been looking me up and down.

'Where are the rest of the people?' I asked. 'Does everybody get dressed all together? It would be helpful to see these clothes being worn, and I don't suppose I'll get the opportunity, stuck down in the kitchen all day.'

'Everyone else comes later. You're here early, which is why I'm here early, and I was up till midnight because of the idiots in the blessed pub across the road, so if I'm not too cheerful you'll know who's to blame. If you want to see the family, you'll need to come some other time as a visitor. Kitchen servants aren't allowed upstairs.'

'The family don't ever pop down to the kitchens to see how dinner is getting on?'

'They've no need to. Lady Fitzwilliam gives me her instructions herself, and I carry them out.'

'Oh. Right. Really, does she give you instructions? How does she do it? Does she write them down?'

'I write them. And then I give them to you and the rest of the kitchen staff — orally, of course. It's not likely that you can read.'

Dear God. A dress like a brown dishrag, a life scrubbing, and no books. Thank goodness I was only pretending.

'Now, go and put that on. Female changing is that door on the left. Leave it open, I'm going to give you my instructions while you're changing.'

Off I did trot according to her orders. The changing room was tiny, whitewashed, and distinctly colder than the staff room. I hung up the costume and kicked off my shoes.

'You will answer to Mrs Collins, the cook,' said Mrs Smudge from the outer room, clearly enjoying projecting her voice. 'However, Mrs

Collins has been noted as a particularly easy-going woman, lax in her kitchen management. It's only her delicate touch with pastry that keeps her in her position, as Lady Fitzwilliam is inordinately fond of choux buns.'

'All of this is historically documented?' I asked, peeling off my jeans. 'Even the choux buns?'

'It's in Lady Fitzwilliam's surviving letters. She wrote that her housekeeper had to keep a close eye on Mrs Collins.'

And the kitchen and scullery maids as well, I was sure, especially the temporary one who wrote for the orgasm magazines. It looked as if I'd be scrubbing with Mrs Smudge breathing down my neck.

Still, it was all material for the article. I stripped down to my undies, pulled the apron off the hanger, undid the long row of buttons at the back of the dress, and discovered a cotton shift carefully hung underneath, along with a petticoat. There was a stiff canvas garment, a bit like a wrap-around sports bra. I assumed it was some sort of corset. A pair of rough woollen stockings were draped over the bottom of the hanger. Fortunately they looked as if they'd been washed since the last wearer scrubbed pans in them.

'Stockings and everything?' I said.

'And everything,' said Mrs Smudge from the next room. Was that smugness in her voice, or was I imagining it? 'According to the rules, you must wear no modern clothing whatsoever.'

None at all? I checked through the clothes

34

again. 'Not even underwear?'

'Not even underwear.'

'But there aren't any knickers here.'

'Knickers,' said Mrs Smudge, and there was definite smug enjoyment in her voice now, 'as we know them, were not invented until the twentieth century.'

I thought about this. Then I stuck my head out of the door, holding my shirt up to myself for modesty's sake. 'Who's going to be looking under my dress?' I asked.

'Nobody, I hope.'

'So it's purely for my own benefit. Is it supposed to help me get more into the part, to have the kitchen air circulating freely around my nether regions?'

'Exactly.'

'And we're cooking food like this? It doesn't seem very hygienic.'

'As far as I'm aware, none of the Fitzwilliam household died from having knickerless kitchen servants.'

'Right.' I went back into the changing room and contemplated this. Somehow, it had never occurred to me that the characters in some of my favourite novels were prancing around without any pants on.

I stuck my head out again. 'Is nobody wearing knickers? Nobody at all, this whole time?'

'Fashionable females, and the better class of servant — which you are not — wear a pair of pantalets. They consist of two separate legs attached to a waistband.'

'Wow.' The mind boggled.

35

'The shift goes nearest your skin, and then your stays. I can give you a hand if you need help getting them on. Then comes your petticoat, and your dress. Your stockings are held up with garters. Fiona should have put them in her apron pocket.'

I put on the shift first. It was light, but no lighter than a normal summer dress. I tied the little string around the neckline and then contemplated the stays. I had no desire to let Mrs Smudge help me get dressed, and surely if a scullery maid could do up this thing early in the morning, I could, too. I tried it, putting my arms through the holes, wrapping it around my chest, and pulling the ribbons. The whole thing tightened around me, and I pulled some more.

'Have you read the information folder?' Mrs Smudge asked from the other room.

'Yes, I've been studying it like crazy.' I'd barely slept last night, going through it all one more time in my head; I wondered if scullery maids were given a cup of tea mid-morning to keep up their energy and spirits. Doubtful.

'How many servants did the Fitzwilliam household employ in 1814?' boomed the housekeeper.

I gave the ribbons one more tug, and then tied them. 'Twenty-five,' I said. 'The butler Mr Munson, the housekeeper Mrs Smudge, a governess Miss Brambles, the cook Mrs Collins, a valet named Frogmore, two ladies' maids named Jane and Mary. There were three housemaids, all called Jenny, and three footmen, all called George. It's too much of a coincidence to think they were all named the same thing, so their names were probably a family tradition for housemaids and footmen. Also, two kitchen maids, Lucy and Gertrude, two laundry maids, Meg and Fanny, a dairy maid named Tamzin, the head groom Joseph and his three assistants John, Will and Matthew, the head gardener Samuel and the under-gardeners Edward, Ben and Joshua, and a scullery maid, Ann Horton.'

There was a long pause from outside. Mrs Smudge evidently did not expect me to know all of this. She cleared her throat. 'There were twenty-four. The governess passed away unexpectedly in April, and apparently Lady Fitzwilliam didn't see fit to replace her.'

'I'm sorry. That wasn't in the notes.'

'No. The research is ongoing.'

'Still,' I said, 'that's a lot of servants. I can see why the characters in Regency novels have so much time to go riding and make brilliant matches.'

'It's more or less typical for a family of this income and a house of this size. The family were fond of riding and kept a large-ish stable; on the other hand, their estate was close to town and so they didn't require a gamekeeper, and Mr Fitzwilliam was fond of managing his own estate and didn't keep a steward.'

I looked down at myself. Actually, the stays did a pretty good job. They pushed my boobs upward, making me look as if I had more there than I really did. I wasn't quite sure why I needed boobs to scrub pots, but I'd take any benefit I could get.

'There's no need for all of those servants this summer,' continued Mrs Smudge, getting back into her stride. 'This is an illusion of a fully working household, not the real thing. Only the kitchen and garden are open to the public, and only two of the bedrooms. The Fitzwilliam family dined fashionably late, around six o'clock, and the house is closed before dinner is served. Of course, the beds are never slept in, and we don't actually have that much linen and clothing to wash. In the house we have the butler, the housekeeper, the cook, one kitchen maid and one scullery maid. Also Samuel the gardener, who is in fact one of the gardeners on the estate, and who works in the grounds. However, for visitors, it's important to maintain the impression that we have a full staff working behind the scenes. You will need to answer guests' questions accurately, and speak as if you are one of many servants.'

'Right. Chat about how the second housemaid Jenny has got a cold, things like that.' I pulled on the petticoat, and then tried to figure out how the garters worked.

'The house opens at ten o'clock. You'll have half an hour to have your lunch in the staff room.'

'Right.'

'The kitchen is fully functioning. We make bread and cakes and pastry, and we sell them in the café and gift shop. This is proving very popular. Mrs Collins also prepares Regency dishes for demonstration purposes, on certain days. You'll be washing dishes, scrubbing floors, tending the fire, and doing whatever else Mrs Collins or I require you to do. I will demonstrate the accurate way of doing these things. And, of course, you'll be staying in role and talking to visitors, which is the most important thing. If you can manage it. If you can't manage it, you'll be keeping your mouth shut.'

I pulled the dress over my head. It had a high waist and buttoned up the front, presumably so its wearer could do it up herself very early in the morning before her day of drudgery. I then tied on the apron and put on the boots. There wasn't a mirror in the changing room, but there was one in the staff room, so I ventured out, cap in hand.

Mrs Smudge was waiting for me. She surveyed me with a critical eye.

'Well, it fits you at least.'

'It's rather fetching,' I lied. I went to the mirror and gathered up my hair. It took both hands to do it; I hadn't had it cut for a little while and my hair goes crazy when I wash it. 'How do I tie this up without using an elastic band?'

Mrs Smudge produced some brown ribbons from somewhere and I got to work. When I'd done the best job I could, she also produced a pin and attached my cap to my head. She was still frowning when we'd finished, evidently disgusted at my offending red hair.

But when I looked properly at myself in the mirror, my eyes widened.

I looked like someone else. Someone prim and neat, someone who worked hard and knew her place. The lowest of the servant class, but so necessary that she had to exist even in a facsimile. She had worked every day since her childhood. She would be up before the rest of the household, and in that brief space of solitude she would think about the people still sleeping upstairs, distant as the Olympian gods and as untouchable.

She wasn't glamorous, but she was interesting. I smiled at her in the mirror, and then I turned to Mrs Smudge and curtseyed again. 'Ann Horton, scullery maid, at your service, ma'am.'

Mrs Smudge grunted. 'Over to the east pavilion with you. I'll show you how to wash dishes.'

★ ★ ★

I was on my knees, peering at the fledgling fire in the grate, when I heard the cheery 'Good morning, Mrs Smudge!' behind me. I jumped to my feet as a good underling should, in time to see a tiny, slim woman in a blue dress and white apron come sweeping into the room. Her grey hair was piled beneath her cap. Her age and her cheerful confidence marked her out as the cook, though I'd been expecting her to be more buxom than elflike. Mrs Smudge nodded at her.

'Good morning, Mrs Collins,' I said. There weren't any visitors in the kitchen yet, but Mrs Collins was clearly in character as she began to unpack the large basket of fruit and vegetables that she carried.

'Morning Ann,' she said. 'Have you done something to your hair?' She gave me the slightest of winks, the only clue in her manner that I wasn't her normal kitchen maid.

'My hair?' I touched the red tendrils that had escaped while I'd been wrestling with the firewood. I hadn't expected to be in role quite so soon; I thought maybe we'd chit-chat in a modern way before the visitors came in. I looked around, but only saw Mrs Smudge frowning.

This was my first test: explaining why I didn't look like the usual Ann Horton.

'I had an awful fright this morning when a mouse ran over my shoe, ma'am,' I said. 'Perhaps that's it.'

She laughed. 'I would have a thousand mice running over my shoes if it made my hair curl like yours. Bone-straight, my hair's always been. I'm too old to care about these things, of course, but I always have fancied curling hair.' She hummed under her breath as she bent over to open a cupboard.

'Where is Lucy this morning?' said Mrs Smudge.

Mrs Collins stood up and looked around. 'I'm sure she'll be here presently.'

'I do believe this floor could use a sweeping. We don't want to attract any more mice.'

'I'll do it,' I said quickly. I went to the scullery where I'd seen a broom leaning in the corner. It was a good-sized room with a flagstone floor, walls lined with dish racks and a deep, wide sink. It had a window where Ann Horton could look out on the courtyard to see the comings and goings as she worked.

I saw a dishevelled person dressed in much the same clothes as I was wearing, running across

41

the courtyard towards the kitchen. She was pulling on her cap as she ran, and with a flutter of interest I noticed that she ran straight past a group of what were obviously the first visitors of the day.

I took the broom and hurried back to the main kitchen. The fire I'd built in the range was already starting to warm the air and fill it with a pleasant tang of smoke. Above the scrubbed copper pots and pans on the far wall hung a large clock with Roman numerals on its face; Mrs Smudge had told me it had been put there specifically so that the servants could prepare the meals on time. As the person I assumed was the kitchen maid, Lucy, clattered into the room, the long hand was already pointing to ten minutes past ten.

'Oh Mrs Collins, oh *Mrs Smudge*, you're here too? I'm so so sorry, I didn't mean to be late, I must have overslept.' She pushed at her cap, which had fallen over her face; a lock of bleached hair slipped out at the back.

'Your hair, Lucy,' said Mrs Smudge in chilling tones.

'Oh.' She pushed it up underneath the cap out of sight as the visitors appeared in the doorway behind her. It was a group of three, and I was surprised at how anachronistic they looked. I'd been in period costume for a bit over two hours, and already their anoraks and trainers and cardigans seemed strange, like objects from another dimension. I wondered if I'd feel that way about my knickers and bra when I put them back on at the end of the day.

The visitors paused, watching the spectacle in front of them: panting kitchen maid, glowering housekeeper, cook biting her lip, scullery maid holding a broom. One of them nudged another, and the third one pointed at Mrs Smudge, who didn't seem to notice, as she was glaring at Lucy.

'I will not have slatternly girls in my employ,' she boomed.

'No, ma'am. Of course not, ma'am. I'm sorry, ma'am.'

'If your behaviour continues in this way I will have to consider whether you hadn't better find a position elsewhere.'

'Oh, no, ma'am, please don't do that. I'll try harder, ma'am. I don't know what happened. I shan't do it again, ma'am.' She dipped her head.

'See that you don't.' Mrs Smudge turned, majestic, and swept past the tourists through the door and out into the courtyard.

'Looks like you're in hot water,' said one of the visitors to Lucy in an American accent.

'Oh, la, sir, Mrs Smudge is always storming on about something or other. Never happy, that woman, if you'll forgive me saying it.' She dropped her voice. 'It makes me feel sorry for Mr Smudge, so it does.'

'*Is* there a Mr Smudge?' I asked. 'She hasn't a wedding ring on her finger.'

Lucy caught my eye and a smile spread over her face. 'Ann, I do believe you've discovered the source of her bad temper.'

The visitors laughed and Mrs Collins suppressed a smile. I'd done something right, anyway. 'Now girls, we have too much work to do to spend our time in idle gossip,' the cook said mildly.

''Tisn't idle gossip to talk about Mrs Smudge's empty bed if she takes out her frustration on us every morning,' said Lucy.

There were a few flashes as the visitors began taking photographs of us, as if we were particularly interesting items of furniture. 'Enough,' said Mrs Collins. 'Will you open the windows, please, girls? It looks like being a hot day today, and we've got the fire blazing, thanks to Ann. I've a mind to make some choux buns so I can spend some time in the pastry kitchen where it's cool.'

Lucy and I went to the windows. They were tall, and deep-set, and opened from the top. Lucy scrambled up on top of the cabinet that sat underneath the windows, her boots carefully stepping between the copper kettles and tureens that were laid out in display on top of it. I followed her, looking down to make sure that my dress and petticoat stuck tight around my ankles and didn't afford anyone a glimpse of my bare bottom. Together we tugged at the coarse ropes that operated the window sashes. I heard the tourists proceed from the main kitchen to the scullery and the larders.

'Mate, I'm so hung over I'm about to start twitching,' Lucy whispered to me. 'I just about popped Mrs S on the nose, forget about the rules. You're good fun though, aren't you? Are you supposed to be Ann for the day? Didn't they say you were writing for *Hot! Hot!?*'

I nodded.

'I'm Kayleigh.'

'Alice.'

'You're doing well to make a joke on the first day. Fiona usually just beetles around like a drudge. I'm telling you, these poor kitchen maids led a miserable life. I've never been so happy to take off my costume at the end of a gig. Glad of the steady work though. I'm in debt up to my eyeballs as usual.'

'Are you an actress?'

She nodded, pulling at the ropes of the second window. 'Theatre mostly, a few adverts. Nothing quite like this before. I'm never taking my microwave for granted again. And it's nothing like learning lines, you have to remember so many random facts. I've got a cheat sheet, look.' She pulled a folded piece of paper out of the bosom of her dress, showed it to me, and stuffed it back in. 'I nip into the larder to check it. Did they make you learn everything just for one day?'

'Most of everything.'

'Not surprised. The worst bit is Mrs S. I think she's got a personal vendetta against me since she caught me saying 'bloody' in front of a visitor. She told me last weekend that if I slipped up one more time I was out of here, and I don't know what I'll do for dosh. Dot is all right though — that's Mrs Collins. She's only ordering us around because that's her role; normally she wouldn't say boo. Keeps quiet most of the day unless there's a visitor in the kitchen. She's dead boring sometimes — I've got to talk to the tourists to keep myself awake. It gets hot in here too, unless it's freezing cold. I have to soak my hands in Vaseline Intensive Care for hours after I get home, and my mate Jessica gave me these glove things that you put on overnight, but they're not helping. Hey, so if you write for *Hot! Hot!* do you get to meet a ton of celebrities?'

I heard a faint shuffle at the door. 'What would you like us to do after this, Mrs Collins?' I called, to interrupt the other maid's flow of modern talk before a visitor heard it.

'We'll need the kettle on the boil, Ann, thank you, and some butter from the dairy, Lucy. Good morning, sir, and welcome to my kitchen. I'm Mrs Collins the cook, at your service. Are you enjoying your visit to Eversley Hall?'

'Ta, mate,' whispered Kayleigh/Lucy, glancing down at the Barbour-jacketed couple who'd come into the kitchen. Out the window, I could see the next visitors arriving, in clumps and groups, clutching cameras and the free leaflet guides.

I smiled and shrugged. 'We scrubbers have to stick together,' I whispered back.

To the Rescue

'What's a pretty girl like you doing in a place like this?'

I didn't stop scrubbing, but I looked up at the visitor. He was in his late thirties or early forties, and his kids had already thundered through the kitchen, chased by their harried-looking mother crying out, 'Watch out for the fire! No, don't touch those tongs, Jeremy! Sasha, come back here, those buns are not for you to eat!' They'd all exited through the scullery door, while the father sauntered leisurely through, and paused beside me.

Five hours in the kitchen of Eversley Hall, and I'd already learned as much about visitors to stately homes as I'd learned about cooking and washing in 1814. I'd made up a catalogue of the different types in my head. Most people were moderate; they looked at everything and enjoyed it, maybe asking a question here or there about what we were doing or the implements we were using. There were the blushers, the ones who were embarrassed by the presence of people dressed in elaborate clothes, and who did their best to ignore you as they walked through the kitchen looking only at the inanimate objects. There were the television-watchers, who stood and stared at you and talked about you as if you were a programme on a screen, not a real person at all; or the photo-snappers, who didn't even ask your permission before they took your picture, or 'instant portrait', as we were supposed to call them.

I'd had an information-gatherer — a woman who asked me question after question, rapid-fire without even blinking, as if she were trying to catch me out not knowing something. I'd had two ladies speak to me in German, which I didn't understand, and one man who insisted on taking apart and reassembling the meat mincer because it wasn't put together properly.

Blushers and starers and watchers and pretenders, who enjoyed the charade of being in 1814. Noisy children and quiet ones, parents who lectured and ones who gave out steady streams of sweets. A glimpse of a baby sleeping in a sling against its mother's chest, a squashed pink face that made me instinctively look away at the copper kettles.

And then there were the jokers. The ones who tried to make us come out of character, to prove their cleverness. I quite liked these, though I knew they were testing us. Mrs Collins had allowed Kayleigh and me to go for our lunch-break at the same time, and over my packed sandwiches and Kayleigh's supermarket sushi she'd told me about the bloke who'd tried to pass her his mobile phone to take a call, and the old fellow with bad breath who'd pinched her arse while his wife's attention was elsewhere. 'Though what she was really interested in was the steel for sharpening knives,' she'd said, popping a piece of sushi into her mouth, 'so with any luck he's got his.'

Now, back in role as Ann, I smiled at the man,

though not more than a modest servant would allow herself to do. He was a joker, I was pretty sure, giving me a pick-up line as if I were in a bar. 'I'm scrubbing pots, sir.'

'Bet you wish you had some Fairy liquid, eh?'

I gave him a blank look. 'Fairy liquid, sir?'

He laughed. 'What are you using to clean the pans?'

'Washing soda, sir.'

'Do they train you to talk like this? All old-fashioned?'

He was staring at my stays-enhanced cleavage. I copied an answer that Mrs Collins had given to this exact same question, asked by another joker before lunch. 'I'm not sure what you mean, sir. I'm talking like any normal person, I hope.'

'And what do you do when you're not — '

'Barry, can you get out here, please! Jeremy's trying to head-butt the fake pheasants in the game larder.'

The man turned his attention to his wife, who was leaning in through the scullery door. 'Jeremy!' he yelled, striding out of the kitchen.

Phew. I'd got away with it, for now at least. I put the baking tray on the side to dry and had begun to wipe my hands on a cloth when Kayleigh/Lucy came in, carrying an armful of bowls and spoons. 'Alice, can you cover for me for a minute?' she whispered urgently. 'I'm absolutely gasping for a fag. Usually I can get through the day all right, but with my head like this it's no good.'

'But didn't Mrs Smudge say that if she caught you — '

49

'That's why I need you to cover for me, all right? If she comes in while I'm gone, distract her until I get back. I'll only be a sec and then I'll poke around in the range for a while right after so I have an excuse to smell of smoke. Thanks, hon, you're a sport. I wish you were here all the time.' She patted me on my cap and ran out of the scullery door.

I washed up the dishes, keeping my head down and my cleavage pointed resolutely sinkward. I hadn't messed up yet, and I had plenty to write about. If I could keep it up for another couple of hours, I'd be able to go home feeling I'd acquitted myself fairly well. Though Kayleigh was right — I'd have to soak my hands in moisturiser before I went out for Liv's pre-wedding dinner tonight. Soda crystals were not easy on your hands, and there were no Marigolds in this kitchen.

And if this article went all right, maybe I could try some other writing for the women's magazines. Nothing too crazy or trendy, nothing about orgasms or anything; maybe I could do some book reviews. That would be up my street, though probably not very lucrative. Then again, I did read a lot. I might as well make a bit of cash out of it. All I needed was something a little different, something to keep me busy and distracted while I was all alone in that big house after Liv went to New Zealand. Maybe even something to think about tomorrow, during Liv's wedding, when I would have to face her brother.

'Ann!'

I heard a bellow from the main kitchen, and I

50

hurried in, wiping my raw hands on my apron.
Mrs Smudge was standing near the big, wide
table where Mrs Collins prepared the food, her
hands on her hips, her ring of keys trembling. A
few visitors stood around her and stared at this
vision of righteous authority from the past.

'Yes, Mrs Smudge?'

'Where is that useless girl Lucy?'

I glanced at Mrs Collins, who had flour up to
her elbows, and was looking helpless and
frightened. 'I don't know, Mrs Smudge.'

'Mrs Collins doesn't know, you don't know,
and yet the girl is nowhere to be found! I don't
suppose she vanished into thin air?'

'I don't suppose so, ma'am.'

'I told her this morning that if I found her
remiss in her duty one more time I would send
her packing! This house is not a pleasure ground
for slatternly girls!'

She was actually red in the face. This might all
be an act, but I didn't think that she would
hesitate to sack Kayleigh in real life if she knew
she'd nipped out for a cigarette. Anachronism
was the Eighth Deadly Sin, as far as Mrs
Smudge was concerned.

'She's no slattern, Mrs Smudge,' I said
bravely. 'Lucy's been working hard all day.'

'That she has,' said Mrs Collins, though I only
knew it from reading her lips, because there was
an almighty shuffle at the kitchen door at that
moment as the visitors inside the room made
way for the visitors trying to get in. For a few
seconds there was a bottleneck, and then it broke
and a whole crowd of people came pouring into

51

the kitchen, all wearing matching royal-blue sweat-shirts saying *Tulsa Area Community Orchestra*. The 't's were made of little grace notes and there was a cartoon of a dancing violin.

A coachload of American tourists. 'Oh look, they're all dressed up as kitchen workers!' one of them said loudly, and I heard the click and whirr of many digital cameras.

Mrs Smudge did not budge. 'Ann, you seem very eager to defend your crony. Since you know so much about how hard she's been working, perhaps you also know where she is right now?'

'No, ma'am.'

Her eyes narrowed. 'I think that you do. And if you don't want to be sent packing yourself, you will tell me. This instant.'

For God's sake, what did she want? For someone who was so obsessed with the idea of historical accuracy, she was pushing hard for me to break it. Then again, if I told her that Lucy was round the back having a fag, she'd have an excuse to sack us both immediately — at the expense of everything she'd said was important. And why? Just to prove I wasn't any good at this?

I wasn't going to let her defeat me. I set my chin. 'I don't know where Lucy has gone, ma'am.'

Mrs Smudge stared at me, fury in her eyes. I didn't drop my gaze from hers.

'What are they fighting about, Chuck?' said one of the visitors.

'No clue.'

'Ann,' called a cheery voice from the scullery, 'you'll never guess who I saw out — oh.'

Kayleigh stopped short in the doorway between the scullery and the kitchen, her hands mid-wipe on her apron, and looked at the scene enacting itself before her. Two dozen Tulsa Orchestra members, Mrs Collins twisting her hands together, and Mrs Smudge and me facing off in front of the blazing fire.

Mrs Smudge spotted her as soon as I did. 'Where have you been, missy?'

'I — ' She cringed, and I saw the triumph on the housekeeper's face. The older woman began to stride towards Kayleigh and I knew that if she got close enough, she'd be able to smell the cigarette smoke on her clothes.

I flung myself between them, narrowly missing a large man in a royal-blue sweatshirt. 'Mrs Smudge, don't!' I cried. 'It's all my fault, please don't dismiss Lucy!'

The housekeeper stopped. 'Aha! I was certain you knew where she'd gone. Out with it, what have you done?'

What *had* I done?

'I — I was — I mean she was ... ' I swallowed. And then I came up with it. Dozens of books and romantic plots came to my rescue.

I dropped my head, as if I were admitting something shameful. 'I asked her to meet my sweetheart.'

'Your *what*?' thundered Mrs Smudge, but around her the tourists had begun to chuckle.

'It's the second under-gardener. Ben. I've — he and I — well, I'm sure he has honourable intentions, ma'am, and I was meant to meet him behind the potting shed. But Mrs Collins has been making those choux buns and she needed the baking trays washed up for the next batch, and so I asked Lucy to deliver my note to Ben for me.'

'Your note? You have been sending notes to the under-gardener?' She eyed me, and then Kayleigh. 'Is this true?'

Kayleigh nodded, wide-eyed.

'And did you collect a note in return?'

She nodded.

'Where is this note?'

The woman was really unbelievable. How she expected Kayleigh to come up with a fictitious note from an equally fictitious under-gardener who wasn't even being portrayed by a real person in costume, I did not know. But then I had another inspiration, and I said, 'I told her to tuck it into the bodice of her dress, ma'am.'

This time the visitors really did laugh. I heard the cameras snapping as slowly, Kayleigh reached beneath the top of her dress and pulled out her folded crib sheet.

Mrs Smudge held out an imperious hand for it, but I beat her to it and plucked the crib sheet from Kayleigh's fingers. 'It's mine, Mrs Smudge, and you may dismiss me for having it, but I'll throw it in the fire before I let you read it.'

'Why, you — '

'Aw, let her have her love letter,' said the big guy next to me.

'Yeah,' said a woman, over near the plate-warming racks. 'She doesn't do anything but scrub dishes all day, she might as well have a boyfriend.'

Mrs Smudge seemed to notice for the first time that the room was packed with modern-day people, most of them nodding in agreement with the two romantics who'd spoken. I could see her quandary registering on her broad face. For one thing, she was meant to keep up the charade of historical accuracy, and nobody could argue that my professed affair between a scullery maid and an imaginary under-gardener wasn't precisely the sort of thing that happened in real life in 1814. In fact, it was exactly the sort of thing that she'd instructed me to do, to keep up the illusion of a full quota of staff. For another, her job was to please the visitors to Eversley Hall, and it seemed as if they were on my side. And for a third, I'd neatly deflected her displeasure away from Kayleigh and onto me, and I was leaving forever in less than — I glanced quickly at the clock, to remind her as much as me — two hours. She'd have her docile Fiona-Ann back tomorrow.

'I love this,' said another of the visitors, not one of the orchestra lot, but a woman in a Barbour jacket who'd been in the kitchen with her pashmina-wrapped teenage daughter before the whole débâcle began. 'It's like being inside a costume drama on the BBC.'

'We should totally come back here again tomorrow to see what happens,' agreed her daughter.

I raised an eyebrow at Mrs Smudge.

'Very well,' she snapped, her face red. 'Keep it. And now *get back to work*.' She turned and strode out of the kitchen, through the door to the rest of the house. A few of the visitors applauded.

'Now, let's get on with our work, girls,' murmured Mrs Collins, and Kayleigh immediately bent to poke at the fire. I tucked the crib sheet into the bodice of my dress, then took a deep breath and pressed my hands to my hot cheeks. The visitors walked past me, smiling, a couple of the Americans patting me on the shoulder and saying, 'Way to go.' The crowd in front of the outside doorway thinned out and then, in between two people in blue sweatshirts, taller than both, I saw him.

He stood in the entrance, straight and true, wearing a dark-coloured coat, snow-white shirt points and cravat, drab breeches and top boots, with a spaniel panting at his feet. His clothes and his face were identical to those in the oil painting in the Hall, his expression the same, so much that I had to blink to make sure I was seeing this in reality.

It was James Fitzwilliam, looking exactly like his own ancestor, life-sized and absolutely stunning. And in his features there was a stillness, an authority, a presence that made the tourists flowing around him seem like ghosts of the future. They glanced at him, even stared, but he seemed not to notice.

His gaze met mine, and my cheeks flamed even hotter. I dipped down, instinctively, into a curtsey. I knew I should avert my gaze to the floor — I knew that Ann would — but I couldn't look away from him.

In real life, in modern clothes, he'd been a

hero. In this life, in Regency clothes, he was nearly a god.

A smile touched his lips and he strode forward into the kitchen, his boots making sharp sounds on the flagstone floor. 'Good afternoon, Mrs Collins,' he said, his voice ringing out with mastery and good humour.

'Sir,' she said, and I assumed she also curtseyed, but I couldn't look away from him.

'My stepmother has sent me to check on the progress of her choux buns.'

'Yes, we've been baking all afternoon, sir. Would you care to try one, sir?'

'No, thank you, Mrs Collins. I have no doubt of their excellence. But Lady Fitzwilliam will devise small errands for any gentleman in her vicinity. I'm pleased that I indulged her; it's most diverting here in the kitchen. Is this the scullery maid?'

'Sir,' I said, dipping again.

He came closer, fully into the kitchen now, within the circle of heat radiated by the range. I could see the weave of his coat, the buttons on his breeches. 'A romance with the under-gardener, is it?'

My heart was palpitating. At that moment I truly was the scullery maid, the lowest of the servants, tongue-tied, blushing, nearly faint. 'Sir, I — '

He spoke quietly in my ear, so quietly that no one else could hear him. 'You haven't been following the script, have you?'

'I — I didn't think there was one.'

He reached out his hand towards my head. All

I could do was to stand, watching, breathing him in, as he touched an escaped curl with one finger.

'I was wrong,' he said, nearly whispering it. 'You're *not* perfect for a scullery maid.'

And then he straightened, though I hadn't thought he'd bent in the first place, and his boots rang out on the floor again. 'Thank you, Mrs Collins,' he called.

'Thank you, sir,' murmured the cook as he left the kitchen.

With him gone, I could see the tourists again, the pots and pans, the platters and dishes and cooking utensils, feel the light breeze from the open windows, smell the scent of washing soda on my hands.

I'd really messed it up this time.

The Happy Occasion

'I love weddings,' my mother was saying. 'I love everything about them. I love the white dresses and the flowers and the music and the nibbles and all the friends and family together in one room, and the first dance and the cake and even when something goes wrong, I think it's wonderful.'

'Nothing is going to go wrong today,' said Liv. She was sitting in a chair in front of the mirror in my parents' bedroom, in her dressing gown. Her wedding dress hung in its plastic wrapping on the back of the door, and my youngest sister Pippi was using curling tongs in an attempt to put a soft wave into Liv's dark, poker-straight hair.

'Your hair will not curl,' Pippi said, pursing her lips and tossing her own curly locks, as if to give Liv's hair a good role model. In theory, Pippi and I had exactly the same hair — thick and curly and bright enough to stop traffic. The hair that Anne of Green Gables hated. The main difference between my sister and me was that no matter what I did with it, my hair always looked like some sort of a nest, and since she'd been about twelve years old, Pippi's hair had been absolutely gorgeous. Today it was in long corkscrew curls around her face and cascading down her back, shiny and perfect.

Pippi wasn't dressed for the wedding yet, or at

59

least I hoped she wasn't, because she wore a tiny denim skirt and an equally tiny T-shirt with the word *Princess* across the breasts in pink sparkly letters.

'Well, whether anything goes wrong or not, I am going to cry and cry and cry,' said Mum, who was already wearing her lilac 'sort of mother of the bride' outfit and was waiting for her nails to dry. She so rarely painted her nails that she was holding her hands in the air in an unnatural spread position, like two spiders affected by rigor mortis. 'I don't even know why I bothered to put on mascara this morning. It's going to be in streaks all over my face as soon you walk down the aisle, Lavinia.'

'I am so going to sit on the other side of the room from the family,' Pippi muttered.

'Celia,' said Liv, smiling into the mirror, 'you've looked after me practically as if I were your own daughter. You're the kindest woman I know. You can cry all you like at my wedding.'

'*You* can say that,' said Pippi, 'you're jetting off to New Zealand right after the reception and you'll never have to be embarrassed by her again. Whereas I have to wait until I finish my A-levels before I can even escape this place.'

'Everybody cries at weddings,' said my mother. 'You're supposed to cry. It's not embarrassing.'

Pippi rolled her eyes. 'Mum, you are the most embarrassing person in the whole world. Why do you think all of your children have moved halfway across the world as soon as they possibly could? Wendy's in Ecuador saving the planet,

60

Heidi's coaching field hockey in Japan, and even Liv's going to another continent.'

'It's not because of Celia,' protested Liv, but my mother got in there first.

'Alice is still in Brickham,' Mum said.

'That's only because — '

'Pippi,' said Liv quickly and warningly, and my sister went quiet. She reached for the hair spray and squirted a huge plume at my best friend's head. The sound of the can was very loud in the sudden silence.

'You know what we need?' I said, getting up off the bed abruptly with no heed of my dress. 'We need more Buck's Fizz.'

'Don't forget your shoes,' said Mum cheerfully. I snagged the shoes from the bed by their thin ankle straps. I had no idea how I was going to wear those things; they were higher than just about anything I'd ever put on before. But it was Liv's wedding, and she'd picked them out, so I was going to do it. I was going to do every single thing that Liv wanted me to do today.

I went down the stairs, carefully, and into the front room. Since Liv was getting married out of my parents' house, the place looked much tidier than normal, which was to say that there were no empty tea mugs scattered around and most of the random odds and ends that usually littered the surfaces had been piled together into the two large wonky bowls that my other younger sister Heidi had made years ago in ceramics class. They overflowed with odd socks, lockless keys, half-combs, name labels, leaflets, expired credit cards, shoelaces — all the legacy of too many

Woodstocks stuffed together into a too-small semi-detached house.

Dad was sitting at the dining-table, his black dinner jacket on the back of his chair. His shirt had been ironed, which was unusual, but I supposed that was because he was giving away the bride. He was bent over a giant jigsaw puzzle of a Hubble telescope photograph of the galaxy; the light gleamed off the bald spot in the centre of his scalp, surrounded by frizzy ginger hair.

'Can I join you for a minute?' I asked him, dropping the shoes and pulling out the chair across from him. He nodded, and his eyes drifted back to his puzzle.

My dad was, by anyone's standard, a geek. He was skinny and wore thick glasses and really awful jumpers and he always, always pulled his trousers up practically to his chest. He drove a horrible Astra and worked long hours as a physicist at Brickham University. I often thought that even out of working hours he was spending most of his brain time on the sub-atomic level; when you'd ask him a normal question to do with the everyday world, for example whether he wanted a cup of tea, he'd have to stare at you for a few minutes, his eyes blank, before responding. For most of my life, he'd been more comfortable fading quietly into the scenery, doing quantum equations or model aeroplanes or jigsaws.

Strangely, all of this made him quite relaxing to be with. If you knew you weren't even on the same planet as your father, you didn't have to try quite so hard to please him, or act chirpy and normal. He always seemed vaguely pleased to see me, when he noticed me, and we never had to bother with small talk. He was also a nearly inexhaustible source of information about model building and chemical processes, which came in handy for several articles I'd written. In fact, it was a contact of his who had got me a start in technical journalism, when I'd first come back to Brickham and was looking for a job.

My mother always said that she'd first spoken to my father because he was the only man she'd ever met with hair as red as hers. It was one of the few things they had in common, aside from us children. While Dad was silent, Mum was noisy. I was about eight years old before I discovered that other people's mothers didn't engage everyone they met — bus passengers, bin men, doorstopping Jehovah's Witnesses — in conversations about piles, or the age at which her children were still bedwetting, or how she quite fancied David Attenborough. Hardly any inner thought remained unspoken, which was good in some ways. You certainly never had to guess how she felt or what she wanted you to do. On the other hand, as Pippi had said, it could be embarrassing at times.

Seventeen years ago, Mum, who'd started out a librarian, had a career change of heart and became the sex education teacher for the local education authority. This was, admittedly, a better career choice for her — since as much as she loved books, nobody could really approve of a librarian who talked incessantly. But it made her daughters' lives more complicated. From an early age, we'd all known where babies came from; sex, like any other topic in our house, was discussed frankly and without squeamishness. But eventually, I realised the rest of the world didn't exactly share this view.

My eldest sister Wendy had begged her not to take the job. Heidi soon added her pleas. In a way, especially at first, I was proud that I had a mother who was brave enough to face sniggering kids and talk about sex. But then Mum made a video of herself demonstrating various contraception methods, and that video was adopted throughout the country as a teaching aid. All over Britain while we were growing up, kids watched our mother putting a condom on a banana.

If being the child of 'The Condom Lady' wasn't enough to tempt you to leave home, I didn't know what was. It was a miracle we all lasted long enough to finish our A-levels.

Pippi was the youngest, and had never had to endure the humiliation and dread of that video being shown in her lessons. But several kind souls had loaded it onto YouTube, where it looked set to remain preserved for ever.

My mother was proud of her status as 'The Condom Lady'. She considered the video a valuable teaching aid. She would say, quite often to total strangers, 'Whenever I think of how many kids have learned how to use a condom because of me, I feel warm all over.'

I picked through the puzzle pieces. They all looked alike: black with maybe a bit of a white star on them. I'd done enough of these puzzles over the years with my father to know that there

64

weren't any shortcuts; they took patience, trial and error and categorisation.

My father chuckled quietly as he fitted a tricky piece. From upstairs, I could hear the buzz of conversation, mostly my mother's, but here it was calm and quiet, with your hands doing something and the logical part of your brain occupied enough so that the rest of your brain could get on with thinking.

My dress pinched me. I'd never tell Liv — the dress was a thing of beauty, and she'd chosen it especially to suit my build and colouring because I was her only bridesmaid. It was the sort of sage green that went really well with my hair, and it was encrusted with embroidery and beads and little shimmery sequins. It was so beautiful, in fact, that I'd been eyeing it with trepidation for weeks now, afraid that I couldn't possibly live up to it.

In the end, I hadn't even been able to live up to a brown dishrag of a dress, at Eversley Hall. I'd finished out the rest of my day there keeping as quiet as possible, washing dishes, cleaning up. And then I'd crept away a few minutes early to change back into my knickers and my modern clothes, and drive home without talking to anyone.

My father cleared his throat. 'How's the new article coming?'

'Really well.' I could write the article without referring to my mess-up, my invented affair with the under-gardener. Or, if I was really good, I could make it seem funny. It didn't seem funny to me right now, but writing it down might make it seem more distant.

'Do you need any help with it?'

'Not this one, thanks. It's not so sciencey. It's more historical.'

He lapsed back into silence. I fingered a black piece with a tiny speck of a star on it and tried to slot it into what Dad had already put together.

I hadn't been a very good scullery maid. But there had been that moment, that one moment, when James Fitzwilliam had reached out and touched my hair. I'd thought he was smiling. But I must have been wrong, because why would he smile while I was flubbing up his special project in front of a crowd of visitors?

The jigsaw piece fitted into place. 'Mm,' my father said approvingly. He reached over and fitted the piece he was holding into mine. He smiled, briefly.

There was a scuffle from upstairs. 'She's going to put on her dress,' Mum called down.

I jumped up. 'Wait for me — I'll be right up with the champagne!' I called back. As I headed for the kitchen, the doorbell gurgled. It had once played a tinny version of 'Here Comes the Sun', but the battery had been dying a slow death for the past few years.

'Alice!' called my mother again. Her voice was slightly muffled, probably by yards of tulle. 'That's the florist with the bouquet and buttonholes — can you answer the door?'

'Okay.' I altered my course towards the front door. Halfway there, Maggie the cat started weaving around my ankles, purring and shedding long grey hair. I raised my feet to step over her and she meowed at me.

'I'm wearing a nice dress,' I told her. She meowed again.

'And will you feed the cats?' Mum called downstairs.

'I want to see Liv putting on her dress!'

'We'll wait for you.'

'Okay,' I muttered, 'I'll go to the wedding covered in cat hair and smelling of Whiskas.' I jumped over Maggie and hurried to the front door before either of the other two cats could ambush me, too.

The florist, Anders McKenzie, was a short, round man with an amazing head of too-black hair and a nose like a tulip bulb. His shop was down the street from my parents' house and I had spent many hours waiting on the pavement outside it while he and my mother had endless gossips. I opened the door and said, 'Hi, Anders,' reaching out my hands to take the boxes of flowers he'd have with him.

The man on my parents' doorstep was not Anders McKenzie.

My smile froze. My body froze. My fingers, stretched in midair, froze.

He was smiling, wide and white like he always did, as if he hadn't a care in the world.

'Hello again, Alice,' said Leo Allingham. Liv's brother. And my ex-husband.

Till Death Do Us Part

I had, of course, thought of this moment many, many times, especially since Thursday when Liv had said he was coming to the wedding. In my mind, I would glance at Leo nonchalantly, possibly raising one eyebrow and pursing my lips slightly in a contemptuous and yet bored fashion. Then I would deliver a short, direct speech, something that was witty and cutting and elegant. I had debated various content for this speech, from a simple, 'Oh, it's you,' dripping with hauteur, to a more authoritative, 'How dare you show your face in my home!'

I'd even relished the possibilities of a breezy, 'Dear me, Leo, you look awful.' Because in my fantasies, he did look awful. Dissipated, older, wearing clothes he'd slept in and four days' worth of stubble. Smelling of booze, probably, and secondhand smoke and cheap perfume. Reaping the wild oats he'd been sowing all over America for the past two years.

In real life his skin was close-shaved and his dark eyes were clear. He wore a Rolling Stones T-shirt, jeans and his leather jacket. He smelled of shampoo, the same one he'd used when we were married, the same one he'd used before that, and he was more real than the Leo in my head, so real that I could see everything about him, even the things I thought I'd forgotten. The small scar in his eyebrow. The shape of his lips.

68

The slight point of his canines, enough to make his smile dangerous.

I couldn't say a word.

'I like that green on you,' he said to me as if we'd met a thousand times since yesterday. 'It brings out the colour of your eyes.'

'What are you doing here?' I said, my voice hoarse and not at all nonchalant.

'My sister's getting married today, didn't you know?' He leaned against the doorway, since I was blocking it. 'Glad to see me, Mermaid?'

'No.'

'Well, that's a definite answer. Sure you don't want to think about it for a little while?'

'I thought you were coming to the wedding. Not the house.'

He shrugged. 'Flight got in early. And I wanted to see — '

I heard my mother cry, 'Leo! Oh my God!'

Leo looked away from me, his smile widening, and my mother came rushing down the stairs. I had to step back to avoid being knocked over. She flung her arms around Leo and they hugged each other, not half a foot from where I stood.

Of course. Leo wanted to see my family.

In my fantasies, Leo and I most definitely did *not* meet again in the company of my family.

Leo was angular where Mum was rounded, dark-haired where she was ginger, taller and stronger, and she held him with tenderness and joy. My best friend's brother, the son-in-law who'd spent nearly as much time in our house as his sister had, growing up. The man whom my mother sometimes referred to as her adopted son.

'I didn't know you were coming to the wedding,' she gasped, looking up into his face and tracing his cheek with her thumb. 'Liv never told us.'

Probably because Liv didn't want me to have to talk about it with Mum. In a dazed way I was grateful.

'I couldn't miss my sister's wedding,' he said.

'Oh, but we've missed you! And look at you — you look the same as you ever did.'

'It hasn't been that long.'

'Two years,' I said.

'Two years, and you never phoned or wrote or anything,' Mum scolded. 'But we've been hearing all about you. I cut out all the articles about you and I kept them — I've got a little scrapbook somewhere especially for — do you know where that is, Gavin? Oh well, of course he doesn't, he never knows where anything is, never mind, it's so good to see you. Come in, do you want a cup of tea? Or wait, what am I thinking of — it's time for champagne! Gavin, will you get out some glasses? Doesn't Alice look beautiful?'

'Yes,' Leo said. 'I was just saying so.' He glanced at me. I glared at him.

There was a rich rustling sound from the staircase. 'Leo?' said Liv.

We all turned to look at her. She'd put on her wedding dress herself.

My God, she looked incredible. Her dress was of cream silk, with a full skirt and a slender bodice that hugged her willowy frame. She floated down the stairs, her skirt flowing behind her. Her shoulders were bare, pale and delicate, a

70

shade lighter than her dress. All of us instinctively took half a step backwards in reverence to this graceful creature in the shabby hallway of my parents' house.

Leo held out his arms to her. 'Missed me, sis?'

'I thought you were coming to the hotel for the ceremony.'

'Ah, but you're glad to see me, aren't you?' He hugged her. Both of them were dark-haired, dark-eyed, with a sort of inbuilt poise. That was where the similarity ended though, because Liv was a decent human being and Leo was not.

Liv whispered something in his ear, I couldn't hear what but it made him shake his head, his smile not altering in the least. When she stepped back she was frowning.

'You're not wearing *that* to the wedding, are you?'

He looked down at his jeans, T-shirt and leather jacket. 'I was planning to.'

'It's my wedding, Leo. You can't look like a scruff.'

'It's part of my charm.'

'Forget your charm.' She checked her watch, a sensible black-strapped thing which didn't go with her dress at all. 'If you hurry, you have enough time to get into town and buy some decent clothes before the ceremony. Go.'

'But we were all going to have a drink,' Mum said. 'Gavin's gone to open the champagne.' She raised her voice. 'Gavin? How are you getting on with that cork?'

There was a vague noise from the direction of the kitchen.

'He'll be here in a minute,' confirmed my mother, seemingly heedless of my father's inability to find things like wine glasses, or that we were all standing in the corridor near the open door. 'You don't have to go into town, Leo. You've only just got here. I'm sure Gavin's got something you can borrow. Gavin?'

'He is *not* wearing something of Dad's.' Pippi pushed through us all, and flung her arms around Leo. 'Ohmigod, I don't believe you're here!' He caught her, with a laugh of surprise and pleasure, his hands spanning her tiny waist.

'Surely not Princess Pippi?'

'Yes! Ohmigod, you look so hot! I love your hair like that, it's all messy and romantic.'

'And you seem to have grown up into a woman while I've been away.'

She'd exchanged her mini-skirt and T-shirt for a teensy tiny pink dress that exposed miles of slim leg and arm. She giggled and kissed Leo on the cheek, leaving a small glitter of lip gloss on his skin.

'Don't get any ideas, she isn't legal yet,' I said. Leo just laughed again. Why shouldn't he laugh, welcomed like a prodigal son and embraced by a burgeoning sex-kitten?

'Have you got a date for the wedding?' he asked my sister.

'No, but maybe you'll dance with me?'

'You're joking. I'd have thought the boys would be flocking round.'

She shrugged. 'Whatever.'

'Have you seen Alice?' Liv asked her brother.

It was a weird thing to say, as if I were ten

miles away instead of six inches, especially since Liv was looking directly at me. I glanced down at myself, to make sure I was really here. That seemed to be my body down underneath my neck, but one could never be sure. I felt like an observer of myself. *That is Alice Woodstock there, standing in a sparkly dress next to the man she used to love, or thought she did.*

'Of course I've seen Alice,' Leo said. 'I was just telling her how lovely she looked.'

And he winked at me.

He bloody winked.

With that, I zoomed back into my body, here and now, losing that sensation of floating and dreaming and observing, to be replaced with burning anger.

He didn't belong here. Not any more. He didn't have any right to wink at me, or even talk to me.

Not after what he'd done.

Pippi was still clinging to my ex-husband. 'You should have visited *ages* ago,' she pouted. 'Just because you split up with Alice it doesn't mean we don't like you any more.'

'Speak for yourself,' I said.

Liv grabbed my arm. 'Come on, Alice, let's go and see if your dad needs any help with that champagne.' She hauled me down the corridor and into the kitchen with a surprisingly strong grip, considering her fairy-like appearance. My father was on his knees, poking around in the cupboard where they kept the cat food.

'We'll take over the drinks, Gavin,' Liv said loudly and cheerily. Dad stood up, nodded and wandered out of the kitchen, brushing off his trousers.

'Did you know he was coming to the house?' I said furiously.

'No, of course I didn't. You know what Leo is like.'

'Yes, I know exactly.' There was a burst of laughter from the hallway. I frowned. 'God, listen to them fawning all over him out there. It's disgusting.'

'How are you? Are you okay?'

'No! My mum thinks he's practically her son, and Pippi's adored him since she was a toddler. Never mind me, the *actual* member of this family.' I pulled open the fridge and got out a bottle of champagne. A jar of mustard fell onto the floor.

'He didn't turn up here deliberately to hurt you,' Liv said, retrieving the mustard and deftly replacing it in the fridge door. 'I'm sure he didn't.'

'No, Leo never thinks that *anything* he does could possibly hurt anybody. He doesn't think — that's the problem. And then he gets away with it.'

Liv touched my hand. 'Alice, I'm really sorry. I should have thought more about you. It was just . . . he wanted to come, so badly. And I . . . I'm sorry if it sounds disloyal, but I miss him.'

Her dress rustled on the vinyl floor. Her wedding dress. It was her wedding day.

I swallowed and squeezed her hand. 'I know you do. It's okay. It was a shock, that's all. I was expecting Anders McKenzie.'

She didn't smile. 'You were so vehement that you're totally over him. To me, to your family. I didn't think that — '

'I am. I'm totally over him. It's all perfectly amicable.'

'But you're upset that your family are so glad to see him.'

'No, not at all, not now that I think about it. I mean, how long were we married? Three and a half years? But he's always been your brother. And you've always been part of my family. So he is too.'

Liv gazed at me for a long time. I could see that she was trying to catch me out. But I was good at this, at appearing all right. I'd been doing it ever since I came back to Brickham.

'Today is about you,' I told her. 'We all love you so much, Liv. We're proud of you. That's all that matters.'

Finally, she nodded and I hugged her. The silk of our dresses was slippery between us.

'You're a beautiful bride,' I said. 'Let's pour the champagne.'

★　★　★

'For better and for worse.'

'For better and for worse.'

I stood on the hotel lawn at the side of the flower canopy, trying to keep upright and steady in my high heels. The sun was hot on the back of my head and there was a lock of hair dangling in my face, but my hands were full of Liv's

75

bouquet and I didn't want to distract from Liv and Yann's vows by fidgeting. I pursed my lips and blew out softly, hoping I could blow the hair away. No luck. It was a beautiful June day, not even a breeze.

'For richer and for poorer.'

Still, it was better to have the hair in my face, because at least I could look at that. I couldn't look at Liv and Yann; my mother's genes were too strong in me and I knew that if I looked at them I was going to burst into tears. I could hear Mum now, in the front row of the chairs that had been set up on the grass, sobbing and sniffing into a bright pink handkerchief and stage-whispering to everyone around her that it was *so beautiful* and she was *so happy* and it reminded her *so much* of her own wedding to Gavin, and did anyone have a tissue because this hankie was *soaked?*

I'd been watching the vicar's sleeve for most of the ceremony, but there was only so much staring at a sleeve that you could do.

I tried gazing over at the groom's side. Yann's family hadn't been able to make it over from New Zealand; his father had lung disease and couldn't travel by aeroplane. Liv and Yann were planning to have another small ceremony for his family when they got to Christchurch. But Yann had still managed to pretty much fill up his side, with their mutual friends from the firm they worked for in London, or fellow Kiwis he'd met while over here. I let my eyes wander over the guests, making myself concentrate on outfits and hairdos, until I saw the baby in the fifth row. A little girl, with a pink sun hat on.

I averted my eyes quickly, but not before I saw the pregnant woman in the fourth row, her hands resting happily on her swollen belly.

'In sickness and in health.'

I closed my eyes. How long did a wedding have to go on for, anyway? It seemed like this one was dragging on forever. Surely when I'd got married it hadn't taken this long. It had been a register office thing, and I could barely remember saying any vows at all. And they still had loads of vows left. I certainly couldn't keep my eyes closed for much longer or everyone would think I'd fallen asleep.

I turned my head slightly and found myself looking directly at Leo, who was between Pippi and my father. He'd never got into town to buy new clothes, but he'd buttoned one of my father's white shirts over his Rolling Stones T-shirt, and Liv had been, while not satisfied, at least willing to accept that. She knew him too well to expect too much in the way of dressing up.

The hotel where the wedding and the reception were being held was near the university, not far from my parents' house, and Leo had walked there with Liv and all of us Woodstocks. Of course we took the shortcut through Donnington Lane, a narrow road that ran between the sides of two terraces. The long brick wall was looped and scrawled with a dozen different colours of spray paint, renewed on a regular basis by the local teens.

Leo dropped back to fall into step alongside

me. He examined the wall as we walked. 'I must have tagged this wall between your house and mine a hundred times,' he said. I didn't reply. I didn't feel like walking down memory lane with Leo, even a narrow graffiti-lined one.

'There,' he said, stopping suddenly. 'That's one of mine, there.' He pointed to a small arch of black and silver, all that was left in the layers of years of other initials and cartoons.

'Quick, call Tate Modern, they'll want to put the whole wall on display.'

He resumed walking. 'Aren't you even the slightest bit glad to see me? The littlest, tiniest, most deeply buried bit glad?'

'No.'

'Come on. Surely you've thought about me once or twice in the past few years?'

'Not if I could help it.' I'd sped up my stride in my high heels, leaving him behind. After a little while he jogged forward and caught up with Liv.

Now he was sitting in a chair in the same row as my family, gazing around, looking utterly and infuriatingly at home. Who knew what he was thinking. He was probably trying to figure out which of the female wedding guests were single, and deciding which one he wanted to take back to his hotel room tonight. There was no doubt he'd be able to pull whoever he wanted to; even in my father's shirt, even though I'd die before admitting it aloud, he was sexy, with his rumpled brown hair and his brown eyes, so dark they were almost black. He'd always been sexy, without even thinking about it. Without even trying. That was part of the problem.

He shifted his gaze to the front of the church, in my direction, and I quickly looked back at the vicar's sleeve. Liv was finishing up her vows.

'Till death do us part,' she said.

Honey, I'm Home

I left the wedding as soon as Liv and Yann drove off in their rented Bentley for the Heathrow hotel they would stay in tonight, before flying to New Zealand tomorrow morning. I went back to the house on Charlotte Street, the house that used to be mine and Liv's but was now only mine. Her suitcases and bags were all gone.

'Welcome home,' I said to myself. The words seemed to echo in the big empty open-plan space. It was very, very quiet, especially after the music from the band at the reception.

I kicked off my shoes and wandered over to the sofa, my dress swishing around my legs as I curled up on the cushions. Now that the wedding was over, I didn't have to keep it crease-free any more. I found the remote and clicked on the wide-screen television that hung on one white wall.

I flicked the channels, not paying much attention to what was on the screen, using the telly for the noise. The party was still going on at the reception inside the hotel. My father had drifted through one dance with Liv while my mother sobbed. Then the music had picked up and Mum stormed onto the dance floor, all tears forgotten. As I left, she was leading the 'Time Warp'. Pippi had been sinking alco-pops as if they'd just been invented. And Liv and Yann had wandered around the room, talking and laughing with their guests, their arms around each other, radiant.

And Leo. I'd managed to avoid him for the whole reception, thankfully. If I knew Leo, and I did, he'd be partying to the small hours of tomorrow morning, and then he would disappear as suddenly as he'd arrived. Then I could get on with my life, without worrying about the past. In fact, from this moment on, my life was going to be about my future.

Onwards and upwards. I'd do my Eversley Hall article and I'd write several more. Maybe I'd take advantage of having the house to myself by doing something like learning to cook properly. Or I could get those yoga DVDs out and do them every day. It was only June, but I could treat this as my own personal new year.

Onwards and upwards.

I stood up from the sofa and walked around on the white carpet.

Who was I kidding? This wasn't a new year. I wasn't making incredible advances. I couldn't even dance at my best friend's wedding. I couldn't even deal with seeing my ex-husband.

I had thought I was over Leo. I hardly thought about him any more and I never talked about him. I'd consigned him to a little box way in the back of my consciousness.

I wouldn't have expected the box to burst open so easily, just with him walking into my parents' house.

I could feel it now. Cold and hot, panic and outrage, fear and hurt, disappointment and jealousy and loss and anger and loneliness. All I'd felt in Boston, all alone after he'd left, after the row when I'd sent him away for good. Days where nothing seemed real except for those feelings and whatever transient sensation I got from sleeping, drinking cups of tea, washing in tepid water. Those feelings were so big and so out of control. It had taken so much of my strength to wrestle them down, to stuff them into that tiny box, to shove them back so I didn't have to feel them or think about them, so I could go on with living and being Alice Woodstock again. With the feelings in a box, I could be human. Not a walking wound.

I hadn't known the box was still so flimsy.

'He'll go away again and it'll all be fine,' I said aloud. That decided, I focused on the telly. It was an old black and white movie, with Cary Grant and Katharine Hepburn trading witty animosity. I curled up on the sofa, resting my bare feet on a fluffy cushion, and let myself relax into the story. A hero, a heroine, a happy ending. The way it was supposed to be.

It hadn't been a movie wedding today — not with the cluttered house, the sunburned necks, the way Yann had dropped the slice of cake he was feeding to Liv. Not to mention the bad history between the chief and only bridesmaid, and the bride's brother. But Liv and Yann were getting their happy ending. I smiled for real for the first time since this afternoon.

The front door opened and a voice called out, 'Hey, honey, I'm home!'

I jumped up, scattering cushions everywhere, and whirled around. Leo stood by the door. He held his leather jacket in one hand and a bottle of champagne in the other. He had an orchid, from Liv's bouquet by the looks of it, tucked behind his ear.

'What are you doing here?' I demanded.

'Celebrating.' He came further into the room, and I noticed his steps were unsteady. Christ.

'Celebrating what?' I snapped.

'Liv's marriage, Pippi's growing up, you and I seeing each other again, the fact that it's Sunday, anything you like, really.' He smiled crookedly.

'You've been drinking.'

'I've been at my sister's wedding. Do I detect some semblance of caring in your words?'

'No, just familiarity.'

He shrugged. 'You wouldn't talk to me. What else was I supposed to do?'

'Why are you here?'

'I'm staying here, of course.'

'What?'

'In my old bedroom,' Leo said. 'The scene of so many happy memories.' Still smiling, he tilted his head back and gazed at the ceiling.

'You are fucking kidding me.'

'Oh, but I am fucking not.' He seemed to think this was hilarious and actually began chuckling.

'But *I'm* using the house! I live here!'

'It's like old times again, isn't it, Alice, the two of us sharing the same space?' He leaned heavily against the back of the sofa. 'This place has changed, hasn't it? I remember it as much darker. I think there used to be a broken hi-fi right about where I'm standing now. Had my dad's footprint through it. How about you get us some glasses and I'll pop open this bottle of bubbly?'

'Leo, I don't want you here. I thought you were staying in the hotel.'

'Why would I do that when I've got a perfectly good house? The leaks in the roof are fixed these days, I assume?' Leo unwrapped the foil from the bottle of champagne. He dropped the foil on the carpet and began twisting the cork. 'Last chance to get some glasses; otherwise we'll have to drink from the bottle.'

'But — you don't have any stuff here.'

'It's upstairs. I dropped it all off before the wedding.'

'You — ' I couldn't breathe properly. 'You can't stay here, Leo.'

'Of course I can. The house is half mine, after all. Left to me by our dear old dad.' The cork popped, and Leo held out the bottle. 'Care to join me in a toast to the elder Allingham? No longer with us and never lamented?' I didn't make a move towards the champagne, so Leo took a swig. 'Not bad,' he said, wiping his mouth with his sleeve. 'Do you remember the days of wine and sunshine, Alice?'

'Shut up,' I said to him.

'If you won't have a drink with me, how about a kiss?' He stepped towards me.

I grabbed the nearest thing, which happened to be a satin cushion, and hurled it at his head.

The cushion sailed past him. He didn't even have to duck. 'You must have thought about me,' he said. 'You wouldn't be so pissed off if you didn't care.'

'This is how much I care.' I reached for the television remote and threw that, too. It went flying and clinked off the champagne bottle he held.

He frowned. 'If you don't mind, I think I'll go upstairs to my room and enjoy a quiet drink by myself.'

'Choke on it,' I said sweetly to his back as he walked away.

'See you in the morning!' he called over his shoulder.

Perfectly Amicable

When I woke up, the sun was high in the sky and the house was quiet.

I checked my clock. It was nearly noon, surely enough time for Leo to have woken up and dragged his hungover self out of the house back to the airport. There was nothing for him in Brickham any more, and he doubtlessly had lots of Very Important Artist activities to do in the States.

Since our divorce, while I'd been in Brickham, living with his sister and writing about amazing breakthroughs in rubber technology et cetera, Leo Allingham had been becoming famous. He'd ditched his more traditional illustration for paintings and installations based on the graffiti and vandalism he'd dabbled with as a kid, and he immediately began picking up major commissions. Most notably, he'd cut an abandoned house in half and filled it with graffiti, called it *inside,* and for some unknown reason this large-scale bit of juvenile insanity won him tons of awards. My mother had all the newspaper clippings.

Bastard.

Anyway, I lay in bed with my laptop for an extra forty-five minutes to be certain he was gone, reading through and tweaking the draft of the article for *Hot! Hot!* that I'd written last night. I'd stayed up till four o'clock, working on it. Even given my errors at Eversley Hall, it was much more pleasant to relive my day in the kitchen as Ann Horton than to think about Leo Allingham lying in the bedroom below mine, dead drunk and probably snoring. And the article wasn't half bad, actually, once I'd given it a more positive slant. It had a shape to it, a narrative, and the way I wrote it, it even had a heroine, the humble journalist-cum-scullery-maid who saved her friend and got to talk with the handsome guy. Well, sort of talk to him. He touched her hair, anyway.

I absently wound the strand he'd touched around my finger, remembering the moment, wondering about it, until I noticed that I seriously needed to pee.

Surely it was safe to go downstairs by now. I listened again, and there was definitely nothing in the house: no footsteps, no voices, no radio playing. I composed a quick email to Edie, the Features Editor at *Hot! Hot!*, attached my article, and sent it off. I found it was generally better to do these things quickly before you could think too much about them, or else you'd never let anything go. Then I pulled on a pair of leggings and a sweatshirt from where they lay on my floor and went down to the bathroom.

The door to the room across the landing from Liv's bedroom was closed. I had never thought of that room as Leo's before, though if I'd thought about it, of course I'd have known it was where he used to sleep as a child. Liv used it as her spare bedroom; she'd redecorated it as she'd redecorated the rest of the house. I paused to listen outside it, but all was quiet. He was either sleeping or gone. In either case, I was safe for the moment at least.

The bathroom was enormous, full of gleaming surfaces, mirrors and graceful potted plants. It had been Mr Allingham's bedroom apparently, before Liv gutted it and plumbed in a sink, toilet and big claw-footed tub. My make-up was still on from the day before, smudged beneath my eyes; I removed it with a pot of cold cream and twisted my hair up into a clip, careful not to leave red strands in the spotless sink. Then I went downstairs. The sofa cushions were still scattered on the floor; the one I'd thrown at Leo was halfway across the living space. I collected them and put them back on the sofa, and looked around for the remote, which was nowhere to be seen. It had probably deflected off the champagne bottle and gone underneath something. Deciding I'd look again after a cup of tea, I headed for the kitchen.

I was halfway to the kettle before I saw Leo. Or rather, his backside. He had his head in a low cabinet, and all I could see was his lower half in jeans, with his arse in the air. He had bare feet.

Something clunked and through the cabinet I heard Leo give a small grunt of triumph. He backed out of the cabinet and kneeled on the floor. He was wearing the same Rolling Stones T-shirt; his hair was rumpled and his chin rough. Overall, he looked much more like how I'd expected him to look yesterday.

And seeing him still made my heart thump and head spin. I'd forgotten how good he looked hungover. It wasn't fair.

He turned Liv's stovetop espresso pot over in his hands, examining it. In the moment before he noticed me, I registered that he was a bit thinner than the last time I'd seen him. His jeans were loose around his waist and thighs. It wouldn't surprise me if he'd spent the past few years on a largely liquid-only diet.

Not my problem. I considered backing out of the kitchen before he saw me, but then decided no. Leo might own half of this house, but I lived here, and he wasn't going to stop me from doing something so basic as getting a cup of tea. I proceeded to the kettle, and he glanced up.

'Morning, Mermaid,' he said. 'Sleep well?'

'Don't call me that.' I snapped on the kettle.

He got to his feet and went to the freezer. 'Have you got any — ah, here it is.' He took the vacuum canister of coffee out, flipped open the lid, and inhaled. 'My favourite roast. Good woman. Do you always have coffee, or do you keep it just in case I turn up?'

'Did Liv know you meant to stay here last night?'

'Well, she was a little bit preoccupied, what with getting married and all.'

I pressed my lips together and put a tea bag in my mug.

'Good morning, Leo. Good morning, Alice. Did you sleep well, Leo? Yes, thank you, Alice, and you? Tolerably well, Leo, and how do you feel this morning? Well, I'm a little bit rough to tell the truth, thanks Alice, but a good espresso should sort me out nicely — would you like one?

Oh, no thank you, Leo, I prefer a nice cup of tea, brewed to within an inch of its life, but I appreciate your kindness in asking.'

I tapped my foot, willing the kettle to hurry up and boil.

'That's how I'd expect the morning conversation to go,' he said, 'if we were being amicable. That's what we're meant to have, isn't it, an amicable divorce?'

Boil. Damn you.

He spooned coffee into the top of the espresso maker. I noted with a certain grim satisfaction that his hand wasn't steady.

'I got the impression that your family believes it was all very amicable,' he said. 'That we just grew naturally apart.'

'I didn't let them think that because it would be easier for you.'

'Why did you, Alice?' He tried to meet my eyes, but I wouldn't let him. I stared at the kettle.

'Would you have liked it better if I'd come back crawling on my knees?' he asked. 'Maybe wearing a hair shirt or something. I probably have one of those around here somewhere. I'll check the wardrobe if you like.'

I said nothing. He put the coffee pot on the hob with a clang, and then picked up the small radio that sat next to the sleek gas cooker and fiddled with its knobs. No sound came out. Leo banged the radio a couple of times on the worktop, wincing slightly each time, then shrugged, pulled out a chair with a bare foot and sat in it.

'So what would you like to talk about, Alice? To be amicable.'

At last, a wisp of steam came out of the spout of the kettle and I could hear the first sign of bubbling. I snatched it off its base and poured water onto my tea bag.

'I don't see any reason why we should talk to each other at all,' I said.

He rubbed his hand against his chin. I could hear the small sound of his stubble rasping on his palm. Against my will, my own palms remembered the feeling. 'Don't you want to know what I've been up to for the past few years?' he said. 'My work, my health, where I've been, what I've seen?'

'No.'

'It would be a very amicable conversation.'

'I told you, I'm not interested.'

'I thought you had better manners than that, Alice. We could talk about something more immediate, if you like. No point in dwelling in the past. For example, you look tired. And you've lost weight.'

I mashed my tea bag viciously against the side of the cup, and poured milk in. It wasn't strong enough yet, but I didn't care. I threw the tea bag into the compost bin and shut it with a thunk.

Leo sighed. 'I can see that it's going to be a fun few months,' he said.

I'd started for the door, but with that, I stopped. And turned.

'What?'

'Well, it's not exactly a laugh a minute around here with you. I'll buy a new radio and that will help, but it would be more pleasant with some real-life conversation.'

'What do you mean,' I said slowly and dangerously, 'a *few months*?'

He smiled at me. 'Ah, some conversation at last. I knew we'd hit upon a topic that interested you, eventually.'

'Leo, are you planning to stay here?'

'Well, with such a warm welcome, I would be heartless if I didn't accept your hospitality, don't you think?'

'Why are you staying?'

'Several reasons, really. One is that I've got a show in London at the end of September.'

The coffee-maker was bubbling, filling the kitchen with its smell. The smell of nearly every morning of my married life, except for when Leo was having his coffee somewhere else.

'It's June. And you plan to stay in Brickham until September? Why aren't you staying in London?'

'I've got a perfectly good house here.' He got up and poured himself some coffee.

'But it's miles away from London here — you'll have to travel.'

'Only half an hour on the train. I can catch up on my reading.'

I tried to comprehend this. Leo was going to be in the house, with me. Every day.

'How long will you be here? Exactly? I need to know how long I'm going to have to put up with this, or if I'm going to have to find a new place to live.'

'Oh, don't do that, Mermaid. I wouldn't want

to put you out of house and home.'

'Don't call me that,' I gritted. 'Just tell me how long you're going to stay. That's all.'

Leo leaned back on the counter, his face serious for the first time since I'd walked into the room. 'I honestly don't know. I've got a lot to do. I want to try to sort things out.'

'Are there some new pubs you haven't visited yet? A few local girls you never got around to sleeping with?'

'How well you think you know me, Alice, and what a flattering picture you paint.' He banged the espresso pot on the side of the compost bin to empty it of coffee, then spooned in some more. He always did that, too: made his second cup of coffee before he'd drunk his first one. 'No, I don't think I'm in a great hurry to sleep with any more local girls. The last time I tried that, I got a bit more than I'd bargained for.'

Meaning me. Getting married had been his idea — he'd proposed to me outside my bedroom window on a night with a full moon and woken up all the neighbours, in fact — but I forbore from reminding him. There was no point going through all of *that*. 'So you'll be here for some time, but you're not sure how long. Definitely till the end of September.'

'That's it.'

'And you don't care that it will seriously inconvenience me.'

'It doesn't have to, Alice. We've lived together, we know how to rub along.'

'That was before.'

'And if there's a before, there always has to be

93

an after.' He put the pot on the burner, and turned it on. 'Or are you going to argue with me about that, too?'

'Oh, forget it,' I said, throwing up my hands in exasperation and turning away. 'I'll get my breakfast in the café.'

'Alice,' he said softly, as I reached the door. I paused, but I didn't turn around. 'Does it really have to be so hard?' he asked.

'You're the one who made it this way,' I said. 'You figure it out.'

My heart didn't stop racing until I was sitting in the Beaumont Café with a pot of tea and a pain au chocolat in front of me. I'd thought chocolate would help, but I made no move to touch it.

Leo was staying. For four months, at the very least. He'd be there every time I woke up, every time I wanted to do anything. The whole downstairs, apart from the kitchen, was open-plan; I wouldn't be able to avoid him unless I stayed up in my room all the time.

And whenever we spoke, it would be a sparring match. We'd try to score points off each other and I would feel like this, dizzy and sick with adrenaline and anger.

What was I going to do? I couldn't work in these conditions, and it wasn't going to do any favours to my mental health, either.

I buried my face in my hands. Why didn't I have a boyfriend? It would be the ideal situation, if I could blithely move out and into the arms of another man. It would get me out of the house and show Leo that he didn't mean anything to me any more. A boyfriend would come in incredibly handy right now. But it was probably too late to go out and find one. By the time we'd reached moving-in stage, Leo might have packed up already.

No, I hadn't been forward-thinking enough to get myself a lover, so I'd have to find another solution.

As if answering my thoughts, my mobile phone rang and I saw it was Mum.

'Alice,' she said as soon as I answered, 'when are you coming over? We've got all the leftover wedding cake still to eat.'

Maybe that's what I could do. Maybe I could move back home for a few months. My old room was a sewing room now, but I could clear it out.

'Actually, Mum . . . ' I began.

'How are you this morning? You looked so tired last night, though I can't blame you, with all the excitement. I hope you got some sleep. Can you believe that Liv and Yann are on their way to New Zealand right now for their second wedding? How do you think her dress is going to do in that suitcase?'

'She's a very careful packer.' I sat back in my chair. At home, there would always be someone to talk with. Mum would cook for me, too. I could do puzzles with Dad, and watch *East-Enders* with Pippi. It wouldn't be too bad. 'Mum, you're not doing too much sewing these days, are you?'

'Now, it's funny you should mention that, because I was just in the sewing room this morning and I found that scrapbook I had of

95

those clippings about Leo. It was in a pile of Wendy's old exercise books, if you can believe that. I'm so proud of him, we always knew he'd make something of himself one day, despite all that sadness at home, poor boy. And Liv too. And of course both of you have been through so much, he deserves all that happiness and recognition, don't you think? I've got you alone right now so I can ask you, and you know you can be honest with me, Alice: how do you feel about Leo being back? Because we're thrilled to see him, obviously, but you're the important one here. I know that you and Leo went through a lot together, and maybe it's stirring up some memories for you. It would be natural if it did. Don't you agree?'

'Um.' I glanced around the café. It was full of people — old ladies with tea cakes, a business-man with a laptop and latte. In the corner was a group of chattering mothers with the newest styles of prams. I swallowed.

This was not the time or place to go through why Leo and I split up. Even if I wanted to.

'It's all right,' I said. 'I just wasn't expecting him. And we . . . haven't got a lot in common these days.'

'Well, you have your entire childhood in common, basically. He was always round the house.'

'Somehow that feels like a very long time ago.'

'You see, to me it feels like yesterday. You never get used to the idea of your children growing up, even though you're there when they're doing it. Isn't that funny?'

My eyes were drawn again to the cluster of prams in the corner. Mum coughed and cleared her throat, and then drew an audible breath to resume talking.

'Anyway, darling, I just wanted to check that you're okay with seeing Leo, especially as he's going to be around now, in the same house as you and everything.'

I sat up straight. 'Mum. You knew?'

'Of course. He told us last night, and I told him he must come round for Sunday lunch every week that he's here. If that's okay with you, of course. It'll give us a chance to know him again.'

She kept on talking, and I let her words babble on through the phone. Of course my family would want to see Leo while he was here. They'd probably invite him round every chance they got. Staying with them wouldn't be any escape at all. I could tell them about the way we'd split up, but then I'd have to discuss it, over and over and over again. *Poor Alice.*

' . . . And Pippi has been throwing up all day. We can't even get near the upstairs bathroom, it's absolutely unhealthy. You should see her, she's the colour of a dishrag and she's got the temperament of a bear. It was all those alco-pops. Do you remember when Heidi and her friends had that party and they were so sick all over the back garden? And in your Wellingtons? I told your father never again, but it was Liv's wedding so I suppose what's the harm? She'll be right as rain by suppertime, and thank goodness her next exam isn't until Wednesday. Still, there are worse things than a hangover,

97

though the bathroom really is like a plague zone. But we've been through worse, I daresay. Do you remember when all six of us came down with food poisoning from that dodgy potato salad that summer? All of us, running at both ends, with only the two toilets in the house?'

I pushed away my cup of tea. There was another one gone to waste. Maybe I'd get to enjoy a cup of tea again sometime, say in October.

'I try not to remember that,' I said.

'So did you get a good night's sleep in the end? When will you be here, did you say?'

'Actually, Mum, I don't think I'll be round this afternoon. I'd as soon avoid the house if Pippi's being sick.'

'That's reasonable enough. Still, you and Leo need some time to get reacquainted. Two years can change a lot, Alice. I imagine both of you have plenty to talk about.'

I closed my eyes. 'If you're hoping that we'll get back together, Mum, it's not going to happen.'

'Oh well, Alice, of course I would never interfere. But the two of you were so attached to each other. Maybe if you spend some more time together you'll discover you still do have a lot in common. You seemed very affected when he turned up out of the blue at the house. Very emotional. Not just tired. That's why I asked, before.'

'I was very surprised.'

'Something more than that, I fancy. I don't think you're going to have to dig very deep to find there are still some feelings there under-neath. Anyway, as I said, I won't interfere, so I'll say no more about it. You just know that your father and I love Leo like a son, and we're happy to have him back in Brickham no matter what the relationship is, son-in-law or just a friend of the family. Whatever, is fine with us.'

I liked it better when she was talking about my sister's puking. 'I've got to go, Mum.'

It took another seven minutes before I could actually put the phone down, but when I did, I sighed. So much for moving into my parents' house.

The only solution was to find somewhere new to live as soon as possible. I got a copy of the local paper from the newspaper rack on the Beaumont's wall and turned to the property section, digging out a pen to circle any likely contenders. I wanted a flat, one bedroom ideally, or even a bedsit; something that wasn't too horrid. I spread the paper out, my mobile phone ready to call any likely numbers. No sense wasting any time.

By five o'clock I had combed through the paper, called several estate agents and visited three properties. I had discovered two things: one, that Liv had been charging me a shockingly low monthly rate of rent considering the quality of the house we were living in, and two, that for the same money, I couldn't afford much. The first flat I visited was a student bedsit abandoned for the summer, and it had no windows and a mouldy carpet. The second was in a new develop-ment on the London Road. It was clean, modern, airy, spacious and light, and it seemed to be in my price bracket, more or less, only a hundred quid more than what I was already paying. I'd have to scrape my bank account clean and sell as many articles as I could, but otherwise, it seemed too good to be true. Until I told the estate agent I'd take it, and he dropped into the conversation that the amount quoted in the newspaper was per week, not per month.

The third flat, which I'd included as a long shot, was in a basement across the street from the Majestic Club, the worst nightclub in Brickham. I'd frequented the Majestic often enough as a student to know that the basement flat windows in the area were prime spots for clubbers to chuck their empty tins of lager or their stomach contents. The first thing I saw when I went down the stairs to the door was a used condom wrapper. Despite this, and the suspiciously scrubbed appearance of the front window, when the agent answered the door he told me that the flat had been taken by the last person to visit.

I bought a prawn sandwich from Marks & Spencer on Broad Street on my way from the basement flat and ate it in Highbury Park. Chewing gloomily, I watched the pigeons watching my sandwich and I concluded that unless I wanted to set up a tent here in the park, my options were few.

My phone rang in my bag, and I took it out, resolving not to answer it if it was Mum again. It was a local landline number, one I didn't know. Maybe it was one of the estate agents I'd called today getting back to me. 'Hello?'

'Alice?' asked a deep male voice on the other end. 'This is James Fitzwilliam, from Eversley Hall. I wonder if you have some time to meet with me this evening, or tomorrow. I have a proposition for you.'

Welcome to 1814

This time, I pulled right up to the front door. James Fitzwilliam was waiting for me on the steps of Eversley Hall, the sunshine in his golden hair. He met me as I stepped out of the 2CV.

'Thanks for coming back,' he said.

I shook his hand. He didn't look cross. He hadn't sounded cross on the phone, either. In fact, he looked quite cheerful. So if I was lucky, he wasn't going to berate me for destroying the historical illusion in Eversley Hall's kitchens and forbid me to send my article to *Hot! Hot!* or ever to darken his doors again.

Or maybe he was the kind of person who looked cheerful when he was actually cross.

'I happened to be free this afternoon,' I said as breezily as I could.

'I'm very glad. Please, come through.'

He led me through the hall, past the portrait of his identical great-whatever-grandfather and over the velvet ropes again. But this time, instead of heading for the discreet servants' door, we went through a vast double set of wooden doors at the far end of the room.

I blinked at the sudden brightness after the muted tones of the hall. The room was vast, red and gold and glittering from the huge crystal chandelier that hung from the gilded ceiling. Floor-to-ceiling French windows opened up to the sunlight outside, letting in a fresh breeze and the muted sound of burbling water. Rich paintings framed in gold gazed down from the deep red walls; a vase of lilies exuded scent from atop a piano.

'The Red Saloon,' James Fitzwilliam said beside me. It was a testament to the impressiveness of the room that I'd stopped looking at him for a moment.

'It . . . sparkles.' Light bounced off two mirrors, each at least eight foot tall, set to reflect the windows. Everything was gold or red: the delicate furniture gilded in gold and upholstered in red silk, the red carpet, the carved gold-painted friezes gleaming along the top of the walls.

'It was designed to dazzle. It's the room for visiting dignitaries or anyone else the Fitzwilliams want to impress. Please, have a seat.'

He was indicating one of the silk and gold sofas. 'Er — here?' I perched gingerly on the edge. 'It's like sitting on a museum piece.'

'A museum piece that's meant to be sat on.' He sat across from me on a matching armchair, and reached over to a glossy side-table where a porcelain tea service sat. Not the violet one I'd used last week, with the hand-knitted cosy; this one appeared Chinese and enormously valuable. 'Tea? Or would you like a glass of wine?'

'Tea, please. Do you — do you actually live here?' I couldn't imagine lounging in this room, reading the Sunday newspaper. Or watching TV. I glanced around again; there was no place to hide a television, anyway. It was all glamorous and historical, and I was certain it was 100 per cent historically accurate.

'There are more modern apartments upstairs that aren't open to the public. My ancestors had more of a taste for splendour on a daily basis than I do.' He poured tea from the pot, added milk, and handed a cup to me. I held it nervously. The last thing I needed to do was splash tea all over this furniture. And the carpet. The carpet must have cost a fortune.

'Listen,' I said, 'I'm sorry about the big scene in the kitchen on Saturday. About the under-gardener and everything. It just sort of — came out.'

He finished pouring himself tea and settled back in his own chair. 'Where did it come from?'

I chewed my lip. I couldn't tell him about covering for Kayleigh; he was the boss, it seemed, and it wouldn't look good for her. And it wasn't my place to complain about Mrs Smudge. 'It seemed like it would be fun. It would liven the kitchen up a bit, to have a little romance.'

'To make it more like those novels you told me you read?'

'Not really. The novels tend to concentrate more on dashing heiresses and rogues. Wayward dukes and innocent governesses. People like that. Not that it wasn't as interesting below stairs, but people like a bit of glitz in their romances.'

'I don't read many novels — I don't seem to have the time. Maybe I should. Was it useful for your article?'

'I did write about it, yes.' I took a careful sip of the tea. It was strong and good — just how I

104

liked it. Though my enjoyment was impaired by the delicacy of the cup, the pricelessness of the furniture, and the possibility that the rich, powerful, good-looking man across from me was about to give me a piece of his mind.

'I was sorry you had to go so quickly on Saturday afternoon,' he said. 'I'd hoped to get the chance to have a chat with you before you left. Nobody stopped talking about your story of Ann Horton and the under-gardener all afternoon.'

'Oh no. I really am sorry.'

James shook his head, smiling. 'There's nothing to be sorry about. The visitors loved it. I overheard several of them saying they'd be coming back, just to find out what happened next.'

'Poor Fiona.'

'She'll be fine.'

'But it's not exactly historically accurate. And that's what you're aiming for.'

'Well,' he said slowly, as if he were considering, 'it's not impossible that it was true. As you said, life below stairs was as full of interest as life above stairs. An affair between the scullery maid and the under-gardener could well have happened. It's the sort of thing that could be true. And it wouldn't have been documented, so we would never know. History is fact, but a lot of it, necessarily, is filling in the empty spaces between facts.'

It didn't appear that I was going to be told off, or warned never to come to Eversley Hall again. 'But you said you were only doing things that were completely documented.'

'I've been thinking about that. And it seems to me that we need to strike a balance. We're presenting history at Eversley Hall, but we're also aiming to be a visitor attraction. It's our first season open to the public and I want to make sure that it's a success.'

'Well, I hope my article can help you. I really like it here, and I think you deserve to succeed. You nearly gave me a heart attack, by the way, when you turned up. I had no idea you were dressing up as your own ancestor.'

James leaned his forearms on his knees. He was clean-shaven and his blond hair was neat. He wore jeans and a pressed cotton shirt, open at the throat. Faintly, I could smell the tang of his aftershave.

'I will do absolutely anything to make Eversley Hall a success,' he said to me, in a voice that was lowered with conviction. 'From the moment we decided to have historical interpreters, I knew I had to do it myself, and that I had to be the original James Fitzwilliam.'

'Because you look just like the portrait?'

'So I'm told. But mainly it's because I care passionately about this house. It's my inheritance, and my legacy. I've devoted the last four years to its renovation. I know more about it than anyone else, and I want to do my best to make my visitors' experience a memorable one.'

I realised, with a catch of my breath, that we were leaning towards each other, with barely as much space between us as in that moment when he'd touched my hair. His blue eyes were earnest and — yes, passionate.

'I admire that,' I said. A man who had a cause he believed in, who would do anything in his power to make it come right. Including dressing up in tight breeches and talking as if it were two hundred years ago.

I more than admired it. It made my mouth water.

'Help me,' he said.

'Yes,' I said immediately, without thinking. Then: 'Er ... how? I've already written my article. But maybe I could pitch something else, somewhere.'

'Yes, please. I would really appreciate that, and it would help. But I was also thinking of something a little more hands-on. The proposition I mentioned on the telephone earlier.'

'What is it?'

'I know you must be very busy. But it's mainly at the weekends, though there will be some evenings during the week for various things like training or dance lessons.'

Dance lessons? 'You — you don't want me to dress up again?'

'You seem to have a talent for it, Alice. You learned everything about the house in just a few days, and then when you were presented with a situation that was outside of your brief, you improvised rapidly, dramatically, and with skill.'

'So ... you want me to be a scullery maid some more?'

'No. I want you to join us upstairs, in the main house.'

'As a Fitzwilliam?'

107

He smiled. 'Not exactly. The roles of the family are all filled.'

'Who as, then?'

'I've been thinking about that quite a bit. I think we can get away with a distant cousin of the Fitzwilliams, an unmarried gentlewoman.'

'Why has she come to Eversley Hall?'

'Her parents have died, and their estate was entailed upon a male relative.'

'Therefore she's homeless?' I could identify with that.

'And nearly penniless.'

'Her only resort is to find a position as a companion or a governess.'

'Or sympathetic relatives who will take her in.'

'It's the beginning of a hundred novels.'

'And a historically accurate situation for an unmarried woman in the early nineteenth century,' he said. 'Are you interested?'

I was practically falling off my seat. I straightened up a little bit, and sipped my tea. 'Tell me more.'

'I think you have to understand the family situation. James Fitzwilliam was the only son of Sir Charles Fitzwilliam. Sir Charles's first wife died in 1784, and he remarried, to Georgiana Norton. The second Lady Fitzwilliam gave him a daughter, Selina, but then Sir Charles died in 1810, leaving his son James in charge of the estate and the family. James bought Eversley Hall as a country residence in the autumn of 1813, and the family moved in for the following spring and summer. That's what we're recreating now.'

I nodded. This was all in the original dossier I'd read.

'In the summer of 1814, Lady Fitzwilliam's daughter Selina, James's half-sister, was eighteen. Her governess, Miss Brambles — '

'Died in April.'

He raised his eyebrows and nodded, clearly impressed. 'Yes. And another wasn't employed that summer. But there wouldn't necessarily be records of an unattached female relative staying in the household, and Lady Fitzwilliam might have found it convenient to have such a person around.'

'An unpaid companion, you mean.'

He shrugged. 'An unmarried, penniless cousin would need to repay the kindness of her relations.'

It still beat seven bells out of a scullery maid. 'So did this person actually exist?'

'No.'

'You're *making up* someone? I thought the whole point was that these people were real.'

'The point,' said James, 'is to draw visitors to the house. And I think you will.'

He was still watching me with that intensity in his eyes. That passion. Despite the breeze from the French windows, I felt my cheeks heating up.

'So you're offering me a job.'

'I believe you'd be brilliant, Alice. I've been thinking about it constantly since Saturday after-noon. It's a paid position, of course. You could fit it in around your writing. And as I said, maybe you'd like to write about it, too. It's for the rest of the season, until the end of September, during house opening hours — ten until five o'clock on Saturday and Sunday. And the evening sessions, as they happen. I'll give you a schedule so you could plan ahead.'

The way he was looking at me made it difficult to think about things like planning ahead. 'What would I wear?'

'Black, I'm afraid. You're in full mourning. But it's a gentlewoman's costume.'

'Doesn't it take ages to make a costume like that?'

'I can have it done by Friday. We're only waiting for you to say yes. I have a contract right here.'

I took a long, deep breath. Then I drank some more tea. In reality I didn't need these pauses to know what I was going to answer. I was going to be a Regency gentlewoman. And a job outside the house would take me out of Leo's path every weekend. It might even make the rest of this summer bearable.

And how could I say no to James Fitzwilliam, who had said he hadn't been able to stop thinking about me?

'Who else is upstairs, besides you and me?' I asked.

'Lady Fitzwilliam. Selina. There are two visitors, friends of the family who, according to records, stayed all summer at Eversley Hall. Miss Isabella Grantham and her younger brother, Arthur.'

'That's it?'

'That's it. We have six of the principal rooms open to the public: the Hall, the Saloon, the

Green Drawing Room, the Library, and two bedrooms. Five interpreters can cover them, but an additional interpreter will be very useful.'

'And what are the evening events you mentioned?'

'We have a variety of lectures and special-interest tours, though it's unlikely you'd be asked to participate in them. The main event is in August and it's open to the public — a Regency ball.'

'A ball?' I nearly clapped my hands together, then remembered my cup of tea. 'Oh my God, what I could write about a ball!'

'Preferably beforehand, so that the tickets would be highly desirable.'

I smiled. 'So Lady Fitzwilliam gets a companion, and you get free publicity.'

'It's win-win all round.'

'Do I get to wear knickers?'

James threw back his head and laughed.

'I don't really want to think about that too much,' he said.

'I'll do it.'

'Great.'

He reached out his arm and took a black folder from a table on the other side of his chair. I hadn't noticed the folder before, but it had obviously been there all along. He gave it to me. 'This is all the information you'll need about the house, its furnishings, and its history. There's also a section about the garden, and a more extensive contextual section. You'll also find a calendar of events planned for the summer, and the contract in the back.'

The folder was substantially heavier than the one I'd had for Ann Horton. I opened it to the title page: *Eversley Hall, 1814: Alice Woodstock.*

He'd been pretty certain of my answer all along, it seemed.

'We've included only the information your character would be likely to know already about the Fitzwilliam family; I think it will be more interesting if you discover what else is to be known through conversation, as if you were really a newcomer to Eversley Hall. The information about you is pretty much as we've discussed already. I'll leave it up to you to invent the necessary details about your life before you came to Eversley Hall.'

'What's my name?' I asked.

He tapped his chin with one finger. 'You're the sole fictional character at Eversley Hall this summer. Do you mind being called Alice Woodstock?'

'That's fine. It's easy to remember, anyway.'

'Thank you, Alice. I appreciate it.' James shook hands with me again. 'Welcome to 1814.'

Radio Silence

When I got back home, the sun was setting. I paused just inside the door to listen, but I didn't hear a radio.

Leo hated silence. He constantly had music on in his studio or wherever he happened to be, using a transistor, his laptop, a stereo or iPod. He didn't care what he listened to as long as it was constant, though he preferred rock music. We'd had a battered boom box in the kitchen of our Boston apartment, its aerial replaced by a bent wire coat hanger. It only picked up WZLX, The Mother of Classic Rock. The soundtrack of our married life.

Of course, he might not have replaced the kitchen radio yet. I tiptoed across the living space into the kitchen, where I stopped dead in the doorway.

The espresso maker was still sitting on the cooker; drops of coffee spattered on the white surface. An empty, used cup sat near the sink, along with a dirty teaspoon and a knife with butter still smeared on it. Toast crumbs littered the granite worktop and the glass kitchen table. But all this breakfast detritus was nothing compared to the chaos of wet laundry that was draped over the chairs, over the radiator, over the tea-towel rail.

There was no sign of the man himself though, and given the choice of the two, I'd rather have

113

his laundry. I made myself a cheese sandwich and a cup of tea, careful not to leave any mess nor to clean up after any of his. I'd bring my sandwich up to my room so I wouldn't encounter Leo if he came back in. I had a lot of work to do before Saturday, and James had invited me to visit Eversley Hall as much as I liked between now and then. There wouldn't be any interpreters working during the week, but I could look over the house and learn more about it. And I also had to get in touch with Edie at *Hot! Hot!* and ask if she was interested in more articles, or if she wanted me to change the one I'd already written to reflect life upstairs.

I put the cheese and chutney back in the fridge, noticed I had a smear of chutney on my hand, and grabbed a tea towel to wipe it off. What was life going to be like upstairs? Fourteen hours every weekend, in the company of the Regency James Fitzwilliam lookalike . . .

The tea towel didn't feel right — it was too light and smooth — so I looked down at my hand. It wasn't a tea towel; it was one of Leo's shirts. A dress shirt in fine white cotton, with a pattern woven into it so subtly that you could only see it from a certain angle.

I knew this shirt. I'd bought it for him myself on Newbury Street in Boston. It was too expensive but I'd bought it anyway because it was his birthday and he never, ever wore anything but T-shirts. It was 14 March and we'd been married seven months, a long enough time that I'd thought of ways I'd like to change him, and a short enough time to think that he would change.

I'd given him the shirt along with a secondhand signed copy of *Waterloo Sunset* by Ray Davies and he'd worn the shirt out to dinner that night in the North End with no jacket even though it was storming outside. We'd walked home, freezing cold and wet through, across the Common and through the streets, and when we'd got back to our apartment I'd taken it off him.

Chutney smeared across the front near the buttons, the place where it had gone transparent from the March rain soaking through to his skin.

I dropped the shirt on the floor and fled upstairs.

⋆ ⋆ ⋆

I was on my second reading of the dossier and had paused to look up a more thorough account of the causes of the Napoleonic Wars on the internet when I heard the door go downstairs. I checked the clock: pub closing time. What a surprise.

Music went on downstairs. I went on clicking links and reading, but I didn't hear anything other than the distant music. Maybe he'd gone straight to bed. Maybe he'd passed out on the sofa. I really couldn't care less.

I was up to Napoleon's banishment to Elba, still keeping an ear out for some sort of horrendous din from downstairs, when I heard a different kind of noise. A soft, careful footstep. I looked up and Leo was standing in the doorway of my office. He had on a red T-shirt and his battered leather jacket.

'This is my part of the house,' I said to him.

He nodded. 'I can see that.'

I waited for him to take the hint, but he kept standing there looking around as if my personal space was some sort of tourist attraction, so I said, 'And I'm doing work in it now. So I need to be alone.'

He didn't move. 'These used to be the attics. We kept all kinds of stuff up here. Liv must have thrown it all out.'

'You were in America.'

He leaned against the doorway, and I made an impatient sound which he seemed not to hear. 'I used to come up here sometimes when I didn't want to be found,' he said.

'Well, you're pretty obvious now, aren't you?'

'Liv's done quite a job renovating the house. I'd hardly know it was the same building. It seems — wiped clean.'

'She likes everything tidy and in order. Modern, with no clutter at all.'

If he hadn't understood my hints about my wanting him to leave, he certainly wasn't going to get this one about keeping the place tidy. Still, it was worth a try.

'I'm betting she doesn't come up here often, then,' he said.

'What are you trying to say? That my rooms are a tip? Everything is exactly how I want it up here, exactly where I can find it.'

'Yes, I remember your filing system.' He gazed around my office.

'There's a dryer downstairs, you know. For

116

your laundry. And a dishwasher.'

'Is that an offer?'

'It most definitely isn't.'

He put his hands in the pockets of his jacket. 'Anyway,' he said, 'enough about me. How about you? How are you?'

'I'm fine. I'd be better if you left.'

'Writing?'

'Yes.'

'A novel?'

'No.'

'You're too thin. Do you eat?'

I exhaled loudly. 'I go to my parents' every Sunday lunch and get stuffed full of food for the week. You didn't come here to ask about my eating habits, Leo.'

'Well, I sort of did.' He stepped into my office, ignoring my glare, and began perusing the books on my shelves. 'I haven't read this one,' he said, touching a spine. 'Is it any good?'

I clenched my fists. 'Leo, in case you haven't picked up the subtext of this conversation, let me spell it out for you. This is my room. It's my space. I don't want you in it, and I want you to leave it. Now.'

'Is this how we're going to live?' he asked me, still running his index finger across the titles of my books. 'Completely staying out of each other's way? Not even speaking unless absolutely necessary?'

'Finally, you understand.'

'You didn't find somewhere new to live this afternoon, then?'

'I — how did you — '

He flashed a smile at me. 'I know you. Trying to find a new flat at a moment's notice is exactly the sort of thing you'd do.'

I shook my head. 'No, Leo. That's the sort of thing *you* would do. Like suddenly turning up in Brickham. You're the impulsive one. I've learned better.'

'I used to like your impulsive side.'

'Well, I've changed a lot since then.'

'Pity.' He began to pull a book off the shelf, then replaced it. 'I'm sorry.'

'What?'

'I'm sorry,' he said again, looking at me now, not the books. 'I'm sorry for what I did to you. That's what I came back to Brickham to say.'

My annoyance vanished, replaced by its much bigger cousin, anger.

'So this is it,' I said. 'You turn up and charm my family and think that you can offer a glib apology and everything will be better?'

'It's evidently not working.'

'It's too late, Leo. And I don't believe you. If you were really sorry, you wouldn't have acted that way in the first place. Besides, I'm over it. I'm over you. I have my own life now.'

He chewed the inside of his lip, as he did when he was thinking. 'Right,' he said, at last. 'Too late. I see. And what — what you want now is for us to avoid each other. No contact at all.'

'You got it.'

He saluted wordlessly. And went back downstairs.

Like It's 1999

The next week was a complete nightmare.

For one thing, Leo was in full-on party mode. At least he didn't spend much time in the house during the day. But he did stay long enough to turn the tidy, well-ordered house I'd shared with Liv into a chaotic man-den. He left dirty breakfast dishes in the sink, he spilled coffee on the floor, he didn't hang up his towel and he forgot to put the toilet seat down. Or maybe he didn't forget; maybe it was all deliberate. He must have done some painting in his bedroom one afternoon, because he cleaned the brushes in the bathtub, a fact I didn't discover until I went to take a shower and stepped in a puddle of cerulean blue.

But the days were the good side. The nights were the worst, when Leo would roll in late, bringing a crowd of people with him. I stayed in my room with the door shut against their laughing and conversation. I recognised some of the voices — old friends of his who lived in Brickham still — people I knew, who had come to our wedding. Some of the others, especially the girls, were strangers. I wasn't going to go downstairs and find out who they were; somehow that felt as if it would be letting Leo win. Upstairs, I read and I wrote my technical articles, doing my best to ignore the muffled voices and music downstairs. And the female laughter. A lot of female laughter.

I didn't exchange a single word with Leo. Nor he, with me. If we met by mistake, we looked away. It was exactly as I wanted it. Well, not exactly . . . but it was the best it was going to get, unless he went away.

And from the looks of it, he wasn't going to go away.

Liv rang on Tuesday, between meeting her in-laws and planning for her second wedding on Saturday. 'I had no idea he was staying for the summer,' she said as soon as I picked up the phone.

I sank onto the couch. It was pub opening hours, so I was safe enough. 'When did he tell you?' I asked.

'He rang last night.'

'And what was your reaction?'

'I tried to tell him that suddenly moving in with his ex-wife probably wasn't the easiest path for either of you.'

'Tell me about it.' I hugged a cushion. 'I've been looking for a flat, but I'm not having much luck.'

'Oh, Alice. I'm sorry. You know what Leo's like when he's got an idea in his head.'

'Yeah, and that idea happens to be 'party like it's 1999', apparently.'

She was silent for a moment. 'He's been out partying?'

'And in partying. He's not picky. In, or out.'

'Have you talked yet?'

'I'm trying my best not to talk with him at all, to be honest.'

'Well, that makes sense, then.'

I dug my fingers into the cushion. 'What makes sense, Liv? What, exactly? Because it seems like a random act of pig-headedness to me. Why would Leo even want to be here in the first place? Surely he could have his fun somewhere else. It's not like the beer tastes better in Brickham, is it?'

'He hasn't told you why he's back?' She sounded surprised.

'Something about a show in London in the autumn. Not anything logical, or reasonable. Why, what did he tell *you*?'

She was quiet again for a moment. In the background, half the globe away, I could hear the faint noise of a television and somebody talking.

'If he hasn't told you,' Liv said at last, 'it's not up to me to say. But it does make sense why he's going out, Alice. You know what Leo's like. If you reject him, he's going to do his best to show you that he doesn't care.'

'Well, that's fine. He doesn't care, I don't care. Everything's dandy.'

'Oh, Alice. I wish I could be there.'

She meant it, and that's when the guilt hit. 'Of course you don't, Liv. You've started your new life. Let's stop talking about this, it's not important. What are Yann's family like?'

★　★　★

The next day, I went to Eversley Hall to learn more about it. During the week, there were no costumed tour guides and only modest numbers

121

of visitors. I wandered through the rooms, the Hall and the Red Saloon and the Green Drawing Room, then went upstairs to Lady Fitzwilliam's bedroom and down again into the east pavilion to the kitchen where I'd already spent a day. I imagined myself in these nearly-empty rooms, standing on the other side of the velvet ropes, using the furniture. Belonging there.

Back at home I wrote another proposal for Edie, and while I was waiting to hear, while Leo was partying downstairs until two or three in the morning, the doorbell going for the pizza delivery guy, I lay in bed with my duvet pulled up and I read about Eversley Hall, and once I had that memorised, I read one novel after another. At this rate, I was going to be spending most of the additional money I earned at Eversley Hall buying more books.

On Thursday night, I couldn't find an excuse to say no when my mother rang and insisted I come round for a meal. Especially as I'd already told her that my Sundays were going to be spent at Eversley Hall for the next few months, and she couldn't watch me eat her rib-sticking roast dinners. Besides, Leo was bound to be out at the pub drinking himself silly.

But he wasn't. When I got to Mum and Dad's, he was there already, sitting on the worn corduroy sofa with a large glass of red wine in his hand. A big scrapbook was spread out on Leo's knees and Mum and Pippi sat on either side of him, curled up close and pointing at different items.

'But how did you do it?' Pippi was asking. She

wore skinny jeans and a tiny vest with sequins on it. 'How do you like basically cut a whole house in half?'

'I used a chainsaw,' he said. 'It took nearly two weeks. It was quite cathartic, actually.' I noticed, with some empty satisfaction, that he looked tired. All those late nights. And he'd missed a bit of stubble on his jaw when he'd shaved. Well, at least that was about 150 hairs that I wouldn't have to gaze at in the sink whilst I was brushing my teeth. He glanced up briefly at me and I went straight into the dining room where Dad was assembling a Sopwith F-1 Camel on part of the table that hadn't been cleared off for eating. Over the years, I'd lost count of the number of times I'd found a bit of fuselage or similar in my mash.

I helped Dad with a tricky bit of the wing and I attempted not to listen to the Leo-adoration going on in the next room. It was a little bit harder over dinner though, what with my mother having placed Leo directly across the table from me. I concentrated on hacking away at my roast lamb and listening to the sound of my chewing.

It was my own fault that this was happening. If I'd told my family the whole story about how and why Leo and I broke up, we wouldn't both be sitting here now. But the thought of talking about it, about all of it, filled me with so much dread I could barely chew my food.

This couldn't last long. One summer, what was that in the great scheme of things? Whenever Leo was around I could just retreat into silence and puzzles or making models with my dad and before I knew it, Leo would be gone again. He probably wouldn't even stick around for as long as he said he would. He wasn't very good at commitment, after all.

I swallowed, with difficulty. And took another bite that I really didn't want.

' . . . and of course it was tricky to get it all done without the CCTV cameras catching me covering the entire building with spraypaint before the sun came up.'

My mother set her knife and fork down. This was always the sign that she was going to hold forth about something or other, generally the thing you'd like best that she never held forth about. 'I just think it's incredible, Leopold. Quite incredible. We always believed in you, we knew you had it in you to be a great artist, but knowing what you had to deal with emotionally, it means even more. It was a triumph over adversity. When I think of what I was like when I miscarried those three times — '

I opened my mouth to speak, though my overwhelming instinct was to jump up and run away.

'*Mum*,' said Pippi. 'For God's sake stop it! Nobody wants to hear *again* about you losing babies while we're trying to eat our dinner. It's gross.'

Leo snapped his fingers. 'Now I remember what I wanted to ask you about, Celia. How are the Finnegans? Do they still have those homing pigeons? Tell me all the latest. I'm dying to hear about them.'

Friday afternoon my phone went at the same time as the doorbell. I had no idea whether Leo was in the house or not, but whoever it was at the door was unlikely to be for me anyway, so I stayed where I was in front of my computer, and picked up my mobile. It was Edie at *Hot! Hot!* magazine. My stomach gave a little flutter.

'Alice,' Edie said, without any preamble, 'I love the Jane Austen-type thing idea. I love the piece you sent about the dishes. Are you at the house now in that fabulous gown or whatever?'

'No, the costume job is for weekends.'

'Great. I want you to do a weekly blog on the website, and a two-part feature in the magazine for July and August. Don't repeat yourself though, new material for both. You on board?'

'Yes!'

'Good. I'm thinking lots of anecdotes, narrative like a story. We'll use your first piece on the blog, and you can send me the July article next Friday. Talk with you then.' She rang off, leaving me clutching my phone and grinning stupidly at my computer screen.

At least my professional life was taking off. James was going to be really pleased with the publicity. And I was going to get to write about something other than photocopier parts and new phone apps. Maybe this could lead to other features, widen my portfolio.

The doorbell went again, in short impatient bursts, over and over and over, breaking into my appreciation of the first good thing that had happened to me since Monday. 'Oh, for goodness' sake,' I muttered, and hurried down the stairs to answer it.

To my surprise, it was Pippi. Her hair was all twisted up on the top of her head in artful disarray, and she was wearing tracksuit bottoms and a jumper. Her face, though, was as carefully made-up as ever. 'What took you so long?' she asked, and stepped into the house without waiting to be invited.

I couldn't remember the last time Pippi had visited me off her own bat. She'd barely said a word to me last night. 'Pippi? Are you all right?'

'Fine.' She shrugged off an enormous backpack and opened it up. 'Mum asked me to deliver these books to you; she said you ran off too quickly last night.' She pulled out a canvas shopping bag full of paperbacks and handed it over. I peeped inside; it was the usual assortment of biographies and autobiographies of people who had triumphed against terrible odds. 'I don't know why you want to be reading that stuff,' Pippi said, settling the backpack on her shoulders again.

'Mum thinks they'll do me good. You came all the way over here to run an errand for her?' I considered checking her temperature.

'No, I need to use your kitchen table to study. I've got an exam on Monday and the house is chaos. Mum's making jam for the WI and Fuzzicat has puked up hairballs all over the sofa.'

'Ugh.'

'It's disgusting.' She looked around. 'Is Leo in?'

Of course. That was the reason she was really here — not to study or do someone else a favour, but to schmooze with her favourite glamorous ex-brother-in-law. 'I don't think so. The radio's not on.'

'Do you think he'll be back soon?'

'I really don't know.'

'You guys don't talk much, do you?'

'Not at all, if I can help it.'

'Weird. It was like a big wall between you at the table last night.' She started through to the kitchen. 'You know that Mum has totally married you two off again, don't you?'

'Yes,' I said, following her. 'Don't you think the library would be less distracting?'

'The library is minging.' She plonked her bag on the kitchen table, shoving over a pile of empty takeaway containers. 'It's full of smelly old people who can't afford to buy their own newspapers, and freaks checking their Facebook pages.'

'What about the school library?'

'I am *not* going into school unless I absolutely have to. Wow, are you in a party mood or something?'

I tried not to glance at the stacks of lager and wine, the empty pizza cartons, the recycling bin full of tins, the three full bottles of whisky. 'That's all Leo's,' I said.

'Hmm. Do you have any hot chocolate?'

'I think so. But Pippi, I'm working today.'

'I don't need babysitting. I'm eighteen years old, you know, even if you do treat me like I'm ten.'

'I didn't mean babysitting,' I said. 'You're welcome to stay and study, but I do have to work, and I can't be interrupted until it's done. So I can't be making you hot chocolate every ten minutes.'

'I can get it myself.'

I had never seen any evidence of Pippi getting so much as a glass of water for herself, but I let this slide. 'Okay, the chocolate is in the cabinet above the kettle, and the mugs are near the sink. Milk's in the fridge; you can heat it up in the microwave. If there's anything else you need, I'm sure you can find it.'

She began unpacking books and folders from her bag, and I went back upstairs. I couldn't start on the *Hot! Hot!* article yet, not until I'd had my first proper day at Eversley Hall, but I had a piece on air conditioning units that needed to be done for next week too, and I wanted it out of the way so I could concentrate on the new stuff.

I only wrote about a hundred and fifty words more before I gave up. At least when it was Leo in the house, I could ignore him with a will. But not my sister.

If my mother had called to ask me to look after Pippi, I would have stayed resolutely in my room. But my phone remained silent; most likely Mum was elbow-deep in jam. She knew where Pippi was, and she was trusting me with something as precious as A-level revision. And I could sympathise with my sister's need to escape a house where she couldn't concentrate. So I went downstairs.

Pippi was sitting at the kitchen table surrounded by books, but she wasn't looking at them. She had her chin propped on her hands and was staring into space. Something about her made me pause in the doorway before I came in; maybe it was the angle she was holding her face, or the paleness of her skin, but her eyes looked huge and thoughtful. It was an expression I'd never seen on my little sister's face before.

'What's the exam?' I asked her, and she blinked and noticed me for the first time. Her face rearranged itself back into its normal teenage coolness.

'Drama.'

'Oh well, you have nothing to worry about then. A drama queen like you.' I saw her preparing a sarcastic answer, so I interrupted, 'Want another hot chocolate?'

'I thought you said you have better things to do than to be making me drinks all the time.'

'Well, I was going to make myself a cup of tea anyway. And you look thirsty.' I put the kettle on and poured milk into a little pan to warm on the cooker. When I turned back to her she was fiddling with a ring binder, opening it and then closing it on one of her fingers.

'Are you nervous about this exam?' I asked her.

'No,' she answered, though I knew Pippi. She'd never answer anything but 'no' to a question like that. And she was nervous about something; I'd never seen her dressed so sloppily, or looking so pensive.

'You shouldn't be. You're really good at drama.

You've got that place at stage camp this summer, and you were brilliant in that play I saw you in this spring.'

'It's a written exam, not a practical, and anyway, what do you know about it?' She pursed her lips. You couldn't win with Pippi these days. She couldn't take criticism, and she was annoyed by praise. And she'd been such a sweet little girl — adorable, full of hugs and happiness, by far the sunniest of any of us Woodstock sisters. Teenage hormones had a lot to answer for.

I stirred the chocolate into the milk. 'You're right,' I said. 'I didn't take drama at school.'

'You spend all your time up in your attic, writing. You probably did that when you were my age, too.'

'Pretty much. I never had a life. It was extremely sad.' I put the hot chocolate in front of her and sat down with my own cup of tea. 'I do know how to write though, and it's a written exam. Maybe I can help you.'

'Why are you being so nice to me?'

'You're my sister and you're under a lot of stress.'

'Oh God, do I look really awful?'

'No, you look fine. I could never do my make-up like that in a million years.'

The compliment, or maybe it was my self-deprecation, settled her. She sighed and trapped her finger in her ring binder again. 'I can do it, but I can't write about it. There are all these theories and everything, and I don't really get them, and it's all people with funny names. Russians and Greeks. I mean, look at this.' She opened her folder near the beginning, to show me her notes, written in careless, bubbly script. 'This is like Ancient Greek! How are we supposed to care about something this old guy said about poetry?'

'Oh, Aristotle's *Poetics*? That's easy.'

'What? What do you know about it? I thought you said you never took drama.'

'I did study rather a lot of English literature though. It's pretty simple. All that Aristotle basically said was that stories exist to make people feel better about their own lives. They get absorbed in the emotions of these fictional people, and that sort of cleanses them and makes their own real emotions more controllable.'

'It's weird.'

'It's not that weird if you think about it. When's the last time you cried?'

She twisted her mouth. 'Why would I cry?'

'Haven't you ever cried at a book?'

Pippi looked at me as if I were insane.

'How about a movie?' I said. 'Or at something on telly? Because it's sad, or even because it's happy?'

'I suppose so.'

'And I bet you felt better afterwards. Lighter. While you were watching these other people you were part of their story, and it let you escape yourself for a little while and feel what they were feeling.'

'Maybe.'

'And that's what this means here.' I pointed to a word she'd written down, and underlined. 'Catharsis.'

'Oh. That's the word that Leo used last night about his painting, wasn't it?'

I pushed her folder away from me. I had no desire to talk about Leo's vocabulary choices.

She flicked a couple of pages. 'What about this guy, then?'

'Stanislavski? You're on your own there.'

Pippi sighed and drank her hot chocolate, opening and closing the ring binder on her finger. It made dents and red marks on her flesh. She didn't seem to be in any hurry to do any actual studying. I stood up to go back upstairs, when she suddenly said, watching her finger, 'Do you think splitting up with Leo completely fucked up your life?'

I sat back down, clenching my hand around my mug. 'What? I thought we were talking about your exams.'

'I've talked about them enough.'

'So you want to talk about my and Leo's marriage, because you're bored?'

She shrugged, still looking at her finger. 'Well, Leo seems to be doing really great, and you do nothing but write articles and build model aeroplanes and stuff. And read books. I was just wondering if, like, you maybe got married too young or something?'

'You were *just wondering*? Pippi, my life is none of your business. What is up with you? You come here to study, I make you hot chocolate, and then you basically tell me I'm a loser.'

'God! You are such a know-it-all. Like it's fine to talk about my exams and all the stress *I'm* supposed to be under, but the minute I mention *you* and maybe the fact that *you* fucked up — whoo! It's like World War Three.' She got up and threw her books into her bag. 'Forget it. I'm finished. Who cares about the stupid exam anyway?'

She flounced out of the kitchen, and I heard the front door slam after her.

Pretending

I still wasn't wearing knickers, and these pantalets were a little draughty, since they didn't actually have a crotch. But my shift was made of finer material, and I had more elaborate stays which laced up the back and pinched my boobs up towards my throat. Mrs Smudge did me up, grumbling something I couldn't quite make out. A petticoat with a drawstring waist, and over that, a black day dress. It was high-waisted, square-cut around the bodice and edged with white lace, with long sleeves gathered with black satin ribbon. The bottom hem was trimmed with a puff of black crepe. I wore black stockings which tied to garters around my thighs, and black kid slippers that looked more or less like ballet slippers, except without the elastic.

It was lovely. It wasn't elaborate, and not as beautiful as some of the other dresses I'd seen on the rail, but it was cut beautifully and made with care, and it fitted me exactly. I'd been up since around six taming my hair, pinning it up and forcing the front bits of it into ringlets around my face. I had no idea how nineteenth-century women did it without a blow drier, a pair of straighteners and lots of product. I draped a black shawl around my shoulders and arms and looked at myself in the full-length mirror.

'Wow,' I said.

It had to be the stays, or the dress, or the

hairdo. My skin looked pale and creamy, my hair bright. I didn't look like Alice Woodstock, obsessive journalist who spent hours in her room typing and who lived in a house with a man with whom she was not on speaking terms. I looked like Alice Woodstock, distant cousin of an aristocratic family, with an interesting past.

'It's trouble,' said Mrs Smudge, and I was surprised that she was still behind me. 'They shouldn't be introducing fake people in here. It makes a mockery of everything we've been trying so hard to do.'

'On the other hand,' I said lightly, 'some might say that we're all fake.'

She scowled, and went away. I hoped that she wasn't going to take it out on Kayleigh.

James had asked me to arrive later than the other interpreters on my first day, about half past one. The idea was that I'd arrived at the house and gone to my room to change out of my travelling clothes. That gave the others a chance to talk about my arrival all morning, and meant that I would be meeting them all for the first time at an hour when there would be a decent number of visitors in the house to hear about it or witness it.

I checked my face and hair and clothes one more time, and then I emerged into the court-yard by the west pavilion. A tall, thin, bald man in black satin breeches and a black coat was waiting for me. He looked a little bit like Lurch from *The Addams Family*, which was appropriate enough, I supposed. 'Miss Woodstock?'

'Yes. Are you — '

'Munson, the butler. I'll announce you to the family, who are in the Drawing Room. I hear they've been talking about you all day.' He started across the courtyard, and I followed.

'Nervous?' he asked me, opening a small door.

'Yes,' I said to his thin back.

He shot me a grin over his shoulder. It transformed his face into something almost jolly. 'No need to be. Once you've got a feel for it, it all flows like a dream. You could do it in your sleep. And I hear you're a natural.'

It was another servants' passage; it twisted and turned and ended at a tight spiral staircase, which might or might not be the same one I'd been up and down with James. We began to climb.

'Have you been doing this dressing-up thing for long?' I asked him.

'About fifteen years. I've set up my own business — I'm a one-man show. Costumed interpreter for hire. On the weekdays I'm up at Wendinham Castle, being an executioner.'

'Which do you like better, being a butler or an executioner?'

'Swings and roundabouts. The history is great at Wendinham, but the mask is annoying. You get a lot less cheeky kids here at Eversley Hall. There are some kids, but most of the visitors are of a certain age, and they don't try to nick your axe.' We reached the first floor and he led me down another corridor, then opened a door and peered out. 'Okay, the coast is clear. Quickly, or it'll look like we sneaked off for a bit of a grope.'

I stepped hurriedly out after him, and he

winked in a very un-Lurch-like fashion. Un-butler-like, too, but it made me like him. We were upstairs in the carpeted hallway between bedrooms, coming out of a small discreet door set into the plaster. 'What's your real name?' I whispered.

'Bill Watkins. Shh, this part here is open to the public.' Sure enough, an elderly couple rounded the corner in front of us and Bill immediately stopped and bowed. 'Madam, sir, welcome to Eversley Hall. I am Munson, the butler. If there is anything I can do to make your stay more enjoyable and comfortable, please do not hesitate to tell me or any of the other servants.'

'Ooh,' said the woman, and the man nodded. They stared at Bill and at me as if we were museum exhibits. Bill nudged me, slightly, behind my back.

'I am just arriving at Eversley Hall myself,' I said to them. 'It's a beautiful house, isn't it? I hear its situation is most beneficial. Have you met Mr Fitzwilliam yet?'

'Er,' said the woman. She looked petrified. The man nodded again. She clutched his arm, and they moved away. Bill waited until they were out of sight, and rolled his eyes.

'This way, please, Miss Woodstock.'

I followed Bill, or Munson as he most certainly was now, down the corridor and down the grand staircase into the Hall. Munson spoke to several more groups of visitors before we reached the open double doors of the Green Drawing Room, having gathered a small crowd at our backs. From my reading and my earlier visits I knew that this was the main room used by the family during the day and for receiving morning callers. Munson courteously waited for a woman to corral her three kids before he stepped through the door and announced, 'Miss Alice Woodstock.'

That, of course, was when it hit me. I was actually doing this. I wasn't just dressing up in a frock for fun and traipsing through the house with the butler frightening tourists. I was working here. And not for a day, as a fill-in someone else.

I was here for the whole summer, and my character was my own. And I was expected to be good at it.

My mouth went dry and I found it hard to breathe. My stays felt as if they were suffocating me. My cheeks heated up and I tried to take a step backwards, but I trod on someone's toes.

'Er, sorry,' I whispered, looking around in confusion. And then, across the room on the far side, I saw him. James Fitzwilliam stood in his finely cut coat, spotless cravat and skin-tight breeches. Our eyes met and held, and I felt my entire body heat up in a blush.

How did he *do* that? Stand so perfectly like a 200-year-old oil painting?

Then he smiled and nodded slightly. A welcome and a reassurance.

'Miss Woodstock, welcome to Eversley Hall,' said a female voice close to my elbow, reminding me that I had just completely stuffed up my grand entrance by treading on toes and turning beetroot red in front of every person in the room, costumed or not. I willed my cheeks to chill out and turned to the speaker with the best smile I could summon. If James Fitzwilliam believed I could do this, I damned well would.

'Lady Fitzwilliam,' I guessed, and bowed. She inclined her head. From the number of choux buns we'd made in the kitchen for her last weekend, I'd been expecting an older woman, probably quite stout, wearing dowdy clothes and a lace cap. But now that I had the presence of mind to notice her, I saw that Lady Fitzwilliam was in her fifties, slim and attractive. She had glossy chestnut hair touched with grey, held back by a velvet fillet, and wore a pretty white day-dress embroidered with small roses.

'I trust you had a pleasant voyage?' she said.

'Yes, thank you, very pleasant, Lady Fitzwilliam,' I replied. 'I took the stage early this morning from Winchester to Brickham, stopping for refreshment at the Red Lion at Basingstoke. Fortunately the roads were dry and we made good progress, travelling the distance of thirty miles in about seven hours.'

All of this burst out of me quickly without a pause for air, and I saw Lady Fitzwilliam's face transform from an expression of bland pleasantness to barely restrained amusement.

'You are a very well-informed young person, Miss Woodstock,' she said, and I flushed even more deeply. There was a ripple of laughter from the crowd of visitors watching us.

Idiot. I'd spat out all of my research in a rush, because I was nervous. This was *not* why I'd been asked to come back.

I forced a laugh. 'Please forgive me, Lady Fitzwilliam. I promise not to expound upon the intricacies of the highway any longer.'

'On the contrary, it is most interesting. May I present your cousin, James Fitzwilliam.'

I felt, rather than saw, him approaching me, and I dipped my head. Should I offer him my hand? What was nineteenth-century etiquette? It all seemed to have deserted me for the moment. 'Sir.'

'Miss Woodstock,' he said, and his voice was warm with humour. 'You are very welcome to Eversley Hall.' Why wasn't every single female in the room swooning at his feet? My palms were damp, but I didn't dare to wipe them on my dress.

I couldn't let a pair of tight breeches put me off my stride. I had to remember that the people in this room were not really frightening members of the aristocracy, who had taken pity on me, and held my fate in their hands. No, they were normal people, just like me, who were doing a job. In the case of James, he did actually own the house — but it was a job. We were all pretending. And I could pretend very well, if I needed to. Look at what I'd done in the scullery last weekend.

And how I'd been living for the past two years.

I glanced at Mr Fitzwilliam, and he was watching me, still with the slight smile on his face. He'd hired me to be amusing and to attract visitors, and he was waiting to see what I'd do next.

'The Honourable Mr Arthur Grantham,' said

Lady Fitzwilliam, continuing with her introductions, and another gentleman stepped forward. His waistcoat was much louder than Mr Fitzwilliam's, his neckcloth more elaborately tied, and his breeches, if possible, even tighter. His Hessian boots were polished to a deep gloss.

'How d'you do?' he said, holding out his hand to me to shake in what I remembered now was complete contravention to Regency etiquette. I heard a female cough, but The Honourable Mr Arthur seemed oblivious to the gaffe he'd made and I gave him my hand in return, grateful that someone else was making silly mistakes around here. He shook it vigorously, and I saw that despite his honourableness, he was quite young, no more than twenty.

'I'm very pleased to meet you, Mr Grantham,' I said, and he beamed at me.

'I was dashed pleased when James said his cousin was coming, though I'll confess I was wishing for another gentleman. You can't imagine how much conversation I've had about needlework and watercolours and deuced gowns! But I can't grudge your gender now that you're here. Sorry, what's your name again?'

'Alice Woodstock.'

'I thought so. Well, Miss Woodstock, an unknown cousin is precisely what we need to liven up this company. Are you horribly accomplished? I hope not. My sister is, you know; there is nothing more terrifying! It makes a gentleman feel quite unnecessary in a drawing room, when the ladies have so much to occupy them.'

'You will never feel a want of occupation as long as you can speak, Arthur,' said a woman standing off to his right.

I had begun to feel myself becoming much more composed, with Arthur's effusive greeting and his own slip-up, oblivious as he was to it. But this woman who had just spoken made me do a double-take despite myself.

It was the lady from the leaflet, and in real life she was even more ice-queen lovely. She had pale blonde hair and cool blue eyes, perfect rose-pink lips, and she wore the gorgeous white and gold gown. And looked about a million times better than I ever could have looked in it. She stood with the grace of someone who'd been wearing gowns and corsets every day of her life.

'Miss Grantham,' Lady Fitzwilliam introduced us. Miss Grantham inclined her head to me.

'Miss Woodstock,' she said. 'May I express my condolences on the loss of your parents, and of your home. How unsettling it must be, to be thrust upon the kindness of relatives.'

I blinked. Had she just called me homeless, in front of everyone, after having met me for the first time?

I was pretty sure that would be considered rude in Regency times. I was pretty sure it would be considered rude in the twenty-first century as well, unless the person was actually selling the *Big Issue* in front of you or something. But she was smiling with her perfect mouth, as if she'd said something inoffensive about the weather, rather than reminding me quite bluntly of my place in the scheme of things.

I smiled back at her, in the most charming way possible.

'Well, it could be worse,' I said. 'I could have been forced to marry my odious Cousin Horace!'

It was Miss Grantham's turn to blink, and I saw that she had expected me to blush and stammer for her, too.

Not a chance, lady, I thought. I've taken on Mrs Smudge, I can handle you.

'I thought for some time that I would have no choice but to accept him,' I continued, 'as Ashbourne House was entailed upon him. In fact, I refused him twice while Papa was still alive, and after Papa died, I didn't know how I would manage to refuse him a third time. But fortunately he went to Bath this spring and found a girl with a fortune instead, which is a much wiser choice for him, and a much more pleasant one for me. Poverty must have some redeeming features, and one of them is, I have not married Horace.'

Miss Grantham looked as if she were struggling to keep up.

'Was he truly awful?' asked the girl standing behind Miss Grantham, the only costumed person, I now saw, whom I had not yet met in the room. She was also young, probably younger even than Arthur, and I smiled at her, knowing this must be Selina Fitzwilliam.

'Truly,' I said. 'I understand that gentlemen in general do enjoy a drink, but one should be more careful when one has a nose as red as my Cousin Horace! Or when one is inclined to fall asleep over the whist table, and actually drool on one's cards. I can only assume that he must have been on his best behaviour in Bath when he met his wife, or perhaps there was a shortage of port.'

The girl giggled.

'Sounds like a capital fellow!' said Arthur. 'Is he a cousin of yours as well, James?'

'No,' said Mr Fitzwilliam. 'It is the other side of the family. But I do hope that Miss Woodstock is not in the habit of abusing all of her cousins so roundly.'

'As long as you can hold off from snoring in public, sir, you have nothing to fear from me.'

'I shall consider myself warned.' Our gaze met, and this time, I hardly blushed at all. Result.

'The relief of not marrying your cousin must hardly compensate for the loss of your home,' said Miss Grantham.

Ah, so she was back in the game.

'Oh, well, we must take blessings where we find them,' I said cheerfully. 'I do love Ashbourne House, but Cousin Horace is too high a price to pay. Naturally when he brought his bride home I was no longer welcome, and so here I am, thanks to Lady Fitzwilliam's invitation. Where is your family home situated, Miss Grantham?'

'Rodean is in Yorkshire, though our time is spent principally in London.'

'How delightful! And are you enjoying Eversley Hall?'

She returned a civil answer, and I enjoyed asking her several more civil questions, all the time thinking about how Liv had never understood why I liked reading Regency novels. She couldn't work out why I would enjoy a whole book full of talking, with no facts or real action. She didn't understand this cut-and-thrust of manners, the subtle jockeying for power.

I glanced over at James; he was watching me and Miss Grantham talking. Mostly her, I was sure; she was bright and beautiful, and I was a scrawny girl with red hair in a black dress.

Then he turned to the man in the anorak beside him. 'I see you admiring the painting over the fireplace, sir,' he said. 'Would you care to know its history?'

'Please excuse me,' Miss Grantham said to me. She crossed to James, where she joined him in a discussion of the painting. Obviously this was some sort of a signal that chatting time was over, and it was time to start paying attention to the visitors; Lady Fitzwilliam immediately started talking to two elderly ladies about the view from the window, and Arthur addressed the man standing beside him with, 'Are you fond of sport?'

There were no visitors close to the sofa, however, so I turned to the girl who had spoken and was now perched on the edge of a cushion. 'We haven't been introduced,' I said. 'I'm Alice.'

'Selina,' she said, quietly. 'Are we meant to be cousins, too? I can't quite tell.'

'Let's say we are,' I said, and sat beside her. She looked very young, about Pippi's age, and I couldn't quite work out whether she was actually shy or whether it was part of her act as Selina.

'Tell me, is Miss Grantham as horrifyingly accomplished as her brother claims?'

'Y — es, I think so.'

'Have you ever seen her net a purse? I believe I can face the rest of her accomplishments with fortitude, but the purse netting gives me pause.'

Selina giggled softly. 'I've never seen her net a purse.'

I gazed across the room, where Miss Grantham was standing with James. They had amassed quite a crowd of visitors and were discussing the finer points of the allegorical painting hanging on the east wall.

'She's certainly well educated about art history,' I said.

'She knows everything about Eversley Hall backwards and forwards. Nearly as much as James.'

I watched the two of them. Miss Grantham stood close to James, talking earnestly about the muse Calliope. They made a very good-looking couple.

'Is her passion only for the house, I wonder,' I murmured. 'Tell me, is her fortune as handsome as her person and her intellect?'

'What do you mean?'

'Is she rich?'

'I — I'm not sure, but I think she's meant to be.'

I nodded. Some things really didn't change, no matter what century you were in. Miss Grantham fancied James like mad.

Of course she did. Who wouldn't? God, that old lady over there was ogling his bum. And that man over there who was pretending to admire the scrollwork on the side-table — he kept on glancing Fitzwilliam-arse-ward as well. I couldn't blame them. It was rather fine. I would probably buy a season ticket to Eversley Hall for that reason alone.

And there was the reason for the bitchiness. Miss Grantham, like everyone else in the room, had seen me blushing at the sight of this Regency god. Despite the fact that I was nowhere near as attractive as her, Miss Grantham took the first opportunity to put me down, to remind me that I wasn't in his league. I was the impoverished cousin, here out of charity; the well-heeled lord of the manor would never look at me twice.

But all of this was self-evident. I wasn't competition for Miss Grantham. So why did she even bother?

The visitors that James and Miss Grantham had been talking to moved on. Lady Fitzwilliam excused herself to go upstairs, and Arthur declared he was going to the Library to see if James had anything worth reading in this house. Evidently the other rooms needed guides in them. Selina didn't seem to have much to say, and I was content for the moment to actually appreciate being here, in this beautiful room with its oil paintings and silk Chinese screens, on a sofa that was as perfect as the day in the nineteenth century it was made. The enormous windows looked out over the acres of green beyond.

'Are these flowers cut from the garden?' asked

a blue-haired lady in a polyester skirt suit and trainers.

'Um — ' said Selina, visibly starting and colouring.

'They're grown in our own greenhouses, madam,' said a calm, masculine voice behind us. I turned to see James standing nearby, with Miss Grantham at what seemed to be her habitual post by his elbow. 'Are you fond of flowers? You would perhaps enjoy a stroll in our garden. The parterre is very fine this time of year, and the rose garden. Do you enjoy gardening?'

'Yes, it's my hobby.'

'Then you should be sure to speak with Samuel the gardener,' said Mr Fitzwilliam. 'Should she not, Selina?'

'Y-yes,' she managed, and looked down at her hands.

'Or possibly with Ben, the under-gardener,' Mr Fitzwilliam said, catching my eye. 'Miss Woodstock, would you like to take a tour of the house?'

'I'd love to.' I stood, and we started together for the far exit of the room. Miss Grantham came along with us, until James paused.

'Miss Grantham, may I trespass on your goodness so much as to ask you to keep my sister company?'

She stopped. Her lovely eyes narrowed at me. 'Oh. Of course, I should be glad to stay with *dear* Selina.' She turned round and went back to the sofa.

'I'm very glad you could join us, Cousin,' said James. He offered me his arm as we strolled through the doorway, and I took it. When I glanced back over my shoulder at her, Miss Grantham was glaring in my direction.

It looked as if it was going to be an interesting summer.

Fictional Families and Married Men

The female changing room was packed with servants and mistresses changing from the Regency to the twenty-first century. Everyone looked up when I came in.

'Hey, mate!' called Kayleigh from the corner, waving. She was half out of her chemise, pulling on her skin-tight jeans. 'Nice to see you got a promotion!'

'Thanks,' I said, making my way over to her. Lady Fitzwilliam was already dressed in modern clothing and hanging up her gown with care, examining it for creases or traces of dirt. Selina was being unbuttoned by a thin mousy girl whom I hadn't seen before, and who I assumed was Fiona, the girl I had replaced as the scullery maid. Mrs Smudge was nowhere in sight, thank goodness, but Miss Isabella Grantham was sitting on a chair, zipping up a pair of high-heeled black boots.

Mrs Collins smiled at me. 'Welcome back,' she said. She was already dressed, too, in jeans and a rumpled cotton shirt. 'Sorry I can't stay and chat, I've got to go and pick up the grandkids. They think Gran is funny for dressing up and cooking all day.'

'How old are they?' I asked. 'Maybe you can get them little outfits and let them run around as Regency kids.'

She shook her head. 'There weren't any children in Eversley Hall in 1814.'

'There weren't any penniless cousins, either,' said Miss Grantham. She raised one of her perfect eyebrows at me, stood up and walked out of the changing room.

'Friendly, isn't she?' I said to nobody in particular.

'She's a professional historical interpreter,' Mrs Collins told me. 'Like Mrs Smudge. She's got lots of degrees in history, and she's not fond of amateurs like us muscling in on her territory.' She picked up a large canvas bag with *World's Best Gran* on the side of it. 'Though I've got a degree in history, come to that, and spent thirty years teaching it.'

'I've got a degree in history as well,' said Lady Fitzwilliam.

'I haven't,' said Kayleigh cheerfully. 'I have got an Equity card though. Ugh, this damn gown has got another stain on it.'

Mrs Collins waved goodbye at everyone. I sat on the chair Miss Grantham had abandoned, taking off my shoes and pulling up my gown to unfasten my garters. 'So not all of you are professional interpreters?' I asked.

'This summer is the first time I've done it professionally,' said Lady Fitzwilliam, 'though my husband and I have been doing Napoleonic re-enactment for years as a hobby.' She smoothed the ribbon trim on her dress.

'That's fascinating,' I said. 'I had no idea everyone had a different background, you're all so into your roles.' Except Kayleigh, of course, who was pulling a pack of gum out of her handbag. 'What about you?' I asked the young woman who was playing Selina. 'Are you an actor, or an historian?'

'Neither,' she said. 'I'm doing my HND in Travel and Tourism, and this summer is an internship. I'm really no good at any of this acting stuff. I'm only doing it because of James.'

'Because of James?'

'He's my cousin in real life,' said Selina. 'I think our grandparents were brother and sister. He must have heard I was looking for a summer placement in a tourist venue, so he pulled some strings. I'm very lucky, of course,' she added quickly. 'Most of my friends are working in hotels or something. This is really unusual, and I get to see the tourist experience from a totally different perspective.'

'Does he — did he hire all of you personally, then?'

'I heard through contacts in my re-enactment society,' Lady Fitzwilliam said. 'And then he held auditions.'

'I answered an ad,' said Kayleigh. 'You too, Fi — right?' Fiona nodded.

'We were all quite surprised to see you,' said Lady Fitzwilliam. 'James only told us you were coming this morning.'

'This morning? I agreed to do it on Monday.'

'He says he prefers us to find out stuff like our characters really would,' Selina said. 'So we show the right amount of surprise or whatever.'

'James told us this morning that he'd received a letter from his cousin Miss Woodstock and that you would be joining us for a visit for the summer,' said Lady Fitzwilliam. 'I had to make up a long list of orders on the spot to give to Mrs Smudge, to prepare for your arrival.'

'Mrs Smudge must have loved that. She and I had a bit of a run-in when I was in the kitchen last weekend.'

'A bit! You practically made her crap her petticoats!' Kayleigh cackled.

'James must have discovered something about a cousin in his research,' Selina said. 'He never mentioned you before.'

'No,' I said. 'There wasn't really a cousin Alice Woodstock in 1814. He made me up.'

'You mean, you're fictional?' Lady Fitzwilliam looked shocked. 'I thought — '

'I didn't think we were allowed to do anything that didn't actually happen.' Selina's eyes were a bit panicked.

All of them were staring at me as if I were a strange and exotic species.

'So the whole Cousin Horace thing,' said Selina. 'You made that up?'

'On the spot,' I confessed.

'Oh my God,' she said. 'That's incredible. I could never do anything like that. I can't even talk properly like a Regency person — I get all tangled up with the words and the long sentences.'

'Do you want help unbuttoning?' Lady Fitzwilliam asked.

'Yes, please. I'm definitely not used to these clothes yet.'

I stood, and she helped me unfasten the back

of my dress. 'So are you a re-enactor, or an interpreter, or an actress?' she asked.

'I'm not any of those things. I'm a journalist.'

'You're really good at all the talking and stuff,' said Selina. 'I can't do it very well, that old-fashioned English.'

'I read a lot of novels,' I said. 'You should try that maybe, reading historical novels to get the feeling of the language.'

'What should I read? I wouldn't even know where to look for those.'

'I'll bring you some.'

'Oh, you don't have to take the trouble to do that.'

'It's no trouble. I'll bring you a bagful tomorrow.'

'That's really kind, thanks.'

'You really have no qualifications at all?' Lady Fitzwilliam pursued, working on unlacing my stays now.

'I think the idea was to introduce a new person into the mix and shake things up a little.'

'Well, today was the most interesting day we've had in a while,' said Selina. 'Usually we spend a lot of time talking about the weather, and the house, and answering the same questions over and over again from the tourists.'

'We also discuss topics of historical import,' Lady Fitzwilliam said. 'Such as the Peninsular Wars.'

'Yes,' said Selina glumly. 'It's fascinating.'

'If you're a journalist, are you going to write about Eversley Hall?' Lady Fitzwilliam asked me.

I spent the rest of my time undressing and dressing talking about the articles and blogs for *Hot! Hot!*. Selina and Lady Fitzwilliam seemed impressed, though Fiona didn't say a word and vanished without saying goodbye. Kayleigh hung around cracking her gum until the others were gone, and then she followed me out of the female changing rooms. I was rather hoping to see James Fitzwilliam in the communal staff area, but the man who played Arthur was the only one there. He sat leaning back in a chair with his feet propped on the table, reading a folded-up newspaper and sipping a cup of coffee.

'Hey,' he greeted us when we came in. 'How was your day?'

In real life his voice was much less Hooray Henry, and he looked even younger, dressed in jeans and a sweatshirt with his hair artfully messed up.

'Very interesting, thanks,' I said.

He put his newspaper down on the table. 'I heard that you don't actually exist.'

'Yup, that's why you can see straight through me.'

'So where are you going now?' Kayleigh asked me. 'I think I owe you a drink, you know, for saving my neck last weekend. You want to go to the pub?'

'Why not?' In fact, I wanted to get home and write up my notes for the day, and normally I'd say no. But a new friend could help get me out of the house and away from Leo.

'Excellent. Do you have a car? I need a lift.'

Arthur was still sitting watching us with his

feet on the table. 'So what's your real name?' he asked me. 'It isn't really Woodstock, is it?'

'It is,' I told him. 'What's yours?'

'Nick.' He ran a hand through his messy hair, and abruptly stood up. 'Well, have fun at the pub, girls.'

'Sure you don't want to come with us?' Kayleigh smiled at him.

'Another time. I've gotta get to the night job. They don't let us gigolos have a moment's rest, I'm telling you.' He tipped us a wink, stuck his newspaper beneath his arm, and left.

'He's a hottie,' said Kayleigh. 'What do you think? Does he look like he's got a girlfriend?'

'He's a bit young for me.'

'Oh well, get 'em young, train 'em up the way you want 'em, right?' As soon as we stepped outside, Kayleigh immediately lit a fag and smoked it, still chewing her gum, as we walked out of the west pavilion and around to the gravel drive towards the staff car park. Eversley Hall basked in the balmy late-afternoon summer sun. It was hard to believe I'd spent all day here, belonging here, and tomorrow I was going to do it, too.

'I'm not convinced that men actually can be trained,' I said.

'Oh. Well, one day, I'm hoping to meet the perfect bloke who'll be all devoted to me and everything, but till then, no harm looking — right?'

I unlocked the door of my 2CV for Kayleigh and she stubbed out her cigarette in the gravel before she climbed in.

'Which pub?' I asked.

'How about the Groom and Horses, near the uni in Brickham? They do a Happy Hour type thing.'

'Fine. That's not far from my house.'

I started up the car and drove down the gravel drive through the grand gates and turned right, towards Brickham.

'What's it like, being with all the posh people?' Kayleigh asked.

'It's a lot easier on my hands so far.'

'You're not joking.' She held up her own hands, which were pink. 'I so swear, I am spending like four days in the nail bar after this gig is over.'

'Mrs Smudge hasn't sacked you yet, then?'

'She is on my case like you wouldn't believe, but I've been lying low. Being the good little servant girl. Poor Fiona though, she was gobsmacked when she came back in on Sunday and found out she was engaged to a non-existent gardener.'

'So what about James Fitzwilliam?' I asked, trying to sound casual. 'I mean the real one, not the historical one. Is he married or anything?'

'I don't think so. But don't ask me, I'm awful at being able to tell if a bloke is married or not. Have you heard about gaydar? Well, I have like absolutely no marriage-dar. I keep on falling for these guys, thinking everything's great and wonderful, and they keep on turning out to be married. I was seeing this last guy, Stuart, for like four months before I got a phone call from his wife at three a.m. or whatever. I had no idea!

157

I had to throw him out on the street in the rain, which I sort of felt bad about, but then again, he had no right to make *me* the other woman, you know? And I had to deal with these phone calls from his wife — who's probably quite nice in real life when her husband's not cheating on her — screeching like a banshee in my ear?' She shook her head. 'I swear, the next bloke I fancy, I'm going to hire a private detective to check him out before I even *talk* to him.'

Being with Kayleigh wasn't unlike being with my mother, what with the constant stream of words. But it was more relaxing, since I didn't have to worry about her going off into flights of praise about my ex-husband. It was like a nice buzz of background music, and she didn't seem to expect me to say much in return. I found a parking spot near the pub and we went in together. The pub was shabby, full of fruit machines and textured wallpaper, with a long Victorian bar that had seen better days. 'What do you want to drink?' Kayleigh asked me.

'Glass of red wine, please.'

She put her hand in her bag, rummaged around, and then grimaced. 'Actually, do you have any cash on you? I've forgotten my purse. I'll get them in the next time, yeah?'

I bought a WKD for her and a wine for me, and was getting my change when she grabbed my arm. 'Hey, don't look now, but there's some major talent standing at the bar. Two o'clock.'

I glanced over and in an instant took in the back of a slender man. He had straight, strong shoulders and muscular legs in jeans. He lifted his pint to his mouth and turned his head slightly, and I stepped backwards, away from the bar.

It was Leo Allingham.

'I do love me a bit of bad boy,' sighed Kayleigh. 'I think he's alone. Do you reckon he's single? Can you see a ring anywhere?'

'He's not wearing a ring,' I said. As far as I knew, he'd thrown it into the Charles River in Boston, or maybe a more exotic river somewhere else in the world. As far as I knew, he'd flushed it down the toilet, like he had our marriage.

Leo took a long drink of his pint, and then said something to the barman, who answered him. My left thumb touched the bare skin on my fourth finger where my own ring used to be. As soon as I realised I was doing it, I straightened my hand.

'What do you think?' said Kayleigh. 'Does he look like the married type? I don't think so, but like I said, I'm horrible at this sort of thing. In fact, I might as well give up now. If I even fancy him he's bound to be married.'

'I think — '

Leo lifted his glass again, but then he put it down. He turned his head, as if he had sensed someone was looking at him. Our eyes met.

I seemed to be doing an awful lot of this meeting of eyes across a crowded room thing today. I felt a flush again, but this time I wasn't going to make a fool of myself. Leo opened his mouth as if he was about to say something, but then he closed it again. I averted my gaze and set about replacing my purse in my handbag.

'He's not married,' I said.

'Are you sure?' Kayleigh asked. 'How do you know? Do you know him?'

I looked back up. Leo had turned away, fully this time. I saw the back of his head and the way his T-shirt tightened against his shoulders as he leaned onto the bar and the barman pulled him another pint.

'No,' I said. 'I don't know him.'

Gone

'But it's all gone.'

It sounded as if he was in the room with me, but when I opened my eyes, he wasn't there. It was dark except for a sliver of light through the crack of my bedroom door.

I sat up in bed. It wasn't the words that had woken me, but the tone.

'No, I didn't think. I — I didn't expect it all to be gone. Everything.'

Why could I hear Leo talking? Who was he talking to? I strained to hear an answer, some clue as to what 'everything' was. But nobody answered.

And I knew what 'everything' was, anyway. I'd lost it too.

'Mm-hmm. I know, I should have said when you were knocking it all down. But I didn't know then. I didn't think I cared.'

He was on the phone, I realised. I reached over and pressed the button on my clock to light it up. It was nearly quarter to three in the morning. It would be in the middle of the afternoon in New Zealand.

He was talking to Liv, who was on her proper honeymoon now. I slipped out of bed, padded to the door, and eased it open. It sounded as if he was right outside my bedroom, but I didn't see him on the landing, so I crept out.

I'd turned out the staircase lights before going

to bed, but he'd turned them on again. I peered through the railings and then drew back quickly. He was on the first-floor landing almost directly below me, a phone pressed to his ear. He had blue paint streaked through his dark hair and there was a glass in his hand. He took a step, staggered, and then leaned against the banister for support.

'You've erased him,' he said. 'It's as if he was never here. As if nothing ever happened.' He listened. 'Yes, well, I can see intellectually that that was the point, but — '

I peeked down again, to see him more clearly.

'But I've come back now, Liv. Yeah, I know. Uh-huh. And — and I'm sorry for that. I am sorry. But I can apologise till I'm blue in the face, and it doesn't really matter. Everything's gone.'

He'd put down his glass. He wiped his hand on his T-shirt, and then ran it through his hair.

'No, I haven't been . . . well, okay, a little bit. Just a couple. It's fucking three in the morning here, you know. What else is there to do? But listen Liv. What's the point of my coming back, if there's nothing here?'

He paused, listening, and shook his head. 'No, she won't. Yes, I know I should. Yes, of course I know I'm a fucking idiot.'

You can say that again.

'But I can't do anything except to remember, and I don't think it's doing any good. I need to see, I need to understand why it happened the way it did, and I can't without — '

Abruptly, he bounded down the stairs to the

162

ground floor. I looked over the banister, but he was out of sight. And I couldn't hear anything from there, except the ever-present radio.

I went slowly back to my bed. I lay down, but I couldn't get Leo's words out of my head. I wasn't sure of the meaning of all his one-sided conversation, but I could work out who 'he' was.

Liv had erased their father after she'd inherited the house. She'd gutted the place and rebuilt it from the inside into something clean and safe, with no memories. It was easier for her that way, and I understood that. Being without memories was easier for me, too.

I didn't understand why Leo would want to remember. He'd hated their father. He'd done nothing but run away from him when he was alive. He hadn't even come back for Mr Allingham's funeral. That was what Leo did: he ran away. He went off and had adventures and left people behind. He'd been swanning around America for the past two years with hardly a word to anybody.

Why would he care if all traces of his father were gone?

But he'd sounded as if he did care. He'd sounded bewildered. He'd sounded lost.

And I should not care about this at all.

I turned over in my bed and pulled the duvet over my head. Leo sounded emotional because he was drinking. People who were drinking got emotional. It was a known fact. And from the evidence, Leo was doing a lot of drinking these days.

What else is there to do?

There were plenty of other things to do. He could get lost, for one thing. He could stop getting on my nerves and making a mess in the house. He could stop waking me up in the middle of the night when I had to be at Eversley Hall the next morning. He could grovel to me and beg my forgiveness. Not a glib 'sorry', thrown in as an afterthought.

Though to think of it, that was about the only time I'd ever heard him apologise for anything at all. That day in my office, and just now on the phone.

I tossed and I turned and I tried not to think about Leo. I thought about Liv instead, and whether she was having a good time out there in a New Zealand winter with the man she loved and her new family-in-law. About to build new houses and a new life.

I thought about how, if she had erased her father, maybe she could erase me, too.

Everything's gone.

All the hope and love we'd had in Boston, all our dreams of what life would be. My best friend and the man I thought was my husband. Their drunken father and all the furniture and papers from all of his wasted life. Everything was gone, and why would Leo care?

Even with the duvet over my head, I could hear bumping and thumping coming from downstairs. It sounded like he was attacking the walls with a cricket bat. Or maybe with his own, very thick, very idiotic head. I didn't get up to see what he was doing. If he was falling down the stairs repeatedly, that was his own damn fault. If he was knocking down the house, he'd just have to pay to get it fixed.

It sounded as if he *was* knocking down the house. Or as if he'd found an elephant from somewhere.

Either way, I couldn't help him. It was none of my business. If he yelled, I'd go down to make sure he wasn't hurt. But if he wanted to dismantle the house in the middle of the night, it was half his, after all. I pulled the duvet up tighter around my ears and curled up into a ball. Eventually, it stopped. Instead I heard strange rattling sounds, things being dropped and maybe thrown. And then that stopped, too. But I didn't sleep, even through the long silence, because the long silence was even louder.

★　★　★

When light began to creep through the curtains, I got up and pulled on my dressing-gown. My head ached and my mouth was dry, as if I'd been drinking too. That would teach me to eavesdrop on conversations. From now on, I was going to wear earplugs to bed. Thank God I had Eversley Hall today, and I could get away from all of this into another century for several hours.

I went down the stairs, peering around as I went. There was no sign of an elephant anywhere. Nor was Leo lying with his neck broken at the bottom of the stairs. The radio blasted, playing some appalling girl band that screeched on my tired nerves. Damn man couldn't even turn the radio off after he'd sloped off, pissed, to bed. I clenched my fists and marched over to snap it off.

I stopped dead.

All the furniture had been moved to one side of the room: the heavy white sofa, the glass coffee table, the standing lamps and the side-tables and the dining-table and all its chairs. The air was heavy with the plasticky smell of acrylic paint and aerosol, and the stale smell of whisky. Spray cans and brushes and tubes and stencils were scattered on the white carpet, leaving red and blue and brown stains. A jar of water had overturned and sat in a wide puddle of sludge-coloured liquid.

These were peripheral. I'd been expecting a mess, anyway. I was frozen in place because of the two men.

One sat in a painted chair, on the white wall. The chair itself was sketchy, fading to mere ghosts of spraypaint at the back and the bottom, though every place where it touched the man it was rendered realistically, in worn brown leather. It almost looked warm from the man's body.

The man had been painted in detail. From here, he looked real, as if he were sitting in front of the wall. He had dark hair streaked with dishwater grey; a pale face with hectic colour on the cheeks. High cheekbones, a nose with a small tilt on the end. Brown eyes that were nearly black, gazing at nothing.

He was his son, twenty years older, with every drink he had taken written in the lines on his face.

Mr Allingham sat slumped in the chair. He balanced a glass of amber liquid on the arm.

He wore grey trousers and no shoes; there was a hole in the toe of one sock. The light on him was muted, as if it were filtered through drawn blinds, while the rest of the room, the real room, was bathed in clear morning. As if he had his own moment and space, his own bleak world.

I had never seen him in this chair — I'd hardly visited the Allingham house when he was alive — but I knew from the painting that he had often sat in exactly this pose. It must be how Leo remembered him, with despair in every line of his body. An old man with hands that had once been strong. His wife had died; he'd let his children grow away from him. A man who had lost everything.

I stepped forward; closer, you could see how it had been painted, with stencils and spraypaint, precise, hasty brushstrokes. Despite the artifice, he still looked real. He could move his hand at any moment, look in my direction, raise his drink to his lips.

Leo had made him beautiful.

Leo lay on the carpet, not far from a stereo speaker that must be blasting in his ear. He had paint on his hands and on his face, and more in his hair. He'd used his jeans to clean his brushes, as he'd used to do when he was working on something important, something that grabbed him so much he couldn't take the time to clean them properly. He breathed gently, his eyes closed, his arms flung out on either side of him, fast asleep.

I stood there, looking from one man to the other. The real man and the memory. The painter and the painting. They looked so damn much alike. And I had seen that nothing in Leo's eyes before.

The song on the radio changed to one by an equally irritating boy band. That was enough to break the spell; I strode over and turned off the stereo. Leo didn't stir. There was a half-empty tumbler of whisky near his arm. He'd knock it over if he moved, so I picked it up and put it on one of the side-tables that had been shoved over to the other side of the room. The carpet was ruined anyway, but it seemed like the right thing to do. On an impulse I grabbed a white knitted throw from the sofa and brought it over to him.

I was draping it over him when he moved his head and opened one eye. 'Thanks, Mermaid,' he murmured.

'You've trashed the house,' I told him.

'I know.' He closed his eye again. 'What do you think of it?'

I looked at the painting again, and then at him. He had used to ask me this every time he finished a painting. With his eyes closed, his face looked both older and younger. How could he do this, imprint a memory on a wall, as if it still existed?

'You're really fucking talented,' I said.

'I know. It doesn't help.' He drew his arms into his body, curling up onto his side under the throw, in his more usual sleeping posture. With one breath that was half a sigh, he slipped from wakefulness into sleep.

I picked up the whisky glass, whose twin was painted on the wall. I brought it into the kitchen and emptied it out.

Plunging In

After a night of no sleep, it took me a little bit longer to do my hair. I was only five minutes or so late, though, for my first proper morning at Eversley Hall. The staff room was full of people chattering and helping each other get into their costumes. As I had yesterday, I glanced around the room to see if I could spot James, but he wasn't there, so I nodded to Lady Fitzwilliam who was, strangely, sitting at the staff-table in only her full-length chemise. She had a cup of tea and seemed absorbed in reading *Vogue*, so I went through into the female changing room.

Selina was in there, standing in her chemise and being laced into her stays by Mrs Collins. She smiled at me, and I set down a large canvas bag next to her. 'These are those books I promised you.'

'Oh, thank you. Do you really think they'll help me know what's going on?'

'Yes. Or they certainly can't hurt, anyway.' I went to the rack of clothing to find my black outfit. 'Why is Lady Fitzwilliam sitting around in her underwear out there?'

'She'll get dressed later, up in her bedroom.' Mrs Collins finished off Selina's stays, tying the laces. 'She puts on a little show for the visitors, explaining the dresses, et cetera, while she puts everything on. She's a re-enactor, it's all about the costume for her, whereas I'm more

169

interested in the social history. Do you want doing up?' she asked me.

'Thanks,' I said, pulling off my clothes and reaching for my chemise. Mrs Collins removed the stays from the hanger with expert hands and helped me put them on.

'You'll be able to do this yourself before too long,' she told me. 'It's all practice. You lace it up in front, then pull it round and tighten the back.'

'It's a shame you have to wear black,' Selina said. 'But at least you don't have to worry about getting it dirty.' She touched the flimsy skirts of her white muslin gown, the same one she'd been wearing yesterday.

'What do we do about washing these clothes, anyway?' I asked.

'Oh, it's all sorted out by some specialist costume people. They come round on a Sunday evening and inspect everything.'

'Not that you're likely to get anything dirty, where you are upstairs,' said Mrs Collins. She gave my laces an extra tug and when I looked down, my boobs were considerably closer to my head.

'Morning meeting, everyone,' called Mrs Smudge through the door and Selina jumped to her feet and hurried out. Mrs Collins helped me put on my petticoats and my gown, fastening the small buttons with deft fingers. When we left the female changing room, the entire staff were sitting in chairs around the room. It had been strange to see them up and milling around, but even stranger to see them arrayed in a line: early nineteenth-century people, sitting on folding chairs in front of lockers with combination locks. Kayleigh was holding a can of Diet Coke. She winked across the room at me.

Selina beckoned me into a chair next to her, and Mrs Collins went to sit on the other side of the room. I settled into my chair, which was not as easy as you'd think, with all the petticoats making my backside about twice as big as normal. I was glad I wasn't in a period where women had to wear crinolines or a bustle. I looked over at Mrs Smudge to see how she managed it, as her arse was pretty large to begin with. She was wedged in, with her customary frown on her face.

James came in, already dressed in his Regency gear. The room went still as he took a position standing in front of us. I clenched my fingers tight together in my lap. He was impeccable. Absolutely perfect. I couldn't imagine a greater contrast to Leo, lying sprawled on the stained carpet.

'Morning, everyone,' he said, and we all murmured answering greetings. Miss Grantham bestowed upon him a dazzling smile. 'Today is Sunday, the twelfth of June, 1814. Just a little reminder of social history. Esme, would you?'

Miss Grantham rose and stood next to James. 'The twelfth of June, 1814,' she said. 'King George III is tragically ill, probably with porphyria though none of us know that; the theory about the disease wasn't put forward until 1966. His son the Prince of Wales is our Regent, and not everyone is pleased with the way he spends money, nor with his many affairs,

171

particularly with the Catholic Maria Fitzherbert.'

Mrs Smudge snorted. Clearly she had strong views about monarchs having affairs with Catholics, though I couldn't quite tell what those views were.

'The Prime Minister is Robert Banks Jenkinson, second Earl of Liverpool,' she continued. 'The most important foreign news is the Treaty of Paris signed last month. I won't go into the details, but essentially it established peace with France. Princess Charlotte, the Regent's daughter, has signed a marriage contract to the Prince of Orange, though there are rumours she's not too happy about the match.

'In more local news, William Parrish, an ostler, has been found guilty in Brickham Crown Court of stealing two saddles and four bridles, and has been sentenced to seven years' transportation. To be historically accurate, it should be much cooler outside. The summer of 1814 was an unusually cold one. But we can't control the weather, I'm afraid.'

She smiled at James again, as if she'd cracked a joke. He put his hand in the small of her back.

'That's wonderful, Esme, as always,' he said to her, and she returned to her seat. 'Now for the family business. As it's Sunday, the family have already been to church and have returned home to change and go about their daily pursuits. According to one of Lady Fitzwilliam's letters that we've found, we're expecting guests, Colonel and Lady Andrews, to dine this evening.

'As far as visitors go, yesterday was a moderate day compared to the last two weekends, though that's not surprising as we had a spike with the Bank Holiday, and then half-term. Still, today we should have a fair crowd. We're expecting two coaches, one from the European Historical Association and one with a tour group from, I think, Texas. Ready for the room draw?'

He held up a small velvet bag and passed it to Arthur, who was sitting nearest him. He reached in and pulled out a card.

'Ugh, the Chinese Bedroom again,' he moaned. 'I always draw the ruddy Chinese Bedroom. When do I get to go outside and do some shooting?'

'I'm not letting you anywhere near a gun,' said James. 'And please don't spend the whole day lolling about on the bed this time. The steward is tired of ironing out the wrinkles and remaking it every day.'

I noticed that the bag skipped over Selina and Lady Fitzwilliam on its way to me. I put my hand inside and pulled out a card. 'The Hall.'

'Are you all right with all the artwork?' James asked me. 'The Hall isn't easy for your first day. Do you want to swap?'

'I'll swap,' said Arthur quickly.

Miss Grantham made a noise very much like Mrs Smudge's snort.

'No, I don't need to,' I said. 'I've studied every room. I'll be fine in the Hall.'

I was rewarded with James's smile. 'Good.'

The bag finished its rounds and everyone performed minor self-checks and adjustments before going off. Kayleigh came over, tipping the rest of her Diet Coke into her mouth. 'You really do look all Gothic. Who died?'

'My parents.'

Her eyes widened. 'Really?'

'Good God, no, my real parents are alive and well. How are you today, Kayleigh?'

'A little hungover. What else is new.' She chucked the can into the bin. 'Well, you know what they say — nothing cures a hangover like a job in a stuffy kitchen wearing five layers of clothing. Not.'

'Did you stay in the pub long after I left?'

'Till closing.'

I didn't want to ask it. But I remembered the caring in his voice. That little softness out of nowhere. 'Did you — did you ever talk with that bad boy at the bar?'

'Oh, yeah. For a little while. He bought me a couple of drinks and I gave him my number, so maybe he'll text me or something and we can meet up.'

'Maybe.' There was another contrast for you. James Fitzwilliam, in control and in charge of all he surveyed, deploying the costumed troops around the house like Wellington himself. Leo, drinking himself into a frenzy and buying drinks for random girls in the pub, before vandalising his childhood home. I could tell which version of manhood I preferred.

Still, there was a twinge there, somewhere down underneath my stays. He'd taken her number. I examined it, trying to tell if the twinge was more than, less than, or equal to the twinge I'd got at Miss Grantham's smug smile. There's no way to measure twinges though, so I gave up.

'I bet he's married though,' Kayleigh said.

'Why do you say that? He didn't mention anything, did he?'

'No. He just seemed sort of . . . morose. Like there was trouble at home or something. And then there's my track record, so it makes sense. Anyway, gotta go or I'll get it in the neck again,' she said. 'See ya around!' Kayleigh scurried off and I walked contemplatively outside, out of the courtyard and on the gravel paths around to the front of the house.

No visitors would turn up for another fifteen minutes; I had time to enjoy my solitary walk through the quiet grounds and imagine what I would look like to someone walking up the drive to the house. My black dress would stand out against the honey-coloured sandstone, but I would look part of the landscape, someone who naturally belonged here amongst the Palladian columns. I ascended the double flight of stairs into the airy portico fronted by Ionic columns — now that I'd studied the dossier, I knew the names of every feature. I paused to enjoy the view of the grounds, the rolling fields and the trees touched by the morning sun, and then I went through the double wooden doors into the Hall.

It was empty. I'd seen it empty before, but not when I'd been dressed like this, as if I belonged here. Now, in the quiet before the visitors arrived, it wasn't difficult to imagine really living here. You probably wouldn't even give the elaborate decorations of this room a second glance. You'd hardly notice the decorated vases on either side of the entrance door, or the chandelier dripping with crystal. I rearranged the flowers that stood on the marble-topped table, freeing the greenery a bit from underneath the blooms. I wandered to the window and looked out over the parkland, which was dotted with trees. What must it feel like to look around you, and everything you see is yours?

I gazed at the portrait of the first James Fitzwilliam. He must feel like that all the time. Imagine knowing that when the visitors left and the gates were shut, this house was your private domain. I remembered the bit in *Pride and Prejudice* where Elizabeth Bennet visits Mr Darcy's house, Pemberley, for the first time, and realises that if she'd accepted his offer of marriage, this house would now be hers as well.

'Mrs Alice Fitzwilliam,' I murmured under my breath, close enough to the window to fog it.

I wasn't in a hurry to get married again, of course. But marriage to someone like James Fitzwilliam, even the modern one, would be so different from marriage to Leo. Less chaotic, less spontaneous. You wouldn't find a Fitzwilliam passed out on the carpet. And they kept the portraits of their ancestors in sensible gilded frames, not spraypainted all over the wall.

Through the pane of glass, I could see the first of the visitors approaching the house. The first couple veered off towards the service rooms in the east pavilion, but the next group of three continued up to the main entrance. They'd arrive in my room in a few moments.

I closed my eyes and tried to remember all I

could about John Carr of York, Chippendale and Wedgwood.

★ ★ ★

Being upstairs was different from being down-stairs, and not only for the obvious reasons that I got to wear a nice (black) dress and talk posh in a beautiful room. I didn't have anything to do with my hands, for one thing: no task to keep me busy while people watched me. If I'd been in the Drawing Room I could have been drawing, or pretending to sew or write a letter, but I was in the Hall, where there was nothing to do but wander up and down the polished floor and talk with visitors.

The visitors behaved differently here, too. In the kitchen, they were surrounded by interesting objects which had a mundane purpose, which they could compare to their everyday experience. Mrs Collins, Kayleigh and I had all been in the kitchen together too, so we could create a bit of banter and camaraderie, the sort of thing you need when you're doing mundane tasks for hours on end. The Hall, on the other hand, had been built and decorated specifically to impress.

People paused here. They gaped. They murmured to themselves and each other in small knots. They would laugh, but in hushed tones, as if they could offend the oil painting of the owner by commenting on his décor. I found myself noticing the disparity of their body language: women clutched their cameras or handbags and men crossed their arms over their bodies, as if they had to hold themselves in reassurance. About one in every five men would act differently, would clasp his hands together behind his back in a charade of feeling at home, and look analytically at the decorations as if finding fault.

'Welcome sir, welcome madam, to Eversley Hall,' I would say. 'I trust you had a pleasant journey? Have you been here before? Well, then, let me draw your attention to Mr Fitzwilliam's portrait on the far wall . . . '

And on. And on. For every new group of visitors who came in. I'd vary the words, and vary the subjects I talked about, and of course I'd answer questions, if they were asked. About half of the visitors listened politely and thanked me, and then carried on without saying anything more. The others, who did speak, usually asked factual questions. I wasn't sure why they were so shy; maybe because this room was first in the normal tourist route of the house, and so the visitors hadn't got used to the idea of interacting with Regency people yet. Maybe it was the room. Twice I posed for 'portraits'. That was a lot less than my day as Ann Horton. Maybe nobody wanted a picture of someone in black.

The only person who wasn't shy was a whippet-looking man in green sunglasses who grilled me about Napoleon and the Duke of Wellington for fifteen fraught minutes, and kept on referring to Waterloo despite the fact that the battle wouldn't occur for an entire year.

It was hard work. I hadn't noticed any of this yesterday; yesterday I'd been fizzing with excitement, I'd been getting acquainted with my fellow inmates, and I'd had a decent night's sleep beforehand. But today I was tired, and my face began to ache and my throat to hurt from smiling and speaking loudly and clearly for hours.

And this dress was hot. And these shoes were thin. I found myself noticing how the tourists were dressed for comfort. They wore cotton T-shirts and jeans, sundresses and little cardigans. Every single one of them had sensible shoes, suitable for walking around a country house on a summer afternoon.

I'd never lusted after trainers before, but I caught myself staring at a pair of Nikes and nearly drooling.

I was glad when, mid-afternoon, the stream of visitors lulled momentarily and I saw Selina approaching me from the direction of the Drawing Room. She was wearing a straw bonnet trimmed with yellow ribbon, and held a parasol, gloves and another bonnet.

'James said that he thought you might like to take a walk with me.' She gave me her spare bonnet, which was very plain, and I tied it under my chin before pulling on the gloves. We went out of the front door in the opposite direction to the flow of traffic, and down the stairway to the gravel drive. The sun was shining and the fresh air felt wonderful against my face. 'James suggested a stroll in the parterre,' she added.

'If James suggests it, so it shall be.'

We walked around the front of the house past the west pavilion. A family was having a picnic in the shade of the large horse chestnut on the west side of the house; they looked up at us and pointed as we walked past, but they weren't in earshot. We were a pretty bit of scenery for them, like the rose garden or the columns of the house.

'Thank you so much for rescuing me,' I said to Selina. 'I think if I had to talk about neo-Classicism any more I would've turned orange.'

'The Hall's difficult,' she agreed. 'Everyone wants to talk with you.'

'Well, maybe I was doing something wrong, but nobody wanted to talk with me. At least, not about anything interesting. There really is only so much you can say about furniture and wallpaper. I tried to get some gossip in about the Prince and Mrs Fitzherbert, but all I got were blank looks.'

'Mrs who?'

I shook my head. 'Never mind. Does Lady Fitzwilliam really get dressed in front of an audience every day she's here?'

'Sometimes she gets undressed again and does it twice.'

'And does Miss Grantham know the full history and meaning of every single artwork in the house?'

'It seems like it.'

I sighed. 'Clothing and art are interesting, but not *that* interesting. I'm much more interested in the people who wear the clothes and look at the art. I didn't get to talk to a single person today about Cousin Horace. Or anything fun like that.'

'I spent most of the morning talking about the carpet,' Selina said glumly. 'There was this lady

180

who was really, *really* into it.'

'Why didn't you choose a room from the bag this morning?'

'Oh. I'm always in the Drawing Room. It's much better for me to be in the same room every time, so I can remember what I'm supposed to say. James thinks it's best, and I don't mind.'

We rounded the pavilion and reached the parterre, which was inhabited by many visitors and several children leaping along the paths between the low box hedges as if they were in a maze. I noticed Selina stiffening, as if she were forcibly pulling her character back on for the audience.

'Of course, you must adore your half-brother,' I said loudly enough to be overheard.

'James is very kind,' she said.

'It was very good of him to invite me here. And I can see why he chose Eversley Hall for your home. It's close enough to London so that eligible prospects will be thrown your way.'

She leaned in close to me and whispered, 'What do you mean by 'eligible prospects'?'

'Men for you to marry.'

'Oh!' She bit her lip and looked around at the visitors, who were watching us with interest. 'Oh. Well, I don't know about that. I mean, I'm still very young.'

'How old *are* you, Miss Selina Fitzwilliam?'

'I'm nineteen.'

'And you haven't yet received any offers? Of marriage?' I clarified.

'Er . . . no.'

'Oh well, not to worry. You have several more

years until you're on the shelf, like me. Of course, you'll probably be snapped up very soon, and if your brother is as good as you say, he will take your own preferences into account.'

'I — I really don't know.'

We were interrupted by an elderly couple who wanted to know the way to the WC. When we resumed our walk, Selina tugged my arm to lead me down the path, slightly away from the visitors.

'Why are you talking about me getting married?' she whispered. 'I don't know anything about getting married. I'm a tour guide!'

'Being a young woman in the Regency period was all about getting married,' I said. 'Isn't that one of the things you talk about?'

'No. We usually talk about more general things. Or Isabella and James talk about history; I'm lost half the time.'

'It wasn't in your dossier, then?'

'No, nothing about getting married.'

'Maybe your character didn't get married until later.'

She looked startled. 'People got married at nineteen? That's ridiculous. I'm twenty-one and I'm nowhere near ready to get married.'

I'd been twenty-two. 'Being ready doesn't have much to do with it,' I said. 'Shall we go into the shrubbery?'

'I think we're supposed to go back inside.'

The sun was warm and my dress was black, but surprisingly, I was much less hot and uncomfortable than I'd been half an hour ago in the Hall. My feet didn't even seem to hurt very much. The walk had been refreshing, but not nearly as refreshing as gossiping with Selina about marriage.

'Seriously,' I said, 'you should read those books I brought for you. They're lots of fun and you'll see how important marriage really was. Come on, a few more minutes outside can't hurt.'

'All right.' We kept on strolling, past the French doors leading out of the Red Saloon, listening to the burble of the fountain on the terrace. Pretty iron tables from the tea room were scattered around the south-facing side of the house, with visitors drinking tea and eating drizzle cake that Mrs Collins and her team had probably prepared earlier in the day. 'Oh look, Harry, don't they look nice,' said a lady with a tea cup as we passed.

Samuel the gardener was bent over a flower bed, digging. He looked up when we approached, a smile on his face which faded when he saw who we were.

'Were you expecting someone more congenial, Samuel?' I called to him.

He touched his cap with his dirty fingers. 'Oh beg pardon, Miss Woodstock, Miss Fitzwilliam. I thought it was maybe Lucy. She takes a little stroll around the flowers sometimes.'

Lucy, also known as Kayleigh, I thought. Coming back from a fag break. But there was a little pinkness in Samuel's cheeks that might not be from the sun. Interesting.

'Sorry to disappoint you. But I can — ' I was interrupted by a ginger blur sprinting across my feet, followed rapidly by a brown-and-white dog.

'Nelson!' cried Selina. 'Oh, he's not supposed to be outside by himself!'

Samuel shouted a word that had been rude way before Regency times, dropped his spade, and took off after the dog. Even from the back, chasing after a cat, Nelson looked familiar. I'd been looking at his oil-painted twin all morning.

'Isn't that James Fitzwilliam's dog?' I asked, and immediately sprinted after Samuel without waiting for an answer. My skirts got in my way, so I hitched them up.

The cat bounded over iron tea tables, around drizzle cake and gasping tourists, with Nelson barking and burrowing through legs and chairs underneath. 'Dog's a bloody nightmare, won't listen to anyone but his master,' Samuel muttered. 'Nelson! Here, boy! Heel!'

'Nelson!' I cried, and grabbed for him when he emerged from underneath a table. I missed, and nearly ended up with a handful of a lady's flowered skirt instead. She let out a muffled squeal. 'I do beg your pardon, madam.'

The ginger cat leaped from the final table and bounded down the terrace, onto the low wall surrounding the fountain and, with a single graceful leap, onto the tall sculpture of an urn in the middle. Nelson barked and hurled himself straight over the wall and into the water.

The splash was terrific, dotting the terrace paving with water. Nelson's head went right under the surface, underneath the decorative lily pads. Only his tail and rear legs were visible.

Samuel climbed onto the wall and grabbed the cat, who hissed at him and scratched at his thick

184

sleeves. 'Get out of here,' he told it, and released it on the other side of the fountain, where it immediately darted across the lawn towards the shrubbery. I leaned forward, ready to grab Nelson's collar when his head emerged from the water.

Only it didn't.

His legs were scrabbling against the stone of the fountain, his plumed tail drooping. He was stuck under the water, probably in the plants. I plunged my hands into the water and found his upper body and his neck, felt for his collar and gave it a hard tug. No luck. He didn't budge.

'Come on, Nelson,' I muttered and pulled again with one hand, with the other trying to find the stem or whatever that had him trapped. The gloves I wore weren't helping, and I was twisted around at an angle perched on the wall. And if I didn't get him untangled soon, he was going to drown.

Screw it. I swung my legs round and got fully into the fountain, kneeling down close to Nelson's head. The water was cold, but I concentrated on the wet dog, his neck, his head trapped under the water, and with my left hand I finally found it: a bit of wire wrapped around the loose end of Nelson's collar. I pulled at it, and he was free.

The dog scrambled up, choking, onto my lap. His wet face drooled water into mine.

'You're all right, boy,' I gasped, holding him tight. He squirmed in my embrace and I heard, for the first time, the people around me applauding.

And realised I was in a fountain, in full

Regency costume, soaked to the skin.

'Nelson!' said an authoritative voice, and Nelson immediately jumped out of my arms. He shook the water out of his coat, showering everyone standing around the fountain, which seemed to be a considerable number of people suddenly, and scampered through the parting crowd to James Fitzwilliam. 'Sit and stay,' he told the dog, and strode to where I stood.

'Miss Woodstock,' he said, holding out his hand. 'Are you all right?'

'I'm fine.' I gathered my skirts in one hand and tried to step out of the fountain, but they were weighted down too much and I had to grab James's hand to keep my balance. His grip was strong as he helped me out of the water. The perfect gentleman.

'You're soaked to the skin,' he said. His gaze dropped down to where my dress clung tightly to my legs and hips, and then lingered for a split second on my chest. The fine white lace covering my pushed-up cleavage had gone totally transparent.

Maybe not such a perfect gentleman, after all.

'Come inside immediately,' he said, 'and Mrs Smudge will find you some dry clothes. Munson!'

Munson appeared, apologising his way through the crowd. The number of people around was quite incredible; the entire house must have emptied itself onto the terrace to witness my plunge into the fountain. 'Sir?'

'We need a blanket, and some towels. And tell Ann to heat some water.' James looked at my face, his blue eyes boring into mine. 'Thank you for saving my spaniel, Miss Woodstock.'

'It's nothing.' It was a warm day, but the water had been cold, and my many layers of clothing were holding it against my skin. I began to shiver, maybe from the cold, maybe from how close I'd come to not saving the dog, maybe from being so close to James Fitzwilliam. It was hard to tell. James put his arm around my shoulders and steered me through the crowd towards the house.

Miss Grantham emerged from the French doors as we approached them. 'Miss Woodstock! My word! What have you done?'

'I — took a little swim,' I replied, my teeth nearly chattering.

She put her hand to her chest. 'Is this your idea of propriety? James, surely you're not allowing your cousin to fling herself into the fountain?'

'He didn't have much to do with it,' I said.

'Please, Miss Woodstock, come inside before you catch your death,' said James, conspicuously not looking at the bodice of my dress.

A puddle was rapidly forming at my feet. 'No,' I chattered, 'I don't want to ruin the carpet.'

'You have certainly ruined your dress!' said Miss Grantham. 'I hope that your reputation may prove to be — '

'I say! Capital sport, Miss W!' Arthur bounded out of the house, his face beaming. 'I saw the whole thing from the upstairs window. You were dashed brave!'

'Yes, you were,' said James Fitzwilliam quietly. 'And I'd be a churl to think of the carpet when you have saved my dog's life.'

Miss Grantham's eyes widened.

'You should have let Samuel do it,' James said to me. 'But I am grateful to you. Arthur, will you please look after Nelson for me?'

And he helped me inside the house, his arm still around my shoulder, the tips of his fingers grazing the bare skin over my collarbone as Miss Grantham, Selina and over a hundred tourists looked on, gaping.

Munson was waiting inside with a giant fluffy towel, and Ann was holding a basin of steaming water. 'I didn't mean your stroll in the garden to be *this* refreshing,' James Fitzwilliam murmured in my ear. I could hear the smile in his voice, and despite my goosebumps and my wet petticoats and bedraggled hair, I smiled too.

Now this was more like it.

Life Goes On

When I walked into the house that evening, Leo was sitting on the stairs. His elbows were on his knees and his hands clasped between them.

'Hi,' he said.

I had no idea how to respond even to this simple word. Walk straight past, pretending not to notice his presence? Launch into a tirade about how he'd kept me up all night and ruined the living room?

He wasn't smiling, and he didn't look smug. He didn't look particularly hungover, or as if he were trying to be charming or wind me up. Any of these things would have made me ignore him or rant at him. Instead, I said, 'Hi.' Guardedly, with one hand holding on to the shoulder strap of my handbag. My hair, frizzy from getting wet, fell across my face and I blew it away, as I'd been doing all afternoon.

'How was your day in 1814?'

'Fine,' I said. I'd had to wear one of Selina's dresses, and the tops of my arms had bruises from where the sleeves of my gown had pulled against me when I'd been tugging at Nelson. But at least there had been something new to talk about all day. 'How do you know where I've been?'

'I picked it up,' he said, and I remembered he'd spoken with Kayleigh yesterday in the pub, before the plunge in the fountain, before the

189

all-night painting. He'd taken her number. I gripped my handbag tighter.

'I'm sorry,' he said.

There it was again. I'd never heard that word from him before, and now I'd heard it three times in less than a week.

'You ruined the living room,' I said.

'I know.'

'You kept me up all night.'

'I did.'

'Does Liv know what you've done to her wall?'

'She will.'

'Why are you agreeing with everything I say? Why aren't you arguing with me?'

'Because I'm in the wrong. You're in the right. There's no point arguing.'

'Damn straight I'm in the right,' I snapped, suddenly absolutely furious. 'But that's never stopped you swearing that black was white.'

'Maybe I've changed.'

'Maybe you haven't at all!'

'No,' he said, and he sighed. 'Maybe I haven't.'

'Spending the whole night in the pub, chatting up girls, drinking the best part of a bottle of scotch when you get home and then painting your memories on the wall. There's no excuse for it, Leo. You're a grown man. It's pathetic.'

'Yes, I think so, too.'

'Aren't you even going to defend yourself? To say it's genetic, or that there was nothing else to do? Or that it seemed like a good idea at the time? Or that you had to do it because every-thing's gone?'

He blanched. 'You heard that?'

190

'Of course I heard it — you were shouting it down the phone on the staircase. And let me tell you, even if you do care that everything's gone, it isn't an excuse, Leo. We're still here. Life goes on. It goes on and you have to deal with it.'

'Is that what you're doing?' he asked quietly. So quietly I could barely hear him.

'Yes. It is. And if we're finished with the self-pity fest, I'm going to go and get myself something to eat.' I strode across the room, leaving him sitting on the stairs.

I pulled the refrigerator door open and slammed a ready-meal from it onto the counter. What was he playing at, with that little boy lost and sorry act? He might have a few brief moments of penitence now. Just enough for me to forgive him a little bit, just enough so that he thought he could begin charming me. And then tomorrow, he'd be right back at the beginning again.

I shoved the meal in the microwave without looking to see what it actually was. Then I reached for the kettle to fill it, to make a very, very strong cup of tea.

I'd had a good day today. A *really* good day. I'd managed to forget all about my messed-up real life for eight hours. Even when I'd been bored senseless in the Hall, it had been better than this.

I heard him coming in behind me, and I willed myself not to look.

'I never dealt with my father,' Leo said behind me. 'I ran away from him and ignored him and got angry with him. But I never found out why he cared more about drinking than his children. And when he died I didn't deal with him either. And now there's nothing left of him and it's too late.'

I didn't turn around. I didn't want to see Leo's face. I watched my meal going round and round in its little box.

'But I won't turn into him,' he said. 'I refuse to be him. That stops now.'

There was a faint sound of bottles clinking together and when I looked despite myself I saw him walking out of the back door carrying the twenty-four pack of French lager with the bottles of wine stacked on top of it. Outside, in the back, I heard the crash of it all landing in the bottom of the wheelie bin.

The microwave dinged. Leo came back in, grabbed the two remaining bottles of whisky, and left. I heard them crash, too. He didn't come inside again.

I chewed lemon chicken and rice without tasting it and when it was gone, I got out a fresh bin liner and put the package in it. Then I swept in the empty pizza boxes, the toast crumbs, the coffee grounds, the stale ends of bread still in their plastic bags. I put every last dish in the dishwasher, whether they were mine or Leo's, and turned it on. I wiped the surfaces and put the dirty tea towels in the wash. When I was finished, the kitchen looked like it had when Liv had still lived here, with no trace of Leo at all.

I didn't think the rest of him would be so easy to tidy away.

For the rest of the week, I worked on my second blog entry and the introduction to my article for *Hot! Hot!*. The account of my day in the kitchen as a scullery maid had poured out of me, but now I had time to think about what I was doing, about the whole scope of the assignment. Writing about my own experiences was very different from doing technical writing. Instead of having facts to organise and explain, I had to present real life, and real people with whom I was starting to form relationships. It was messier.

My first draft sucked. It was technical, it was explanatory, it was dead. I deleted it immediately and started another, trying to be looser and more narrative in my style. I printed it off, went to bed, and read it when I woke up the next morning. It was also terrible: a stilted, overblown parody of a Regency novel that even I didn't find amusing or clever.

I spent several hours staring at the computer. I typed sentences and then deleted them. I even started one version with the words *It is a truth universally acknowledged* and immediately banged my head against the desk in punishment for using such a barefaced cliché. I was not Jane Austen. Not by a long way.

I was me, and I didn't know how to write anything except for articles about ball joints and grommets. I was being defeated by a blog post.

A blog post. And I'd once wanted to be a novelist.

I shoved that thought aside quickly. There was no point dwelling on failures when you needed a success.

Eversley Hall and this article were the only successes I had at the moment. I couldn't afford to muck them up because my personal life was a mess. My ex was back in the picture, my family thought he was God, my youngest sister treated me like a freak, and my best friend was half the world away.

I suddenly missed Liv. Not in a niggling, *I wonder what she's doing now* way, or a *does she miss me at all* way, but in a whole-body, *where is my best friend* way. I checked the clock, did a mental calculation, and then picked up the phone next to my computer. She answered after several rings, and as soon as I heard her 'Hello?' my heart did a great thump of gladness.

'Hi, Liv,' I said. 'It's me.'

'Alice! Oh, it's so good to hear your voice.'

'I didn't want to interrupt your honeymoon.'

'Mmm. Yes.' She sounded all warm and smiley. Oh, I missed her.

'How's Yann?'

'Great. Yann's family are all so sweet. And we went out to the site this morning to have a walk round. It's so exciting to be here, Alice. Like a big starburst. I hadn't realised how stuck in a rut I'd been with my thinking. I've had more ideas here in two hours than I have for the past two years in Brickham.'

'Wow. That's great.'

'Yes. It is.'

Was I part of the rut? I didn't ask it; I didn't

194

want to hear the answer. I knew, anyway. I could feel it in the pit of my stomach, like a poisonous seed of failure.

'I was scared,' she said suddenly. 'It was such a big move to make. All through the wedding, I was terrified. Could you tell?'

'Not really.'

She laughed. 'I must've done a good job of hiding it by being Bridezilla. But Yann was wonderful, all of you were wonderful, and now that I'm here, I can see it was absolutely the best thing to do. You know, I've been thinking about it and I've come to the conclusion that if something's scary, it's worth doing.'

I ignored that feeling in my stomach. 'Dear God, Liv, you'll be diving off buildings next.'

'Not quite that. But you're right. I'm happy. I wish I didn't have to leave everyone behind to do it though. I'm . . . ' I could almost see her pausing, weighing her words. 'I'm worried about you and Leo.'

'Me and Leo, together? Or separately? Because you don't have to worry about the first one. We barely speak to each other.'

'Both. Leo called me drunk the other night.'

'I heard.'

'Do you know where he'd been?'

'I don't know about the whole night, but I saw him in the Groom and Horses earlier on in the evening.'

'Oh.'

'You say that like it's significant. Is the beer more alcoholic there? He was royally pissed.'

'I don't know what the beer is like. That's

where our father used to drink.'

It was my turn to be surprised. 'Oh.'

'We'd go in sometimes to find him when we were kids.' She paused, and I heard a creak, as if she were sitting in an old wooden chair. 'Leo will never ask for help, you know, Alice. He needs to do absolutely everything himself.'

'You don't need to tell me anything about Leo's personality, believe me.'

'And he's harder on himself than anyone else.'

Now this, I had never seen any evidence of. But Liv was his sister; she was biased. I had no desire to argue with her, so I said, 'He's turned the living room into a studio. It's going to need redecorating.'

'That's not surprising.'

'He painted your dad on the wall.'

She laughed dryly. 'That makes sense. He's always used his art to express himself. Do you remember the cartoons he used to do of Dad when we were kids?'

'No.'

'They were horrendous. But funny, in a horrendous way.'

'Well, this painting isn't horrendous.'

'Maybe he's growing up a bit.'

'I wouldn't hold my breath. Liv . . . I'm sorry I didn't notice you were scared at your wedding.'

'It's all right. I hid it well. I think we're both good at hiding, don't you, Alice?'

I bit my lip. I listened to the distance between us.

'How's Eversley Hall?' Liv said at last.

I brightened up. 'It is absolutely excellent. It's like being in a novel. Heaving bosoms and men in tight breeches everywhere. Can you believe I flung myself into a fountain on Sunday?'

'That's a little extreme, isn't it?'

'I was saving a dog. It was interesting.'

'Hm. And what about that gorgeous guy, the one who owns the house?'

'He's . . . very nice.'

'Very nice.' She chuckled. 'I think that's the first time in a very long time I've heard you call a man 'very nice' in that tone of voice.'

'Liv, he's my boss.'

'You've been spending so much time by yourself. Not getting out, not trying anything new, just working. Maybe this Eversley Hall is exactly what you need.'

We talked for a while, about Yann and his family and their visions for their project and their exploration of her new country; about James Fitzwilliam and Miss Grantham and Selina. When I put down the phone, I realised I'd probably talked with Liv long distance for longer than I'd talked with her when she'd been living in the same house with me.

⋆ ⋆ ⋆

I sat down with a pen and paper, and did what I often did when I was writing for a new client about a new subject: I jotted down who the audience was, what they expected, the purpose of the article, the content of the article, what I could bring to it.

197

What I could bring to it.

That was the question, wasn't it?

I had lots of material. Even after only two week-ends, my head was overflowing with Eversley Hall. But where was I in it?

That was what readers wanted. They wanted to identify with me, they wanted to put themselves in the midst of this experience and this fantasy. I needed to be personal, and yet factual; true, and yet entertaining. I needed to be the heroine of my own tale and also the observer.

But that was easier said than done, because I also had real life to deal with. For example, how did I portray Isabella Grantham? To my eyes, she was a snob and a bitch, and portraying her that way could definitely add interest to my article. I could even play it up, really make her a villain; that was the way I'd described her to Liv. On the other hand, I had to work with her for the rest of the summer, so I didn't want to alienate her if she should read my article. And the opposite problem — what if I expressed honestly how attractive James Fitzwilliam was? Wouldn't that make me look like a completely lovelorn puppy in his eyes? But wouldn't showing the truth make the story much more compelling reading, something more than a few lines about dressing in a historical frock at the weekends?

If I was going to tell this story properly, I would have to flex some writing muscles I hadn't used in a very long time.

The memory, this time, wasn't so easy to shove aside. I was sitting in our Boston apartment, staring at a computer. It wasn't this computer; it was an iMac, one of the original ones in apple-green, which I'd bought secondhand and which wheezed and whirred whenever its memory was overloaded, which was just about every time I called up the document containing my novel. The Novel. The one I'd come to America with Leo to write, the one that was going to get me published, make me A Novelist, put my name in *The Sunday Times* and who knew, maybe even onto the longlist for the Man Booker Prize. Oh, okay, the *shortlist*.

It was the story of a young woman in New England, a poet, and her love affair with her country and with a mysterious, impulsive hero. There were scenes on the top of the Prudential Building, at the funfair at Old Orchard Beach in Maine, an elaborate first meet in Cambridge over a copy of *Wuthering Heights* that had used to belong to Sylvia Plath. Sometimes I had to drag the words out and force them into being; sometimes they flew out of me like a spirit onto the page.

I had a Post-it note stuck to the front of the apple-green computer. *Be truthful*, it said.

'I can edit the draft,' I would explain to Leo. 'As long as I write the truth, even when I'm writing fiction, the real truth that's inside me, everything else is just technique. I can revise the structure and the dialogue. But I can't revise the truth.'

Be truthful. As if that would save the world.

God, I'd been so naïve.

Being truthful hadn't got me anywhere with my novel. Being truthful was too painful, and being truthful felt like it had little to do with a young girl in Boston and a copy of *Wuthering Heights*.

Truthful was having love and losing it. It was long hospital corridors and your husband with nothing in his eyes.

I launched myself out of my chair. Fresh air, that was what I needed. I'd take a walk and blow the memories and the failures away and tackle this job, refreshed.

The radio was playing downstairs. Leo and I hadn't crossed paths since Sunday evening; I went down the stairs quickly and out of the house without looking around for him.

It was much easier to walk in leggings and flats than in two petticoats, stockings and kid slippers, and I didn't have the boundaries of propriety to dictate my pace. I jogged down Charlotte Street and Berkley Street, along London Road past the sandstone hospital that looked like Eversley Hall's grubbier cousin. It was a sunny day and I pulled the air into my lungs and walked as fast as I could, down through brambles and under a bridge to Waterloo Meadows, cutting onto the steep incline of Alpine Street with its Victorian terraces built for factory workers. Upwards, and nearly running. When I was a kid, this hill had been fenced off when the tunnels dug to feed the Victorian brickworks had collapsed and holes had started to appear in the road and under the houses. It was all filled in now. I forced myself to think about the article, and nothing else.

The thing was, if I did it right, it could be excellent. I was a better writer now than I had

been in Boston: more disciplined, more experienced, more structured. The technical writing
had done that for me, at least. I could almost see
what the story could be like — no, I could
almost *feel* what it would be like, an emotion
hovering outside my peripheral vision, a cloud
waiting for me to mould it into shape.

If I could do it.

I thought of what Liv had said: *I've come to
the conclusion that if something's scary, it's
worth doing.* I flung myself down on the bench
at the top of the street, on the little green that
looked out over Brickham. A small brass plaque
said it was in memory of Ida Smith, who loved
this place.

Writing something small, a blog post or an
article, wasn't too scary. It was a little scary, but
maybe that was because it was worth doing. And
if not this, if not now — what and when?

I pulled out the little notebook I always carried
in my handbag and found a stumpy pencil pushed
into the spiral binding. I opened to a blank page.
Sitting there on a bench in memory of someone
I'd never known, I began to write about Eversley
Hall and Miss Alice Woodstock.

The Most Dangerous Thing In The World

'Have you ever been in love?'

I looked up from my book at Selina, who was sitting beside me on the sofa in the Green Drawing Room. Rain streamed down the windows, making the large room seem smaller and warmer. There were some visitors with us, in clumps and pairs, most of them distinctly damp, but they were Observers and Murmurers, and we hadn't spoken with them at all, as if we were all in cahoots together to keep the room peaceful and cosy, an illusion of an idle Saturday afternoon in 1814.

Selina's cheeks were pink and her eyes were a bit nervous. 'Have I ever been in love?' I repeated, loudly enough so that everyone in the room could hear me. 'Why, my dear Selina, whatever put that question in your head? Have you been reading the novels I lent you?'

'Yes. That is, I've been reading one of them. It's — interesting. And especially after what you and I were talking about last week, in the garden . . . '

'About your finding a husband, or rather one being found for you.'

'Yes. So I was just thinking . . . about love. It seems that that's all they talk about in these novels, being in love and marrying the right person.'

We had piqued the interest of the Observers and Murmurers and they pressed closer, observing and murmuring.

'There is nothing more important for a female than to marry the right person,' I said. 'Think about it, Selina. Unmarried, we own no property. We must be chaperoned in everything we do. We cannot live alone; we cannot pursue a career without risking censure, and even then, the options are limited and unappealing. A woman cannot hope to have an influence on society unless her husband is of some importance. An unmarried woman is dependent on her family and the kindness of others. She's a figure of derision and pity.'

'But you're unmarried, and you're not a figure of derision and pity.'

I laughed. 'I am in some quarters. Especially soaking wet to the skin.'

'So why aren't you married?'

'I'm red-haired and have no accomplishments, home or prospects. I'm not exactly a catch.'

'I love your hair, and you weren't always homeless. And marriage can't be as important to you as you say it is. If it were, you'd have married your Cousin Horace when he asked you, and you'd still be in your own house now.'

'True. The only reason to marry my Cousin Horace was the fact that he owned my home, and I discovered that I loved the house much less when he was in it.'

'So you wouldn't marry without love, even if it was logically the best decision.'

'When it came to Cousin Horace, definitely not.'

'So — have you ever been in love?'

I glanced around the room. Selina's questions had drawn even more visitors around us, listening to our every word. A nice intimate conversation about love and marriage between two Regency ladies, eavesdropped upon by several dozen people wearing dripping anoraks.

I smiled. Selina had been doing more than reading my novels; she'd got herself a bit of nerve, too.

'I have been in love,' I said, quietly enough to make the visitors shuffle a little bit closer to hear.

'Then why aren't you married?'

'He . . . wasn't suitable.'

She settled more comfortably onto the sofa. 'It sounds like an exciting story. Was he handsome?'

'Extremely.'

'Was he rich?'

'He was the heir to a substantial property.'

'What was his name? Tell me all about him. Where did you meet? What did you do?'

'His name was Henry . . . ' I looked briefly around the room, for inspiration. ' . . . Pelmet. We met at a ball at the Assembly Rooms in Winchester.' I had no idea whether Winchester even had Assembly Rooms in the nineteenth century or any other time, but as it was unlikely that anyone in the room would contradict me, I carried on. 'He was in the country visiting his uncle and aunt. You can imagine the sensation created by the arrival of a young, handsome eligible bachelor.'

'What did he look like?'

I made my eyes go dreamy. 'He had brown hair, and eyes so dark they were nearly black. He dressed like a romantic hero, with a sort of careless elegance.'

'So what happened? Did your eyes meet across a crowded room, or something? Did you dance every dance together?'

'No. He was far too popular. Before we could be introduced, he was dancing with nearly every lady in the room, *except* for me.'

'How did you meet, then?'

'Ah. Well, my Cousin Horace had paid us a spontaneous visit, and I had made the mistake of accepting the first dance with the vicar's son, and after that, I could not refuse Horace when he asked me to dance. If you accept one invitation, you know, you have to accept everyone who asks you afterwards,' I explained to the woman standing closest to us. 'I was in a fair way resigned to having to use a crutch for the following fortnight, he trampled my toes so badly. In the quadrille he dealt my foot such a crippling blow with his boot that I actually tripped and fell, and would have gone sprawling onto the dance floor. But I was caught by a strong pair of arms.'

'Mr Pelmet,' sighed Selina. I wished I'd chosen a better name for this romantic paragon, but it was done now.

'Exactly. He carried me to a chair and although my pride was more hurt than my foot, he refused to leave my side all evening, quite cutting out Horace, and handed me up into our carriage at the end. He called the very next morning.'

'That is so romantic,' she said. 'Exactly like in a book.'

Not surprising, since that was probably where I'd got it. 'Of course, I could hardly fail to fall in love immediately.'

'And was it wonderful?'

'It was . . . magical.'

'Oh,' she breathed.

Shy Selina had been transformed, somehow. She was shining-eyed, smiling, enjoying herself immensely. I studied her. A novel or two couldn't have wrought this change, could it? She wasn't this good a play-actor. She must be thinking of something real. Or fantasising about the man who would come and rescue her in his strong arms, sweep her away into endless bliss.

'Have *you* ever been in love?' I asked her in my turn. 'Truly in love? Do you know what it feels like?'

She shook her head.

'It's madness,' I said. 'When you're in love, you're no longer in control of your thoughts or your emotions. You might do anything. Your happiness, your entire being, is wrapped up in one person. You're at their mercy. Being in love is the most dangerous thing in the world.'

'Why would anyone want to do it, then?'

'Because when you're in love, you don't see it as dangerous at all. Or you love the danger. And that's exactly what makes it so dangerous.'

'What was so wrong with Mr Pelmet? He sounds perfect — handsome, charming and rich.'

'He was too charming. He blinded me to his faults.'

'But wasn't he a respectable gentleman?'

'No. He appeared respectable, but really he was a rake. A . . . painter of oils. Of some genius, but with too artistic a temperament. He lived a life of constant flirtation, unable to resist any woman who smiled at him. If I had married him, I might have been happy for a few months, or even years. But the rest of my life would have been misery.'

'He couldn't have been that bad, could he? If he asked you to marry him, he must have meant to reform.'

'A man like that does not ever reform.'

'Did he ever truly love you?'

'I — I'm not sure.'

'But you still love him. Even though he wasn't worthy, you still think of him all the time. That's why you refused your Cousin Horace. It wasn't because he drank and he snored. It was because if you couldn't have Henry Pelmet, you wouldn't have anyone.'

'No. Cousin Horace was a pig.'

She gave me a knowing smile. I clasped her hand.

'You must be careful about falling in love, Selina. If you're in love, you won't be able to keep your head. You must make absolutely, positively sure that you have chosen the right person. Because you will be tied to him for life. Do not marry without love. But do not fall in love with the wrong person.'

Her shining, curious expression was gone, melted into a frown. I realised I was squeezing her hand far too hard, and that the visitors around us had leaned still closer. One of them was practically propped up on the back of the sofa with the sleeve of her anorak so close to my ear that I could hear its rustling.

'But enough of this,' I said, releasing Selina's hand and standing up. 'Shall we talk about the present, and this wonderful house? I notice you are admiring the sofa, madam. May I interest you with the details of its manufacture?'

★　★　★

I had never meant to fall in love with Leo Allingham.

I'd been out of uni for a year or so, drifting from temp job to temp job. Liv was in London making a splash in her architecture firm and I was spending that particular summer working in an insurance office. I was sharing a flat with two other temps, kicking around, writing notes for my novel in my lunch-hour and after work while my mother rang to worry about my future and suggested I follow in her footsteps of becoming a teacher. Not a Sex Ed teacher — an English teacher. It was the only straight-forward solution to the problem of what kind of job to get with a degree in English Literature and Creative Writing, and the feeling that Mum was right hung overhead like a thick dark cloud.

But it was a distant cloud, easy to ignore. I was sure I had time to write my novel and get it published before I had to look seriously at teacher training. My tutors on my creative writing course had, on the evidence of my short stories, told me I had some talent and a certain skill with observation and empathy. It wasn't exactly effusive praise, but I knew they had to be cautious in such a subjective field. Since then, I'd had two stories published in literary magazines and one in a women's magazine, which paid better. I'd written some feature articles for *Berkshire County* magazine, though I didn't consider the non-fiction as proper writing. It was an apprenticeship, not the real thing.

The picture of myself as a novelist, drinking cup after cup of stewed tea while painting fantastic visions in words, sitting in a bookshop with a stack of my hardback novels to be signed, was much closer in my head than the black cloud of doing teacher training. Alice the novelist had a golden glow around her; she observed conversations with a knowing eye, dropping witty sentences in like small diamonds. Alice the teacher had pencils chucked at her by spotty teenagers in the back of a classroom. There was no contest, really.

I filled up notebooks with notes and observations — always the elastic-bound Moleskine ones, written in HB pencil, since I'd heard in a lecture from a visiting author that it was important to have your own writing rituals. I typed furiously on my student laptop with its broken S key. I drifted around with my head full of voices wondering which one I should choose, making plots out of thin air.

The problem was what to write about. The world of fiction was so vast, so boundless. How could you confine so many possibilities into only one narrative, roped to the three-act structure of set-up, complication, climax, resolution? When any one character, one moment, could go in any direction imaginable, and some that hadn't been imagined yet?

This was the problem I had been wrestling with for months, when Leo came back.

I say 'came back' but he'd never really been gone, entirely; he'd been working and painting in London, doing a lot of commissions for illustration. He invited my family to his shows there, though we never went. Even then, my mother collected all his press clippings. He had been on Radio 4 as a young artist to watch, and he'd illustrated two children's books, which I thought was a laugh, considering he'd never been what you would consider innocent. Occasionally I'd see him when I dropped in on my parents, discovering he'd dropped in too and stayed a couple of days. Or Liv would tell me she'd seen him. Sometimes I saw him in a town centre pub on a Saturday night with some of his Brickham friends and a girl I assumed he'd brought from London, never the same one twice.

He moved, as he always had, around the periphery of my life, liable to appear and disappear at will in his own mysterious way. Sometimes, walking to my parents' house, I'd see a fresh tag of his name on the alley wall. When we saw each other we'd chat and have a laugh, like old friends who didn't really know each other any more, and then he'd go away and I wouldn't see him again for months.

So I was surprised one Thursday lunchtime at my temp insurance job when I got a call from reception telling me I had a visitor, and found Leo waiting in the lobby for me. He had on torn, paint-spattered jeans and a grey T-shirt, a black leather jacket over it, and carried a large canvas holdall. In the ultra-modern glass and steel lobby he looked like a visitor from some other chaotic world. He was chatting with Janet, the reception-ist, who had gone all starry-eyed and fluttery at the sight of him.

I kissed him on the cheek as always, his unshaven skin rough on my lips. 'Hi Leo, what are you doing here?'

'It's a sunny day and I thought you might like a picnic. I've got my bike outside, come on.'

Janet asked, 'Is this your boyfriend, Alice?' She looked from Leo to me, as if trying to figure out how the geeky temp got someone so gorgeous.

'No, it's my brother,' I replied, and laughed, and followed Leo outside to where he'd parked his motorcycle. It was as battered as his jeans, dented, with dust on the wheels. But the seat was clean and the chrome gleamed. He gave me a leather jacket, too large for me, and a helmet.

'You take this,' he said, putting the holdall's strap over my head, 'and hang on tight.'

I was still laughing at Janet's swooning and at the suddenness of Leo's appearance and invita-tion as I tucked my hair underneath the helmet. 'Why are you here? Did you drive all the way from London?' My voice sounded both loud and muffled, and my head was heavy, as if my neck wasn't quite strong enough to support the added burden of the helmet.

'Yes. I've got nothing on today and I fancied

seeing the countryside. Come on, let's go.' He straddled the bike and I got on behind him. I'd never been on a motorcycle before, and I had to pull up my skirt to do it. My legs fitted around his, and my feet, thankfully in flats, found places to rest.

'But why are you here? Why are you taking me?'

'I was going to take Liv, but Liv's working and can't stop, so I'm taking you,' he said, and kick-started the engine. And then we were off, weaving through the streets of Brickham and then up the hill out of town with me holding on as tight as I could so as not to fall off.

The engine was too noisy to talk, but it was no use questioning anything that Leo did anyway. We twisted along country roads and through villages. Everything seemed so much more real and close when you were riding on a motorcycle instead of cocooned in a car. He stopped the bike eventually at the side of the road near a hedge, and we dismounted. Without my helmet on I could hear the engine ticking as it cooled and the sound of birds. Leo pointed to a gap in the hedge and we squeezed through into a field of grass.

'Here we are,' Leo said, taking the bag from me, opening it, and spreading a woollen blanket on the ground. I kicked off my shoes and sat, feeling the sunshine on my bare arms, legs and face, while he unpacked the rest of the bag: two baguettes, apples, wax-wrapped cheese and a tube of salt and vinegar flavour Pringles. When he pulled out a bottle of red wine and a

212

corkscrew I protested, 'I've got to go back to work, Leo.'

He raised his eyebrows. 'You don't mean to tell me that your job in that horrible place is more important than this.'

'What do you mean, this?'

He gestured with the corkscrew, and I looked around. Green velvet grass, blue skies, sunshine, a view over the valley, with the Thames glinting between trees below. A ladybird alighted on my bare knee and tickled my skin with her pinprick feet.

The cork popped. 'I didn't bring any glasses,' Leo said, and held out the bottle to me.

'Look, if I lose this job, Mum is going to be even more on my back about starting a teacher-training course.'

'Don't worry, I'll get you back before dark.'

I sighed. I wasn't likely to see Leo again for months and months, and after all, he was right. My job wasn't more important than a sunny afternoon in July.

I took the bottle and drank.

'That's my girl,' said Leo when I gave the bottle back to him. He unwrapped the cheese, broke off a piece of bread and handed it to me. Then he flung himself down beside me.

'I haven't seen you for ages,' I said. 'I thought you'd be back for your dad's funeral.'

'Nope. I hate funerals. Never go to them.' He tore off a chunk of bread with his teeth.

'Have you been to the house?'

'Why would I?'

'Liv says she's going to renovate it and live

213

there. It's bigger than anything she could ever get in London, and the commute's pretty easy.'

'Hmm.' He took a long drink from the bottle, and we lapsed into silence.

As I ate, sipping occasionally from the wine, I wondered what we were supposed to be talking about. I'd known Leo so long that I didn't have to worry about being quiet with him, but I saw him so rarely that I didn't really know what to say, now that we'd exhausted the topics of his father's death and the house. I felt I should repay his effort in taking me out by entertaining him. But he seemed content enough to be outdoors eating his lunch.

I sat upright with my legs crossed while he lay back on the blanket, his hand resting on his stomach as he used the other to pop pieces of bread into his mouth. He had a long thumb and square nails, a smudge of oil on his finger, a thin silver-white scar against one of his knuckles. It looked like a stranger's hand.

'I've never really looked at your hands before,' I said, more to break the silence than anything.

He lifted his hand and looked at it, as if it was as strange to him as to me, and then he put it back down. 'I've looked at yours,' he said. 'They have freckles on them. Thin fingers. I gave them once to a mermaid I was painting.'

I put down my cheese in surprise. 'You did?'

He shrugged. 'When you're making things up, you re-use bits that you've observed and remembered. Sometimes it's easier to put a combination of features together than to find something from life.'

214

'Why were you painting a mermaid?'

'It was for an illustration, but I'm trying to get out of that now. I don't like following someone else's imagination.' He gazed up at the sky. 'So what are you doing this summer, besides working in an insurance agency and trying to avoid your mother's career advice?'

I picked a blade of grass and ran it between my fingers. My hands, which in another world, belonged to a mermaid. 'I've been planning my novel.'

'A novel? Liv never mentioned that.'

'I haven't told many people. I don't want to have to answer lots of questions about it.'

'Fair enough. Why have you told me?'

'You're creative, you're a painter, I thought you'd probably understand.'

'Might.' He handed me the bottle and I drank a bit of courage down with it.

'If you tell people, they ask you what it's about. And then they try to give you their own ideas about it, which are always completely wrong. Or they ask if you can put them in it. And they assume you're going to find a publisher just like that, or even worse, that you never will, or they tell you how they always meant to write a novel when they got around to it one day.' I drank more wine. 'And then every time you see them, they ask you have you finished it yet. As if a novel is something you can whip out in about a week.'

'And then they ask you if writing is a profitable occupation. As if anyone took up anything creative to make money.'

'Exactly.'

He propped himself up on one elbow. 'So, how much money are you planning to make on it?'

'Oh, squillions. Of course.'

'And what's it about, Alice?'

'I don't know yet,' I said.

He only raised an eyebrow, and took the wine from me.

'There's too much to write about,' I explained. 'I've got so many ideas and I don't know which one to use. I was writing a story about a woman who has these two lovers, and she has to choose between them, but I sort of hit a brick wall with that one, so I decided maybe I'd set it in the past and so I was doing some research about the war. Then I got interested in stuff about evacuation, and I came up with this great character who's a little boy who gets evacuated and loses his memory, but then I couldn't go on. It's too big, Leo. So much stuff can happen, the story is just this huge feeling in my head. And when I write it down, I have to start making choices, and that makes it so much smaller. It's like I'm battering my head against the limits of what I can do. Oh, I'm not explaining it very well.' I snorted. 'And I want to make a living with words. Good luck, Alice.'

'I know what you mean though,' Leo said. 'That's why the illustration is frustrating me. It's too small. This town is too small. This *country* is too small.'

'I want to make something extraordinary. I want to *be* something extraordinary. Not another callow unpublished novelist with a manuscript that she keeps under her bed.'

I slapped down my hand onto the blanket to emphasise my point, and the bottle toppled over. 'Whoops!' I cried, and grabbed it, slopping wine over my arm.

Leo laughed. 'You are drunk,' he told me.

'It's your fault.'

'You can blame me. Or you can blame your extraordinary self.' He reached into his pocket and pulled out his mobile phone. 'Call work and tell them you won't be in for the rest of the afternoon.'

'I'd better not, Leo. Mum — '

'Your mother would know, if she thought about it, that nothing extraordinary ever happened to a person while she was working as a temp in an insurance agency.'

He held my gaze, as if he were challenging me with his dark eyes. They seemed subtly different from every time I'd seen them before, maybe because of the closeness. Maybe because of the wine.

I took the phone.

★   ★   ★

Sometime after that, we drank the wine to the dregs, ate the picnic to crumbs, and lay back on the blanket next to each other, looking up at the clouds.

'Remember those times when you and Liv came with us on picnics?' I asked him, lazily twirling a daisy stem in my hand. The sun soaked into my body and bees droned. The wine had

217

made me both sleepy and alert to the small things around us.

'Of course I remember. I always got roped into being Pippi's horsey. Completely ruined my reputation, being a toddler's plaything.'

'So when do you have to get back to London?'

He shrugged. 'It doesn't matter. I'm not staying in London for much longer anyway. I'm going to America for a while.'

'That's brilliant, Leo.'

'It'll be fun. I'll go over next month to find a flat, and move over in the autumn.'

'I'd love to go to America. I've never been.'

'Except in novels,' he said with a smile in his voice. 'You could visit, as research. I promise I won't ask you what your book is about.'

'You'd better not.' I rolled onto my side, facing him. 'Why haven't we ever talked before?'

'We've talked quite a bit, haven't we? It would be odd if we hadn't. I'm your brother, after all.' He rolled over to face me too, his eyes teasing.

'No, I mean like this. The two of us.'

'I really don't know, Alice.'

'Why did you come and get me?'

'I honestly haven't a clue. I just felt like it.'

'Do you always do things just because you feel like it?'

It sounded like a challenge, but I hadn't meant it as one. After my own summer of wanting and writing and crossing out, of waiting for the right story to hit me, I honestly wanted to know.

He laughed, a deep, chuckling Leo-laugh that nevertheless sounded new today though I'd heard it a million times. 'When I can,' he said. A lock of my hair fell across my face and he brushed it away, and in the same movement, as if it were a natural part of taking the hair out of my face, he leaned over and touched his lips to mine.

A casual kiss. A friendly kiss. Except my heart stammered and my body flushed, and Leo didn't take his lips away from mine as I'd expected him to do, as you would with a casual kiss. He stayed. And stayed. And I forgot how to breathe, looking into his eyes that were as surprised as mine must have been.

He blinked and pulled back, gently and slowly, and I touched my lips with my finger.

'I wasn't expecting that,' he said.

'I wasn't either.'

'May I . . . ' He swallowed. 'May I do it again?'

Without the question, and probably without the hesitation, I probably would have jumped to my feet and started talking about getting back. I would have remembered that Leo was my best friend's brother and that every time I saw him with a girl it was a different one. I would have wondered how I would write about it in my Moleskine and would have put it down to another instance of Leo following his impulses, without thinking about the consequences.

But he asked. And more importantly, he hesitated. And his face didn't have the slightest bit of mockery in it, no teasing or laughter. He looked, in fact, as stunned as I was.

So I said, 'Yes.'

And he put his hands on either side of my face and he kissed me again, but properly this time.

Not a peck on the lips that grew into something else.

A proper kiss. With his lips soft and strong against mine, his body as warm as the sunshine. The caress of his thumbs on my cheekbones as gentle as the breeze. And something opened up inside me, something bigger than a story, something more possible. An answer I'd been looking for without knowing it, all summer. Maybe all of my life.

I kissed him back, opening my mouth for him, and we grasped for each other, hungry. 'Oh my God, Alice,' he whispered, 'I didn't know,' and I nodded, still kissing, because I hadn't known either but I was feeling it, too, blossoming all at once between us.

Two Portraits

Three months later we were married, to the delight of my family and the surprise of his sister. Three and a half years after that we were filing for divorce, and just under six years from the day we'd first kissed in a field I was sneaking down the stairs of the house that had belonged to Leo Allingham's father on a Sunday morning, hoping not to wake my ex-husband so we would not have to speak.

Time passing showed you everything. It exposed all the cracks and holes you weren't able to see at the time. How could I have thought that falling in love as Leo and I did, on an impulse, under the influence of wine and sunshine, could ever be a good thing?

I hadn't been looking for love that day in July. I'd been looking for experience, though I hadn't known it. I couldn't decide what to write in my novel because I'd never done anything at all. I wanted life, some excitement, and I'd found Leo.

No time, and all time, had passed since then. I rarely remembered it because I knew better than to torture myself, but when I did, prompted for example by questions like Selina's, I could recognise myself on the back of that motorcycle and lying stretched on the grass. That Alice seemed like the same Alice I was now. And yet that Alice hadn't lived at all and was thirsty to feel; and this Alice, if offered the warm red wine straight from the bottle, if offered the tickle of a ladybird on bare skin and the glance of a pair of brown eyes, nearly black — this Alice would turn it away.

I was older. And wiser.

'I should never have married your son,' I said to the painting of Mr Allingham on the wall. 'I thought I knew him so well, and I didn't know him at all.'

Mr Allingham gazed at his painted glass of whisky, balanced on the arm of his chair, as if it held all the answers. Or none of them.

The kitchen was still clean. The bottles of alcohol and the pizza cartons hadn't made a reappearance. From the evidence, Leo had actually been buying and cooking food, and cleaning up after himself. I hadn't seen it with my own eyes, because we timed our sojourns in the kitchen so they wouldn't coincide, but unless he'd been hiring elves to do it for him, Leo had housebroken himself.

He hadn't been out partying, either, I mused as I put in some toast and brewed a cup of tea. Or at least not in an obvious way. For all I knew he was still spending most of his waking hours at the Groom and Horses. He wasn't out carousing with Kayleigh, because she'd told me he'd never got in touch, but he could be out with a whole bevy of other beauties. But he wasn't bringing them back here. He was lying low. *He's harder on himself than anyone*, Liv had said.

What was he doing drinking in his father's pub, anyway? Was he trying to climb into his father's shoes? Was painting Mr Allingham Leo's

222

effort to understand him?

I spread marmalade on my toast and put the thought out of my head. It was none of my business. Our marriage was over, and Leo had given up all right to my thoughts and wonderings when he'd chosen not to be with me when I needed him most.

But why was he here? Why was he revisiting the past, when all I wanted to do was stay far away from it? My own personal past, anyway. I had no such reservations about spending as much time as possible in 1814.

★ ★ ★

'Can I open my eyes yet?'

'No. Keep them shut.' I checked to make sure Selina had her hands held tight against her eyes, and then I resumed my watching and waiting.

We were alone in the Hall. There hadn't been many visitors today, for some reason. It was a brilliantly sunny day; maybe people didn't want to waste the sun by walking around a stately home. Or maybe there was a big football game on, or a sale in the shopping centre in Brickham. I was a little disappointed; my first blog had published on Monday, the one about my adventures as a scullery maid, and I'd been hoping it would attract a flood of visitors to Eversley Hall.

But the brilliant sun suited my purposes just fine.

'What is it?' Selina asked. 'Why is it a mystery?'

'You'll see in a minute.' I kept my eyes on the oil painting of James Fitzwilliam and his dog, who I was sure had also been called Nelson. The real-life Nelson did look extraordinarily like the painted one. Either James had chosen him specifically to match, or the Fitzwilliams were genetically programmed to favour brown-and-white springer spaniels.

The sunlight streaming through the tall windows reflected off the crystal chandelier in bands and dots of rainbow. I checked the ormolu clock on the marble mantelpiece: fourteen minutes past two o'clock. It was nearly time.

I suppressed a giggle.

Slowly, inevitably, the small band of rainbow crept across the oil painting, its movement mirroring the passage of time. It had probably been making this exact same journey for 200 years.

'Does it have anything to do with Henry Pelmet?' Selina asked.

'No, nothing to do with him.' She'd kept on bringing up that name since I'd told her my story. I sort of wished I'd never mentioned it, or at least chosen a better surname.

But this should give her something else to talk about.

'Just a little bit more,' I whispered, waiting for the world to revolve, waiting for the exact moment.

Now. I grabbed Selina's arm. 'Open your eyes.'

She took her hands away and opened her eyes. Then her mouth dropped open.

'No way,' she said.

'Way.' I gazed with her at the painting of Mr James Fitzwilliam. Who now sported a six-inch coloured band of light at a highly suggestive angle, superimposed on the crotch of his breeches.

'Oh my God.'

She began to giggle, and I joined her.

'How did you know it was going to happen?'

'I saw it last week. And it stands to reason that it would happen again, whenever the light hits the chandelier in the right way, on certain days of the year. You can practically tell the time with it. It's like Stonehenge.'

'A sundial,' breathed Selina. 'Oh my God, I don't believe it. Does James know?'

'I haven't told him, but maybe it's a Fitzwilliam family secret. Maybe they designed it this way.'

'I don't believe it. A rainbow erec — '

A footfall on the marble floor. 'What are the two of you conspiring about?'

Selina jumped away from me, blushing. Isabella Grantham had come in. She was looking beautiful and disapproving.

'N-nothing,' Selina said. 'Alice wanted to show me something.'

'Didn't James say you were to stay in the Green Drawing Room?'

'Oh, yeah, I mean, yes I am.' Selina immediately fled the Hall. The other woman regarded me.

'Miss Woodstock,' she said. 'I'm surprised to find you still here.'

Still in the Hall? Still in the house? 'I'm still here,' I said cheerfully.

'Wouldn't you rather be off swimming?'

'Well, you've got to admit, it worked for Colin Firth.'

She didn't seem to find this funny. 'You have a very strange idea of what it's like to be in character.'

'Apparently that was exactly why I was hired.'

'And you seem to be filling that girl's head with all sorts of equally strange ideas.'

'She's a grown-up. She can fill her own head.' I glanced at the portrait; the rainbow had moved on, and was now inhabiting an innocuous spot near James Fitzwilliam's elbow.

She followed my glance, and frowned a pretty frown. 'I came to warn you that Rosemary Phipps is in the house.'

'Thank you. Who's Rosemary Phipps?'

'She's one of the world's greatest experts on Napoleonic costume and a consultant at the V and A.'

'Ah yes.' I nodded. 'The seam-checker.'

'So you do know her?'

'No, but a woman wearing a hideous cardigan was in here earlier and demanded that I turn around so that she could examine the seams in the back of my gown. I'm assuming that's her.'

'I hope you allowed her to look at your gown.'

'I couldn't help it, she grabbed me practically by the throat. I thought she was going to wrestle me to the floor.'

'From past evidence, you might actually enjoy that.'

'Depends who's doing the wrestling.'

She pursed her lips. 'Of course, when you're a professional, you realise what a privilege it is to have contact with world-renowned authorities.'

'I'll remember that next time.' I grinned at her, a wide and unladylike grin. She turned and left the room with a swish of her fine white gown.

As soon as she was gone, I quickly checked my hair with both my hands. Thank God, there were no foreign objects left in there by mistake today. Heaven only knew what the godlike Miss Phipps or the professional Miss Grantham would make of a cocktail stirrer.

I went out of the front door and stood on the portico, looking out between the columns. I wasn't the only one who'd been taking advantage of the lull in visitors: on the lawn near the drive, James Fitzwilliam was throwing a stick for Nelson to fetch. I sighed happily, leaned my elbows against the stone railing, and watched him. Now that was a sight: James's shoulders moving in his perfectly fitting coat, his long legs in his impeccable breeches and boots. The stick went flying through the air and Nelson bounded after it. From a distance, I could hear James laugh.

Heaven.

I heard footsteps behind me, and Arthur appeared. 'Hello, Miss Woodstock, have you seen the crazy lady?'

'Check your seams, did she?'

'I beat a hasty retreat before she decided to check my flies, as well.'

I laughed. He leaned on the balustrade next to me. I'd have expected him to have a smile on his face, given that he'd just cracked a joke, but for some reason he looked rather serious. He studied me for a moment, as if he were trying to figure something out, and then looked away, at James and Nelson.

'Are you all right?' I asked him. He'd gone so quickly from cheerful to grave.

'Oh, me? Yes, fine, fine. Thinking. Always dangerous.' He drummed his fingers on the stone railing, and then perked up, with almost exaggerated energy. 'I say, is that some stick-throwing going on?' He bounded down the stairs and across the drive, in a credible imitation of Nelson.

I rested my chin on my hands and watched them for a while.

At moments like this, it was almost possible to believe that I really did live here. If there had been a true-life Regency Alice Woodstock, she would have paused here to watch her cousin and his friend. She would have felt the sunshine on her face and considered whether she could be bothered to get her bonnet to prevent freckles.

She would have thought about Arthur's strange stillness just then, and wondered if it meant that he had some sort of a secret. In a novel, he would. He'd have gambling debts or an unfortunate hidden engagement, or he'd have been sent down from Oxford for some awful prank, and he'd need help to extricate himself. I hadn't been given any backstory about any of the Fitzwilliams or Granthams; for all I knew they'd gained their wealth through piracy on the high seas. Maybe Arthur's constant jocularity was a front to disguise a deep well of guilt and sorrow.

Or maybe he was just a good-humoured bloke who had been slightly traumatised by having his seams unexpectedly checked.

But on the topic of backstory: exactly why was it that I, who had no backstory at all for my character and could make up anything I wanted, had chosen to make myself fall in love with a rake who broke my heart?

Well. Because I wanted to tell Selina a story, of course. And there was nothing unusual about falling in love with a rake who broke your heart. It happened all the time in novels. And 'rake' did sound a whole lot better than 'heartless infuriating bastard'. Still, I resolved to be more inventive with my inventions in future. Fiction was better than real life; that was the whole point.

Catharsis.

I heard a scrape of metal on rock and looked down. Samuel the gardener was near the front of the house, neatening the grass edges with a long-handled tool. On a sunny day like this, he was ridiculously over-dressed for manual labour, but that was Regency propriety for you. I wondered if he was looking forward to the autumn, when this re-enactment would be over and he could get back to his gardening in sensible old clothes and rubber wellies.

Or maybe he had something else on his mind. Making a quick decision, I skipped down the stairs to the gravel drive. 'Afternoon!' I called to him.

He straightened up, then looked around to see if there were any visitors in earshot. 'Hi,' he said warily.

I strolled over to him. 'A heads-up, there's a costume expert kicking around the house today.'

'Oh. All right, ta.' He tugged at his collar.

'How do you feel about this whole costume lark, anyway?'

He looked around again. 'To tell you the truth, it's not really my thing.'

'What about Kayleigh?'

His face went bright red. So I hadn't been imagining things. He had broad shoulders and capable hands: the strong, silent type. Quite hunky, actually.

'Has she said anything?'

'No, I think she's completely oblivious.'

'She's always chattering,' he mumbled, his eyes on the grass. 'Don't think she's even noticed me.'

'Are you married?'

He blinked. 'Pardon?'

'Are you married? Please be honest, it's quite important.'

'No, I'm not married.'

'Engaged? Steady girlfriend? Casually dating?'

He shook his head at all of them.

Nelson barked, and Arthur came running up to us, panting. 'Incoming coach,' he said, and sprinted up the stairs to the house.

'I wouldn't give up so easily on Kayleigh, if I were you,' I said to Samuel, and hurried after Arthur.

Princess

Whistling, I bumped open the front door with my backside, dropped my shopping bags on the mat and shook my hands to get the blood back into my fingers. Why was healthy food so much heavier than ready meals?

But I'd been walking through town and passed a fruit and veg stall, and the colours had called out to me. Red, green, yellow, orange. It all looked so vibrant, so alive, and I couldn't help thinking about 200 years ago, before air freight and Marks & Spencer, when people ate what was in season from their own gardens.

I filled two bags with asparagus, dimpled strawberries, hothouse lettuce, a phallic cucumber. I touched glossy tomatoes and then recalled from somewhere that people had thought they were poisonous back in George IV's day. Instead I'd selected a big spiky pineapple. The Georgians were into pineapples. Eversley Hall had once had a pinery.

I paused to listen for Leo's radio, as I did every time I entered the house these days. I couldn't hear it, so I picked up my bags of goodness and brought them into the kitchen, where I unpacked everything onto the kitchen table.

My purchases looked as bright here as they had on the market stall, though somewhat more minimalist. I arranged them into groups of fruit and veg and then by colour, feeling ridiculously pleased with myself. I couldn't remember the last time I'd brought home something that wasn't wrapped in cellophane.

Liv had been right: Eversley Hall was good for me. I felt alive, with something to look forward to. As if I had a challenge in front of me. As if I were a little bit in love. But this love was safe; this love was for a job, a game, a house, a time.

And the writing, too. Edie had liked the article, and the second blog post, the first one about being Miss Alice Woodstock, published today. I could look forward to a nice juicy cheque soon. My block was gone. I didn't have to stick with writing about grommets any more. I'd probably never be a decent novelist, or any novelist at all; but at least I could write something people liked to read.

I could eat healthy food. I could go out for long walks. I could have a perfect summer and ignore my ex-husband, and pretty soon he'd give up on whatever he was doing and go away again, and I could get back to my nice peaceful existence, except even better.

I didn't have a clue how to cook asparagus though. I'd have to ring Mum and ask her. I swept everything into the fridge for now and went upstairs to have a wash in the bathroom, because my skin felt sweaty and gritty after lugging shopping bags all over town. Halfway up the stairs, I paused.

Someone was crying.

'Liv?' I said automatically, before I remembered that she was over 10,000 miles away.

It wasn't Liv. But it was someone female,

someone sounding young, like a girl who'd been hurt. Where was she? I ran up the rest of the stairs to the first floor. The bathroom door was open, the door to Liv's room was shut, and the door to Leo's room was ajar. The crying was coming from there.

I gritted my teeth. What the hell was Leo doing, bringing his girlfriends back here and breaking up with them? I'd evidently been too optimistic about him. He'd learned to clean up after himself, but he still hadn't learned basic manners.

The girl, whoever she was, let out a long wail, as if her heart had split in two. The end of it was muffled. She'd buried her head in a pillow, or maybe against Leo's chest.

'Hey,' I heard Leo say, his voice so gentle it made me clench my fists as well as my teeth. 'It'll be okay. It'll be all right.'

Enough. I didn't need to use the bathroom that badly. I turned on my heel.

'But Leo, what am I going to do?' wailed the girl.

I spun back around. I knew that voice. I should have known the crying.

'Pippi?' I said, shoving open Leo's door.

They were both on his bed. Leo had his arms around my sister and she was clinging to him. They looked up, startled.

'What the hell are you doing here?' I demanded of my sister.

Pippi jumped off the bed. She had dark tear-trails down her cheeks; she wiped at them with her hands, which only smeared her mascara worse.

'It's none of your business,' she sobbed. She grabbed her backpack, which was sitting next to Leo's bed, and stormed out of the room.

'Princess, wait,' Leo said.

'I want to be by myself!' shouted Pippi, already going down the stairs.

Leo launched himself off the bed after her. I stretched out my arms to block the doorway. 'Where are you going?' I asked him. 'I think you've done enough, don't you?'

'She can't go anywhere in a state like that. I need to — '

'She's *my sister*, Leo. If anyone's going to go after her, it's me.'

If he'd tried to push past me, I couldn't have stopped him. But he stepped back.

'She's not in a good way,' he said.

'I've noticed. We'll discuss this later.' I turned and ran after Pippi as I heard the front door slam. By the time I got out of the house, she was far down the street, running.

I sprinted after her. Normally, I wouldn't have had a chance, with the length of her legs, but she was wearing wedge sandals and I was wearing trainers, and I caught up with her on College Hill in front of an off-licence.

'Pippi,' I gasped, grabbing her hand so she had no choice but to stop and face me. She was breathing hard, still sobbing, her hair in disarray and the panda smears around her eyes even worse. 'Are you all right?'

'Leave me alone, I don't want to talk to you.'

'Why are you crying? Have you been hurt?'

She shook her head.

'Why were you at my house? Were you looking for me?'

She shook her head again.

'What were you doing in Leo's bedroom?'

She shut her mouth, stuck out her lip and glared.

'Did he say something to upset you?'

No answer.

'Pippi, I know you've always had a crush on him, but he's not right for you. You're too young. And he's — '

'Oh, shut up! Shut up! Stop treating me like some kind of a childish — *whore*!'

She broke free from my grasp and began to run again.

'Pippi, wait. You have to — '

'Leave me alone!' she screamed at me over her shoulder.

And she ran off. There was no point following her, and she wasn't physically hurt, as far as I could tell. She was going in the general direction of home, anyway. I'd ring my mother and tell her to look out for her.

Meanwhile, I had another person to deal with. I turned around and marched back to the house and straight up to Leo's room.

He was sitting on his bed, which was, I saw, made. Of course he could have made it while I was out of the house. But I seemed to remember it being made when he and Pippi were sitting there.

Not dishevelled, as if they'd done anything on it. And they'd both been fully dressed.

That didn't mean anything, of course.

Leo's hair, though, was a mess, tugged this way and that, and his face was worried. I was glad he was worried, because if he thought I'd been angry at him when he broke my heart, that was absolutely nothing compared to the piece I was going to tear out of him if he had done anything to my youngest sister.

He stood up when I came in. 'Is she all right?' he asked.

'That's what I should be asking you.'

'No,' he said. 'No, she's not all right.'

His voice was so grave, so not-Leo, that panic ripped through me again.

'Jesus, Leo, should I have called an ambulance or something?'

'No, nothing like that. She's not hurt.'

'She certainly looked like she was hurt.' I clenched my fists and stood up as tall as I could. 'Leo, you need to tell me the truth. This is really important. This is my family. Did you — did you try to get off with my sister?'

My voice shook. Leo's face got even grimmer.

'I'll leave aside the opinion you have of me for the moment,' he said. 'There's something I think you need to know. Sit down, Alice.'

It was a big room, but Liv had decorated it minimally, and there wasn't anywhere to sit but the bed and the floor. I perched on the side of the bed, apprehension gnawing at my insides. 'What do you need to tell me?'

He sat beside me. His hands had traces of paint on them, and he reached slightly towards me as if he were going to touch me, but then he thought better of it. 'Pippi came here to talk with

236

me,' he said. 'Nothing else. She needed someone to confide in.'

'It looked like she was doing more crying than talking.'

'Yes, well, I think she needed to do that too.' He took a deep breath. 'Listen. She's your sister.'

'Yes, I know that, Leo. Will you get to the point, please?'

'I don't think she wants you to know what's happening with her. But you're going to find out anyway, sooner or later.'

'Why? What is it? Is she in some sort of trouble?'

'I can't actually tell you. She asked me not to tell anyone.'

'Leo!' I cried, frustrated.

'But if you guess, that's not my fault.' He gave me a significant look.

'She's crashed my parents' car.'

'No.'

'She's in trouble at school.'

'No.'

'She didn't get a role she wanted in a play.'

'More serious than that.'

'She's had a fight with someone. Mum. Her friends.'

'No. It's more . . . permanent than that.'

'Leo, just tell me.'

'I can't. Guess.' He was watching me intently with his dark eyes, as if he could make me guess correctly by willing it.

I tried to think what I would have been upset about at Pippi's age. I'd been teased a lot at school — a red-haired bookworm with an equally geeky best friend and a mother who demonstrated condoms was never going to be wildly popular, but I didn't think that was a problem for Pippi.

'She's got a disease,' I said. Leo shook his head. 'She's addicted to drugs,' I went on. 'She's in trouble with the law. She owes a lot of money. She's pregnant.'

Leo nodded.

'She's pregnant?'

I couldn't help it. I didn't want things to be this way. I had tried so, so hard to make it change. But my first reaction, when my ex-husband confirmed that my eighteen-year-old sister was pregnant before she'd even finished her A-levels, wasn't shock. It wasn't surprise, and it wasn't anger, and it wasn't even concern.

It was *She's going to have a baby and I'm not.*

Burning, gutting jealousy.

Followed immediately by self-loathing.

I should have been used to this response by now. I felt it all the time. When I ran into a schoolfriend and her children in the park. When my cousin turned up for a birthday party blooming and round. When I heard the cry of a newborn in the supermarket, on a bus, in Eversley Hall even, and my entire body reacted to it with longing and loss and shame.

My arms wrapped around myself, covering my belly. I didn't have a single stretchmark. Not even that, to remind me. My breasts had shrunk to normal, my bump melted away, as if Clara had never grown inside me. As if I'd never been a mother, not even for six short days.

Breathing

Clara Allingham was born at twenty-six weeks' gestation, at 9.34 in the morning of 23 February, in a headlong rush of fluid and pain and fear, too early for her heart and lungs to have formed properly. She lived for six days in the neonatal intensive care unit at Boston Memorial.

On the evening of the day she was born, I sat in hospital slippers and paper scrubs, holding her tiny hand. She lay on her back, boxed in a plastic cot. She wore nothing but a tiny preemie nappy. Tubes ran out of her body to machines that helped her breathe, monitored her heart, fed her fluids and medicines. It was very warm in the ward, but her hand was cool as she grasped my index finger.

I kept on looking at her fingers. Each one of them was perfect. They had little wrinkles where they bent at each knuckle, and paper-sharp nails. How could her fingers be perfect, and not her heart? I couldn't work it out. It made no sense. But nothing had made sense, not since the contractions had begun the night before, in the middle of dinner with Leo. We were eating takeout eggplant parmigiana I'd bought from the sub shop on the corner. We'd been talking about Boston's underground train system, which was called The T, wondering what the T really stood for, and Leo had just suggested Terrifically Fucking Freezing. I'd dropped my fork and cried out as something squeezed and tore at my back and belly.

And now here was our baby. The child who'd been so strong kicking inside me was skinny and frail out in the air, here in the real world. I'd been told I could hold her, and I planned to, when I felt braver and less as if I'd break her. She was the newest baby in the ward and she was in the cot closest to the door to the outside world. The other babies had bright quilts in their plastic cots, hand-knitted bonnets and booties. Clara had nothing: white sheets, a nappy, and tubes. We hadn't expected her yet, not for another three months at least. We weren't ready.

Her eyes were closed now, but she'd opened them when I'd first touched her hand. They were dark like Leo's, but clouded and tired, as if she'd come a long way and needed to rest. She had a tiny slick of hair that might be red, and almost-invisible eyebrows.

I watched her face, trying to trace resemblances, as if knowing who she looked like would make her stronger. My hair. Leo's eyes. Her nose was too tiny to tell, and her mouth was scrunched up, like petals that hadn't yet unfurled. Her breathing was rapid and shallow. I breathed with her, copying her rapid rhythm. In, out. In, out. My lungs could help hers. My breathing would give her oxygen, help build her lungs. I could will life and strength into her, if I tried hard enough. And look, there — the small whorls of her ears. Those were like my ears. Just like my ears.

I stroked her fingers with my thumb. I could

help her. My breath would nourish her. I would pump milk for her and watch it make her grow. If I stayed here, beside her, every minute, I could create a womb of love around her and she would live.

The nurse glided between the cots on crêpe soles, checking machines and making adjustments. She had introduced herself to me; she was called Monica or something similar, or maybe Brenda. Distantly, I heard her saying something to me, but I shook my head. I was busy breathing.

But I knew when Leo arrived.

He stood in the doorway, watching us. He wore paper scrubs like mine, and his hair was wet. Somewhere out there, out where the world wasn't measured by breaths, snow fell.

'Have you got the bonnet?' I asked him.

Leo shook his head. I saw what was in his eyes.

I'd known him for most of my life and I thought I'd seen everything his eyes had to show. I'd never seen this before. It was nothing. Not a great and mortal weariness, like in Clara's eyes. Not worry or love or even despair.

It was nothing. A blank and powerless nothing. An absence of hope.

'She needs a bonnet,' I said to him. 'She needs something of her own. Something colourful. You need to get it, I can't leave her.'

Leo closed his eyes. Their eyelids were the same, the same gentle U's. Another little resemblance to make Clara real.

'I can't do it,' he said.

The paper scrubs he wore rustled as he walked away. The door closed after him with a soft, cushioned click.

I couldn't get up to follow him. We could do without a bonnet. I had to stay here and hold Clara and breathe in the silence he'd left. Through the beeps of the machines, the small cries of the other infants, the murmured conversations and the distant hum of the hospital. I had to breathe, and hold a little bit of her, these perfect fingers.

I couldn't let her go.

Pippi

I tried never to think of it, never to think of her, but for a moment in Leo's room, hearing the news about my sister, I could hear the beeping again, feel the pain. My breathing went fast and shallow and I bowed my head.

'Alice? Are you okay?'

I squeezed my eyes shut, hard. This was about Pippi. My sister. Not my daughter, who'd died on the sixth day, no matter how much I breathed.

A hand touched my shoulder. 'Mermaid?'

With an effort, I uncrossed my arms and focused my eyes on Leo, who was watching me, touching me gently. I forced all thoughts of Clara back into their box.

'So . . . ' I cleared my throat. 'How far along is she?'

'Nearly three months, she thinks.'

'What's she going to do?'

'I don't know. She didn't tell me. I think she's been very frightened, Alice.'

'She's done an expert job of hiding it.' I sighed. 'Who's the father?'

'I've no idea.'

'Does she even know?'

'I don't know.'

'You don't know much, do you?' I realised that Leo's hand was still on my shoulder. I shook it off and stood up. 'Why did she tell you, anyway?

243

Why didn't she tell Mum, or me?'

He frowned. 'I suppose it's because she knew how you'd react.'

'And how is that, exactly?'

'Just like you're reacting now. She probably didn't want to have someone bombarding her with questions. She probably wanted someone to listen.'

'What? You're her ex-brother-in-law, she hasn't seen you for two years, and you're saying that you're better for her than her own family?'

'I'm not saying anything. I'm assuming that she didn't want a lecture, and she knew I wouldn't give it.'

'She's incredibly stupid and she needs a lecture!'

'No, she doesn't.'

'And now you're the expert on teenage girls, are you?'

'Don't lash out at me because she chose to tell me. It was her decision, not mine. If she doesn't feel she can talk to you, that's not my fault.'

I thought about her coming to study at my kitchen table. Making snarky comments. *The minute I mention you and maybe the fact that you fucked up — whoo! It's like World War Three.*

Had she been trying to say something? And had I cut her off by getting angry?

Stop treating me like a childish . . . whore.

I bit my lip.

'Well, we were all going to find out sooner or later, if she's planning on keeping it,' I said. 'Is she planning on keeping it?'

'I don't know.'

I sat down again, and put my head in my hands. 'What are we going to do?'

'Are you okay?' Leo asked.

'Stop asking me that! Of course I'm not okay. My teenage sister is pregnant.'

'I'm not talking about how you feel about Pippi.'

He was watching me. I could still feel the warmth on my shoulder where he'd touched me.

'I'll have to talk with her,' I said. 'If I can find her.'

'I'll come with you.'

'No.'

'Yes.'

I started to argue, but then I thought better of it. If Pippi trusted Leo, for whatever reason, she was more likely to act reasonably if he was around. 'All right. But I'd wear protective clothing, if I were you. She's going to be furious when she finds out that you told me, and she's got a much worse temper than I have.'

He got up off the bed and picked up his leather jacket from the floor. I thought I heard him say, 'I doubt it.'

★   ★   ★

'Do you think we should call your mother again?'

I shook my head and indicated left. The 2CV's indicator made a sound like a sick beetle clicking its wings. 'If I ring twice asking for Pippi, Mum will twig that something's up and she'll go crazy.'

'Maybe that's an appropriate response to this situation,' said Leo.

'She's only been missing for half an hour or so. We'll find her.' I craned my neck out of the window as we drove past Highbury Park, looking for a glimpse of red hair in the clumps of teenagers sitting on the grass.

'You all keep secrets from your mother, don't you?'

'She's a worrier. She freaks out about the least little thing, and then she talks about it incessantly. It's easier if she doesn't know.'

'Is that why you didn't tell her why we got divorced?'

I nodded and drove around the other side of the park. 'It wasn't to protect you, believe me.'

'But you didn't tell Liv either. Not everything.'

'I didn't want to go through it, okay? Anyway, this isn't the time or place to talk about our divorce. We're in a car, looking for my pregnant sister.'

'You've been giving me the silent treatment; I'm just grabbing the chance while I've got it.'

Instead of answering, I kept on peering out of the window. 'Pippi can't have gone that far on foot.'

'She could've taken a bus, or a taxi.'

'The thing is, I have no clue where she might have gone.' I banged the steering wheel in frustration. 'No wonder she didn't want to tell me she was in trouble. I don't even know where she hangs out, or who her friends are.'

'Plus, you're driving a 2CV.'

I shot him a look. 'What's wrong with my 2CV?'

'Nothing, it's exactly what I would expect you to be driving. But its top speed can't be much faster than a teenager in a strop.'

'What do you mean, it's what you'd expect me to be driving?'

'It's completely impractical and outdated, and hugely sentimental.'

'Of course it's practical. It works, doesn't it? And I'm not sentimental.'

'Mmm-hmm.' He ran a finger over the frayed roof fabric around the passenger-side window.

'Shut up, Leo. This isn't helping us find my sister.'

'Do you know how much I've missed winding you up?'

'I'm not wound up, I'm righteously and justifiably annoyed. Anyway, you're one to talk, you've never even owned a car.' I gave up on the park and drove up Duke Street, because it was the only direction we hadn't tried yet.

'I don't even own a motorcycle any more.'

'You crashed it, eh?'

'I sold it in Kentucky.'

Leo and I had gone everywhere on that motorcycle, the one he'd bought in Boston. Someone in Kentucky was riding it now. I pictured the black gleaming body, the chrome tailpipes, a long-legged Southern girl climbing onto the seat behind a stranger I'd never met. Roaring away, into their own story. Maybe it had a happier ending than ours.

'Why'd you sell it?'

'It had too many associations. I thought I'd rather walk. Where are we going, by the way?'

I stopped the car. 'I have absolutely no idea. And you're really not helping.'

He leaned back in his seat and bit the inside of his lip. 'I've got an idea.' He unbuckled his seat belt, got out of the car and walked around the front of it to my side.

'What are you doing?' I asked him through the open window.

'I'll drive. Get out.'

'You will not drive — are you insane?'

'We'll get there a lot quicker if I drive.' He opened the door. 'Come on, let's go.'

'You are not driving my car, Leo. Do you even have a licence to drive a car?'

'Yes. I think. Somewhere.'

'Have you driven a 2CV before? You need a master's degree to change gears in this thing.'

'I've been watching you.'

I held tight to the steering wheel. 'You aren't going to drive my car.'

He shrugged and said, 'Okay, then,' and went back round to his side.

'Was that your great idea?' I asked him as he rebuckled his seat belt.

'It was one of them. The other one is this. Turn around and drive back towards the house.'

'You want to give up?'

'We're not giving up. I'll need you to turn right on the Oxford Road.'

I put the car in gear and did a careful three-point turn. 'What makes you think she might have gone up the Oxford Road?'

'Something you said about worrying your mother. It made me think about being a kid, and it made me remember the Oxford Road. Park up here, behind this van.'

I did. This part of the Oxford Road wasn't far from Liv's house, but it might as well be a different world from the leafy streets where I lived. It was a procession of betting shops, convenience stores and takeaways. We got out of the car and Leo led me past a plumbing supply shop and to a café signposted as *Kebab Korner*.

'You think Pippi is in a kebab shop?' I asked as he opened the glass door. The scent of roasting grease assailed me.

'It's as likely as anywhere else.' He greeted the man behind the counter, who was wearing a paper hat and a stained apron and standing near the revolving skewer of doner kebab. 'Hey mate, do you still do chocolate milkshakes? Can we have two of them? Thanks.' He put a five-pound note on the counter and then led me past tables and plastic chairs and a giant rubber plant, to a doorway in the back.

'Leo, I can't picture my sister in this place in a million years. And if she's pregnant, don't you think she'll be steering clear of the smell of kebabs?'

'Let's just check, okay?'

The back room was bigger than I'd expected. It had three more giant rubber plants in it, posters of scenic parts of Turkey on the walls, more plastic tables and chairs, two ancient pinball machines in the corner, a jukebox, a table football game, and my sister Pippi sitting at a table sipping something through a straw.

She looked up as we came in, started, and

stood up. 'Why are *you* here?' she said to me, and then glared at Leo. 'You didn't tell her, did you?'

I stared at her stomach. Her maxi-dress was pretty maxi, and I couldn't see any signs. But it was there. I knew it.

She's going to have a baby and I am not.

I tried to swallow it back, and failed. 'I guessed. You can't keep something like this hidden for ever.'

'I trusted you,' she said to Leo.

'Alice is right, Pippi. Your family need to know.'

'Oh my God, I don't believe this is happening to me.' She clutched her head and sank back down into her chair.

'That's funny, because I don't believe you could be so monumentally stu — '

Leo grasped my arm and I stopped, as the man in the paper hat came in with two takeaway cups with straws in them, identical to Pippi's. 'Thanks mate,' Leo said, taking them and his change. 'Come on, let's all sit down and have a drink and talk about this like grown-ups.'

'I'm never telling you anything again,' Pippi said to him. 'I thought you were cool and now you're spinning all this bullshit about being grown-ups.'

'If you're going to have a child,' I said, 'you'd better start thinking of yourself as a grown-up as soon as possible.'

'This is so what I didn't want to happen,' Pippi moaned, and sucked some more of her drink from her straw. I wondered what it was. I hoped it was nutritious for the baby. I thought of all the pre-natal vitamins I'd swallowed so that I'd ended up with a perfectly nourished, premature baby with a faulty heart and lungs so weak she couldn't breathe without a tube.

Stop it.

'Who's the father?' I asked her.

'I don't want him to know.'

'Why on earth not? He's got responsibility for this too.'

'No, he's got his own life. I'm not going to mess his up as well.'

'Seems like he's done a pretty good job already.'

Leo kicked my ankle under the table.

'All of you Woodstock women are exactly alike, as stubborn as mules,' he said cheerfully. 'Listen, Pippi, we're not here to read you a lecture. We're *not*,' he added, shooting me a dark look. 'We're here to help you. That's all.'

'I don't think anybody can do anything.'

'Have you thought about whether you're going to keep it?' I asked her.

She set her chin. 'You're asking me if I want to have an abortion? You think we need more dead babies in this family?'

I choked on my own breath. 'Pippi,' Leo said, and his voice had an edge to it I'd rarely, if ever, heard before. 'Watch your mouth.'

I stood up. 'Forget it,' I said. 'Forget I ever said anything, forget I ever tried to help. You're on your own here.'

'Alice, you don't mean that,' Leo said.

'Watch me.' I started for the door. Leo jumped

up and grabbed my hand before I could get past the first rubber plant.

'She's eighteen,' he murmured. 'She's full of hormones. Breathe.'

Much as I hated to take Leo's advice, he was telling the truth. I breathed in kebab-scented air, three times. Then I turned around. My sister's eyes were big, and young, and scared. It made it easier to ask, 'What do you want to do, Pippi?'

'Don't tell Mum and Dad.'

I came back to the table. 'They're going to find out, sooner or later.'

'I know. But I've still got two exams to take, and if Mum and Dad find out, everything's going to blow up. I can't take my exams like that. Just . . . ' She drew in a shaky breath. 'Wait till I've finished my exams. Then we can tell them.'

'You're going to need to see a doctor.'

'Not Dr Seaton.'

'It doesn't have to be our family doctor. Just a doctor, or a midwife. You need to be checked out.' She bit her lip. 'Do you need me to sort that out for you?' I asked.

'No, I can do it.'

'Will you though?'

'Yes.'

I didn't believe her. 'I'll do it. Text me your exam times and I'll make an appointment. Sometime this week, if I can.'

'Okay.' She was sulky, but she went back to sucking at her drink, which was apparently all the thanks I was going to get.

'What are you doing now?' Leo asked her. 'Do you want a lift home?'

'No, I want to stay here for a while. By myself.'

'Fair enough. Come on, Alice, back to the Batmobile.' Leo picked up our untouched drinks and we got up to go.

'Alice,' Pippi said quietly, and I paused. 'I'm sorry I said that.'

She didn't need to explain what. I nodded.

We left Pippi sitting on her own in the back room. 'How on earth did you know she was going to be there?' I asked Leo.

He shrugged. 'It was a guess. I used to go there when I was a teenager.'

'What were you doing there?'

'I liked the chocolate milkshakes. And playing the pinball machines. It made me feel like a kid.' He opened the passenger door of my car and folded himself inside. 'Have you ever considered trading this in for a nice two-seater coupé, maybe? Something made less than twenty years ago?'

'No.'

'We were a good team in there,' Leo said.

I buckled my seat belt with a firm click and put the key in the ignition. Should I go back inside, on my own this time?

'She'll be okay,' Leo said.

'I wish I could think that.'

'Drink your milkshake.' He held it out to me.

I took a sip through the straw. It was thick and rich and chocolatey.

'I'm a bit more concerned about you at the moment,' Leo said. 'You look pale.'

'Well, I appreciate that, but it's none of your business any more.'

'Like fun it's not. You're about to drive me home in this bucket of bolts. One more drink before we go, build your strength up. My life is in your hands.'

I took another sip of the milkshake. Comfort calories. Then I gave it back to Leo and turned the key in the ignition. The 2CV started up with a cough and I pulled away from the kerb.

'Thanks,' I said quietly, with my eyes on the road.

The Biggest Problems
In The Room

I wished I'd never volunteered.

I sat on a blue plastic chair in a light blue room with one small window at the top. A fake pot plant sat in the corner and Pippi sat next to me flipping through the pages of an *Elle* magazine from last Christmas.

None of these things were the problem. Well, Pippi was a problem, but right at this very moment she wasn't the biggest problem in the room. The biggest problem was that the other blue plastic chairs were all taken up by pregnant women and their blissful partners.

It was a midwife's clinic, after all. I really shouldn't have been surprised. But I hadn't thought that far ahead when I'd rung to make Pippi an appointment. I'd thought I'd pick her up and drive her to the appointment, wait in the waiting room, go in with her and watch her have her blood pressure taken et cetera, then drive her home, stopping at a chemist's on the way to buy some prenatal vitamins.

I hadn't reckoned on all the pregnant women.

'Anil Lee to the midwife please,' said the voice over the intercom, and the woman across from us lumbered out of her chair. She was hugely pregnant. Her feet were too swollen for anything but sandals, and she had trouble catching her breath. She looked like she was overdue by a couple of weeks, at least.

I saw Pippi glance up at her as she waddled past, and then she quickly looked back down at photographs of last season's shoes. She was trying not to think of what she'd look like by the time she was that far along.

I'd never got that far along. I watched the woman leave the room and I envied her swollen ankles and her sticking-out navel and her breasts that dangled to her distended belly. I envied every twinge and discomfort, the heartburn and the inability to tie her own shoes.

I swallowed and looked down at my own book. Beside me, Pippi turned the page of her magazine. I wished she'd say something. I'd tried to have a conversation with her in the car, but she'd just glowered and fiddled endlessly with the radio. As if it were my fault that she had to come here, instead of her fault that I did.

I was trying to read a book about Georgian women's costume. It was a mistake; I should have brought something with a story, something I could get absorbed by. It was too tempting to look up, like having a sore tooth that you poked and poked and poked at with your tongue, over and over again until it bled.

And I should have tried to get a morning appointment instead of an evening one. Surely in the morning there wouldn't be so many husbands and boyfriends. Look at that one over there, actually stroking his woman's pregnant belly as if it were some sort of cat. And leaning down and talking to it, while its owner smiled and giggled.

There was no call for that kind of behaviour in public. It was almost . . . pornographic in its happiness. I'd rather watch them strip their clothes off and have sex in time to whacka-whacka music, in fact, than have to witness these cloying parents-to-be antics.

I averted my eyes again. 'Are you all right?' I asked Pippi quietly. 'Do you want a glass of water or anything?'

'Will you get off my case? I've come here because you wanted me to, okay? I don't need to be treated like an invalid too.'

Charming. I stuffed my nose in my book again, trying to be interested in the manufacture of vegetable dyes.

I should have told my mother, regardless of what Pippi wanted. She was pregnant, she was a teenager, and she had massive amounts of hormones coursing through her body; she wasn't the best person to be making decisions about anything. If I'd told my mother, she could be here with Pippi right now, wringing her hands and talking a mile a minute about the future and what to do with the baby and drinking milk for healthy bones, taking in every twinge of all of her own pregnancies on the way. Pippi would be cringing in embarrassment, and I could be safely at home reading, without a single pregnant woman in sight.

I glanced up again, prodding the metaphorical toothache. The woman to my left was reading a book called *Breastfeeding the Natural Way*; an older woman sitting next to her, obviously her mother, was knitting a tiny pink cardigan. They both wore identical long patterned Batik skirts. On the other side was a round-bellied woman trying to distract her toddler with a doll while her older brother ripped pictures out of the stack of magazines.

Clichés. We were all clichés. The earth mother, the knocked-up teenager, the happily marrieds. I was a cliché myself: the woman who'd lost a baby. The divorce statistic. The irrelevant. There were waiting rooms like this one all over the country, all over the world, and nobody in them was any different. People had babies, people lost them. It wasn't anything new. It wasn't a big deal.

I wiped my palms on my jeans and flipped through my book to look at the pictures.

'Pippi Woodstock to room number four,' said the intercom, and my sister put down her magazine and stood up. When I stood too, she frowned.

'You're not coming in, are you?'

'Yes.'

'I can do this by myself.'

'It's a good idea to have someone with you. All of the information can be a bit overwhelming.'

She shrugged, and headed for the door of the waiting room. Taking this as assent, I followed her. Room four was on the first floor, and she knocked on the closed door and walked in without waiting for an answer. A comfortably rounded woman behind the desk smiled as she came in, and stood up. 'Hello, Pippi,' she said in a West Indian lilt. 'I'm Marianne.'

'I don't want any lectures,' Pippi said, without even a hello. 'I don't want to talk about what I'm going to do with the baby and I don't want to talk about the father or having an abortion. I just came here to make sure I'm healthy. That's all.' She sat down on one of the two chairs, and crossed her arms.

'Pippi!' I said, shocked.

'Oh, that's all right, it's no problem,' said the midwife. 'We don't have to talk about anything right now. We'll fill out some forms and do a little examination. This is your sister here?'

'Yes, I'm Alice.'

'Well, please have a seat, Alice. Nice of you to come along.'

At least someone thought so. I sat on the second chair, the one provided for fathers. Marianne produced a new plastic wallet sleeve and extracted a long form from it. She got straight down to business, asking questions about Pippi's age and her year in school in a pleasant, non-judgemental voice that even Pippi couldn't object to. With a little bit of detective work and a circular sliding calendar they determined that she was about twelve weeks pregnant.

'How are you feeling?' Marianne asked.

'Fine.'

'No morning sickness?'

'Not now. I was pretty sick for a couple of weeks though.'

'Do you smoke?' asked Marianne.

'No,' Pippi said. 'Not any more.'

'Not any more?' I cut in. 'Since when?'

'Since I found out I was pregnant. More or less.'

'And when was that?'

'About a month ago.'

'You *smoked* during most of the first trimester of your pregnancy?' I was nearly out of my chair.

'What does it matter to you? You wanted me to have an abortion.'

'And you were drinking, too. You were completely pissed at Liv's wedding. What were you thinking, Pippi?'

Marianne cleared her throat and said, 'Your sister asked for no lectures.'

'Yes, but she — '

The midwife gave me a look that said *I have delivered hundreds of babies and you had best do what I say.*

I bit my lip. I sat back down.

'I know it was stupid, okay?' said Pippi. 'I suppose I thought that if I ignored it, it would go away.'

'That's a strategy that only works with men and stray puppies,' said Marianne, 'and often not even with them. Do you understand now why you should try to avoid alcohol and cigarettes?'

Pippi nodded. 'I've stopped. I've definitely stopped.'

'How about drugs?'

'I don't take those.'

'All right then. Let's move on. Can you look at this list of conditions and tell me if you or anyone in your family has had them?'

They might be moving on, but I wasn't. I sat there, fuming. Not only was Pippi pregnant, but she had deliberately put her baby at risk by doing stupid, pointless things. Didn't she know how precious the life inside her was? How delicate and fragile? How if anything, absolutely

260

anything, went wrong with this pregnancy and this child, she would spend the rest of her life wondering what she could have done differently?

The doctors had said premature birth was just something that happened, sometimes. That it wasn't my fault, it wasn't anyone's fault. But what if it was?

I'd missed a prenatal appointment because I'd slept through it, and didn't schedule it again. I'd felt well and thought I didn't need it. I'd seen my mother pregnant and thought I knew what a healthy pregnancy was like.

Maybe if I'd gone to that appointment, they'd have caught whatever was wrong, and Clara would have lived.

Maybe if I'd come back to England as soon as I'd got pregnant, and seen another doctor, they would've spotted something, done something, and Clara would have lived.

Maybe if I hadn't taken that long walk the day before I went into labour, I would have held off for a while, and Clara would have lived. Maybe if I'd stopped drinking caffeine, Clara would have lived. Maybe if I'd thought about her all the time and not about my novel or my husband, Clara would have lived. Maybe if I'd said something different, thought something different, been a different person.

Maybe something could have helped.

Pippi stood and I looked up, startled. 'Are you okay?' I asked.

'Yes, I think I can pee in a cup by myself,' she said and left the room.

Marianne was watching me from behind the

desk. 'Are *you* okay?' she asked.

'Me? Oh. Yeah, I'm fine. It's just — this whole thing with Pippi is a bit of a shock.'

She nodded. 'I can understand that. Your sister does seem like a sensible girl though.'

'Sensible? Pippi? You obviously don't know her that well.'

'You're angry at her now, but I see quite a few teenage girls in here. She's actually doing really well. There are resources available for young mothers, if she wants them. Is there any reason why she doesn't want your parents involved? Something I should know about, some history?'

'No, nothing like that. My parents will freak out, but they'll help her. She just doesn't want the lecture until she finishes her exams.'

'See? Sensible girl. I think she's going to be all right, you know.'

But what about the baby? I wanted to scream. I swallowed. 'I'm glad you think so.'

'And it's good that you're here for her. She must really appreciate it.'

'Now I'm certain you don't really know Pippi. She'd cheerfully kill me for even knowing about this.'

'If she doesn't appreciate it now, she will.'

'Maybe.'

'Do you have any children yourself?'

How did I answer that question? A 'no' was a betrayal, and a 'yes' was torture. It wasn't meant as a hurtful question. But it always, always was.

'No,' I said.

The door opened and Pippi reappeared. 'Ew, that was so gross,' she said, handing the full plastic cup to the midwife, who brought it over to the sink to test.

'You'd better get used to peeing in plastic cups,' I said.

'And being prodded around,' Marianne said cheerfully. 'Your body's not your own once you've got a baby in it.'

Pippi pursed her lips. She didn't like that idea.

I shut my own lips to stop myself from saying anything, and crossed my arms over my body which was all my own now. Every inch of it empty.

★   ★   ★

In the twilight, the big house where I lived looked like a shadow. I opened the door and dropped my handbag and keys inside. They made a hollow sound on the wooden floor.

The downstairs was dark. I wished Liv was here, in the kitchen with a cup of herbal tea, reading a big book. We wouldn't have to say anything; she wouldn't demand details. She'd smile at me and we'd chat and everything would feel normal again. As normal as it ever had been. Maybe I could have persuaded her to watch a movie with me. A romantic comedy, or a period drama. Anything, as long as it didn't include anything to do with babies. Watching a movie took even less effort than reading a story.

I could watch one by myself; the sofa and the DVD player were in their normal places. Mr Allingham was a dark blob on the far wall. More ghosts.

It was nearly half nine. My mother had intercepted me when I'd brought Pippi home and dragged me inside to sit at her kitchen table and listen to her talking. Pippi had escaped upstairs, the prenatal vitamins and the notes in the plastic folder hidden inside her handbag. Mum had tried to feed us, but we told her we'd had a bite already. 'I'm so glad you sisters are spending time together,' Mum said, sipping contentedly at a cup of tea, and I looked at her and I thought, She's going to give you a grandchild and I couldn't.

It was a stupid thought. Mum didn't want Pippi to be a teenage mother. She was going to be in for a shock. But I couldn't help thinking it, and I couldn't help feeling the burning jealousy that came with it, and the memory of how happy Mum had been when she'd heard I was expecting and the little white crocheted matinée jacket she'd made for Clara. The boxes of baby clothes and the mobile made of fluffy sheep, all of it sent by post from Brickham to Boston. All of it packed away, given away, never used. Would she wish I'd kept it for this baby?

Fortunately, I didn't have to say much as my mother had enough news stored up to tell me, so I didn't have to let out any of the envy or self-loathing I was feeling and I could just sit there and not drink my tea and listen. Irrelevant.

Now, at home, I considered finding myself something to eat and decided I couldn't be bothered. I'd curl up under my duvet and read. As usual.

When I approached the first-floor landing the

door to Leo's room opened. He wore jeans and a clean white T-shirt and he was barefoot. 'Hi,' he said.

'I — I didn't think you were home,' I said, pausing on the steps. 'I didn't hear the radio.'

'I haven't got it on. I was listening for the door. How is she?'

'She's fine.'

'Good. She's a tough one. How did it go though?'

I could have repeated, 'Fine,' and carried on upstairs. I could have said something snarky about minding his own business. They were both on my lips to say. But he was watching me carefully and I knew he wasn't asking about Pippi.

And he was the only one who knew.

I stepped off the stairs onto the landing. 'She is so bloody stupid! She's been carrying on as if she wasn't pregnant at all, Leo. She's been doing absolutely everything wrong, and if I hadn't dragged her to see the midwife, God knows when she would've even got a check-up.'

'But she's okay though, isn't she? She's going to be okay.'

'We don't know that! We don't know anything. Everything could go wrong, it can go wrong at any time. She has no clue at all.'

He bit his thumb. Then he rubbed his hand over his chin. He hadn't shaved and I could hear the faint rasp of his beard stubble.

'Do you want a cup of tea?' he asked.

'No. Yes. I don't know what I want.' Alarmingly, I felt tears burning my eyes.

265

No. No crying. If I cried, that would be it. I would be right back to what I'd been in Boston. I would have that big unfillable hole inside me open again. I would rip the scabs off it and the grief would come pouring out, the grief that blinded you, stopped you from breathing. It would have followed me here, into my life that used to be safe. I stepped forward to get away and felt something warm.

It was Leo. I'd walked into his arms by mistake. They closed around me and he said, 'Tell me.' I heard the words as they rumbled through his chest.

'It's so unfair,' I said — no, I wailed it. Like a child who's lost a toy, who's been sent to stand in the corner, because I should know better by now than to expect life to be fair, and the tears welled up and they were about to fall and I had to do something to escape it so I grabbed Leo's T-shirt in both fists.

He kissed me. Full on the mouth, his lips on mine, and it was so familiar that I forgot to be shocked for a moment. And then I was shocked, even more so because I'd forgotten at first, and then I felt a surge of anger and something else, something more like relief, and I kissed him back.

He was warm and alive, immediate and now. I pulled up his T-shirt and ran my hands over the skin and muscles of his back. Leo held me tighter and kissed me deeper and together we stumbled off the landing and into his bedroom, onto the bed.

I didn't want to cry. I was hungry, lustful,

wanting. Leo had always done this to me — from zero to one hundred miles per hour in a split second, with one touch. One kiss. My body ached. I wanted his hands all over me. I wanted him inside me, stopping me from thinking and feeling, lying on top of me and pressing me into the bed.

I fumbled with his flies and he pulled my shirt up around my neck with one hand, pulled my bra down with the other, and his mouth was on my breasts. I arched my body into the warm wetness of his tongue, his beard stubble scratching my skin.

No thinking. I pulled open his jeans and took him into my hand and heard him gasp. Fast, now. Right now. I helped him wriggle me out of my jeans and knickers and I wrapped my legs around him and cried out when he entered me. No words. Just a cry and our breathing, the taste of Leo and his scent that I knew as well as my own.

Yes. This was what I needed. Hard and fast, my body straining against his for forgetfulness. I came almost right away, eyes squeezed tight shut in a shaking moment of oblivion, and then I dug my fingers into his buttocks and urged him deeper. Went to a world where there were only two bodies moving, shuddered and let myself come again, snatched in a breath and another kiss. Leo tangled his fingers in my hair, thrust. Sweat slicked between us. He groaned and I felt him jerk inside me, deep inside where I couldn't be empty any more.

He collapsed on top of me, his heart pounding

against mine. Pulled my palm to his mouth and pressed a kiss into its centre.

⋆ ⋆ ⋆

I opened my eyes. Leo's dark hair was damp and his eyes were closed, though his breathing was ragged. My shirt was around my neck and I had my socks on. He was still wearing his clothes, his shirt rucked up around his chest and his jeans tangled around his calves. My legs were wrapped around his hips.

What had we done?

I pushed him off me and sat up. 'Oh God,' I said.

Leo opened his eyes. 'I've missed you, Mermaid.' A smile creased the corner of his mouth. He reached for me, and I flinched away.

'That was — that was an enormous mistake.' I tugged my bra and shirt back into place.

'Alice?'

His voice was cautious, now. That made it worse. I crawled to the side of the bed to look for my jeans. There they were, on the floor, turned inside out in our haste to get them off me. My stomach twisted.

'I think we need to talk about this,' he said.

'No.' I pulled on my knickers and tried to sort out my jeans, with trembling hands. 'No. We shouldn't have done it. It was wrong.'

Leo sat up and pulled his own jeans up, though he didn't fasten them. He ran his hands through his hair, throwing it into even further disarray. 'There's obviously something still between us.'

'No, there isn't. We're finished. We were finished as soon as you started going out with other women.'

'That's one of the things we need to talk about.'

'No.' I tried to put one leg into my jeans and nearly lost my balance. I sat on the floor. My whole body was shaking now.

'When Clara was in hospital — '

'No!' My leg tangled in my jeans. 'No, you don't get to talk about Clara! You don't get to talk about us!'

'I was there, Alice.'

'No, you weren't there, and that's the whole problem. You weren't there at all.'

'I'm here now.'

'That is also the problem.' I got my other leg in, and stood up to pull my jeans on, staggering.

Leo was kneeling on the bed now. His hands were tight on his thighs and his dark eyes snapped. 'Alice, you just had sex with me. We had sex. You can't run away.'

'It's never seemed to be a problem for you before.'

'You're not going to put all of this on me. You were the one who — attacked me just now.'

'I didn't attack you! I was trying to — '

To run away. To absolutely the worst place I could run.

'You're not the only one who can feel, Alice,' said Leo. His voice was low, and angry, and dangerous.

'I don't want to feel anything,' I choked, and I fled the room.

Picnic In The Sunshine

'What do you call this contraption, sir?'

'It's an electric wheelchair.'

Holding his battledore racquet out of the way, Arthur stooped down to examine the fat rubber tyres of the visitor's wheelchair. 'I wouldn't fancy these wheels on a curricle. How on earth does it work?'

'Er, well, I'm not quite sure. It has a battery attached.'

'A battery?' Arthur looked alarmed. 'Dear lord, sir, I hope you don't mean to tell me that you have a host of armed men to pull you around in this thing?'

'No, no,' said the visitor, laughing. 'It's a — a sort of square box, with electricity coming out of it.'

Arthur frowned.

'Electricity,' the man explained. 'It's this — oh, I don't know — it's this invisible power. Like lightning.'

'You have a lightning-powered conveyance.'

'Yeah, that's it. More or less.'

Arthur turned to the man's wife, who was standing beside them. 'Madam, you have my unalloyed sympathy. Does he often succumb to these delusions?'

The group of visitors laughed. There were lots of them; it was Bring A Picnic Day at Eversley Hall, and the weather was cooperating by being warm and sunny. Blankets and garden chairs dotted the lawn in all directions; there were several impromptu games of football and cricket going on in the lower fields. The inhabitants of Eversley Hall had a more formal picnic, laid out on a table with silver and porcelain, and set up under a small canvas tent to shield the ladies' complexions from the sun. The visitors formed themselves naturally around us, as if we were on stage and they were the audience.

I'd been looking forward to this weekend. In fact, since last night and my disastrous encounter with Leo, I'd been doing my best to think about nothing but Eversley Hall. I didn't want to remember what Leo and I had done. I certainly didn't want to analyse it. Nor did I want to think about Pippi and how angry I was at her, how anxious I was for her unborn baby. Or any of the memories that all of this stirred up.

Thinking about it, talking about it, would be like reaching inside and grabbing my pain with both hands and dragging it, throbbing and cowering, into the light of day. I didn't know how big it was. Inside me, it felt small and safe, something I could control. But if I dragged it into the open, how much would it grow? Would I ever be able to contain it again?

I much preferred it hidden away.

The nineteenth century was so much more sensible. I glanced down at my black dress. If someone died in 1814, you changed your clothes and your behaviour. You wore black. Everyone knew you were in mourning. You had a schedule to follow, with a prescribed amount of time given to grieve. And then, when that period was over, you changed your clothes and your hair. You put aside your sadness with your black dresses. You started going to balls and parties again. You began to think about how to move on with your life.

You didn't go crazy from seeing a bunch of pregnant women and then have sex with your ex-husband.

No. You mourned moderately and with propriety, and meanwhile you sat on the lawn under a tent, drank lemonade and had a civilised conversation about current events and wheel-chairs powered by lightning.

'It was the Duke of Wellington's ball last night in London,' said Lady Fitzwilliam, fanning herself with an exquisite silk and sandalwood fan. She was wearing a shell-pink day dress with seed pearls and ruffles of lace. In the weeks I'd been working here, I hadn't seen her wearing the same outfit twice. Unlike Selina and me, who wore the same thing every day. I plucked a twig of lavender from a crystal bud vase and rolled it in my fingers, smelling the scent.

'There were nearly two thousand people at Burlington House,' added Isabella Grantham. She wasn't as well-outfitted as Lady Fitzwilliam, but she did have three day dresses and several different bonnets. Today she was in an apple-green dress with scalloped edging, with a spray of roses on her straw bonnet.

'Do you wish you could have been there?' I asked her.

'Of course I wouldn't wish myself anywhere

but in the present company,' she said to me. 'But it must have been a grand spectacle.'

'Imagine the dresses,' sighed Lady Fitzwilliam.

James put down his battledore racquet and bent to stroke Nelson's silky ears. 'Were you there, sir?' he asked a visitor sitting nearby, on a fold-out lawn chair.

'No, I'm afraid not.'

'Are you familiar with the event?'

'No.'

'It was a great masked ball in honour of the Duke of Wellington, celebrating the Allies' final victory over Napoleon, and only one of a series of events in London this summer to celebrate one hundred years of Hanoverian rule and the end of the Peninsular Wars.'

'Next week there will be a Service of General Thanksgiving for the Allied Victory in St Paul's Cathedral,' said Isabella.

'And there is to be an enormous public celebration in St James's Park on the first of August, with fireworks and a re-enactment of the Battle of the Nile.'

I rolled the lavender in my fingers. History, history, history, although to be fair, it was pretty interesting history. I'd read at least one novel which began during that celebration, with a young lady rescued by a dashing young man from being trampled in St James's Park.

We'd been coached and instructed to talk about all these things, however. They were in our dossiers. Isabella Grantham had reminded us this morning. I had them memorised, too. The next thing would be about the Temple of

Concord in Green Park.

'And the illumination of the Temple of Concord in Green Park,' added Isabella, ostensibly speaking to a woman sprawled on a blanket. 'Have you seen it, madam? It is a sight to behold.'

'Makes you proud to be English,' said Arthur, reaching over his supposed sister to snag a bunch of grapes. 'We've routed the Frenchies, Boney is on Elba, and we're showing those Yankees who their masters are.' He flung himself down on the lawn, heedless of stains to his light breeches. Nelson immediately jumped on top of him and started licking his face. A cordon of three small children joined the action, pig-piling on top of Arthur as he laughed.

'No! No!' he sputtered. 'Not the British Army and the British Navy! Help! Take me back to Elba, Jacqueline, please!'

I twisted the lavender. Clara would have been about the age of that girl with the black plaits, the one holding on to Arthur's boot. A phantom child, with Leo's eyes and my hair, my hands and his laugh, a trillion possibilities of nature and nurture that would never exist.

I stood up and strode over to Selina, where she stood under a parasol. The sunlight caught strands of her light brown hair and turned it to gold. I tucked a relatively intact blossom of lavender into the ribbon of her bonnet.

'Have you read any good books lately?' I asked her.

'Yes! I'm reading that *Friday's Child* that you gave me, and I love it. I love how George is always fighting duels.'

'Shh.' I lowered my voice. 'It's a great book, but Georgette Heyer wrote it in the forties.'

'The eighteen-forties?'

'Worse, the nineteen-forties. Don't let your brother catch you discussing it.'

'Whoops.' She put her hand to her mouth and twirled her parasol in consternation. I squeezed her hand.

Why couldn't my sister Pippi be like this?

Arthur had stood up and was running around the lawn, chased by Nelson and the children, to the amusement of almost everyone except for Isabella. He obviously loved kids; he was a kid himself.

Leo used to be like that with Pippi when she was a little girl.

And we hadn't used any contraception last night.

'Ladies, may I interrupt your conversation to challenge Miss Woodstock to a game of battledore and shuttlecock?' James Fitzwilliam was beside us, holding out the racquet that Arthur had abandoned, and smiling. My heart, which had been in my stomach, leaped into my throat.

There. That was what I should be thinking about. Playing a lawn game with a perfect man in the sunshine.

'I don't know how to play,' I told him.

'I'm certain you'll pick it up quickly. You have an admirable facility for adaptation.'

I reached for the racquet, and someone spoke in a very loud voice.

'But the war wasn't over in 1814.' It boomed out over the picnickers, and we turned to look at the man who'd spoken. He was standing a few metres away, wearing a short-sleeved buttoned-up shirt and jeans and round glasses. He looked like a secondary-school history teacher. 'Napoleon escaped in early 1815.'

'Did he?' murmured a woman near me, to her daughter. 'When was Waterloo?'

'Thousands of people were killed,' the man said. 'All the celebrating in London in the summer of 1814 was horribly premature. The Prince Regent, the King of Prussia, Tsar Alexander I, all the other Allied leaders — they were partying for nothing. People were still going to die. Over two million, in total. And the Temple of Concord caught on fire.'

A hush descended. Over the picnics, over the sun-drenched grass, over the flowers and the beautiful dresses.

'Sir,' said James calmly, 'you are remarkably knowledgeable about events that have not yet occurred. I congratulate you on your prescience.'

'The British didn't win the War of 1812 against America, either. We lost over eight thousand people.'

At this, there was a murmur. 'We're trying to have a picnic, here,' said a man next to the history teacher.

'I'm just pointing out what really happened,' the teacher protested, but the visitors around him were beginning to give him dirty looks. A couple folded up their picnic blanket and moved towards the other side of the lawn.

'How rude,' said Lady Fitzwilliam.

'Well,' I said, 'I never liked the Temple of Concord anyway. Horrible, ugly thing.' I took the racquet from James and smiled at him. 'Shall we play?'

★ ★ ★

It is impossible to think about anything else when you're batting a shuttlecock back and forth with a tall, handsome Regency gentleman in the sunshine. For one thing, my stays, the construction of my dress and the slippery leather soles of my shoes meant that I had to plan each swat at the shuttlecock with ridiculous precision, or else I'd bust a seam or fall over.

For another, James Fitzwilliam was laughing, and that was a sight to behold. His entire face lit up, his blue eyes sparkled. He had on a new satin waistcoat that was exactly the colour of the summer sky.

Between the costume and James Fitzwilliam, I was dropping a lot of points.

'I meant to thank you,' he said to me, when I paused to pick up the shuttlecock yet again from the grass. 'You've been very kind to my sister. I think she's grown very attached to you.'

'I'm very attached to her.'

'There has been a certain heightening of her spirits since you arrived at Eversley Hall.'

'That's probably all the talk about Cousin Horace.'

'And the famous Henry Pelmet.'

I tried to swat at the shuttlecock, and missed. 'You've heard about Henry Pelmet?'

'I've heard enough to think that he was a very great fool.'

Dear lord, he was looking at me. He was looking at me with those blue eyes sparkling with 1814 sunshine and he was saying that the fictional person who dumped me was a very great fool, which meant that he thought that I wasn't worthy of being dumped. Fictionally.

Or really?

My pulse fluttered and I hit the shuttlecock hard enough to send it flying over James's head, through the middle of a group of picnickers, and straight into a plate of sausage rolls.

'Don't eat it!' I called to the startled visitors. They laughed. James laughed. Everyone laughed. The history teacher seemed to have slunk off somewhere else.

It was a picnic in the sunshine, after all.

'Would you like some lemonade, Miss Wood-stock?' Kayleigh was standing nearby, holding a tray with glasses and a pitcher.

'That would be perfect, thank you, Lucy.' I took one and sipped.

'I resign the game to you,' James said. 'The sausage-roll gambit was a work of such genius that I could never hope to match it.'

'That is very gallant of you, Mr Fitzwilliam, but I'm not the sort of woman who accepts a victory she hasn't earned.'

'Oh, you have earned it. And do call me James.' He helped himself to a glass of lemonade, and went to retrieve his shuttlecock. I watched him go: the long legs in the pale breeches, the perfect cut of his coat. The master of a better age, where courtship was ritualised and respectful, leisurely and polite.

'Still got a thing for the lord of the manor?' Kayleigh whispered to me. It was a bold thing for her to do, seeing as we were being watched by about a dozen people at least.

'I've been thinking about devotion, Lucy,' I said to her aloud. 'It is such an admirable quality in a man, don't you think? For example, devotion to one's relations, or to one's house.'

'That's Mr Fitzwilliam, all right,' she said.

'But there are other types of devotion. Take, for example, the quiet, patient devotion of a man who works with nature. Who sows seeds and tends them and waits for them to grow; who gently trains his plants with hours of care and passion.'

I gazed pointedly across the lawn, past the picnickers, to where Samuel was working. He was digging in a flower bed, an action that made the most of his broad shoulders and capable hands. As we watched, he put down his spade and bent over to examine something in the soil.

Demurely, I finished my lemonade and replaced the glass on the tray. I lowered my voice. 'And he's not married, either.'

Kayleigh was staring, her eyes widened.

'Mr Fitzwilliam!' I called. 'What about a rematch?'

★   ★   ★

There was no question about it. The 1814 me was a better person than the real me. In 1814,

Alice Woodstock could form an attachment to a young girl. She could wear black gracefully; she could help a servant find what might be true love. She was witty and inventive and interesting. Her heart could flutter at a compliment from an eligible man.

She was out of the pages of a novel. She was my picnic in the sunshine. And I wanted to spend as much time as I possibly could in her company. So at the end of the day, after the lawn was cleared and the visitors had gone home, I went into the staff room, which was still buzzing with energy, and said, 'Who wants to come to the pub?'

'Yeah!' said Arthur, who was wrestling with one of his Hessian boots. 'That's a great idea.'

Lady Fitzwilliam, with her expertise on robing and disrobing, was already dressed in her day clothes, a well-cut linen shirtdress. She checked her watch. 'Jerry's doing the tea tonight, so I've got time for a quick drink.' Several of the others nodded.

'Excellent,' I said. 'What do you say to the Duke of Wellington?'

The Duke of Wellington was a country pub about midway between Eversley Hall and the village of Lidbury. It had timbered walls and a thatched roof and was pretty much perfect for a meeting of people who dressed up in historical costumes. I ducked my head under the hanging baskets over the door as I went inside.

I saw Arthur first, at the bar. He was wearing baggy jeans and a red T-shirt and he waved at me. He looked younger out of costume and with his hair messed up with gel, barely old enough to be holding the pint of lager he was ordering. 'Hey, Alice,' he called. 'Nice one! It's my round, what do you want?'

'A glass of red w — actually, an orange juice, please. I'm driving.'

He nodded. 'This was a great idea, to go to the pub together. I made sure everyone knows. We could use a bit of Regency bonding time.'

'Haven't you ever been before?'

'Well, yeah, to the pub, obviously. But not with the Eversley Hall crowd. I thought of asking before but I'm such a whippersnapper compared with everyone, I thought nobody would want to come with me.'

'Selina's your age, isn't she?'

'Oh yeah, Selina is, that's true. They're in the beer garden — I'll bring your drink through.'

Was James Fitzwilliam here? I craned my neck to spot him as I went through the lounge bar towards the garden at the back of the pub.

I didn't see him, but I did see Samuel waiting at the bar. I slipped into place next to him. 'She drinks WKD,' I murmured, and smiled at his surprised expression before going out to the garden.

They'd taken over two adjacent tables, though it took a small moment of non-recognition before I placed them all. Selina, Lady Fitzwilliam, Mrs Collins, Munson. Kayleigh, already halfway through a bottle of WKD. And of course there was no mistaking the flawless Miss Grantham, with her blonde hair falling in smooth waves over her shoulders and a mobile phone pressed to her ear. Slender, mousy Fiona the scullery maid was on the other table, texting furiously into her mobile.

No James. On the other hand — no Mrs Smudge, either.

I found a chair next to Selina. 'Thanks for inviting me,' she said to me. 'I haven't had a chance to get out to the pub since I've been in Brickham. I don't really know many people down here.'

'I don't believe we haven't been before,' said Munson cheerfully. 'I suppose we'll all have to learn each other's real names now.'

'Oh no,' panicked Selina. 'I've only just got used to everybody's fake names. I'm sure to mess up if I know who you really are.'

'Let's keep our Eversley Hall names,' I suggested. 'That would be more fun, anyway.'

'And this one will get to be called 'Lady' all the time,' said Arthur, arriving with my drink. He winked at Lady Fitzwilliam.

'Did anybody get the chance to invite James?' I asked.

Isabella snapped her phone shut. 'I have,' she said. 'He had one or two things to sort out at Eversley Hall first. He's very busy.' She was wearing an ivory sleeveless dress, exquisitely cut, and a string of jade beads. I felt distinctly under-dressed near her, in my jeans and sandals and flowery top.

'So, how did you get involved in Eversley Hall?' I asked her. Maybe if I made an effort to be friendly in real life, she'd be a bit nicer to me in costume.

'James invited me personally,' she said. 'He had seen my work at Warwick Castle, and I helped him with some of the aspects of setting up this summer's project.'

'I got roped in by my aunt,' Arthur said cheerfully. 'She's in the re-enactment society with our Lady here.'

'I believe that James was very particular about whom he chose,' Isabella said. 'That is, in most cases.' She shot a glance at me and Selina.

Hmm. So much for being nice. I turned to Selina. 'I've got some Jane Austen you can borrow, when you're finished with the bag of books I gave you.'

She looked doubtful. 'It's old English, isn't it? I mean, it's not really easy to read?'

'They're marketing Austen as chick lit at the moment,' said Isabella scornfully. 'I think it's such a degradation to one of our great literary treasures.'

'Well, there are worse things you can do with a book than put it into pink covers,' I said. 'For example, making people think it's fusty and not fun to read.'

'The films are wonderful,' said Lady Fitzwilliam. 'I watch them just for the costumes.'

'We should totally have a Jane Austen film fest,' I said. 'I've got nearly all of the Hollywood ones, and the BBC *Pride and Prejudice*.'

'Oh no,' said Arthur, 'I feel a Colin Firth versus Matthew McFadyen argument coming on. *Again*.'

'We should get together and watch them,' I said. 'It would be inspirational.'

'I'd like that,' said Selina. 'I love watching movies.'

'Excellent! I've got a nice big — ' I suddenly remembered Mr Allingham, painted on the wall across from the television. 'Actually, I don't have any place to watch them.'

'I do,' said Mrs Collins, from the next table. 'Our grandchildren are going away for the summer holidays, and the house seems very big. It would be nice to have people over.'

'Hey, there's a chair over here,' Kayleigh said suddenly. Samuel was hesitating in the door of the pub, looking very unsure, but she waved at him and he came over and held out the bottle of WKD. 'That's my favourite drink! How did you know?'

I smiled into my orange juice.

Isabella stood up and said, in a warm voice, 'James.' She lifted her handbag off the chair beside her.

With my spying on Kayleigh and Samuel, I hadn't noticed James Fitzwilliam arriving. He wore a cream linen suit with a white shirt open at the neck, all of it perfectly tailored to his body. Not every man could get away with cream linen, but it looked, if possible, even better on him than the breeches and waistcoat. In each hand, he held a wine bucket with a bottle of Veuve Cliquot.

'Congratulations, everyone!' he said. 'I've been going through visitor numbers with Quentin, and today was our best day ever. We've got a lot to celebrate.'

One of the barmaids put down a tray of

champagne flutes on the table, and James opened the first bottle with a deft twist and pop. I watched him pouring. He did it without spilling a drop, and gave a glass to each of the Eversley Hall people. When he handed one to me, his fingers brushed mine and his smile almost made me drop it.

'Thank you, everyone,' he said, holding his glass aloft. 'From me, and from all of the Fitzwilliam family. This first summer is crucial in making the house a going concern, and every one of you is helping to make it work. To you.'

We drank. 'And to old Boney rotting on Elba,' added Arthur. 'Who believes all that 'the-war-didn't-end-till-1815' rubbish anyway?'

James slipped into the seat between me and Lady Fitzwilliam. It was the only empty chair, aside from the one Isabella had put her handbag on. I glanced over in time to see her eyes narrow.

'Your idea to go to the pub, I hear?' he murmured. He smelled delicious; linen and sandalwood.

'Yes, it felt like a festive day.'

'It was wonderful. You did a fantastic job. Thank you.'

'It's fun. I'm having a great time at Eversley Hall. We were just arranging a Jane Austen film splurge, do you want to come?' I crossed my fingers under the table. Imagine cuddling up next to James Fitzwilliam on a sofa, watching love stories, sharing popcorn, licking the salt off each other's fingers . . .

'I'll have to check my diary,' he said, smiling. 'Make sure you leave some time open, too; we're going to start some dancing lessons before the Eversley Hall Ball in August.'

'Ugh, I'm not looking forward to those,' groaned Selina. 'I've got two left feet.'

'You don't have to worry,' Lady Fitzwilliam told her. 'We'll do the simple ones. You follow what everyone else is doing, and of course your partner will lead you.'

'Promise I won't step on your toes,' said Arthur.

'Nor will I,' added James. 'Not like Cousin Horace.'

'Cousin Horace has a lot to answer for,' I said. 'Dancing lessons will be fun.'

'I'll do some extra with you if you like,' Lady Fitzwilliam said to Selina. 'And you too, Alice. You can come to our re-enactment meetings, too, if you want.'

'You're going to have a very busy social schedule,' James said. He was sitting close enough to me that I could feel the warmth of his thigh next to mine under the table.

'That's just how I like it,' I said.

'And how are your articles for *Hot! Hot!* going?'

'Great. The first one will go on the stands in two weeks. My first two blogs are already up on the magazine website.'

'I've read them,' he said. 'They're excellent. I felt that you really captured the flavour of Eversley Hall, especially in your one about your day in the kitchen. It read almost like a novel.'

'Oh, it was fun to write.' I'd ended up describing his entrance in quite romantic terms.

Now that I thought of it, I believed I'd used the words 'masterful' and 'handsome'. My cheeks flushed. Literary bravery was all well and good, but a bit embarrassing when you were down the pub with your subjects. 'Edie told me — I mean, Edie is my editor at *Hot! Hot!* — she said that she wanted me to, you know, emphasise all the romantic bits.'

'It's very romantic,' he told me. 'I hardly recognised myself.'

'Um, well, you know . . . you have to make it interesting for the readers.'

'Have you read them?' he asked Mrs Collins. 'I think you'll enjoy them. Alice described you exactly. Here, I'll write down the website for you.' He pulled a pen and a business card out of his pocket, and began to write down the address.

'Did you write about jumping into the fountain?' Selina asked me.

'Yes, that'll be in the magazine.'

'I think the articles will bring us a lot of extra visitors,' said James. 'So thank you, Alice.' He held up his glass to me and then drank his champagne, holding my gaze with his. It was electrifying.

'I'm very pleased you're enjoying yourself so much,' he murmured. I swallowed some orange juice, caught in his spell, until he smiled suddenly and looked away. Across the table, Isabella was glowering, her champagne untouched.

'How are you doing?' James said to Selina, who sat on my other side. 'You seem to be feeling more comfortable with the costume these days.'

'Yes, it's getting better. I do try to study all the stuff you gave me. And everyone's being really nice about it. Alice lent me lots of books, and then Mama — I mean, Lady Fitz — I mean — '

'Lady Fitzwilliam?' James said. 'You're not on a real-name basis, then?'

'Oh, it's my f — ' said Selina, but I interrupted her before she could deprecate herself any further.

'It was my idea,' I said. 'I thought it would be easier if we all kept on using our historical names. Then we won't slip up by mistake while we're in Eversley Hall.'

His smile deepened. 'You love the illusion, don't you?'

'I think it's a lot of fun. Yes.'

'I knew you did. That's why I wanted you to come back. Of course, you and I have it easier than everyone else as we're the only two using our real names. James Fitzwilliam and Alice Woodstock.'

'James Fitzwilliam and Alice Woodstock,' I repeated, not because the information was new, but because I wanted to hear, again, how those names sounded together. They sounded good. As if they belonged together.

'James,' said Isabella across the table, 'it's getting late.'

'Yes, it is.' He stood. 'Very sorry to leave so early, everyone, but I hope you'll enjoy the rest of the champagne without us.'

'We're going to the opening of the Declan Hannon show at the Parkside Gallery,' Isabella told everyone as she came around the table to join James. 'It's so wonderful to find someone who appreciates art as much as I do.'

'I'm sure it is,' I murmured.

'Bye!' James and Isabella left together. She didn't need to shoot me a triumphant glance; it was all over her posture and the way she walked, conscious of James's hand in the small of her back.

I refilled Lady Fitzwilliam's flute and passed the bottles around the table.

'So,' I said to Arthur, 'are you going to join us for the Austen movie fest? We can restrain our Darcy-lust for you.'

'Sounds good, but only if it's a Monday or Tuesday. I've got a gig most other evenings.'

'A gig?'

'Yeah, it's at a new comedy club in Brickham. I do some standup, some sketch stuff. Nice people.' He checked his own watch. 'Fact, I should get my skates on. We're on in ninety minutes. Catch you tomorrow!'

'He's a comedian?' Selina said after he was gone.

'We should go and see his show,' I said. 'All of us.'

'I've been with his mother,' said Lady Fitzwilliam. 'It's good. You would like it. I'll go again, if you like.'

I did have a full social calendar. Or I could have, quite easily. I might not have a hope in hell of nicking James off Isabella if they were dating in real life, but these people were nice. They would be good to have for friends. If I played my cards right, I wouldn't have to cross paths with Leo at all. I could carry on being the better Alice Woodstock.

Accomplished

'No, not like that, like this . . . Make sure the needle is over the thread, then pull through. Then back inside the loop and bring it up again, over the thread. See? A chain.'

I watched Lady Fitzwilliam's hand dextrously moving over the embroidery needle and tried to copy her. When I pulled the needle through the material, my green floss tangled itself into a snarl.

'Bother!'

'Keep practising, dear, you'll get it eventually.'

'I wouldn't be so certain about that.' I looked gloomily at Selina's sampler, sitting on a side-table. She'd only just begun today, too, but she'd picked it up immediately.

'Didn't your governess insist upon your learning needlework?' asked Isabella from the other side of the room. It had started raining overnight, and today most of us were gathered in the Green Drawing Room demonstrating typical indoor pursuits for the few visitors who had braved the weather. Isabella had set up a candle and a screen, and had taken James's silhouette with many tender strokes of her pencil. He sat watching now as she did Selina's. Lady Fitzwilliam was trying unsuccessfully to instruct me in one of the key female arts.

'We mostly concentrated on reading and writing,' I said.

'Music? Drawing? French?'

'Not so much.'

'Oh dear,' said Isabella, glancing over from her screen with simulated concern. 'That shan't make it easy for you, I fear.'

'What do you mean, Miss Grantham?' asked James. She favoured him with a smile. I wondered how their date had gone last night.

'I was thinking about poor Miss Woodstock's prospects,' she said.

'Her prospects?' Selina said, trying not to move her lips too much.

'How kind of you to be concerned about my future, Miss Grantham,' I said as sweetly as I could. 'I am sure I'm very lucky to have such solicitous friends. Selina, Miss Grantham refers to my present situation. Though she is too delicate to spell it out, I am homeless, penniless and single. My future is in doubt.'

'It is no such thing,' said Lady Fitzwilliam. 'You're welcome to make your home with us for as long as you wish, Alice.'

'It's a tempting offer, Lady Fitzwilliam. But I have no desire to be a burden upon my relations.'

'You aren't a burden,' said James.

'After the summer, you'll be going to London, and an additional unmarried female on your hands will be an expense and a nuisance.'

I pulled at the tangle of green floss. Ironic I should be arguing about my stay in Eversley Hall being temporary, when I'd decided to spend as much time in this world as possible. Of course, it was temporary. The contract only went till the end of September. Leo might be gone by then, or maybe he wouldn't.

I didn't want to think about that future. The point was, Miss Alice Woodstock wouldn't want to be a burden on her relations. She was too spirited, too independent.

'If you saw the bills I receive for my stepmother's gowns, you'd hardly call yourself an expense,' said James.

'Why are you homeless?' asked a young woman next to me, and I paused to explain to her the plight of an orphaned young woman whose home was entailed upon a toe-treading drunk.

'My options, therefore, are limited,' I concluded. 'Even if I were wealthy, I couldn't live alone, or not without a great deal of social censure.'

'If you are determined not to rely upon your relations,' said Isabella, 'perhaps Mr Fitzwilliam or I know of a suitable family who require a governess.'

'Not a *governess*!' cried Selina. 'That's *horrible*!'

I restrained myself from bursting into laughter. Selina really had been absorbing the books I'd lent her if she knew that being a governess was a fate worse than death.

'Selina — the silhouette, please,' said Isabella, and Selina rapidly composed herself and tried to sit exactly as she'd been sitting before. 'Of course,' Isabella continued, 'they would have to be a relatively undemanding family, or perhaps a bookish one, since you're unable to teach drawing or music or needlework.'

'I'm not quite accomplished enough to be a paragon of governesses,' I admitted. 'On the other hand, it's almost a pity you have a fortune, Isabella, since with all your many talents, what a wonderful governess *you* would have made!'

Isabella frowned, not quite sure if I'd insulted her or not.

'You will not be a governess,' said James to me. 'You are too valuable a companion for Selina.'

'Until Selina gets married,' I said. 'Miss Grantham is right; maybe you should make some enquiries about a suitable family for me.'

He got to his feet. 'I will do no such thing. You are not meant for that life. You are too — '

'Troublesome?'

'I was going to say extraordinary,' he said, smiling. 'But perhaps they are the same.'

'I don't want Alice to be a governess,' said Selina. 'Please, James, don't let her be a governess.'

'For goodness' sake, Selina, they don't positively torture governesses,' snapped Isabella.

'I tortured mine,' said James. 'No, Selina, don't worry. I won't allow our Cousin Alice to become a governess.'

'In that case, you have an infinitely more difficult task in front of you,' I replied. 'Almost impossible, I would have said. But as I have the highest estimation of your abilities, perhaps you can accomplish it.'

'What's that?' he said, drawing closer to me and placing his hand on the back of my chair. I studied his handsome face. What was going on

293

with him and Isabella? Were they a couple?

I held his blue gaze with mine. 'You will need to find me a husband.'

OMG! I want a mr f!!! ☺
I wouldn't want him to find me a husband, I would want him to BE my husband!
I want a Mr Fitzwilliam too, goin to Evrsly Hll nxt wkend 2 get him
Can we have pics pls!??!
This is really fun, can't wait for next instalment. More!
Gonna buy magazine just 4 this.

I shouldn't be reading the comments on my blog on the *Hot! Hot!* website — it was probably the height of vanity. Let alone Googling it to see how many times it had been Tweeted and linked to online. But it was such a novelty to see anything I wrote actually attracting any interest beyond commentary by a handful of geeks. And since the third instalment of my blog had been posted this morning, it had — I refreshed and rechecked — 346 comments.

346.

Okay, I was no J. K. Rowling. But people were reading what I wrote. They were liking it. They were going back and finding the earlier blogs and commenting on those, too.

My phone rang, and I answered it without looking away from the screen. 'Hello?'

'Alice! Three hundred and forty comments!'

Three hundred and forty-seven now, I didn't say. 'Hi, Edie.'

'I love it! It's fantastic! We are going to sell magazines like crazy! You really need to play up this romance angle for the rest of the stuff you write. How gorgeous that Mr Fitz is — all the flirtation. People are eating it up.'

'Um.' I remembered James in the pub, saying he was reading everything I wrote. 'Do you think?'

'Definitely. Listen, I need you to come to a party.'

'A party? When? I have some Regency dancing lessons and stuff.'

'Oh, ha ha! That's sweet. This is on the twenty-eighth, it's the week after the issue with your feature comes out. The Chico Club.'

'The Chico Club? Is that the place where all the movie stars and celebs hang out?'

'Yes, isn't it exciting? So you'll be there, right? It's our tenth anniversary party, love to see you, I'll send you an invite in the post. Can you bring the divine Mr Fitz?'

'I . . . don't know.'

'Try. It would be wonderful. All right then, keep up the good work! Byee!'

I put down the phone, dazed. Was this what it was like to be popular?

I'd never been a big party girl, or had a busy social life. I'd always liked hanging out with Liv, or reading, or writing. The quiet girl in the corner who laughed at inappropriate moments and who had the weird family. And now — I refreshed the screen — I had 350 people who thought my life was extremely cool. I also had a big Jane Austen Monday-night movie fest this evening, which I had organised, and an invitation to hang out with the beautiful and famous in the Chico Club.

My laptop beeped, reminding me it was time to go out. I ran a brush through my hair, got it stuck, decided on second thoughts that I'd stuff my hair into a clip, and ran downstairs and out of the front door. I was digging in my handbag for my car keys as I walked down the front steps towards my 2CV, and bumped full-on into someone at the bottom.

'Careful,' said Leo. He put his hands on my shoulders to steady me. 'It would be a shame to fall on your face when you're so dressed up.'

'I'm going out,' I said, backing away from his touch. I wasn't dressed up, anyway. It was just a nice top and clean jeans. He was being sarcastic.

'So I see. You've been out quite a bit since Friday night, haven't you? It's enough to make me think you're avoiding me.' His voice was light, but I knew Leo.

'I *am* avoiding you.'

'Frightened you won't be able to resist jumping into bed again?'

'That's not going to happen.' I looked back into my bag and began to walk away.

His hand on my arm stopped me. 'Alice, wait. We can't keep doing this. Sooner or later we're going to have to talk with each other.'

I pulled away. 'Or alternatively, you could go back to wherever the hell you've been for the past two years.'

'For the past two years, I've been running away. I've been running away for my whole life.

I'm finished with that now.'

'Do you want a medal or something?'

'I don't want anything except for you to talk with me. We don't talk, Alice. We never talked.'

'Are you joking? We talked incessantly the whole time we were together. We never stopped talking, except maybe when we were asleep or — ' *when we were making love.* I flashed back to his breath in my ear, the wordless groan as he sank into me.

No.

'Not about the important things,' he said. 'Do you realise we never once had a fight? That whole time we were married? Not until — '

'The day I kicked you out. I'd have thought that was enough.'

'I think by then it might have been too late.'

I crossed my arms. 'And that's my fault, is it?'

'It's your fault you won't talk now. Jesus, Alice, on Friday night I thought — '

'Thought you had another notch on your bedpost? Oh wait, does it count if you've already had sex with me before? Well, never mind, I'm sure you'll make up for lost time.'

His eyes narrowed. 'I've been putting up with your accusations for weeks now, because God knows I deserve some of them, but it's becoming ridiculous. You seem to think I've spent the last two years drinking and shagging my way across America, and that I've come back here specifically to make your life hell.'

'Haven't you?'

'No.'

'You must have a natural talent for making my

life hell, then, because you're doing a really good job. Now excuse me, because I don't feel like arguing in the middle of the street, and I've got to go.'

He grabbed my hand. He was warm, always so warm, Leo. 'I didn't know what else to do.'

'Let me go.'

'No. You have to listen to me this time, Alice. You think that I never cared about you or about Clara. But I did. I cared too much. I couldn't handle it that Clara died. And I couldn't take it that you were so angry with me, that you wouldn't talk with me. I needed something to do, something to take my mind off everything I was feeling. That's why I went out to all those bars in Boston. I wasn't out having fun.'

'I saw you, don't you remember? That night. I saw you through the window of the bar. You were laughing, Leo. You had your arm around a woman. You were having fun, all right.'

He shook his head. 'I don't even remember most of it. I have no idea who that woman would be. I have no memory of her. She didn't mean anything. Nothing meant anything except for you and Clara.'

'You certainly had a funny way of showing it.' I tried to pull my arm away from him.

Leo tightened his grip on my hand. His eyes were serious.

'You hadn't talked to me in weeks,' he said. 'Not since Clara — not since you'd come home from hospital. You didn't even notice me when I was there. You sat in that one chair reading and reading, great stacks of books piled all around you, and every time I spoke to you, you had this expression on your face like you couldn't wait for me to be gone. As if I were an annoyance, or irrelevant.'

'You couldn't have tried very hard to talk to me,' I shot back. 'I don't even remember you being there. You were too busy *making friends*.'

'I couldn't sit there and watch you. I had to get out.'

'It's a nice trick, Leo, turning all of this around so it's my fault. How long did it take you to think it up?'

'It was wrong. But you need to understand why I did it. You froze me out, like you're freezing me out now. I was lonely and sad.'

'How do you think *I* was feeling? I wasn't exactly desperate to cheer you up. You weren't there when your child was dying. Your own child.'

His hand went limp, and I snatched my arm away.

'And if I mattered so much, you should have been there when I needed you. But no. The drinking was more important. The bars. The having fun, with someone so unimportant that you can't even remember who she was.' I backed off a few steps, my hands on my hips. 'You know what, Leo? I would have rather you did know who that woman was. I'd rather you were in love with her, that you'd left me for her, because that would actually make you someone with feelings.'

'I have feelings. I tried to talk with you about them. You shut me out. Just like you've done since I got back here.' He reached for me again.

'Don't talk to me,' I gritted. 'Don't touch me, don't even look at me. I've got to go.'

'Right. Go ahead, do it again. Only, please, do me the courtesy of acknowledging that there's more than one method of running away.'

'Goodbye, Leo.'

I stormed to my car. Behind me, I heard the house door slam.

My fingers were shaking as I tried to fit the key into the car door, and after I got in I had to sit holding the steering wheel for a few minutes, trying to calm myself.

How dare he blame me for what he did. How *dare* he? If I'd spent all my time reading, it was because that was what I'd needed to do. I couldn't rely on him; I'd learned that from Clara's first day alive, when he'd walked away. I'd had to do whatever I needed to, to make the days pass.

My fingers were white on the wheel. Why couldn't he leave me alone? Hadn't I made it clear enough to him? We were finished. There was nothing left but the arguments. And if we'd never argued when we were married, it was because we knew deep down that our love was too fragile. It couldn't survive nights in the neonatal ICU. Or the long months afterwards.

It couldn't even survive my reading a few books.

Goodnight, Moon

I didn't read while Clara was in the hospital. I couldn't bear the thought I might miss her opening her eyes, or clasping her tiny hands. I needed to see every single breath, and keep her flawed heart beating with my will and my love alone.

I slept in a cot in her room in the NICU. I watched her. I touched her when I was allowed. I talked with the doctors and nurses about her. I forced milk from my breasts into a machine to keep for later when she could be fed it through a tube in her nose. I persuaded my mother not to fly over from England because I knew that if she was there, she would talk and I would have to pay attention to her, and I needed all my attention for Clara. Leo wasn't there. I didn't know where he was. My baby needed me.

I only read one book: *Goodnight Moon*. It was the only children's book I had. I had bought it when I was pregnant, a single slim orange-and-green volume. I could have bought more books for Clara, but I couldn't bear to buy anything for her when she was lying, small and helpless, in the neonatal ICU. I promised myself I would buy her more books when she was home. When it was safe to plan for a future.

Meanwhile, I would read her *Goodnight Moon*. With pauses between the pages to check her breathing, to touch her tiny perfect hand beside all the wires and tubes. I read it and read it and read it to her, thinking about my voice only, how my voice was helping her hold on, and it was only near the end of her short life that I realised it was a book of goodbyes I had been reading to her all that time.

Goodnight.

When she died, I began reading in earnest. I walked along a narrow bridge created of words and stories, spanning the gulf that had no bottom, the hole I couldn't look at, because I would fall into it and never come out. I read novels to push myself forward. I read novels to think of something else because I could not think of what was happening to me. What had happened to Clara.

I found novels everywhere, in bookshops and secondhand markets, in the library and in drugstores. I read books I had never seen before, books I'd read a dozen times. Stacks and towers and walls of them. When I was finished with a book, I tossed it aside and picked up another, with no time in between to digest. I read every waking moment, and when I was asleep, I dreamed of what I had read.

I must have also eaten, and walked, and taken buses and used the telephone. I must have spoken with Liv and my parents when they came to see me; I must have signed the release forms for the autopsy and the cremation and sat through the service that my mother arranged, in a row in a pew between my father and Leo. I know these things logically, because they had to have happened to get me from point A in the hospital with Clara hooked up to machines, to point B, where I was now. But I don't remember these things.

I do remember the unknown Ajax, and a time machine, and a speckled band, and a bicycle-riding bear. I remember Jeeves and Wooster and Lord Peter Wimsey and Jean Valjean and Emma Woodhouse, with very little to vex her. I remember the Grand Sophy and her thorough-bred horse, Salamanca. I remember tunnels and spaceships and castles and wizards.

And novels saved me. Other people's stories saved me. They brought me to the other side, to the safety of attic rooms in Brickham and a life writing about facts.

I owed my life to novels.

The Perfect Husband

'How's the search for a husband going?' asked the girl in shorts and a strappy top.

'Slowly,' I said. 'Though perhaps we should enquire of Mr Fitzwilliam.'

James looked up from the letter he was writing, while several other young women admired his handling of the quill. There seemed to be a lot of young female visitors today. In fact, it was quite a marked difference in demographic.

'Have you found her a husband yet?' asked one of them. James raised his eyebrows at her, and I saw her simper.

'Shouldn't be too difficult,' said Arthur from an armchair where he was lounging, toying with a book. 'I know she's got no money, but she's a dashed fine girl. I'd marry her myself if I could.'

This was the point where Isabella Grantham would normally protest, but she wasn't in the room, so I said it myself. 'That's very kind of you, Arthur, but you're too young for me. Besides, your mama is planning on your making a brilliant match, I'm sure.'

'Good point there,' he said cheerfully. 'So she is. Can't let the mater down.'

'I'm in no hurry to find Miss Woodstock a husband,' said James. 'Especially since I've been told that she must marry for love.'

'Maybe you should marry her, then,' said the girl in shorts, and there was a chorus of giggles.

I was quite interested in what James thought of this suggestion, but then again, I didn't want to hear it if he was going to laugh, so I hurriedly said, 'Love is unpredictable, but not wholly irrational. If you provide me with a likely candidate or two, I shall do my best to contrive to fall in love with one of them.'

'Perhaps I may manage to invite one or two prospects to our ball next month,' James said, smiling. 'What are your requirements in a man you'd like to fall in love with?'

I considered. 'Well, of course he should be amiable, and intelligent, and rich. Not too rich, mind you — I'd hate to be forever tripping over footmen. A house in the country, and a residence in London. I don't aspire to Grosvenor Square — not with my red hair and my age, and no fortune. But if we could manage to *glimpse* Grosvenor Square in passing, perhaps from an upstairs window, that would more than suffice.'

'I see,' said James. 'Do continue.'

'He should have a sense of humour and be able to dance. He should be lively and patient. After Cousin Horace, I should prefer it if he didn't drink to excess. He should be kind, and principled, and responsible, and — '

'Good-looking?' suggested the girl in shorts.

'Of course. Handsome as an angel.' I tilted my head at James. 'Are you writing this down, or do you have someone in mind already?'

'I am searching my brains to come up with a single person good enough for you.'

'Do you prefer brown hair, or fair?' Arthur asked.

'Oh, either.'

'And dark eyes?'

'Light,' I said quickly, thinking of Leo's dark eyes snapping with anger. 'And he must be scrupulously faithful. No actresses.'

This searching for a fictional husband was much more pleasant than the realities of having one. No wonder so many stories were written about it.

'Sounds like Lord Rackham to me,' said Arthur. 'Don't you think so, James? Racky has blue eyes, don't he?'

'But he does live in Grosvenor Square,' James said.

'True. Well, that needn't be an obstacle if Miss W really does like him. Now Colonel Forsythe, he's got grey eyes, and is teetotal to boot. Though maybe a bit past it, since he's fifty if he's a day. And Bertie Barnaby, he's devilish good-looking.'

'A rake,' said James shortly.

'Ah well, you could reform a rake, couldn't you, Miss Woodstock?'

'I think I'd prefer to start with someone who didn't require taming.'

'Ah yes,' said James. 'I recall the story you told Selina, about the charming but unfortunate Mr Pelmet.' He folded his letter. 'Come along, Arthur, before you try to match-make any more. I need your help upstairs.'

Arthur groaned. 'I'd much rather help Miss Woodstock find a husband.'

'You'll have her married off to the worst fellows in England if you have your way. And

Cousin Alice, your lists are comprehensive, but you are forgetting one very important thing. Blue eyes and Grosvenor Square notwithstanding, while you're a resident of my house, I shall not consent to your marrying any man unless he is also in love with you.'

'Ah, well, that is even more difficult,' I said. 'Perhaps I should be resigned to becoming a governess, after all.'

'It's not as difficult as all that,' said James, and then stood. 'Come, Arthur.'

He left the room, trailing Arthur and all the young women with him. 'James,' I heard Arthur saying as they went through the door, 'don't *you* have a house in Grosvenor Square?'

★ ★ ★

'Mr Darcy. Definitely Mr Darcy.'

'I don't know,' I said, though of course I agreed with her. 'There's a certain something about Mr Knightley, too. He's alpha, but not as flawed as Mr Darcy.'

'That's why I like Mr Darcy. The flaws.' A spat of rain hit the windscreen of the BMW, and Lady Fitzwilliam turned on her wipers. 'It's probably because I've been married long enough to appreciate the idea of a man who's willing to change.'

'What do you think?' I turned in my seat to talk with Selina, who was sitting in the back of the car. She was wearing cropped jeans and a vest top, with her hair pulled into bunches. On her feet were a pair of plimsolls, for an evening of

Regency dancing lessons.

'I don't know,' she said thoughtfully. 'I really thought that Marianne got a rough deal in *Sense and Sensibility*. Willoughby wasn't right for her, and Colonel Brandon would be perfect, except he's so *old*.'

'He isn't old!' Lady Fitzwilliam and I cried at the same time. 'Alan Rickman is gorgeous,' she continued.

'I don't know, I just keep on seeing him as Snape. Ew.'

'Colonel Brandon is lovely,' I said. 'He's loyal and passionate and totally romantic. He falls in love with Marianne at first sight, and all he wants to do is make her happy, even if that means he can't have her.'

'You've really thought about this stuff, haven't you?'

'Of course I have. Heroes are important.'

She curled her feet up on the leather seat. 'I bet we all know who *your* favourite hero is in the world of Eversley Hall.'

'No comment,' I said.

'Do you have a boyfriend, dear?' Lady Fitzwilliam asked Selina, as she put on her indicator to go on the M4 towards Newbury.

'No, not at the moment. And I've never had a serious relationship. I haven't really had time, and I suppose I've never met the right person.'

'Haven't had time? You're twenty-one, how can you not have time for boys?'

'My mum and dad keep me really busy. They run a small hotel up in Cumbria, near Derwent Water, and they need all the help they can get.'

'Is that where the course in Travel and Tourism comes from?' I asked.

'Yeah, they want me to follow in their footsteps.'

'And is that your dream? A little romantic hotel up in the Lakes?'

Selina frowned. 'I'm not sure. I've sort of done it all my life, you know? You spend so much time doing the same thing over and over. But they think it's best for me so they're probably right. It's in my blood.'

'But you're James's cousin, aren't you? So stately homes and aristocracy run in your blood too.'

'Maybe. We're only second cousins or whatever.'

'What about you, Alice?' asked Lady Fitzwilliam.

'Oh, I haven't got any stately homes in my blood. Middle-class through and through, that's me.'

'No, I meant, do you have a boyfriend?'

'I'm single. So what can we expect from this dancing evening, then?'

'I'm an awful dancer,' said Selina. 'I hope I don't hurt anyone.'

'No, no, you have nothing to worry about. The Berkshire Regency Dancers are a wonderful group and they'll make you feel right at home. We'll walk through every dance first and then Vera will call it, so all you have to do is follow instructions. You'll take to it like a duck to water. Nick's been doing it since he was a lad — under duress sometimes, mind you.'

'Nick?'

'The boy who plays Arthur. His mum and dad are in the group.'

'What got you into re-enactment?' I asked her.

'The clothes. I was always a good seamstress, and a friend of mine asked me to help her make a pelisse. She was going to the Jane Austen Festival in Bath. The more I started researching, the more interested I got, so I started making my own costumes, and then Jerry was always interested in history and battles, so he joined a regiment and we started going to events together, and that's how it all began.'

Selina sighed. 'My mum and dad don't do anything exciting like that. They just stay in and take care of the hotel.'

'It's probably just as well,' I joked. 'They're much less likely to embarrass you that way.'

Lady Fitzwilliam chuckled. 'If you'd grown up with parents who were Napoleonic re-enactors, you'd probably have thought it was embarrassing too. Crazy people dressing up in costumes for fun.'

'No! I'd love it,' Selina told her.

'It could be a lot worse,' I agreed. 'My mother is the Condom Lady. Have you seen the sex-education film on YouTube?'

'No!' gasped Selina again, and she and Lady Fitzwilliam started laughing.

'Careful, the car's going to go off the road,' I said, but I was smiling, too. It felt good to share things with friends. To have a laugh. I'd never been a hugely sociable person, not like Pippi or Heidi or my mother, but I'd always had Liv. And lately, I hadn't even had her. I'd been lonely.

'I love Mum,' I said, 'but it wasn't the most

sensitive career choice for a mother of four to make.'

'At least you never had to worry about unwanted pregnancies,' Selina giggled.

I opened my mouth. Then I closed it again.

'It's good to have you girls to talk to,' Lady Fitzwilliam said, after a brief pause. 'It's been fun, these film evenings and the pub after work. I can't help but think . . . ' She moved into the left lane and signalled for the junction. 'I can't help but think that if Jerry and I had had any children, they would have been about your age.'

I glanced at her. Her soft, pretty face was lit up by the dashboard lights. She kept her eyes on the road, her hands on the wheel. But for a moment, her mind was somewhere else. Somewhere I might know.

'I'm glad we're friends too,' I said.

A Most Inconvenient
Engagement

When I entered Lady Fitzwilliam's bedroom she was standing in front of the pier glass in her petticoats and chemisette.

'The chemisette is used for modesty during the day,' she said to the assembled crowd, mostly female, who packed the bedroom, some leaning against the walls, some seated on the rush carpeting. 'As you can see, it's a sleeveless garment, almost like a bib, of fine cambric, which ties at the waist — like so. And now, I am ready to select my gown for the morning.'

It wasn't my imagination; there were lots more young female visitors here this week, and more families, too. A girl of about thirteen and a girl of about seven stood next to Lady Fitzwilliam, each holding one of her gowns.

'Shall I have the figured French muslin? That's yours, dear. Hold it up so we can see it. It's very pretty, isn't it? Or perhaps the jaconet muslin with the embroidery up the front, and the coral-coloured ribbons? Which do you think? The jaconet? I agree, that's a splendid choice. Thank you. Now, young lady, would you mind assisting me in putting it on?'

I watched as Lady Fitzwilliam recruited two teenagers to lift her gown over her head, adjust it, and button it up the back. She kept up a running commentary about buttonhole styles, methods of button manufacture, the difference between a flounce and a pleat, and how textile manufacturing had been affected by the Peninsular Wars. I hadn't been up here before when she was getting dressed; mainly I'd been assigned downstairs rooms. But Munson had carried me a message that she'd wanted to see me.

'Thank you,' she said at last to her helpers. 'If you will pass me that lace cap — thank you — I shall put that on, and my toilet will be complete. If you wish to — yes, how kind, of course you may have your portrait taken with me. I should be most flattered. Is that a new fashion from London, can you tell me, those boots? Ah, Miss Woodstock, how good of you to attend me here. If you will wait until I have finished with this portrait, I have something to discuss with you.'

'Are you Alice Woodstock?' whispered a woman next to me.

'I am.'

'Oh my God, I read your column online! This place is great! I can't wait to meet Mr Fitzwilliam. Is he really as gorgeous as he sounds?'

I realised that the entire room was looking at me. 'The most prudent answer to that question is to say that the portrait downstairs is a most faithful representation of his person.'

'Including the *rainbow*?'

Whoops. Maybe I shouldn't have blogged about that. 'Perhaps we can discuss that after I have my conversation with Lady Fitzwilliam,' I said.

Lady Fitzwilliam took the cue. She sat on the

chair in front of her looking-glass, and motioned for me to pull up another one next to her. The crowd in the room settled into silence, watching us.

'I hope you are happy with us here,' she began, in a polite and confiding tone which nevertheless carried so that everyone in the hushed room could hear it.

'More than you can possibly imagine, Lady Fitzwilliam,' I said.

'And I'm pleased to see you growing so fond of Selina.'

'Very fond. She's like the sister I never had.'

'You also seem to be fond of James.'

I inclined my head, not wanting to be too forward for my Regency self. But the visitors laughed, so I said quickly, 'My cousin has been very kind to me.'

Lady Fitzwilliam folded my hand in hers.

'My dear,' she said, 'I'm not sure how to tell you this. I didn't think, when James invited you, that it would come to — I mean, we expected someone quite different.'

'What do you wish to tell me, Lady Fitzwilliam?'

She sighed, and fiddled with the lace on the cuffs of her gown. 'Lord Grantham was one of my husband's oldest friends. Lady Grantham's mother and mine were very attached to each other. Indeed, it was at the Granthams' house that I met my dear late husband, not long after his first wife, James's mother, died.'

'You must owe the family a debt of gratitude.'

'Our attachment goes further than that. The

314

families are much connected. You see, you must know . . . ' she paused, 'that my husband and Lord Grantham settled it between them that one day, James and Isabella should marry.'

There were rather a lot of people in the room, and more had entered while we had been talking. They were all completely silent.

'Ah,' I said. It wasn't a shock, of course, but Lady Fitzwilliam seemed to think it would be, because she hurried on, 'We have always thought them very well suited to each other. They share so many interests. A love of art, and of history.'

'And of course she is so very beautiful. And accomplished. And rich. Everything,' I added with a smile, 'that I am not.'

'Oh Alice, don't talk so. You know how fond we are of you. But I would not want to see you growing too . . . fond of James.'

'Isabella is a brilliant match,' I said. 'You must be very happy. And her preference for James is clear. Have you noticed a similar preference in James for her?'

'James knows his father's wishes.'

'And he is nothing if not dutiful. Yes.' I acted calm, but I was squeezing my fingers together in my lap. 'Well. I shall have to congratulate them.'

'Oh, it's not formally settled yet. But it will be, by the end of the summer, I am confident.'

'That's why the Granthams are staying here,' I said. 'To get Isabella and James together.'

'That is one reason, I'll admit. Of course we like having them here, as well. And also — '

'And also Selina and Arthur?' It was so obvious now. And slightly ludicrous, given the ways these two characters were being played — as children, not in the least ready to marry each other. 'Selina told me she wasn't thinking of marriage yet.'

'Arthur will come of age next year, and naturally . . . '

'Naturally it makes sense for both the families to secure an engagement before he comes into his fortune and other young ladies set their caps at him.' I nodded. 'How convenient, and how pleasant. Two sisters and two brothers. A double wedding.'

'We are not so far advanced as to be planning the weddings yet.'

'I suspect Isabella has already chosen her gown.' I sighed out a deep breath. 'Does Selina know this yet? Or Arthur?'

'Arthur is aware. Selina doesn't know yet. We wanted her to become better acquainted with Arthur. James thinks it will be time to tell her soon.'

'James thinks.' I stood up, suddenly angry instead of dismayed. '*James* thinks, that love is important in finding a match for *me*. But for him, a person of consequence, it seems not to matter at all. Does James think of love, in any of this? Isabella may make him richer, she may make him more admired, but will she make him happy?'

Lady Fitzwilliam watched me sadly, as if this wasn't all play-acting, as if she hadn't been given all this information in her dossier. 'I'm sorry, Alice, I truly am. But it's settled. It's best for everyone.'

What Is A Heroine To Do?

I ask you, dear readers: what is a heroine to do? I am penniless, homeless, red-haired and can only wear black. Whereas Isabella Grantham is rich, talented, blonde and beautiful, with frocks coming out the wazoo.

Of course, she's also a total bitch.

I stopped typing and considered. Maybe it wasn't good to call my colleague a bitch in print, true as it was. Especially as I had evidence now that people were actually reading my columns and coming to Eversley Hall on the strength of them. I amended my text accordingly.

Of course, I can't help but be jealous. So is it jealousy that makes me think that James Fitz-william wouldn't be happy with her? Is it jealousy that makes me imagine he's been flirting, maybe a little bit, with me?

I don't have to imagine my own feelings: I fancy him like crazy. Who wouldn't?

So there's my dilemma. Do I stand back and let James make the logical choice, the wise choice, the only choice for any sensible gentleman in 1814? Or do I stand up and somehow try to prevent it?

In short: do I behave like a real Regency gentlewoman, or the heroine of a Regency novel?

I read it back. It was fun, it had the right tone, it invited reader participation. James would probably read it when it was posted online next Monday.

I highlighted it and hit the Delete button.

Edie had asked me to focus on the romantic aspect of Eversley Hall, but blogging for the whole world to see about how I fancied a bloke was a bit too blatant. It was one thing to describe James objectively as attractive, and quite another to go all giggly schoolgirl on him.

So what did I write?

I sighed and pulled out a piece of paper. I'd write down the facts. That usually worked for my technical writing.

1. I did actually fancy James Fitzwilliam.
2. Lady Fitzwilliam had told me that James and Isabella were as good as engaged. But she hadn't told me right away. Not until, in fact, it was clear from my blogs and from my behaviour in the house that my character fancied his. Instead of telling me the facts from the start, she'd waited until the most dramatic moment to tell me.
3. I had some evidence that James preferred withholding information from his interpreters so he could get more genuine, spontaneous reactions from them. He hadn't told the family about my arrival, for example. And Selina had no idea her character was supposed to be getting engaged.
4. Therefore, had he actually told Lady Fitzwilliam to tell me the news about him marrying Isabella, *at that moment*?

318

I paused. That was an interesting idea. It implied that he wanted me to be disappointed. It also implied that he wanted me to write about the whole thing. Was he doing it all to create excitement, to stimulate visitor interest?

5. The Regency James Fitzwilliam acted like he fancied Alice Woodstock. There were the glances, the little flirtations about finding me a husband. The small ways he seemed to prefer me to Isabella. Not to mention that lingering look at my cleavage after I'd jumped in the fountain.
6. And the real James Fitzwilliam had flirted with me too, hadn't he? In the pub. Sitting close, telling me how much he appreciated what I was doing.
7. Just before he went off on a date with Isabella.
8. Whom he was supposed to marry in 1814.

I sat back in my chair. So was all this to increase visitor interest too? Was he enacting a flirtation in 1814 to create some drama, and then playing at it in real life, so that I'd write about it for *Hot! Hot!* and attract more people to Eversley Hall?

Or did he mean it? Did he actually like me? Because if he actually *liked* me, the whole revelation took on a different light. It seemed less like something staged, and more like a challenge.

These are the facts, he might be saying. *What are you going to do about them, Alice?*

This was not helping me write my piece, at all. I was right back where I'd started with the words I'd deleted.

'Aargh, men,' I grumbled, and got up from my chair. As usual, I paused at the top of the stairs and listened for the radio before I went down. I could hear it, but it was muffled, which told me Leo was in his room. When I crept past I could smell the faint aroma of paint, so I knew he was working too.

He'd been doing a lot of that, the past few days, I reflected as I filled the kettle in the kitchen. Not partying, not drinking. Not out having fun. Not making a mess. Just working, keeping himself to himself. Not talking to me.

Like he said I hadn't talked to him after Clara's death, even though he said he'd tried.

All I remembered about the months after we'd lost Clara was the reading. I had books all over the flat, one stashed in every room so I would never have to spend more than a few moments out of some fantasy world or other. I didn't remember Leo being there at all. Did I?

I closed my eyes and pictured myself there in Boston, curled up in a chair with a book. It was a thick book, with illustrations — one of the Gormenghast novels, by Mervyn Peake. A nice long book, one of three nice long books in the series. I saw myself reading, pictured the page as I turned it over.

In the background of my memory, I heard a radio. Classic rock.

So the radio had been on. So what? So that proved that Leo had been in the flat once, while

I was reading. He was in the house now, too. Again: so what?

But now that I thought of it, I could remember other times. Emerging from a story for a moment, long enough to register guitar solos, footsteps, the smell of coffee. Leo's face, hair dishevelled, chin rough. Eyes dull.

He was there. Had he tried to talk to me as well?

Enough. Really, enough. I shook myself. I needed to write, not puzzle through the mess of my marriage. My ex-marriage. Leo was probably lying about all of this anyway: blaming me for shutting him out, to make me feel bad and make himself look good.

Except as long as I'd known Leo he'd never cared what other people thought of him. He'd never justified his actions or made up reasons for his impulses. Unlike Liv, who worked by consensus and logic, who smoothed things over, put on the best face. Leo did what he wanted without excuses.

Why would he lie now?

I was pouring boiling water over my tea bag when something Liv had said popped into my head. As if I didn't have enough going on in there already.

I think we're both good at hiding, don't you, Alice?

I'd pushed Liv away for two years too. I'd hidden up in my attic and I hadn't talked with her. I'd never told her exactly why Leo and I had split up, not all the details. Even right now, at this moment, I wasn't about to pick up the phone, dial her number and tell her that my sister was pregnant and it was stirring up all kinds of emotions in me, so much so that I'd jumped into bed with her brother and then had a huge row with him in the street.

She was 10,000 miles away, and I was still hiding from her. My best friend.

I finished making my cup of tea as quickly as I could and went back through the living room, past Mr Allingham's picture on the wall. 'I'll tell her later,' I said to him. 'I really will.'

He didn't answer.

On my way up the stairs, I met Leo coming down. I stepped aside, without looking at him. I'd had good reasons to push him away, if I had. I'd had the best reasons in the world.

'Sorry,' I muttered, passing him, my head down, feeling his body as a presence all the way up my left side as I went by.

Automatic words. Made of nothing but air.

★　★　★

Anyway. I didn't have time to worry about all this stuff. I had a brand-new social life to live — the comedy club to see Arthur, the cinema with Selina, dancing lessons with Lady Fitzwilliam. The *Hot! Hot!* magazine with my article in it came out on the Wednesday; I bought three copies and marvelled over the glossy pages with my words and photographs of James and Lady Fitzwilliam, Selina and Arthur, Isabella, of course, and even me.

And I had work to do. I wrote my blog post

the best I could, leaving my attraction to James firmly between the lines. I reported the upcoming engagement between him and Isabella in factual, unbiased terms, leaving the readers to make of it what they would. And they did.

For myself, I'd made my decision as soon as I'd got back upstairs to my room. I was going to take up James's challenge. Somehow or other, I was going to prevent James and Isabella's betrothal. The Regency Alice Woodstock would do no less.

But how did you prevent a betrothal, anyway? The commenters on the *Hot! Hot!* blog were full of ideas: spill ink down Isabella's dress (unlikely to make much difference), trip her down the stairs (tempting), steal her fortune (impossible), grab Mr Fitzwilliam and give him an all-out, tonsil-tickling snog (even more tempting). Actually, the last option was remarkably popular with readers, who seemed aware of the mores of Regency society; I had several suggestions that if James and I were discovered in a compromising situation, we'd be forced to marry to avoid scandal.

I gave the theory some careful thought. In the end, I saw there were only two ways it would work. One, I would have to be an all-out seductress and tempt him into trying to get into my pantalets in a house full of a hundred or more visitors. This was unlikely. Or two, I had to manipulate events so that it looked as if James and I had compromised ourselves, when we hadn't. And this didn't appeal, because it didn't involve James choosing not to marry Isabella. A forced marriage was worse than no marriage at all.

No, I had to work out a stratagem that would show Isabella's true nature to James. And also, at the same time, demonstrate to him that his poor Cousin Alice would make a much better wife.

In a novel, you could do it. You could introduce some kind of sub-plot that would throw the hero and heroine together. But I couldn't, for example, embroil us in a spy plot about stolen government documents. I couldn't arrange to be kidnapped by highwaymen and my life to be placed in mortal danger. I couldn't even introduce a love rival for me, or a richer prospect for Isabella.

I was stuck with what I had, which was twelve costumed characters, a lot of visitors, and a restored house.

I was no closer to a solution on the following Saturday, which was as well because I drew the card that meant I spent the entire day outside by myself in the shrubbery and parterre. Samuel had called in sick, and perhaps not coincidentally, so had Kayleigh, so I supposed it was my own fault in a way. The sun was shining fiercely, so I stuck to the shade, where it was a little bit cooler. It was particularly busy again; several people knew my name.

It was a little bit weird to be this kind of a quasi-celebrity. I spent a lot of time discussing my Cousin Horace, whose story was becoming more elaborate: he now had a wart on his chin, a flatulent dog and an unhealthy dependence on his valet — and trying to avoid the kind of questions that a Regency gentlewoman would never answer. For example, whether Isabella was as bitchy as all that, and quite a lot of contemplation of the merits of tight breeches.

In my few moments of solitude, I tried to cool myself with the fan Lady Fitzwilliam had lent me, and took sips from a glass of water I'd stashed behind a statue of a Roman dog. Under my bonnet, I watched the windows of Eversley Hall reflecting the summer sun and wondered what was going on inside. Was Isabella using her feminine wiles on James? Was Selina being told she had to marry Arthur? I tried asking some visitors but they didn't have much useful information so I paced and fretted. On the lawn outside, tea-tables were filling up and I could smell something delicious baking. My stomach rumbled, and I took advantage of a gap in traffic to nip over to the staff room in the west pavilion to find my packed lunch and a large glass of water.

It was a little cooler in there. The clock on the wall said it was nearly two, and it looked like everyone had had their lunch already because the room was empty. I splashed my face with cold water before I sat down at the table, unwrapped my Marmite sandwiches and took a big bite. Maybe I could eat quickly and then go inside to persuade someone else to take my post, for example Isabella, and then maybe I could somehow arrange for Nelson to get into some other scrape that she was too snobby to rescue him from. Though that didn't seem particularly kind to Nelson. It might be better to volunteer to take Nelson for a walk and then let him jump on Isabella's lap with his mucky paws. She'd freak out, and surely James could never marry someone who valued a clean dress more than his dog, could he?

The door to the staff room opened and I looked up, chewing my sandwich, my mind still on dog paws.

It was James. Not the James I'd been thinking about all day, who was a character to be played with. This was the real James, with his blue-sky eyes and his devastating smile. He was in costume, but not in character.

'Hi,' he said.

I swallowed my mouthful. He pulled out a chair and sat across from me.

I'd wanted nothing more than to see him and talk to him all day, but now that he was here, I was flustered. More the real Alice than the fictional one.

'Have you come for lunch?' I spluttered.

'No, I had lunch earlier. It's been really busy in the house, or I'd have come out to see you. How's it going outside?'

'Hot. This dress isn't made for sunbathing.'

His brow creased. 'I'm sorry. Come inside for the rest of the afternoon. I'll go out in the garden with Nelson.'

'No, that's okay. Anyway, you're having a Fitzwilliam and Grantham pow-wow about the engagements, aren't you?'

'Well, yes.' He rested his arms on the table. 'But it would've been much more interesting with you there.'

'What, so I could throw ink on Isabella's dress?'

He laughed. 'I read that. Your fans have a lot of ideas, don't they?'

'I think they're your fans, actually.'

'No, they're yours. You had a steady stream of them in the garden; I could see you through the window.'

He'd been watching me through the window? I went hotter, and hoped he hadn't seen me wiping sweat off my upper lip or biting my nails or anything. 'No, believe me, James, they're all *your* fans.'

James was looking a little bemused. 'It's strange, to be honest. Every week I find myself more and more like the hero of a romantic novel.'

'Well, you *are* like one,' I said, and then felt myself blushing even more.

'No, Alice. I'm really not. I'm — ' He looked away from me, at the clock on the wall, and abruptly stood. 'I've got to go; we've got a tour group coming through in five minutes.'

'Okay,' I said, but he didn't move. He just stood there, his hand on the back of his chair, looking at the clock, and then looking at me. I gazed back at him.

'I should really go,' he said.

'Okay.' I thought about asking him what was wrong. I'd never seen him hesitate about anything before. 'What's — '

'Are you free for dinner?' he blurted.

'Er . . . ' I blinked. 'What?'

'Dinner? Tonight? Are you free?'

'You mean, can all of us have dinner tonight together? After going to the pub?'

'No, I mean you. Having dinner with me. I can pick you up at eight, if that gives you time to change after having a drink with everyone.'

'I — yes, it should. I mean, yes.'

He nodded. 'Good. Okay. Good. I'll see you then.' He turned and rapidly strode from the room.

It was quite a few minutes after he left before I could get up out of my chair and go back to the garden.

Dating

Why didn't I ever shop for clothes? Why why why?

I examined myself again in the bathroom mirror. I used to like this dress quite a bit — it was floaty, strappy, flowery, summery, perfect for a rare hot English day. I hadn't worn it in years though; it was probably out of fashion. Plus, it was a bit big for me around the bust and waist. And it had a fraying hole under one arm.

'Damn!' I didn't have time to stitch it up and James would be here any minute. I was rubbish at sewing anyway, even the pointless recreational Regency kind. I'd just have to keep my arm down. On second thoughts, I ran upstairs for a cardigan. If I was lucky, the restaurant would have air conditioning.

I was pulling it on whilst going down the stairs when the doorbell rang and I nearly tripped over my feet. Between the cardie and my clumsiness I had to watch where I was going so I only noticed Leo when I'd reached the bottom. He was wearing a pair of jeans and nothing else — no socks, no shirt. He carried a pint glass of iced water and was heading for the door to answer it.

'That's for me,' I said.

He stopped when he saw me. 'Oh. I didn't know you were here. I didn't hear you come in.'

'Well, I am, and I did.' I hurried to the door. The last thing I needed on our first date was to have James greeted by my live-in half-naked ex-husband. I put my hand on the doorknob, waiting for Leo to disappear. 'I'm going out again in a minute.'

He stood there for a moment, looking at me. His mouth turned down at the corners. His skin was tanned, and the muscles of his arms and chest were well-defined. He never did something so normal as go to a gym, but the way he painted made him athletic. A trail of hair led down his belly to underneath the waistband of his jeans. Familiar, yet strange. I noticed he had a small tattoo on his left upper arm, the place that would normally be covered by a T-shirt. I couldn't make it out from here, but it was new. He'd never had a tattoo before.

Odd to think his body had changed since I'd known it, I thought, and then the doorbell went again. Leo turned and went up the stairs, carrying his water. The ice cubes made fragile glassy sounds.

I waited until he was definitely gone, then I counted to ten, after which I opened the door. James Fitzwilliam was there, wearing a beautifully tailored suit with a snow-white shirt open at the collar.

'Hi,' I said, a bit breathless, on edge in case Leo came back downstairs.

James smiled at me, that smile which transformed his face from an oil painting's to a man's. 'You look lovely,' he said. 'I don't think I've ever seen your hair in all its glory.'

'Oh.' I touched it where it lay loose on my shoulders. 'That's a nice way to describe a ginger bird's nest.'

'I like red hair.' He offered me his arm.

I looped my arm through his and we went down the steps. 'Is that your car?' I asked, spotting a silver Mercedes coupé parked next to my 2CV.

'Yes. But I thought we'd walk, if that's all right. It's no fun to drive in the centre of Brickham on a Saturday night.'

'Oh. Yes, of course.'

I did my best to hide my sinking heart. I hadn't expected to stay in Brickham for our date. The centre of Brickham was all chain restaurants and theme pubs. It was dominated by the huge new shopping centre, lined with noisy bars filled with binge drinkers. Not exactly the spot for a Regency gentleman to whisk a girl off her feet.

But maybe he didn't want to whisk me off my feet. He hadn't exactly made a big production of asking me; he'd seemed a bit uncertain about it, to be honest. Maybe he just wanted to have dinner. He'd never said this was a date. Maybe this was the way he dressed all the time, to go down to the pub with workmates or whatever.

I glanced at him as we walked. His blond hair was neat, his cheeks and nose touched by a bit of sun. He had a strong chin and broad shoulders. I'd never really been on any dates, not proper grown-up ones. Leo and I had never dated; we'd rushed from friends to lovers to spouses with no gaps in between. It could be very possible that I'd completely misread this situation.

Or maybe he thought that the centre of Brickham was a pleasant place to spend a Saturday night. 'Do you know Brickham well?' I asked him.

'Not really. I didn't grow up in Eversley Hall but in London. I used to come shopping here when I visited my grandmother. We bought embroidery floss at Jackson's and had tea and cake at Mumbles.'

Both long gone, concreted and built over in the name of progress and chain stores.

Oh well. Date or no date, I knew enough about etiquette to be sure it wasn't polite to suggest to the person who'd invited you that it might be a better idea to get in the car and drive somewhere a hell of a lot nicer.

He cleared his throat. We walked on. Interesting that when we were dressed up in costume in front of an audience, we could trade banter like nobody's business. But here, walking down the street with him, I couldn't think of a single thing to say.

'You live in a beautiful house,' he said. Oh no. Had he been expecting me to invite him in?

'The house isn't mine,' I said. 'It's my friend's. And it's very modern inside — she did tons of renovations.'

'Did she? I imagine she had to jump through a lot of planning permission hoops.'

'Yes, I think so.'

'I know what it's like. I've become an expert in red tape.'

'Did you have to do much restoration on Eversley Hall?'

He nodded. 'It wasn't the fixtures and furnishings so much. My family never throws anything away. It was more the general wear and tear, and bringing the interior back to what it looked like two hundred years ago. We had generations of redecorating to undo. And structural neglect.'

'That was really something to take on.'

'It's a labour of love.'

And he must be rich as anything, I thought, if he could undertake a project like that. Rich, handsome, charming, clever. What on earth was he doing out with me?

We crossed the Duke Street bridge over the canal and were immediately assaulted by thumping music and flashing lights coming from the pub on the corner. A cluster of open-shirted men and women wearing skin-tight dresses smoked fags and shouted at each other outside.

'Do you come out in Brickham often on a weekend?' James asked, seeming not to notice them as we walked past.

'No, not at all, to be honest.'

There was another pub right next door, this one with a bouncer arguing with two females in not much but high-heeled shoes. 'Nah, you gotta let us in, we got our mates in there, they bought us shots already!' one of them was bawling.

'I can't imagine why,' James said. 'Don't you feel you're missing out?'

I laughed, loudly enough that one of the bawling females stopped yelling and looked at me. James quickly steered me to the other side of the street, and down a side road between two brick buildings. We came out in a square near the park. Though it wasn't dark yet, the trees were strung with fairylights twinkling in their leaves, and suddenly, it was quiet.

'Where are we going?' I asked him.

'The Highbury Hotel.'

Oh. The Highbury Hotel. The most luxurious hotel in Brickham, though I knew this only from rumour as I had never been inside its huge oak doors. James led me under the arch of sparkling trees and up its stone steps, and opened the door for me. Inside, someone was playing a piano. The floors were polished marble, the walls lined with gilt-framed mirrors. In them, James's reflection looked perfectly at home. I tried my best not to look at myself. I was really going to have to keep my cardigan on to cover that hole, if there were enough mirrors to give a 360-degree view.

The maître d' led us to a table in the corner of the restaurant. James pulled out my seat for me, and I sat down, dazed.

Maybe this *was* a date. The restaurant was gorgeous, decorated in modern decadence, with raspberry and gold velvet wallpaper and leather seats. This wasn't a place you took casual work colleagues, was it? A waiter handed me a menu.

'Champagne?' James said.

'Oh — er, I'm not drinking, I'm afraid.' I hoped he wouldn't ask why. Explaining that I could be pregnant wouldn't start this evening on the right foot.

'Sparkling water, then,' he told the waiter, who immediately disappeared to do his bidding and was back within seconds with a chilled bottle of water, and pouring it for us.

'Here's to you,' James said, holding up his glass.

'Um. Thank you.' I touched glasses with his and drank. Good thing it was water; being so close under the scrutiny of those blue eyes was doing my head in quite enough. 'Why?'

'Well, for one thing, your articles have been wonderful. I love the blogs, and I was absolutely blown away by the one in this week's issue of *Hot! Hot!*.' He smiled wryly. 'Though I never expected to buy a copy of that particular publication.'

'I hope you bought a copy of *GQ* or something at the same time, to assert your manliness.'

'*GQ*, *Man's Monthly*, and the *Extra-Manly Man's Mag*.' He refilled my water glass. 'Seriously, Alice, you're a very talented writer.'

'Well, it's all about being in character, isn't it?'

'That's exactly why I brought you on board after seeing you in the kitchen. But you've done even better than I'd hoped. The whole project has become much more lively since you've joined us.'

'Really?'

'You've been there long enough to know what it can be like on a daily basis, doing free-flow interpretation. It's a challenge. You have to repeat the same information so often, it can be easy to glaze over or slip into anachronism. You've kept us on our toes, whilst staying completely true to the timeline. Emphasising the relationships within the house is a wonderful idea; it keeps visitors coming back to find out what's happening.'

'Like a Regency soap opera.'

'Something like that. We've sold more annual membership tickets in the past two weeks than in the whole summer up till now.'

'I'm glad I can help. Novel reading pays off, doesn't it?'

'It's not just reading novels. You have a talent for identification. You throw yourself into your character. It sweeps up the visitors, and also the interpreters. They really believe you. It's quite extraordinary.'

'Thank you. I like being the Regency Alice Woodstock.'

He lowered his voice. 'I like her very much, too.'

I wished I could take off my cardigan. Instead I gulped my water to cool down. I wasn't deluded; James Fitzwilliam was actually flirting with me.

Or was he flirting with the Regency Alice Woodstock?

Well. Of course he was flirting with the Regency Alice. He didn't know the real Alice. He'd only ever seen the better me, the brave me, the imaginative and impulsive me. If he knew the real me, he'd know I didn't belong in places like this, having dinner with a man like him. He'd know I was actually a pretty boring writer, with a specialism in grommets and glue, who spent most of her evenings out doing jigsaws with her dad.

Whereas James . . . I dropped my gaze to his hands on the table. James was perfect. His broad shoulders and strong arms, the fresh fairness of his skin. The understated cufflinks. How did you take off cufflinks, anyway? Was it something you could do quickly, in the heat of passion, or was it more a leisurely foreplay sort of thing?

'What do you fancy, Alice?'

'I — ' I looked up quickly, to see that the

waiter was standing near our table again, ready to take our order. 'Oh.' I seized my menu and chose a starter and main course pretty much at random. By the time the waiter had left, I couldn't remember what I'd ordered. But that was okay, because there was something much more important on my mind. Even more important than cufflinks.

'Are you dating Isabella?' I asked. Well, more like blurted out before I lost the courage.

'Isa — you mean Esme?'

'Yes. In real life. I know you went to that art show together, but are you properly dating?'

He took a sip of his water. I watched him swallow.

'We have . . . spent a lot of time together.' He sounded as if he was speaking carefully. 'And I like her very much. I owe a lot to her — she was the one who suggested I take on the role of the original James Fitzwilliam, for example. I'd never thought of doing it myself.'

'That was a good idea,' I said grudgingly.

'But I'm not dating her right now. I'm not dating anyone. It wouldn't be fair.'

'What do you mean, it wouldn't be fair?'

'I'm too busy,' he said. 'This summer, nothing means more to me than making Eversley Hall a success. It's all I can commit to. I've explained that to Esme, that I can't get into anything romantic for the moment.'

I glanced around the restaurant: low lighting, intimate tables, muted music, sparkling crystal. 'Not anything?' I said.

James took a deep breath. 'I got divorced five

years ago, and if I'm honest it was my fault. I was working in the City at that point. It was incredibly stressful, and incredibly exciting. I had to put in long hours; I was thinking about it all the time. I put my job before my marriage, and it split up. That's why I've promised myself never to do the same thing again. I'm not going to have another relationship until I can give it my full attention.'

'But you're not working in the City any more, right?'

'No. I inherited Eversley Hall. And that's even more demanding than my old job, because this time it's my own heritage that I'm working on. It's my legacy, too.' He leaned forward. 'Alice, can I tell you something in complete confidence? Something that can't go into anything you write?'

'Of course.'

'We've had to spend a fortune to restore Eversley Hall. And it's not just the Regency decoration; all that is cosmetic stuff. The place had been neglected for a long time. My father never cared for it, and I loved my grandparents, but they weren't practical people. There were structural repairs that needed to be done, if the whole thing wasn't going to fall down around our ears. I'm not exaggerating when I say I *need* this summer to be a huge success. That I will literally do anything to make it a success. Because if it isn't, I could lose everything.'

I opened my mouth to express my surprise, but at that moment our starters arrived. Oddly, mine appeared to be chicken livers on toast.

'Is there something wrong with your starter?' James asked me immediately.

'Oh no, not at all. I'd forgotten what I ordered. But I love liver.' I didn't. But I picked up my fork and took a bite; it wasn't that bad. Of course I was hardly going to taste anything in these circumstances anyway. 'Delicious.'

He picked up his own fork. 'Anyway,' he said, 'I'm not just working for me this summer. I want the house to be a success for my son.'

I choked on a mouthful. 'Your son?' I gasped, reaching for my glass.

'Are you all right?'

'Fine. Fine. You have a son?'

'Yes, Charles is seven. He's a bit young to appreciate Eversley Hall now, but he will.'

'I . . . I didn't know you had a child.'

'He spends most of his time with his mother. His school is in London with her, and all of his friends.' He reached across the table, and I realised he was passing me his phone. I took it. There was a photo on the screen: a young tow-headed boy, squinting at the camera with his blue eyes.

I never knew what to say about photographs of children. They made me think of the photographs I could never have. 'He's lovely.'

'Thanks. Do you have children, Alice?'

'No.' I passed the phone back to him and resumed poking at a chicken liver.

'It changes the focus of what you do. I don't think I would have put on a silly costume and pretended to be my ancestor, if I didn't have the idea that somehow, it was helping him. It'll all pass down to him, after I'm gone. I have to know that I'm doing everything I possibly can.'

Poke, poke at a liver. Don't ruin the evening, Alice, by being resentful of someone else telling me what it's like to have children. He doesn't know. There's no reason for him to know.

'It must be his school holidays now,' I said. 'You should get him an outfit and have him living in 1814 with us sometime.'

'No, there wasn't a child in the house in 1814.'

'Well, I wasn't in the house in 1814 either. Surely you could make another exception.'

'You're there for a very specific reason. I don't think people want to come to Eversley Hall to see a schoolboy running around playing. And it wouldn't be fair to make Charles work during his holidays.'

'Well, you must have plenty of time to spend with him anyway, since the house is only open on weekends.'

James shook his head. 'No, the weekdays are even busier, if you can believe it. We have marketing and development strategies to discuss, meetings with investors, ongoing restoration projects . . . and Charles is at the age when he wants to spend time with his own friends. He'll appreciate it when he's older.'

I put down my fork. My heart was hammering in my ears. 'So basically you don't get any time to spend with him at all?'

'It's hard, but I'm doing everything for him. He's my first priority.'

'But how can you say that . . . ' I reached for my water glass, needing to do something with my hands, something so I wouldn't say too much, and heard the unmistakable sound of a rip underneath my arm. Oh no.

'Excuse me a minute,' I said, and jumped up from my chair to head for the ladies' room.

Once in the cubicle I was relieved to see that the hole in my dress had only grown by a centimetre or so. And I'd had an even closer escape with James. Had I really just been about to have a go at him in the middle of an expensive restaurant, during what to all intents and purposes appeared to be a date? About not seeing much of his child, which by the way was none of my business in the first place?

I breathed deeply and slowly. I knew that I had a different perspective from people who had healthy children. If you had a healthy child, you could take him or her for granted. You could plan to spend more time with them in the future if you didn't have time now. You could do things like devote an entire summer holiday to creating a legacy for your son.

It was a passionate and noble thing to do. I was only getting all upset because I didn't have that option. I couldn't look forward to another summer. I'd only had six days, and they were all gone. It tended to warp your viewpoint of what normal parenthood was.

I pulled my cardigan back on. 'Right,' I said to the beautifully papered walls. Then I realised that there might be someone else in the toilets so I kept the rest of my thoughts in my head and went out to check my make-up.

As expected, I was slightly shocked to see

myself in a place of such splendour. I reapplied the only lipstick I owned, and gave myself a little talking-to. I'd spent two years post-divorce hiding myself away in an attic, and now I was having a night out with an eminently gorgeous man. It was a new start. A heroine wouldn't pick an argument. A heroine would be a well of sparkling conversation and wit.

I walked carefully back to the table, keeping my cardigan firmly anchored beneath my arm. James actually stood when I got to my chair.

'Are you all right?'

'Yes, absolutely fine.' I sat down. Fortunately what remained of my chicken livers had been whisked away in my absence.

James sat down across from me. 'What were you saying, before you left?' he asked. His brow was slightly creased with concern. It was an expression I never, ever wanted to see him directing towards me.

'Absolutely nothing,' I said, and smiled.

⋆　⋆　⋆

James Fitzwilliam had a talent, he really did. You could talk about anything — novels, films, growing up in Brickham, dogs versus cats, your penchant for killing house plants, having three sisters with names out of children's literature — and he would watch you and respond to you as if you were the most interesting person on the planet. As if you were, indeed, a heroine. Part of it was impeccable manners. The rest must be a gift. All I knew was that I was through with a main course of some kind of lamb, a dessert of some kind of ice cream, we'd had coffee, he'd paid the bill and we were getting up from the table, before I seemed to come up for breath.

He guided me out of the restaurant with a hand at the small of my back, where my cardigan ended. Had any man done that to me in two years? My skin tingled with the touch, and what with the shining mirrors and the sparkly trees I felt brave enough to ask another question that had been preying on my mind.

'What is the deal with you marrying Isabella?' I said.

'Are you chilly?' he asked me. 'It's got cooler now that it's dark.'

'No. I'm fine, thank you. I do want to know about you and Isabella though.'

We began walking back the way we'd come. The thumping music from the row of bars and pubs was even louder than it had been hours before, but I wasn't focused on that right now.

'It's an historical fact,' he said. 'James Fitzwilliam and Isabella Grantham became engaged to be married in August 1814.'

'But you don't actually get married, do you?'

'You mean, *didn't they* get married?'

'Yes. Right. The historical people.'

'Yes, they married in 1815.'

'But you can't!'

'Why not?'

'Because Isabella is awful.'

'This is my great-great-great-great-grandmother we're discussing,' he pointed out.

'Oh. Yeah, sorry. I mean — I'm sure the real

one was very nice. Did Selina and Arthur get engaged too?'

'Yes. Watch out.' He took my arm and guided me around a kebab splattered on the pavement.

'Have you told Selina about it yet?'

'She picked it up from a visitor yesterday,' he said dryly. 'I don't believe she's been reading your blog, so it was a big surprise.'

'I don't think there's a whole lot of attraction between her and Arthur, to be honest.'

'In 1814, marriage wasn't about attraction.'

'But surely it helps?'

'It always helps.' He glanced at me as we crossed the bridge over the canal.

'And I do notice you chose someone really beautiful to be Isabella.'

'Esme has a strong resemblance to the real Isabella Grantham, actually. I remember a miniature that my grandmother used to own.'

'And why not choose someone gorgeous if you're going to be spending so much time with them. And marrying them and everything. It makes sense.'

'Esme is an incredibly talented and experienced interpreter. She knows the Regency period inside out.'

'I'm not jealous or anything. I mean, I know it's ancient history, and it has nothing to do with me anyway. It's just that you set up this whole thing with Lady Fitzwilliam telling me about the engagement, so of course I have to make a big deal out of it.'

'I thought the drama would be useful.'

'Yes, I love it. And Isabella's a babe. It's

344

fortunate that history and real life have coincided so nicely for you.'

'It is,' he said, and though I wasn't looking at him I heard his smile.

'Of course though, you're not dating her at the moment.'

'I'm not dating *anyone* at the moment. I told you, I don't have time.'

So what was this, right here? I walked on for a moment. We were out of the worst of Brickham's carnage, in the quieter residential streets. 'Do you have any idea whether the real James really loved the real Isabella?'

He paused before he answered. 'I don't. There are letters, but James Fitzwilliam was very courteous. It's difficult to read between the lines.'

'And doesn't that bother you?'

'Alice, you know as well as I do that status and wealth were more important than love back then.'

'Are they to you?'

We'd reached my house. 'The most important thing for me right now is that this summer goes well. I want to be able to preserve Eversley Hall for Charles. My own feelings don't come into it.'

'Oh. Of course,' I said, feeling foolish.

James opened the gate for me. He'd been doing that all night: opening doors, pulling out chairs, waiting for me to go first. He was a gentleman.

And I'd been pretty much hounding him to tell me how he felt about Isabella. Someone with worse manners and no sense of humour would have told me where to get off by now.

'I'm sorry,' I said. 'I shouldn't be grilling you

about your feelings. I think it's wonderful that you're doing all this for your son.'

'Thank you.'

'And I had a really lovely time tonight.'

'So did I.'

I looked at him. He looked at me. He was tall and perfect in the gathering darkness.

He looked almost as if he were going to kiss me.

'I'll walk you to your door,' he said gently.

'Oh. Yes. Okay.'

He walked me up the steps, his hand in the small of my back a guiding touch that could easily turn into something more. He knew I was attracted to him; he'd read the articles.

We paused by the door. If he was going to kiss me, this was the time and the place. His body was a whisper from mine, his gaze intent on my face.

'Why — ' I began, but my throat was dry. I swallowed and started again. 'If you don't have time to date, why are you out with me tonight?'

'I tried not to. But I really couldn't help it.'

Slowly, he touched my face. Just the side of my cheek, with his thumb.

I shivered.

Through the door, music suddenly swelled. I could hear Bruce Springsteen singing 'Born to Run'.

Great. Just great. Tonight, of all nights, Leo decided not to go out, and to turn up his music.

'I'm sorry,' I said. 'I can't invite you in for coffee.'

The moment was gone, thumped away with

Springsteen guitar chords.

James nodded and smiled. 'Well,' he said. 'Thank you, Alice. I really had a good time. I'll see you tomorrow.'

'Yes, see you tomorrow.'

He was still waiting for something, so I dug in my handbag for my keys and unlocked the door. I didn't open it though. Not with Leo inside.

James started down the steps. Halfway down, he paused and turned. 'For what it's worth,' he said, 'I think that if there really had been an Alice Woodstock in Eversley Hall in 1814, my ancestor would have been strongly tempted.'

Then he got into his car and I watched him drive away.

A Nice Guy

I couldn't keep still. My feet seemed to pace themselves around the Green Drawing Room. To the window, to the sofa, to the fireplace. To the table with the vase of flowers, to the card-table. Back to the window.

'You really don't have to stay,' said Selina.

He was somewhere in the house, but I hadn't seen him yet. Dressed in his hero clothes, walking around, talking courteously to visitors to his ancestral home.

What would have happened if Leo hadn't been at home, and I'd been able to invite James inside? Had he really been planning on kissing me? Why had he said he couldn't help going out with me?

I paced. My questions weren't new. In spirit, at least, they were the same questions asked by every heroine in every novel. Every real woman too, after every first date. Well, almost every first date. It wasn't like that with Leo, for example. I'd known how he felt about me, because it was the same way that I felt about him. At that point, anyway. We'd kissed that first time and then we'd been together, inseparable, for what we believed would be for ever.

And look how that turned out. So probably it was better to have this fizzing excitement, this uncertainty, as if I was walking on little bubbles that could pop at any moment. It was more of a mystery. It was a better story.

'I really think I'd be fine on my own, if you'd like to go somewhere else,' Selina said.

'Do you know where James is this morning?' I asked, peering out of the door to the Hall. He wasn't there, just a group of tourists listening to Isabella hold forth about a vase.

Isabella. He wasn't dating her, but was that only because he was so busy, as he'd said? They'd spent a lot of time together in the past, and he seemed to think a great deal of her. Were they finished, or were they just sort of taking a break?

'No,' said Selina. 'Though I'm sure he'll be in to check on me soon. He's always checking up on me.'

'He's very protective of his family.' And then there was the whole thing about his son, Charles. I'd been too harsh on James, in my head anyway, for not spending enough time with him. They probably had a great relationship. James knew what was best for his own son. He was bound to be a wonderful father — he was so responsible and dedicated.

'Yes, he is,' said Selina. 'He's only looking out for my best interests, I know he is. And I appreciate the help, I really do. But — maybe I'm being silly, but I almost feel as if he doesn't quite trust me to make any of the right decisions myself. As if I'm a child or something.'

I looked at Selina for the first time. She was pleating the skirt of her muslin gown between her fingers. There were a few visitors in the room; not too many, but they were watching us.

'You heard about you and Arthur yesterday,

349

didn't you?' I asked. 'That you're meant to marry him.'

She nodded.

'How do you feel about that?'

She fidgeted, and glanced at the visitors around us. 'Well, it's . . . you know, it's a little bit of a shock. I feel that I could have been . . . you know, informed.'

'Perhaps James and Lady Fitzwilliam wanted you and Arthur to get to know each other, without the pressures of a betrothal.'

'Yes, but if I'd been told, then I would have known how to behave with him. Now I'm too shy even to look at him. Did he know all along, do you think?'

'I think he did, yes.'

'Oh no.' She buried her face in her hands.

I went to her and put my hand on her shoulder. 'Dear Selina, you have nothing to be ashamed of. Your behaviour has always been everything that is appropriate and charming.'

'I don't think I'd like to learn out of the blue that I had to marry some bloke,' said one of the visitors, a girl in a jumpsuit.

'Well, that's how it happens, isn't it?' said Selina, half to the visitor and half to me. 'In those — in these days, I mean — your family chooses your husband for you. They choose everything for you. And Arthur is very nice — I have nothing against him. It's just that I sometimes feel like a doll or something. You know, the way I'm never left alone, or . . . ' She bit her lip.

'James is simply looking out for you,' I said.

'We all are,' said James from the doorway, and Selina sprang apart from me, as if we'd been caught doing something wrong. He entered the room and my heart leaped. He'd tied his cravat a different way, and there was something else different about him, though I couldn't quite tell what. Maybe it was only me, the way my eyes instantly focused on his mouth. Had he been planning on kissing me?

'We only want the best for you, Selina,' he continued. 'You must trust me, sister.'

'I do trust you, I do! But it's just . . . I don't feel that *you* trust *me*.'

'Why is that?' James asked gently.

'I'm never alone! There's always someone with me, watching over me, making sure I'm doing the right thing.'

'This is 1814, and it's a modern world,' he reminded her. 'Young women require a chaperone.'

'I know that, but this is supposed to be my own home, isn't it? And I think I've learned enough to comport myself correctly.'

He nodded. 'I see what you are saying. Would you like to go outside in the garden? It is not so hot out there today as it was yesterday, is it, Miss Woodstock?' He glanced at me and my pulse sped up.

'It seems much cooler outside,' I agreed.

'In the garden by myself?' Selina asked.

'That is what you wanted, isn't it?'

'Well . . . yes. Yes, it is. Thank you, James.' She bustled out of the room, leaving me and James together.

351

Along with a dozen tourists. Our eyes met, and I edged closer, wondering how I could ask any of the questions I'd been thinking of.

'I'm sorry that . . . the coffee was not available yesterday,' I said. James smiled.

'It was a disappointment,' he said. 'I'm very fond of coffee. But I hope one day we'll be able to share a cup.'

I swallowed. I was close enough to touch him, if I wanted to. And I really did want to.

'Perhaps . . . ' I began, clenching my hands by my sides to keep from reaching out. The air felt heavy, hot. Full of anticipation and sexual tension.

'Hey, it's nearly quarter past two,' said one of the visitors suddenly, and they all hurried out of the room, leaving us alone.

'What was that?' James asked.

'Quarter past two is when the rainbow hits the . . . er . . . '

'Oh, that's right. Quite an event, apparently.'

'We could probably tempt them all back in with a prism and the real thing,' I dared.

He laughed. 'I think that experiment might destroy the illusion of dignity I've got going on here.'

Alone in the room, unchaperoned, with James. No tourists, no members of the family, no Leo behind a closed door. I glanced at a silk screen embroidered with dragons and old Chinese men carrying water buckets and things. I could grab his hand and pull him behind it with me. I could kiss him there, in thrilling secret.

Would Miss Alice Woodstock do it?

And what if we were caught behind the screen by half a dozen witnesses? That would keep him from marrying Isabella. But I'd already decided that wasn't a good idea.

'Dignity is sometimes overrated,' I said.

'Not in 1814.'

Hmm. I sidled forward and whispered, my heart thudding wildly underneath my stays: 'I'm going to a party in London next Thursday. At the Chico Club. Do you want to be my date?'

He shook his head. 'I'm sorry. I can't. I don't have a single spare hour for the next few weeks.'

'Oh,' I said. If he couldn't even come to a party, grabbing and kissing was definitely out of the question. Definitely. But still . . . here he was. Right here. And he was looking at me that way, the same way he'd looked at me last night on the doorstep, before he'd spoken of temptation.

'But I will,' he said. 'Let me know what time it is and I'll clear my schedule.'

Footsteps, approaching the room. I stepped back quickly and James crossed rapidly to the far side of the room. He took a book from the low shelf against the west wall and opened it, ready to be graciously interrupted by the necessity of greeting his guests.

I cleared my throat and prepared my smile for the visitors.

★ ★ ★

Pippi met me at the door of my parents' house. 'I haven't told anyone,' she said.

'Okay.'

353

'And I'm not going to. Not tonight. So don't even.'

I looked at her baggy jumper, worn over leggings. 'You're not going to be able to hide it for much longer, you know. And your exams are finished.'

'Try telling me something I don't know.' She turned and stomped down the corridor. I popped my head in the kitchen, where my mother was grating carrots. She was surrounded by little flecks and curls of orange. When she looked up, there was a shred of it adhering to one eyebrow.

'Oh, you're here,' she said. 'Thank goodness, it was a nightmare trying to find a night when we could all sit down to dinner, now that you're working on Sundays. Come here and give me a kiss.'

I kissed her soft cheek and flicked the carrot off her eyebrow. 'Need any help?'

'Oh no, not with the cooking. Everything's finished except for this, and I've already set the table — maybe you can tell everyone to come in and sit down. I'm glad you're here so I can get a decent meal into you. Tell me the truth, Alice, have you eaten *any* vegetables in the past month, or just those horrible Pot Noodle things?'

'I have, I bought a lot of fruit and veg at the market the other day.' Though come to think of it, that was back in June, and I hadn't actually got around to eating any of it; there had been too much upset once I'd bought it, what with Pippi and my doing my best to be out of the house all the time. It was probably still mouldering in the fridge. 'And I went out for dinner on Saturday night. I think I had some salad then.'

She sighed. 'I'm going to have to watch every bite you put into your mouth tonight, aren't I? Not one of you except for Heidi has ever known how to feed yourselves properly, which I can't understand because I've always had plenty of good food here for you to choose from. Thank God Pippi seems to have developed a sudden taste for something nutritious. She ate two pomegranates yesterday, I don't know what brought that on.'

'It's a mystery,' I said grimly.

'You've got some freckles — you've been out in the sun, I can see. Are you hungry now? Here, have this carrot, it won't spoil your appetite while you tell everyone to come in and sit down. And it's vitamin A.'

'Right.' I took it and wandered into the living room, where the television was going. My father was watching the blank space somewhere to the left of the screen, and Leo was sprawled on the sofa with one of the cats, Maggie, purring on his stomach while he scratched her favourite spot between her shoulder blades.

Of course he would be here too. My mother's two dearest wishes for me: to eat more fruit and veg, and remarry Leo. He looked up at the sound of me crunching my carrot.

We hadn't spoken since our brief exchange on Saturday night. I was expecting some sort of cheeky comment. Instead his eyes briefly flickered to the corridor where the staircase was, and I knew what he meant: Pippi. Hiding upstairs in her room in her baggy jumper.

355

I shrugged slightly and he shook his head. *What is she thinking?* On that one topic, at least, we were both in total accord.

'Mum says dinner is ready,' I said.

'Oh? Oh, hello, Alice.' My father blinked and stood up from his chair to give me a kiss. 'Nice to see you, love. Is Pippi here?'

'I'll get her.' I went to the bottom of the staircase and shouted, 'Sister! Dinner!'

When I got back, my mother was already pushing a tray of steaming dishes through the serving hatch from the kitchen. Leo jumped up and started to carry the dishes to the table. 'Oh don't, dear,' she protested. 'You haven't got a potholder, you'll burn your hands.'

'I've got a thick skin,' Leo said, placing a massive bowl of gratin potatoes in the middle of the dining-table.

'Oh but you haven't. Here, use this tea towel at least.' She shoved one emblazoned with a cat through the hatch for him. 'Gavin, can you please move that biplane from the sideboard? I want to put the crumble there.'

I pulled out my chair. There were eight chairs at our dining-table — one for each of the Woodstock family, and two for guests — despite the fact that there really wasn't enough room for such a big table and all those chairs in the dining-living room. Especially since Wendy's and Heidi's chairs never got used these days, as my two sisters had moved to the far ends of the earth. I always sat at my father's right hand, with Liv next to me when she was here, and then there was Heidi's empty chair, occupied at the moment by the other two cats, Tim and Fuzzicat. Wendy's empty chair was across from mine, with a stack of newspapers on it, and then Pippi and Leo had their places at my mother's right hand.

The seats were non-negotiable. If someone were to research the Woodstock family in 200 years, they would definitely get this bit right, because our places at the table were extensively documented in photographs of birthdays and Christmases.

But what about the other things, I wondered, as Pippi slouched into her seat and Leo draped the tea towel on the back of his chair. Would the historians know anything about the secrets, or would they make their decisions purely on the records that survived, births and deaths and marriages, my mother's famous video, my father's aeroplanes and formulae, my articles and maybe even Leo's paintings? Maybe they'd find shreds of carrot fossilised under the kitchen table. Maybe a card tucked between some pages as a bookmark and forgotten.

They'd know the fate of Pippi's baby, but they wouldn't know how she kept it secret from everyone but two people. They'd know Leo and I divorced, but they wouldn't know every reason behind it. They'd never know about our moment of madness in his bed, or the way I'd looked at James Fitzwilliam and longed to drag him behind the silk screen. The things that made up our daily lives were too ephemeral to be recorded anywhere but in our memories, and those would disappear when we did.

'Leo, darling, sit down and let me dish up. Gavin, would you pass over the serving spoon, please? No, dear, that's a fork. Pippi, are you having wine or water? Water? What about you, Leo? Water too? Alice, you too? Looks like I'm the only one having a glass of wine. You'll have to make sure I don't drink the entire bottle or I'll be drooling into the custard. Leo, will you carve, please?'

He took the knife from my mother. As he was sitting across from me, I could hardly avoid seeing him. He was wearing a Led Zeppelin T-shirt with cat hairs on it, and he had a streak of greenish paint on the outside of his left elbow. The tattoo I'd seen was covered by his shirt-sleeve. I wondered where that had happened, and when. I wasn't going to ask him. In fact, I was going to do my level best not to speak with him at all if I could help it, as every civil word we exchanged would be yet more evidence for my mother that we were still madly in love.

Meanwhile, she kept up a running commentary about everything as she loaded plates. My father was examining the tablecloth, and Pippi was rolling her eyes, her arms crossed on her chest, though I noticed she started tucking in as soon as she was given her food, without waiting for the rest of us. Mum passed me my plate, which was practically running over with gravy, she'd put so much on it. Oh well, at least if I was stuffing my face, I didn't have to deal with conversation. Maybe that was Pippi's strategy, too. Or maybe she was just hungry.

Mum surveyed the table to make sure everyone had a full plate, before she sat down herself and poured a glass of wine. 'Wanda McLoughlin from Drama in Action rang me this afternoon,' she announced. 'She said you'd pulled out of your gap year with them, Pippi.'

None of us had started eating yet, but Pippi kept on sawing at her roast beef with her knife. 'Yeah, so?'

'Why would you do that, dear?'

'It's boring.'

'But you were so looking forward to it. You haven't talked about anything else for months. You kept on saying you couldn't wait to go. Travelling all over the place, putting on shows, seeing the country.'

'Yeah, well, it's boring now.'

'What are you going to do next autumn? You can't change your UCAS applications now, you've only applied for deferred places at uni. Even if your A-levels are amazing, which I'm sure they will be, darling, but even if they're incredible, you're still going to end up hanging around in Brickham waiting for a whole year. And you know how competitive it is to become an actress; if you're serious about doing that, you can't afford to give up any little bit of experience you can get.'

Emotion flitted across Pippi's pale, perfectly made-up face. I could see her thoughts clear as day: she wasn't doing a gap year with a travelling youth theatre company when she was pregnant. And the baby was going to put paid to any dreams of being an actress, for good. She set her jaw.

'Have you changed your mind about being an

actress?' Mum pursued, passing round a bowl of peas.

'I — '

'Mum,' I spoke up, 'if Pippi doesn't want to do the gap year, that's her choice, isn't it? She's old enough to make these decisions herself now.'

'Well yes, but it seems so out of character, I'm wondering if there's something you're not telling me about it. Did something happen with the other people in the group to make you change your mind?'

'Nothing happened, Mum.'

'There was that boy, wasn't there? The one you liked?'

'Nothing *happened*.' Pippi stabbed her fork into a potato.

'She doesn't need to keep busy all the time,' I said. 'It's important just to *be* sometimes too. To have a little quiet time to think over your life. Isn't that right, Pippi?'

'You're one to talk,' Mum said. 'You're so busy you can't even eat properly. Does she even spend any time at home, Leo?'

'Not much,' Leo said quietly.

'Well,' I said, 'you should be happy, Mum — you've been telling me I've spent too much time at home for the past few years. I'm really busy and it's exciting. Next week, for example, I'm going to a party at the Chico Club in London for the magazine and there will be all kinds of celebrities there.'

'You are?' Leo said.

'Yes.'

'Who's going to be there?' asked Mum.

360

'Well, I'm not actually sure,' I admitted. 'But there are supposed to be famous people.'

'What are you going to wear?' was her next question.

'I don't know. I'm going to have to do some shopping, I suppose.'

'I'll help you,' said Pippi suddenly. 'I'll do your hair for you, too. If you want.'

I looked at her in astonishment. 'Yeah, okay. That would be great.'

She nodded and went back to her dinner.

'It sounds like my kind of party,' said Leo. 'Do you have a date?'

'Yes,' I said firmly.

'Is that for *Hot! Hot!* magazine?' Mum asked. 'I read your article. It was really very good. I was telling Aisling McAuley about it this morning, and she said she was going to buy a copy for her niece who just loves that sort of thing. You read it too, didn't you, Gavin?'

My father looked up, a bit startled. 'Mmm. Yes.'

'I was saying to Aisling, I've been so lucky that my girls are all so talented. Wendy's so clever, and Heidi's so good at sport, and Alice at the writing, and Pippi with her acting, although I'm not very happy about the theatre-group thing, Pippi. I do think you could have discussed it with me first.'

'It's a good article,' Leo said, 'but Alice is much more talented than that. Your novel was incredible, Alice. It was one of the most beautiful things I've ever read.'

I stared at him. Where had that come from,

out of the blue? A compliment?

'You should pick it up again,' he said. 'Writing it used to make you really happy.'

'I've got other things to make me happy now,' I said quickly, and forked up some peas.

★　★　★

Pippi sidled up to me as I was opening the door to leave, after saying my goodbyes. 'Thanks,' she murmured.

'I can't distract attention for ever,' I said. 'Nobody can help you until you come clean.'

'I know. But not yet.'

'You said after you'd finished your exams, and you're finished now.'

'I know! I said! Jesus, can't you leave it for like a split second?' She flounced off.

I sighed. Hormones, I reminded myself. Also, she got enough nagging at home — and it was only going to get worse. I vowed to stop stating the obvious to Pippi, if only for my own sanity's sake. Plus, it would actually be nice if she stopped being stroppy with me for long enough to help me shop and do my hair for the party.

I had reached the corner of the road when Leo fell into step beside me. 'Hey, why didn't you wait?' he said.

'I didn't think we were on speaking terms.'

'Of course we're on speaking terms, Mermaid. We were just speaking over dinner, weren't we?'

'"Please pass the coleslaw" doesn't count.'

'We said a few things more than that.'

'Not much.'

'Well, you said it so charmingly. Besides, we're going to the same place. We might as well walk together.'

'I thought you were going to spend some more time in the bosom of my family.'

He laughed. Roast beef and au gratin potatoes had put him in quite a good mood. 'Your mother has given me recipes,' he said, showing me a stack of index cards bound with an elastic band. 'Her theory is that if I cook for you, you might end up eating something. I tried to explain the egg explosion thing, but she wasn't having any of it.'

'Only you would put a whole egg in a microwave.'

'At least I don't buy a whole fridge full of fruit and veg and then let it go to rot.'

'You didn't tell her, did you?'

'I wouldn't.' He stuffed the recipe cards in the back pocket of his jeans. 'I love it in that house.'

'I know,' I said, because I did.

'Thank you for not taking it away from me. You could have made them hate me, but you didn't. I appreciate it.'

Walking beside me, Leo seemed very different from when we'd argued. Not angry, not accusing. Somehow the time with my family had relaxed us both enough to bring us back, nearly, to the time when he'd been my brother.

Of course, another argument could erupt any time.

'Your parents paid for me to go to art college, you know,' he said. 'I wouldn't take the money from my father, and I had decided not to go, just to spite him. But your mother made me. Did she ever tell you that?'

'No.'

'See? I think she can keep her mouth shut when she wants to.'

'Not as well as her daughter,' I said. 'I don't know what Pippi's playing at. She's wearing those smock tops and eating pomegranates, of all things. And the gap-year thing — how did she think she was going to get away with that?'

'She'll come round. She can't hide it for much longer, anyway.'

'My mother is going to *freak out.*'

'You might be surprised.'

'I don't think so. And what was all that stuff about my novel?'

'It was true,' he said.

'That never went anywhere, and you know it.'

'It could. And you're braver now than you were then.'

I didn't know what to say to that. We walked together down the hill, under the trees. The evening hovered between light and darkness, with a smell in the air of warm pavements and grass.

'Who was your date this weekend?' he asked me. 'Is it that guy from the house?'

'His name is James.'

'And you're going to that party with him, too?'

'Yes, if you must know.'

'Nice guy, is he?'

'Yes, he is, very nice.'

We reached the house, and Leo paused at the gate. 'You deserve a nice guy, Alice,' he said.

'Yes, I do.'

Leo opened the gate for me, but he didn't go through it after I did. 'I need a bit of a walk,' he said. He left, walking down the street in the gathering dusk. I could almost imagine there was something defeated about the way he held his shoulders, the way his hands stayed in his pockets. And my heart almost went out to him.

Then I gathered it back in, where it was safe, and went inside. I sat down on the sofa, next to Mr Allingham.

'You messed him up, you know,' I said to the painting.

Mr Allingham didn't disagree.

All Dressed Up

'No. No. Too big. Too red. This is cute, but it's not you. You can't wear this with your freckles. This one's too frumpy, ugh. This one's good, though. Okay, we'll try this and this and this. Come on.'

Shopping with Pippi was astonishing. A revelation. She was some sort of retail genius. She'd made straight for the shops that I'd never even walked into before, the ones which catered for the trendy and the solvent. She didn't even ask my size, just plucked piles of clothes from the rails. I followed her into the changing rooms, where she took a plastic tag from the attendant and pointed to the big curtained-off cubicle in the corner.

'You don't have to come in,' I said.

'Oh, yes I do. I don't trust you at all, you have horrible taste in clothes.'

'It's not that bad, it's that I never have the chance to dress up, except at Eversley Hall, and those aren't my own clothes.'

'You don't need an excuse to dress up to get decent underwear. Ugh, Alice, that bra is like twenty years old. We're getting new lingerie after we find a frock.'

'M & S?'

'Puh-lease. No, that one looks awful on you. Try this one.'

'That looks like a sack.'

'That's because it's not zipped up, der.' She did up the zipper and looked at me critically. 'No, it's a sack on you. You're too scrawny. Mum's right, you need to eat more. Not that I can say anything. I'm turning into this totally fat cow.'

'You're not fat, you're pregnant.'

'Ew, don't remind me. I'm all like, 'Goodbye, perky tits.''

Keeping my mouth shut produced serious dents in my lip from my teeth. Soon she was directing me to another shop, this one blasting pop music, where she yanked yet more dresses off the rails.

'I would have given up about an hour ago,' I said, taking off my jeans for what seemed like the fortieth time.

'And that is why you dress like a slob. It takes time and patience to find exactly the right outfit.'

'You and Lady Fitzwilliam would have lots to talk about.'

'Lady who?'

'One of my friends in Eversley Hall. She gets dressed several times a day, just so she can change outfits and explain them to people.'

'That sounds like good fun. I always thought that if I got famous, I wouldn't get a stylist or anything. I'd want to do it all myself. Like have my own signature look.' She sighed and passed me a dress. 'No point thinking about it now. It's never going to happen.'

I pulled the dress over my head and looked at my sister in the mirror. I felt bad for her. She wanted to be a famous actress, and yet here was I, the nerdy writer, going to this party, while she was stuck at home with my parents incubating a baby. It probably never occurred to her that I'd give a million or more fancy parties at A-list hang-outs to be pregnant again, for the first time, innocent of all the knowledge of what could go wrong.

I'd started my period this morning. Seeing the small smear of blood, I'd had such a maelstrom of emotions that it was hard to pinpoint the individual ones. Relief that felt like disappointment. Regret that felt like release.

'Why are you keeping the baby, Pippi?' I asked her, in my gentlest voice. 'Do you want it?'

She zipped me up. 'I don't know. I don't actually have much feeling for it, right now. It's sort of a lump, you know? It doesn't seem . . . real, yet. But I can't have an abortion. I just can't.'

'Why not?'

'This dress isn't right, it's all saggy in the back. Try the next one.' She handed it to me, and frowned. 'It's like ever since I can remember, Mum's been going on about the three babies she miscarried. One before she had Wendy, and two between Heidi and me. She mentions them all the time.'

'I try not to listen.'

'Yeah well, me too, obviously, but she's been talking about them all my life. I used to think about what they would have been like, you know? My three extra sisters.'

'They might have been boys,' I said, but I knew they weren't. The Woodstocks were all sisters. 'I wonder what she would have called

368

them. She's used up a lot of children's literature heroines already.'

'Oh, I had that all worked out. I thought probably Susan and Lucy from *The Lion, the Witch and the Wardrobe*, because she always read that to us, and then I couldn't decide who the last one would be. Maybe Jo, from *Little Women* or Anne of Green Gables or Hermione from *Harry Potter*.'

'Or something right out there, like Cinderella or Mrs Tiggy-Winkle.'

She laughed, and then looked startled that she'd done it. 'Anyway, those babies were all so real to me. It didn't matter that she'd lost them so early — in the first trimester or whatever it's called — I couldn't do that to another baby. And then there was you.'

I had taken a dress, silky and creamy in my hands, like milk froth. I didn't put it on. 'You mean, when Clara died.'

I could hardly believe I'd said it. But my sister's eyes were so frank, and I'd never seen her face so serious before.

'Yeah. I mean, I wasn't there obviously, but I heard all about it from Mum, and it was like the saddest thing ever, and when you came back from Boston, you were just . . . '

'A loser?'

'You weren't yourself any more. And I'm not going to do that. Not an option.'

'Pippi,' I said quietly, carefully, 'you don't have to have a baby because I lost mine. Or because Mum lost hers. It's your choice. We'd both understand.'

She blinked. 'Der. I know that. It's my decision, it's what I'm going to do. Like I'd let you decide for me.'

But I'd seen that split second before she went into teenager mode. She'd wanted me to see it. The Pippi underneath the strop and the swagger, the sister who felt and heard and thought and feared.

'I'll stand by you whatever you do,' I told her.

'Yeah, well, thanks, but right now you have to like try these dresses on before the shops actually close, because we still need to get bras and shoes and everything.'

'Yes, ma'am.' I pulled on the frothy cream dress. Even before I finished tugging the skirt down, I knew it was the one. It had an Empire waistline and slightly puffed sleeves, and a skirt that ended above my knee.

'Yes, that's it,' Pippi said immediately. 'Modern Regency girl. You're modern and old-fashioned at the same time, like the articles you're writing. It's your signature style.'

'Wow.' I smoothed down the skirt. 'I have a signature style.'

'You'll totally stand out and it's a great colour for your hair. Plus, it's nice and loose around the belly so I can borrow it off you.'

'Do you want to come?' I asked her.

'Come where?'

'To the party.'

'I thought you had a date.'

I did. It was my big thing with James, my chance to get him alone again. He was rearranging his schedule. But I suddenly really wanted Pippi there, too.

'I'll have two dates. I'm sure nobody will mind.'

'Really? I can come?' Cinderella had never looked as surprised and pleased as Pippi did to discover she was going out for an evening. She seized my jeans from the floor. 'Come on, come on, get dressed, quick. I need to shop now too.'

★ ★ ★

James looked more than a little surprised when he pulled up in front of my house and saw two redheads waiting for him.

'This is my sister, Pippi,' I said. 'She really wanted to come, too.'

'I'm dying to meet celebrities.' She shook his hand. She was wearing a black dress which was both sophisticated and slimming, and heels that were even more ridiculously high than mine.

'Very nice to meet you,' he said to her, and gave me a swift and thrilling kiss on the cheek before he opened the car door for both of us. It was a two-door coupé, and fortunately Pippi climbed in the back, because I didn't think I'd be able to manage the gymnastic moves necessary, wearing this dress and these shoes. I settled into the passenger seat, still feeling James's lips on my cheek and breathing in the trace of his aftershave.

'She's not a chaperone,' I murmured to him once we were going. 'She's just had a hard time lately and I thought she deserved a treat. You don't mind, do you?'

'Not at all, I get to escort two beautiful women.'

Pippi leaned forward from the back seat. 'So are you the dude who has the rainbow penis?'

'Pippi!'

'So they tell me,' James said.

'You're hot. Do you fancy my sister?'

'Pippi!' I said again. Thank God she had sworn not to mention the existence of Leo, let alone that our mother wanted us to get back together. I hadn't thought to swear her to silence on any other topic though. Silly me.

'I never answer questions like that while I'm driving,' James said. He glanced over at me, caught my eye, and mouthed *Yes*. I just about melted into my seat.

It was just as well I had a bit of lust to distract me, because Pippi spent the entire journey down the M4 and into Central London grilling James about Eversley Hall, the family tree, his former job in the City and all the famous people he had ever met, bumped into, seen from a distance or merely heard of. James answered it all with good-tempered amusement. It was another plus point on his list: Puts Up With Sister. I wondered how he'd cope with my parents. I wondered how I'd get on with his kid.

Hold on, I was getting way ahead of myself, here. This was only our second date, and my sister was with us. Then again, Leo had been out when we'd left; maybe he'd be sensible enough to stay away for the rest of the night, and I'd be able to invite James in for that coffee, after all. Et cetera. Though Leo tended to stay in these days. Maybe, to be safe, I could suggest that we dropped off Pippi when we got back to Brickham, and we could go back to his place for a coffee. His place being Eversley Hall.

I was only listening vaguely to James's and Pippi's voices in the background and imagining various interesting uses for silk-upholstered early nineteenth-century sofas when James pulled up in a parking spot.

He opened the door for us and Pippi immediately grabbed my arm as soon as she got out onto the pavement. 'He's nice,' she whispered. 'And he's very good-looking, isn't he? Posh as anything.'

'Pippi, shh.' Though underneath, I was quite pleased she thought so. I had a feeling I'd been upgraded several notches from 'loser' in her eyes.

'I like Leo better though. He's not as polished. More fun.'

I looked over at James, desperately hoping he hadn't heard any of this. He was certainly pretending not to. He strolled beside us on the busy pavement; tourists and weeknight revellers parted to let him pass.

'Ooh look, it's the Chico Club!' Pippi cried, pulling me in her haste to get to a small doorway between two other doorways, which looked distinguished in no way whatsoever.

'How do you know?' I asked, teetering after her.

'Magazines.'

James opened yet another door for us, and we were met inside by a besuited man holding a clipboard. 'Name?' he said.

'Alice Woodstock. I've got two guests.'

It was an age of my wobbling on my heels before he found my name. I glanced over at Pippi; her eyes were shining, her lips open. I'd often thought recently that she looked like a little girl in a woman's body, but this little girl was in awe and amazement, as if she'd glimpsed a magic fairy castle for the first time. Much as it was likely she would embarrass me, I was glad I'd brought her.

'Says you've only got one guest here,' said the doorman.

'Um yes, well, another came at the last minute. I'm sure it will be all right.'

He shook his head. 'Alice Woodstock Plus One. That's what it says.'

I bit my lip. 'But — I've got two.'

'Looks as if you'll have to choose who you like best.'

James put his hand on my shoulder. 'Don't worry, I've got an invitation of my own. James Fitzwilliam.'

The doorman took considerably less time to find James's name. 'Have a fun evening,' he said, and stepped aside for us.

'You had an invitation?' I asked James.

'Yes. Though I hadn't planned on going until you asked me.'

'Oh.' I wasn't sure how I felt about this. Did this mean that James was now no longer my date for the party, but instead merely a fellow invitee?

Someone arrived at the door behind us, so we had to move forward to avoid being caught in a crush. The corridor leading to the club was lined with mirrors, no doubt so the famous and beautiful could check themselves for spinach in their teeth or whatever before they made an appearance with the other famous and beautiful.

I caught a glimpse of myself from the side in one mirror and nearly stopped to double-check. Pippi had done up my hair in a Regency-ish Grecian style, but she'd made it artfully messy, with curled and somehow glossy tendrils falling around my face and bare neck. Thanks to the sage-green court shoes she'd picked to go with my dress, I was about four inches taller, and make-up faded my freckles and brought out the colour of my eyes. And because Pippi had gone on eagerly ahead, I was standing right beside James, tall in his dark suit.

'You look beautiful,' James murmured in my ear.

I swallowed. It was difficult to believe this was really me. I nodded, and whispered, 'You do too.' Then I let him escort me through the banks of mirrors to the terrifyingly loud party going on in front of us.

The club was surprisingly small, and the room was already very hot. I could feel my hair curling up and my cheeks flushing. Pippi rushed over to us; she already had a glass of orange juice in her hand. 'Oh my God — did you see Johnny Depp? I think I am going to die.'

'Johnny Depp is here?' I asked, in a daze, though for the moment I seemed to have forgotten who Johnny Depp actually was. All of these people. All with perfect clothes and hair, all of them shouting at each other and laughing and air-kissing.

Maybe this hadn't been such a great idea after all.

A waiter came by with a tray of champagne glasses and James took two and gave one to me. I sipped it. James, by my side, seemed totally at ease; Pippi was vibrating with excitement. It was all I could do not to bolt for the door, or at least the ladies.

'Is that Alice?' A very tall woman separated herself from the crowd and approached us. She wore slightly frightening horizontal stripes and a pair of half-clumpy, half-spiky shoes which I couldn't quite understand but which made Pippi audibly draw in her breath in wonder beside me.

'Edie?' I guessed.

'Great to meet you! Knew it was you right away because of the hair and the dress — fantastic.' She air-kissed me and turned to James. 'And you're the hunky Mr Fitz — so glad you could come.'

'Lovely to meet you too,' said James.

'This is my sister, Pippi,' I said. 'Pippi, this is my editor, Ed — '

'Can you introduce me to Johnny?' Pippi interrupted.

'You're adorable. No problem. Let me introduce Alice and Mr Fitz to some people first. This is Brigid and Valerie, our Fashion Editors. Brigid and Valerie, this is Alice Woodstock, correspondent in Jane Austen land, and her fabulous sexy hero Mr Fitz.'

Two rail-thin women with perfect asymmetrical hair air-kissed me. 'Love your blog!' one exclaimed.

'Love your dress!' exclaimed the other.

'Love *you*!' exclaimed the first one to James.

'Er, thanks,' he said.

'Thanks,' I said too. They were important people, I knew, but already I couldn't tell them apart.

'Mr Fitz, I need to introduce you to the Marketing Manager to talk about some cross-promotion,' said Edie, latching on to James's sleeve.

'Of course, that sounds very exciting,' said James. 'I'll be right back,' he said to me, touching me fleetingly on the waist before Edie drew him into the crowd.

Pippi went with them, saying, 'But Johnny first, right?'

'You must write more for us!' exclaimed Valerie (or Brigid).

'We need more pictures of the clothes!' exclaimed Brigid (or Valerie).

'Okay,' I said.

Oh dear. What had happened to my Regency manners of being able to chit-chat about anything? I racked my brain for inoffensive topics: the weather, the journey, current events. I only knew current events from 1814.

'Er, what a very nice party,' I said.

'Yes! So I said to Sophia, you must talk to Augustus, he knows everything there is to know about Kurt, so talk to him just discreetly, you know, and then she goes right up to Kurt anyway herself!'

'No!'

'Yes! Wearing those jodhpurs, can you imagine!'

'In front of *Kurt*?'

'Yes!'

'Oh my God!'

This was evidently some code-speak, designed to separate the truly cool people from the wannabes. I backed away discreetly, sipping at my wine and looking around for my sister or my date. The heel of my shoe came down on something soft.

'Oof, darling, if you're going to go backwards, do you think you could put red lights on your arse?'

I whirled around to see the large man whose foot I'd trodden on. 'Oh, I'm so, so sorry.' My face flamed.

'Oh, no harm done, you're just a titchy thing darling, aren't you?' He smiled at me. He was actually enormous, roughly the size of Frankenstein's monster, crammed into a linen suit and with a sheen of sweat on his massive forehead. He held a glass of champagne which looked like the size of a toy in his hand.

'Bryce Burton,' he said, holding out his other paw. I shook it, feeling the size of a toy myself.

'Alice Woodstock,' I said.

'Yes — I thought so from the dress. Oh, it's so good to meet you, darling — you're the one who's doing those columns about life in that Regency house, aren't you?'

Being recognised by a stranger, here, was so odd that for a moment I thought he was probably talking about someone else, most likely wearing jodhpurs. 'Yes,' I said finally. 'Yes, that's me.'

'But they're wonderful, darling! Who are you, are you a fiction writer or a journalist or what? Should I have heard of you, Alison?'

'Alice. I'm a technical journalist and a copy writer. You haven't heard of me.'

'Have you ever thought of writing a novel, darling? You have such a way with words.'

'Well, I . . . I used to. Write novels. But none of them were ever published. Why, are you a writer?'

'Oh no no no, I'm an agent. Here's my card.' It appeared between surprisingly dextrous fingers. 'Listen, Alison darling, if you want to write that novel, get in touch. We'll meet up and discuss it, if you like. Or just send it to me, and I'll give you a ring.'

I took the card. 'Are you joking?'

'No, darling, deadly serious. If you can write fiction like you're writing those articles, you'll be sensational. Trust me, I've got a nose for these things.' He tapped his huge, rather crooked nose and winked. 'It's why I'm so fabulously rich.'

'Um . . . er . . . ' I gulped, then remembered my champagne, and swallowed some of that instead. 'Um. Thanks.' I stashed the card in the clutch bag that Pippi had also made me buy, and had a quick glance around for James or Pippi. Nowhere to be seen. That said, Bryce was blocking rather a lot of my vision.

'My pleasure,' he said. 'Oh look who's arrived, it's Reuben. Reuben, come here, darling, you must meet this little Regency girl. Isn't she adorable?'

Reuben was dressed all in black, and had a

goatee. He looked a little bit like a magician. He let Bryce give him an extravagant kiss on the cheek, and then he shook my hand. 'She's very adorable. You are . . . ?'

'Alice Woodstock.'

'That sounds familiar.' He looked at me thoughtfully, stroking his goatee with his finger. 'Now where have I heard your name?'

'A children's book and a famous music festival?' I suggested.

Someone tugged on my arm. 'I met him!' Pippi squealed in my ear at about a gazillion decibels.

'Wow. That's great.'

'He is so much more gorgeous in real life. This is so incredible. Thank you so so so much, Alice.' She threw her arms around me and gave me a big kiss on the cheek.

'Have you seen James?' I asked her.

'No, but — well, yes, I did actually — he was talking marketing plans or something boring. Oh my God, is that who I think it is over at the bar?' She was gone in a flash. Bryce and Reuben looked on, evidently amused.

'Sorry,' I said to them. 'My sister. She likes spotting actors.'

'They're pop stars, I think,' said Reuben.

'Reuben is directing *One Cherry Summer*,' said Bryce. 'It's a costume drama set in . . . what, Reuben? 1810?'

'1812.'

'You should come to Eversley Hall,' I said promptly. 'I'm working there for the summer as a costumed interpreter, and everything is set in

380

1814. It's extremely historically accurate. Except for me, but I don't really count.'

'It would be inspirational for you, darling,' agreed Bryce.

'Interesting,' said Reuben, but he was still stroking his goatee, and I got the impression he hadn't heard my invitation.

'Are you a theatre director?' I asked.

'Film.'

'He's *extremely famous*,' whispered Bryce loudly, and I put it together: Reuben Rogers. I had one of his DVDs, a romantic comedy called *The Throbbing Member of Parliament*. I bit my lip, suddenly wordless. If I couldn't even talk to a couple of magazine editors who were actually in the same business as me, what was I going to say to a film director?

'I've got it,' Reuben said, snapping his fingers. 'You're Alice Woodstock. Chemical-curing adhesives.'

'Pardon?'

'You wrote a series of articles on cements, didn't you? For *Model Aeroplane World*?'

'Er . . . yes.'

He beamed. It made him look less like a magician and more like a normal person. 'They were classic,' he said. 'I was in the middle of a Sikorsky Hoverfly Mark 1 at the time and you don't know how much they helped me.'

'I'm not actually a glue expert,' I explained. 'I just put the information together.'

'Well, that's a skill in itself. I'm no expert in Somerset in 1812 either, but I've got screen-writers and researchers and costume designers to do all that for me. This woman,' he told Bryce, 'is a hero. She absolutely saved my helicopter. What is it you're doing now?' he asked me again, this time paying attention.

'I'm spending my weekends dressed up as a penniless orphan and trying to prevent a marriage,' I said.

'Now that's even better than glue,' he said. 'Why are you trying to prevent a marriage?'

'Because the woman is a total cow, and I want the man for myself.'

'Ah. Have you tried telling him?'

'It's difficult, because he did really marry her.' I filled him in on the Isabella-James problem, with Bryce adding in details, because apparently he had really been reading my columns. And he was a real-life agent, one who knew film directors. Like the one I was talking to, quite easily, right now.

And then it hit me — the most brilliant idea I had ever had in my life.

'You have to come to the ball!' I gasped.

'Cinderella,' announced Bryce, with a sweep of his hand.

'No, I mean the Eversley Hall ball,' I said. 'It's August Bank Holiday weekend. A big Regency ball to round off the season. The Fitzwilliams actually gave it in 1814, and we're recreating it, with dancing and everything. I've been taking lessons.'

'Thank you for the invitation,' said Reuben, 'but I have a feeling that you have a particular reason for my being there.'

'Isabella is a professional historical performer,'

I told him. 'I bet she's dying to get into films. If you go to the ball, she's bound to recognise you. We can announce you as some amazing rich Earl or Duke or something, and you can ask her to dance, and she won't be able to resist you at all. She'll totally be all over you, and James will see that she's really only out for herself and what she can get. Oh my God, you can even borrow a costume from your film set and everything, if you want to. All you need to do is flirt with her a little bit. And she's seriously beautiful, so it won't even be a hardship.' I thought for a moment. 'She might not even be a bitch in real life. This whole thing might bring out the worst in her. I bet she's really nice when you get to know her properly. Unless you're married or something?'

'No,' said Reuben, his actually quite handsome face suffused with amusement. 'I'm between girl-friends at the moment.'

'So you might even like her! And she's supposed to be very good at her job, so she might even be able to help you with your movie. And then it's a win-win situation all round. James will see her true colours, and you'll have a fun evening. Oh, please say you'll come!'

'How could I possibly resist?'

'Hooray!' I jumped up and down, paying no heed to my heels. 'This is the best plan ever.'

'More champagne,' declared Bryce. He looked round for a waiter, just as I caught a glimpse of James in the crush. He spotted me at the same time and made his way over. He had his mobile in his hand.

'I'm so, so sorry, Alice,' he said, 'but I'm going to have to leave.'

'Leave?' I repeated in dismay.

'Yes. I got a call from Quentin. The alarm's going off at Eversley Hall.'

'Oh no.'

'There's no emergency. The fire and police have already been, everything checks out. But the alarm won't stop. The wiring's ancient,' he explained to Bryce and Reuben.

'But if everything's okay, then someone else can — '

'No, I'm sorry, I really am, but I have to get back right away. I know this puts you in an awful position, Alice. What would you like to do? I'll understand if you don't want to come back with me.'

I peered over to the bar. Pippi was talking animatedly with a man and a woman who were dressed in identical clothes.

'I think Pippi will really want to stay, so we can get the train home.'

James hesitated. I could see though that it was just politeness and that he was eager to get back to Eversley Hall.

'Go ahead,' I said. 'We'll be fine.'

'Thanks.' He kissed me swiftly on the cheek again, and then he was gone.

I sighed. Two swift kisses and a compliment were evidently my lot for romance tonight.

'He's the man who's marrying the cow, isn't he?' Bryce said sympathetically. 'Here, darling. Have some champagne.' He handed me a glass. I drank it, and he handed me another.

Space And Time

I woke up at the sound of the doorbell ringing. It seemed to echo, as if my hangover had scraped out the inside of my skull, leaving only an empty cavern. Which hurt.

I groaned and stayed right where I was, under my duvet. I should never, never, never, never drink champagne. It had seemed like such a good idea, especially when it had been given to me by a famous film director and a man who believed I could write a novel. I had vague memories of being poured into a cab amongst many air-kisses, and staggering on Pippi's arm to catch the last train home. Somehow I must have made it home from the station, because here I was in my own bed, and it was obviously morning.

Why hadn't James stuck around? If he hadn't left, I might have ended up in bed with him, and I'd be feeling wonderful now. Had Pippi got home all right? I couldn't remember. I'd have to ring, as soon as I felt a little better. I burrowed my head under the pillow.

The doorbell rang again. 'Leo, get the door!' I shouted, and that echoed around in my brain too. I winced and stuck one arm out of the duvet to grope for a glass of water. There was one on the bedside table, full and cool, a whole pint glass. I dragged myself semi-upright and drank the whole thing in a series of grateful gulps.

There went the doorbell again. 'All right, I'll get it,' I muttered and swung my legs out of bed. I appeared to be wearing my pants and bra; the cream dress was draped carefully over the back of a chair. My hair was loose and in my face. I didn't remember getting undressed or taking down my hairdo, or fetching the glass of water, but I must have had good instincts, to take care of my new clothes. Maybe I'd been learning something from Lady F.

I grabbed a pair of jeans and a T-shirt from the floor and flung them on. The doorbell was still ringing in time to the throbbing of my head as I ran downstairs. 'If this is for Leo I'm going to be really cross,' I said, but when I opened the door, it was Dad standing in front of me, blinking.

'Dad?'

'Oh, hello, Alice.' He looked vaguely surprised to see me, which was nothing to how surprised I was to see him. Of course he'd been here before, but never alone. I peered behind him, but Mum was nowhere to be seen.

'Um, hi. Come in.' He nodded at me as if I'd said something profound and stepped inside. 'Do you want a cup of tea?'

'That would be nice.' He followed me through towards the kitchen. 'That's new, isn't it?' he said, pointing at Mr Allingham on the wall.

'Er, yes. Leo did it.'

'It's a good likeness.'

In the kitchen, I put the kettle on and rubbed my eyes. My head ached, and despite the water, my mouth felt like sandpaper. Dad pulled out a chair and sat down at the table.

Had he wandered here by mistake? He didn't seem to have anything urgent to say or do; he was tapping his fingers gently on the glass surface of the table, seemingly absorbed in the patterns of light and shadow that they made.

Oh well. At least he was quite restful, though not as restful as being in bed asleep. Dad liked his tea brewed strong, like me, so I waited till the liquid had gone very dark brown and then mashed the tea bags up some more before I added the milk. Then I put one mug in front of my father. For a second I wondered if he would even notice if I went back up to bed with mine, but filial duty prevailed and I sat down across from him. It felt a little weird to be sitting with him at an empty table, without a jigsaw or a model in front of us.

He took his tea with a small sound of thanks and sipped it. I sipped mine. At least it was making my head feel a little better. And there were worse things for hangovers than silence. The only sound in the kitchen was the wall clock ticking. I raised my mug to my lips and let the steam warm my face.

'How far along is Pippi?' my father said.

Slowly, I lowered my mug.

'Pardon?'

'How pregnant is Pippi? No, that's wrong, pregnancy is an absolute, not a relative state. What I mean is, how many weeks pregnant is she?'

'She's . . . she's about fifteen weeks, I think.'

Dad nodded. He sipped his tea. It was as if we were talking about a fuselage.

'How do you know?' I asked.

'It's fairly self-evident.'

'Does Mum know?'

'No.' He gazed down at his tea. 'Your mother is a good woman, Alice, but she doesn't always have the patience to observe.'

'Oh my God.' I clutched my pounding head. 'It's going to be a nightmare when she finds out.'

'A nightmare?' He looked faintly puzzled. 'No, I don't see that. What is Pippi planning to do?'

'I'm not sure. She's definitely having the baby.'

Dad nodded. 'And how are you?'

'How am *I*?' I didn't think I'd ever heard him ask a question like this.

'Yes.'

'I'm . . . okay.'

He lapsed into silence.

'Dad? Why haven't you told Mum?'

'I was waiting.'

'But why? I mean, I haven't been able to tell you because Pippi swore me to silence, but I've been trying to get her to say something. Why didn't you?'

'Because . . . ' He tapped the tips of his fingers together, as if they would spark the right words. 'Because sometimes talking is better. That's what Celia does. She gets it all out, all out on the table and she deals with it. But sometimes silence is better. Space and time.'

For the first time since walking into the house, he looked up, straight into my eyes. And for the first time, maybe ever, I saw what he was trying to say.

Silence and waiting. All those hours doing

puzzles, building things together. He was giving me quiet and time and peace. He was watching me and waiting for me to work things through. To get used to my grief. To come back to myself.

I swallowed, hard. Dad reached out with his long theorist's fingers and touched my hand.

'Thank you,' I murmured, and he squeezed my hand. His gaze slipped from my eyes to focus somewhere behind me. I turned to see Leo in the kitchen doorway. He was holding a carrier bag.

'I'm sorry,' he said. 'I'm interrupting something. Hi, Gavin.'

'Dad knows about Pippi,' I told him.

'Good. It's about time.' He came into the kitchen and put the bag on the worktop. 'How are you feeling this morning? That champagne is a bugger.'

'I've got a fuzzy head,' I said, and then realised what he'd said. 'How do you know I'd been drinking champagne?'

'You told me. And also you breathed it in my face all the way up the stairs.'

'You carried me up the stairs?'

'You'd rather have slept on the doormat?'

'Oh God.' I tried to run my fingers through my hair, but they got tangled. 'What else did I say?'

'You said something about an agent who was interested in your writing. But mostly, you snored.'

'I don't snore.'

'You do when you've had a few.' He pulled out the grill pan and looked at it. 'Where do you

389

keep the aluminium foil?'

I got up and found it in the drawer near the cooker. 'Did you undress me too?' I asked him in an undertone, handing the foil to him.

'Nothing I haven't seen before.'

Well. At least he'd left my underwear on.

I looked away from him and started poking through the carrier bag he'd put down: bacon, eggs, mushrooms, bread rolls, apple juice. 'Are you planning on making breakfast?'

He shrugged. 'I thought it was the least I could do, seeing as you let me cop a feel last night.'

I punched his arm, and he laughed. 'More tea, Gavin?' he asked Dad. 'And a bacon roll?'

'Yes, thank you, that would be nice.'

Leo snapped on the kettle, got out the espresso maker, and started laying rashers of bacon on the grill pan. 'Still like your eggs with the yolks broken, Alice?'

'Yes, please,' I sat down again. Amazingly, it seemed that Leo had everything under control. He clattered around the kitchen as if he'd been doing it for years and soon the aromas of bacon and coffee filled the air, and there was a fresh mug of tea in front of me.

'We need to tell Mum,' I said.

'Pippi needs to tell your mum,' Leo said.

'Yes,' said Dad.

'How are we going to get her to do it?' I asked.

'Is she home today, Gavin?' Leo asked. 'And Celia too?'

'Should be.'

'We can go over there after breakfast,' I said.

'It might be better to do it here, you know,' Leo said. 'She's less likely to be able to disappear up into her room.'

'If I call Pippi and ask her to come over, she's going to know something is up.' I considered. 'Unless I offer to lend her my new dress, maybe.'

'I'll do it,' said Leo. He cracked eggs into a pan. 'I'll go and get Pippi and your mum and bring them here while you're both having breakfast. They'll come with me if I ask them. Then you can all talk it over together.'

Dad nodded. Leo did have a point. 'All right,' I said. 'Thank you.'

Leo held out his hand to me. 'What?' I said.

'Car keys. I don't have any wheels, remember?'

'You can't drive my 2CV. You can walk, it's not far.'

'And give Pippi all that extra opportunity to run away?'

'I'll drive, then.'

'With the amount you had to drink last night, you're probably not legal yet. Come on, Alice. You've got to trust me with something, sometime.'

'Do you have a licence to drive a car?'

'You weren't so argumentative about this last night,' he said.

'You *drove my car* last night?'

'Pippi rang me from the station to come and pick you both up. I wasn't going to do it on a bicycle.'

I stared at him.

'And I do have a licence,' he said.

'Oh, all right then.' I got up and went to find my car keys. He'd put them back in my normal handbag, the one I'd left behind last night because I was using the little clutch bag. When I got back with the keys, he put them in his jeans pocket, and then slid eggs onto plates. The yolks of mine were broken and cooked all the way through, how I liked them.

'Don't crash the car,' I said.

He smiled at me. 'It'll be all right,' he said. 'Everything will be all right. You'll see.'

★ ★ ★

But I still held my breath when my sister said the words. Sitting on the white sofa, one parent on either side of her, with me in a chair and Mr Allingham on the wall.

I watched my mother. I waited for her to jump up, to start yelling, to talk and scold and lecture and lament the future and mention the proper way to put on condoms.

She didn't. Mum took Pippi's hand and she said, 'Oh love, you must have been so worried. I'm sorry I didn't notice. Let's talk about what we're going to do.'

On Pippi's other side, watching and waiting, my father nodded.

On The Warpath

Quickly, I opened the desk drawer and rifled inside for papers, my ears on the alert for the sound of Hessian boots. An unfinished letter, a rough sketch of improvements for the servants' quarters, a list of items to order from Weston the tailor in Bond Street . . . the pounding of my heart was louder than the rustle of papers as I glanced up to see who'd come into the Library. Just a couple in Barbour jackets and Wellingtons, carrying guidebooks about the house. I went back to my rifling.

I didn't have long; while I'd been in the Hall I'd overheard James announce to Arthur that he was taking Nelson for a walk around the garden. No sooner had I seen him stride outside, spaniel at his heels, than I'd slipped into the Library. Five minutes, that's all I needed. Somewhere in here, there was a list of the 1814 guests invited to the ball; James and Lady Fitzwilliam had sequestered themselves in the Library last week to draw it up. They'd arranged to invite the Berkshire Regency Dancers and other costumed re-enactors as additional guests. As many of them as possible would be assuming the characters of real people who had been invited to the ball in 1814.

If I was going to assign an identity to Reuben, I would need to know who was actually going to be there in the present day, and then find an historical figure he could be. I foresaw many hours in the Brickham Public Library in my future.

But it would be worth it, if it showed up Isabella for who she really was.

'What are you doing?'

I started at the male voice. But it wasn't James; it was the man in the Barbour jacket.

'I'm looking for the list of guests to the ball next month,' I told him. 'I'd like to make an addition to it. But please don't tell anyone else. The Library is meant to be the exclusive domain of the male of the household.'

'I'm not sure I can condone snooping in someone's desk,' said the man.

'Ah, yes, but James is meant to be finding me a husband, you see, and forewarned is forearmed. I'm trapped by etiquette. Once I've accepted one invitation to dance, I must then accept the hand of any male who asks me. If James has invited anyone revolting, I shall know to refuse all. You wouldn't condemn me to an evening of dancing with a horrid potential husband, would you, sir?'

'Fair enough,' he said, laughing. 'Your secret is safe with me.'

'Thank you.' I opened another drawer. More unfinished letters. If this were really 1814, I would suspect James of being an awful correspondent, but as I knew that he was writing to long-dead people at addresses that probably no longer existed, I could forgive him for not posting anything.

The note I'd found tucked inside my locker this morning was in the same handwriting. *So sorry about Thursday night*, it said. *I'd much rather have stayed. I hope you had a good time after I'd gone. You looked spectacular. J x* There was a rose pinned to it, one of the sunrise-pink ones that were in bloom in the garden.

As apologies went, it wasn't too bad. And it wasn't as if he hadn't warned me beforehand that most of his time was taken up by the house. But I was still disappointed that he'd had to leave.

It did make me rather more determined to pull this off. To show that I was someone to be reckoned with.

I found what I was looking for in the third drawer: a list of names, an assortment of Sirs and Ladies and other less distinguished Misters and Misses. I nearly cheered. Aside from that alarm going off at Eversley Hall, my luck had been pretty good lately. Meeting Bryce and Reuben at the party, for example. Even the conversation between my parents and Pippi had gone well.

Amazing how these things that you were so afraid of could turn out all right after all, I thought. How someone you thought would definitely act one way, could act in a completely different way. For example, Leo carrying me upstairs and putting me to bed, being careful of my dress. Buying breakfast to cook for me and fetching Pippi and Mum, and then melting into the background to let the Woodstock family get on with what we needed to do.

I pulled the guest list out of the drawer, grabbed a pen and a fresh piece of paper and started to copy it.

Tried to. I hadn't used an ink pen since I was a schoolgirl, and even then it had been a fountain pen, not one that you had to dip in ink. I uncapped the bottle on the top of the desk, dipped the nib in, wiped it on the side of the bottle, and applied nib to paper. A splotch.

God. I tried again, and got a spidery scratch and another splotch, this one staining my fingers.

I should have been taking writing lessons as well as dancing lessons. Even if I managed to get anything legible down on the paper, I was going to have to blot it, if I didn't want ink running down the inside of my bosom when I'd stashed the list. And James would notice the soiled blotter. I looked up; the Barbour couple were still in the room, looking at some of the titles on the shelves.

'Pardon me,' I said, 'but do you happen to have a pencil I could borrow?'

Mrs Barbour dug in her handbag. 'How's this?' she asked, holding out a biro.

I hesitated. Anachronism was bad. Using a biro was tantamount to jumping onto the table in the dining room, striking a Kylie pose, and singing 'Can't Get You Out of My Head'. But surely it didn't count if the guest actually gave you the modern item?

This was an emergency. 'On the hush hush,' I said, and took the biro. I scribbled down the names in a rush of perfect plastic ballpoint ease. Excellent. Now all I had to do was to find someone incredibly rich, who had really existed, who could conceivably have gatecrashed the ball. It wasn't strictly historically accurate, because if this person was so important, he would have been mentioned in the contemporary documents. But I wasn't above bending the rules a little bit, for a good cause. As long as there weren't two people claiming to be Sir Wilfred Watlington or whatever, we would be fine as far as I was concerned. Never let the truth get in the way of a good story.

I folded up my list to tuck into the bodice of my dress, listening all the time for James's boots on the polished marble floor of the Hall. 'Thank you so much,' I said to Mrs Barbour, holding out her biro.

'James!'

It came from the Hall, in a high-pitched nearly hysterical scream. The cry of someone in a panic, or whose dress had been set on fire. I forgot about returning the biro and ran as fast as I could, skirts permitting, into the Hall.

Lady Fitzwilliam was standing there, surrounded by a crowd of alarmed-looking tourists, her face pale and her embroidery dangling unheeded. 'Alice!' she cried when she saw me emerge from the Library, and she hurried over to me. 'Have you seen James?'

'He went out for a walk with Nelson,' I said. 'What's the matter?'

'Oh dear,' she said, wringing her hands together. I wasn't sure how she was doing this without dropping her embroidery, until I looked a bit more closely and saw that it was actually sewn to her dress.

'What is it?' I asked.

'What are we going to do?' she said. 'James

will be so displeased — and my friends, the Granthams . . . All our plans, the whole summer. We can't let this happen, Alice.'

Granthams? James? Surely Isabella hadn't broken off the betrothal agreement? 'Dear Lady Fitzwilliam,' I said, putting my hands over hers, 'please come and sit down. You'll do yourself a mischief if you run around the house in this state.'

'I need to find James,' she insisted. An even bigger crowd had begun to congregate around us. Of course — it was nearly rainbow-crotch time. Lady Fitzwilliam couldn't have chosen a more dramatic time and place to have hysterics. *If* she'd chosen it. I wasn't so sure; she looked genuinely alarmed.

'I'll fetch him,' I said, and turned immediately for the door. Only to be met by a ball of curly fur jumping up at me, wagging his tail profusely.

'What's wrong?' asked James, who was following immediately after his dog. His voice boomed through the room, over the panting of Nelson, above the murmuring. Lady Fitzwilliam ran to him.

'Oh James,' she gasped, 'I don't know what to do. Selina says she won't marry Arthur!'

James frowned. I took a step back in surprise. Even the dog seemed a bit shocked.

'When did she say this?' he asked.

'Right this second — in the Drawing Room, as we were doing some embroidery. I thought she'd seemed a little distraite all morning, but I put it down to the weather, and I was trying to interest her in talking about her trousseau, when out of the blue she said it. 'Mama,' she said, 'I have decided not to marry Arthur.''

James's frown deepened. 'And did she give any reason for this decision?'

'She says she doesn't love him! She says she has been thinking it over, and she has decided quite vehemently that she cannot marry a man whom she does not love. I tried telling her, James, that love was not the work of a moment, but rather the outcome of years of mutual respect and admiration, not to mention the requirements of a shared duty, but she refused to listen. She was adamant!'

'And what does she think that love is, pray?' said James. His voice was low.

'She has some very decided ideas,' said Isabella. She had appeared behind Lady Fitzwilliam, and spoke with high dignity. 'She seems to believe that love requires the meeting of eyes across a crowded ballroom, or some such missish notion.' Isabella shot me a poisonous look, and I recalled that I was holding a plastic biro. I whipped it behind my back.

'I never expected this of Selina,' said Lady Fitzwilliam.

'It is entirely unexpected,' agreed James. His eyes flickered briefly to me.

'You've got to talk with her, James,' insisted Isabella. 'She'll listen to you. She must. My parents will be beside themselves — it could jeopardise the entire agreement between our families.'

Really? I gripped the biro behind my back.

'I'll speak with her,' James said. 'Where is she?

The Drawing Room?' Lady Fitzwilliam nodded and he strode down the Hall, Lady Fitzwilliam and most of the tourists tagging along behind him. Isabella, though, stayed put.

'This is your fault,' she said to me. 'You've filled her head with your novels and your stories about love. You've set yourself up as some sort of tragic heroine and now all she can think of is finding the love of her life. Whatever that means.'

'I believe, and have always believed, that Selina is old enough to make up her own mind,' I returned.

'So she can displease her family, fly in the face of every convention, and no doubt end her days as a dependent spinster — like you?'

'Or perhaps marry a man who loves her more than anyone else in the world, and with whom she has much in common — *unlike* you?'

Her eyes narrowed, and I knew that the gloves were off now. This was war.

'And you really believe that James Fitzwilliam could prefer *you*?' she spat. 'A penniless girl with no accomplishments nor any sense of propriety?'

I thought of the rose that had been tucked in my locker. 'I cannot presume to know my cousin's heart. However, being penniless has one advantage, at least: I know that any man who cares for me has been attracted by my own merits, not for my fortune.'

'And your partiality for James is in no way connected to his fortune.'

'It must be tiresome to be so mercenary, Isabella. Tell me, are you certain that James's fortune is enough to justify *your* partiality? It must be a little galling to have spent so many years perfecting your accomplishments only to bestow them on a mere gentleman. Don't you think there might be an Earl or a Duke whom you could learn to prefer?'

She opened her mouth, but there was a distant wail from the direction of the Drawing Room. 'I must go to Lady Fitzwilliam,' she said, and flounced off.

'Nice one,' said a girl with a ponytail as she passed me, and then the rest of the visitors filed after, not wanting to miss the drama. I stood, breathing rapidly, watching them go.

Isabella being a pain was nothing new. But Selina standing up for herself! I smiled. 'Good for you, girl,' I murmured.

I had to see this for myself. But the Drawing Room was bound to be packed out, and I had no real desire to make my entrance in Isabella's wake. Maybe I could slip in through the French doors to the garden. I turned towards the exit and for the first time noticed Arthur standing beside it.

'Oh,' I said. 'Are you — did you — how long have you been here?'

'I came in with James,' he said.

'So you heard . . . '

He came to stand next to me. We were the only two in the Hall now, if you didn't count the portrait of the first James Fitzwilliam gazing down at his dominion. Arthur's face was pensive, his voice muted, his movements slowed, as if all the puppyish verve had drained out of him.

'I can't blame her,' he said. 'I've made Arthur

such a clown that I can't imagine anyone wanting to marry him.'

'I think he's charming.'

'Well, it's been more fun for me this way, and I'm good at playing everything for laughs.'

'What are you going to do?'

'Arthur would take it in good humour, I think. I don't think he's the marrying type anyway. I'll play along with whatever happens; there's enough drama around here as it is without my adding to it.' He sighed. 'It's just my luck though, that the fictional me has got dumped as badly as the real me.'

'Oh, I'm sorry,' I said. I remembered his strange pensiveness, weeks ago, on the day when I'd shown Selina the rainbow. 'Your heart wasn't broken, was it?'

'A bit. Well, a lot.'

I touched his arm in sympathy. 'Was it last month?'

Arthur nodded. Then he looked down, and smiled slightly.

'It's history. Unlike this.' He plucked the biro from my hand and slipped it into his jacket pocket. 'You don't want to be carrying things like this around when Isabella is on the warpath.'

'She really is.'

'I'm probably in for it too, especially if I don't work up sufficient outrage for the Grantham family honour.'

'Maybe we'd better enjoy a few minutes of peace while we've got them,' I said. 'I'm sorry you've had a rough time of it recently. You haven't shown it at all.'

'They tell me I'm a good actor. It's a blessing and a curse.' He held out his arm. 'Would you care to accompany me on a walk in the garden, Miss Woodstock — before all hell breaks loose?'

★ ★ ★

'But it's not historically accurate,' declared Lady Fitzwilliam, clad in a flowered blouse with a cashmere cardigan draped, 1950s style, over her shoulders. 'The whole point of this re-creation is the accuracy. Everything's been researched, every single thing.'

'Except for Alice.' Selina sat beside me at our usual table at the Duke of Wellington. She was pale, but there were two flushed spots on her cheeks, and a sparkle in her eyes I hadn't seen before, as if she were simultaneously exhilarated and frightened by her own rebellion. 'Alice isn't an historical figure. If she can do made-up things, I don't see why I shouldn't too. If I want to.'

Lady Fitzwilliam, James and Isabella sat at the other side of the table. If there hadn't been drinks in front of them, they would have looked like some sort of jury. Arthur, prudently, had chosen to sit at the other table with Mrs Collins, Munson, Fiona, Kayleigh and Samuel. He was drinking his normal pint of lager and telling them some sort of long, involved story which, from the sound of their frequent laughter, was hilarious.

Isabella was practically grinding her teeth, especially every time the next table laughed.

'Alice is there for *publicity*,' she said. 'She's a journalist. She's not really part of the story.'

'She is now,' James said. 'As much as the rest of us, if not more. Is that why you decided to speak out, Selina? Did you want more attention, like Alice is getting?'

His voice was kind when he spoke to her. I hadn't heard any of the conversation that had gone on in the Drawing Room while I'd been out walking with Arthur, but I could tell he'd been calm and gentle, as he was being now. He was protective, and Selina was in fact his relative; he couldn't be anything but kind, even if this messed up his plans for the summer. I caught his eye and smiled at him.

'It's not attention as such that I want. I'm just tired of being shadowed all the time, as if I can't be trusted on my own.'

'Pulling a stunt like this is a brilliant way of assuring that you'll never be left alone again,' Isabella snapped.

'Is that how you feel?' James asked. 'I'm sorry. That's not what I intended.'

'You did hire Alice to look after me, didn't you?'

'Well.' He glanced at me. 'Partly. But you're right. You deserve to be left on your own, if that's what you want. Point taken.'

'So you're rewarding her for stepping out of role?' Isabella demanded.

'I wouldn't see it as a reward. It's greater responsibility, which is more difficult.'

'I'm ready for it,' said Selina.

'You have to admit,' James said, 'the visitors

404

did love the drama. It'll increase our numbers, I have no doubt, especially if Alice writes about it.' He glanced at me again, and I nodded. I couldn't *wait* to write about this. 'It could significantly increase our ticket sales for the ball. Maybe . . . ' He lapsed into thought.

'But it isn't *accurate*,' Lady Fitzwilliam reiterated. 'Everything we've done — all the clothes, the research, the dossiers. Selina and Arthur are supposed to get engaged. It's historical fact.'

'I think I've got it,' Isabella said to Selina. 'You need to have a little rebellion and you're fully intending to do what you're supposed to do by the end of the summer. Then we can have the extra pulling-power of the conflict, as James says, but it's historically accurate in the end. Everyone wins.'

Selina shook her head. 'No. I don't think Selina *would* marry Arthur. It doesn't feel right. And I'm not going to be bullied into doing something I don't want to do just because someone else thinks I should. I didn't want to do this costume thing at all in the beginning, but my parents and my tutor thought it would be a good idea, and James was being so kind I went along with it, but I haven't been happy. Not till Alice came along, and I got to know everyone better. And now I really do like it, and I'm not going to let anyone else ruin it for me.'

I felt like applauding; instead I squeezed Selina's hand under the table. Lady Fitzwilliam, James and Isabella all looked at each other. Over on the other table, Arthur had paused his story and the other group had all been listening to Selina's speech too.

'Well, I understand where you're coming from, love,' said Lady Fitzwilliam, 'and I can't blame you. But it's really a pity. All of those hand-made gowns. Every one of them researched and authenticated. I might as well have been wearing something from British Home Stores.'

★ ★ ★

I gave Selina a lift home from the pub afterwards. She was living in a studio flat in the village of Eversley, a summer sublet and close enough to the Hall that she could walk to work. 'I think you're being very brave,' I told her. 'And I'm one hundred per cent behind you, both now and in 1814.'

'Thank you,' she said. 'I was terrified this morning, knowing I was going to speak up. But actually you know it's not that bad? I'm a little nervous, but it feels good to know that I'm not some useless person in a pretty dress.'

I smiled. 'It was the books, wasn't it?'

'No. Well, a bit. But really it was you. You've always seemed so fearless. You see what you want, and you go for it. I want to be a person like that.'

'Oh, I'm really not very brave,' I told her. 'That's the 1814 Alice Woodstock. She's a fantasy figure. In real life I'm pretty timid. A geek.'

Selina shook her head. 'No, you're brave in real life too. Look at how you got us all going out together. And the way you write, and how nice you've been to me. I think you're amazing.'

'No, Selina. You're the amazing one, not me. Look at you — you've come all the way down here, to spend the summer with people you don't know. That's not easy to do.'

'I'd never really left home before.' She sighed. 'James was right. It's more responsibility, being independent. I've spent my whole life in my mum and dad's hotel, helping them out, and they've always said that when I was older, it would be mine. That's why I'm doing this Travel and Tourism thing, so I can be qualified and grow the business if I want to. It all seemed so simple and obvious. But now that I'm down here, doing something different . . . I wonder if the hotel is what I want to do, after all. It's their whole life, Alice.'

'Maybe that's what this summer is meant to be for you,' I said. 'Time away, to figure out what you really want.'

'Maybe. But that's not what my parents intended it to be, I know they didn't. They thought it was a nice little internship with a member of the family. If I go back at the end and say, 'I'm sorry, but I don't want to do this course any more and I don't want to take over the business,' they'll . . . well, they'll freak out.'

I remembered my mother, quiet and support- ive when we'd expected her to be hysterical. I remembered my father, who'd been spending all that time I'd thought he was oblivious, watching and understanding, giving me the space I needed in the family.

'Everything will be all right,' I said. 'You'll see.'

It was only after I'd dropped Selina off that I realised I'd said the same thing that Leo had said to me the day before.

Looking Up, Looking In

Selina's rebellion did shake things up. Although James was acting the concerned yet tolerant older brother, Lady Fitzwilliam found herself duty-bound to scold her wayward daughter in public fairly often. Lady F's face looked so apologetic while she did it though, that anyone could tell that her heart wasn't really in it. Outside of character, the two of them were often together and it was obvious that Lady F wasn't holding a grudge against Selina for supposedly making her wardrobe irrelevant.

Isabella, however, really was on the warpath. For one thing, the threat to total historical accuracy gave her the perfect excuse to sequester herself with James for hours before and after the visitors came, and probably during the week, too. It was a good tactic if she did want to revive their relationship: James didn't have time to date, but he'd always have time to discuss Eversley Hall. In costume, she took every opportunity to discuss her betrothal and look down her nose at Selina.

Her battle with me was waged mostly in looks and acid comments, though one time I came back to my locker in the staff room to find that all of my modern clothes were soaking wet, as if they'd been thrown into the fountain. I wasn't going to play into her hands; I borrowed a belt and a denim jacket off Kayleigh and wore my shift as a maxi-dress, as if nothing was wrong. From the way Isabella pretended not to glare at me in the changing room, I knew my suspicions were correct and she'd done it.

It made me even less inclined to let her get the guy in 1814. So I was busy on my little plan. I emailed Reuben, who confirmed he was definitely coming to the ball, and I bought him a ticket at the same time I bought my family's, so nobody would notice the extra one. Then I got down to the serious business of finding out who he could come as. This was where my days as a technical journalist came in handy. I might not know very much about history, but I knew how to do research.

I went down to the British Library for the day to ask some careful questions, and spent the afternoon examining a copy of Cary's *New Itinerary to the Great Roads* to find a list of the family homes of the nobility and gentry in Berkshire in the period. Then, once I had a list of names that I knew didn't correspond to the names on my purloined guest list, I attacked a copy of *The Peerage* for details of the families as they were in 1814. I ended up with two likely candidates: Ernest Edward Barratt, Fifth Earl Addlesborough, and George Fotheringay, Second Baron Fotheringay. They were both unmarried in 1814, and both had houses in Berkshire. Addlesborough had a country residence near Newbury, and Fotheringay had just built a massive family seat outside Sonning. When I dug more, I discovered that Addlesborough married a Miss Jane Smithers in 1816, who appeared to be from America. An

American heiress, probably, which meant that Addlesborough wasn't as loaded as he seemed to be, and so not a good enough prospect to tempt Isabella.

Fotheringay, on the other hand, owned endless coal mines in Wales. Not that he'd get his hands dirty there himself, but they obviously made him a good enough income so that he could build a grand pile in Berkshire. And we all knew what a single man with a handsome fortune was in want of.

He did marry in 1819, someone called Lady Angelica Abbot, but that didn't matter. All I needed was someone rich enough, important enough, and single enough to attract Isabella in 1814. I typed up a brief dossier on George Fotheringay and emailed it to Reuben.

All of this was excellent distraction. So excellent, in fact, that it was the day of Pippi's scan almost before I had any time to worry about it.

★   ★   ★

'Are you all right?' Mum whispered at me for the seventy-eighth time. There wasn't enough space in the waiting room and we were sharing a plastic chair, crammed up against each other. She was soft and smelled of cinnamon. While the hospital itself was a specialised form of torture, this part was actually nice. It was like a cuddle with Mum, the kind I had tried to avoid for such a long time because I thought it would make me break down.

But I wasn't breaking down. 'I'm fine,' I said, and surprisingly, it was true. This hospital didn't actually remind me too much of the hospital in Boston where I'd had my own twenty-week scan. The memory was there, of course, but it was more like an echo than a full-volume shout. Maybe because that hospital had been modern and glossy, whereas this maternity unit was drab and built in the 1960s. Maybe too it was because I was literally surrounded by my family and didn't have time to remember.

The woman at reception had looked surprised when we piled into the waiting room. All five of us: Mum, Dad, of course Pippi, me and Leo. Pippi had insisted. It was as if now that the secret was out of the bag, she'd swung 100 per cent in the opposite direction and had resumed her traditional role as the centre of attention. She now wanted the entire family to know everything about what was going on with her and the baby apart from the identity of the father, who should have been there too.

Leo produced a yellow bag of jelly babies from a pocket in his leather jacket and passed them round. He'd been extremely chipper all morning. A bit unnaturally chipper, to tell the truth, as if he'd had several too many espressos. Maybe he had; he'd been up before me, showered and dressed and sitting at the kitchen-table with his foot tapping underneath it and the radio turned nearly all the way up. As soon as I walked in the room he'd started talking to me. Talking at me, really. He kept up a running commentary on every song that came onto the radio as I made myself a cup of tea and some toast.

'You sure you need that?' I interrupted a story about how when he was a kid he'd thought that Elton John's 'Island Girl' was called 'I Like Girl' which was ironic given Sir Elton's sexuality, though come to think of it, as the song was actually about a prostitute, Leo's interpretation seemed quite sweet and innocent, though not grammatically correct obviously. Leo stopped, a little out of breath, in the middle of reaching for the espresso pot.

'Need what?' he said.

'Another coffee. You're wired.'

'No, it's fine. At this point, coffee is only going to help. Anyway, caffeine doesn't have any effect on me, you know that. I could go to sleep right now if I wanted to. Though I won't, because your dad's going to drive up any minute to take us to the hospital. Oh, listen to that, it's Dirtysweet. I stayed in the same hotel as the lead singer in Chicago once; he had the room right next to me and I thought I wouldn't get any sleep at all because he'd be tossing televisions out of the window and such, but actually he was very quiet and when I walked by the next morning I swear the whole place smelled of lavender. They don't make rock stars the way they used to, do they?'

'Maybe you should stay at home instead of going to the hospital.'

'Home? Why would I do that? Pippi said she wanted me there, so I'll be there.'

'Then maybe you should go out and have a bit of a run round to get rid of some of this energy before Dad turns up.'

413

'Why?'

'You're not exactly a relaxing presence right now.'

'I'm not? Right, I'll go to the shop. Do we need milk?'

We were already all stuffed into the car when he returned, without any milk, and climbed in with us. I was sitting beside him, and his leg kept on bouncing up and down. I put my hand on his knee and pressed down to stop him, and he stayed still, though he was fidgeting and making crackling noises in his pockets. Evidently because he'd filled them full of sweets, to produce now in the waiting room.

Just what he needed on top of all that caffeine — sugar. But Pippi took one and smiled and put it on top of her belly, which was quite prominent now that she wasn't wearing baggy clothes any more to hide it. 'Jelly baby,' she said, smiling, and passed the bag to Dad. When it came to my turn I picked out an orange one because it was my favourite and gave them back to Leo.

The plastic chairs were arranged around all four walls of the waiting area, and they were filled with pregnant women and their partners. We were the only family, and I could feel everyone's eyes on us, especially as Leo produced a bundle of liquorice laces and began to pass them round too. As I took one I caught the eye of a woman sitting across from us. She quickly looked back at her *Woman's Own* magazine.

Staring at the teen mother. Wondering, no doubt, how such a nice middle-class family got

414

itself into such a dilemma. Maybe she thought that I was Pippi's mother, and that teen pregnancy ran in the family. Maybe she thought that we were all red-headed inbred freaks. Except for Leo, with his dark hair and eyes; she probably thought Leo was the father and was thinking disgusting things about a grown man having an affair with a young girl. Choosing to ignore the fact that I'd even briefly thought the same thing myself, I glared at the top of her head, chewing my liquorice lace fiercely.

'She's eighteen,' my mother said to the woman. 'And she's being very sensible. Our house is absolutely stuffed with prenatal vitamins. Did you know that even condoms are only ninety-four to ninety-eight per cent effective?'

The woman blushed furiously. 'I — I didn't, no.'

'Numerically, there is more chance of getting pregnant whilst using a condom than there is matter in an atom,' said my father,

Leo produced a bag of cola bottles.

The woman on the other side of us cleared her throat. 'There's always not having sex,' she said under her breath to her husband.

'Have you ever *been* a teenager, or did you come out, like, already middle-aged?' Pippi asked.

I snorted. *Don't mess with the Woodstocks.*

'Pippi Woodstock?'

Pippi leaped to her feet, half a liquorice lace hanging out of her mouth. 'Come on,' she said to us, and we stood and followed her, en masse, across the waiting room to where the ultrasound technician stood in her white uniform.

'Um,' she said. 'We can only have one person in the room at a time. The father, perhaps?' She glanced at Leo.

He shook his head. 'It's not me. Care for a sweet?'

'No, thanks. Maybe your mother?'

'I want my whole family in with me,' Pippi said.

'It's regulations, we can't do it. Besides, the room isn't big enough.'

'Haven't you read all the stuff about teen pregnancy?' Pippi said. 'I'm a vulnerable youngster who needs all the help and support she can get. But hey, if you'd rather isolate me from my entire support network, that's your choice. I'll just have to go home without finding out whether my baby is healthy or not. Come on, everyone.' She made to walk away.

'Oh, all right then,' said the technician. 'You can all come in. No, thank you,' she said to Leo, who was still holding out a liquorice lace to her. She clocked his dark hair, as opposed to the ginger hordes of Woodstocks. 'Are you actually part of the family?'

'Yes,' said Pippi vehemently, and went into the scanning room, with the rest of us trailing behind her. The technician wasn't joking; there was only enough room for us to squash together, pressing against the wall as Pippi lay down on the padded table and the technician took her place.

I ended up squished between Dad and Leo,

breathing in a mixture of leather jacket, ancient wool and sweets. It had been chilly in the waiting room, but in here, it was stifling, close and warm. I'm not going to think about doing this, I told myself. Not going to think about seeing Clara for the first time, a grey moving shape in a dark pool of shadow. Her tiny limbs, the cord attaching her to me, and how one of her hands had seemed to wave.

I shook my head. I'd just told myself *not* to think about it. Across the tiny room, my mother was holding Pippi's hand, but she caught my eye. 'You all right?' she mouthed. I nodded and pointed back at her, raising my eyebrows. She nodded too. I wondered if she'd had scans for the babies she'd lost. Did they even have scans back then?

On the table, Pippi was having gel squirted on her belly. 'That feels weird,' she said. 'Like warm frogspawn.'

The technician put the bottle of gel back in the warmer and ran the instrument over the swell of Pippi's stomach, pressing down. We all looked away from Pippi's belly and leaned towards the screen. It swarmed with cloudy shapes, indistinguishable and faintly moving, as if someone were trying to show a black-and-white film but hadn't focused the projector properly. I held my breath. And then, all at once, there was a baby.

The round dome of its head, a snub nose and pouted mouth in profile, a curved white ridge of spine. It appeared and then went out of focus, and then the technician moved something and it

417

appeared again. Inside my sister, inside her baby, a heart throbbed like a small flickering light.

I heard my father drawing in a deep breath of wonder. I leaned forward. I'd thought this was going to be hard. But that black-and-white image wasn't Clara. This was another baby, my sister's baby, my niece or nephew. Someone new, an empty slate, a completely fresh beginning. The pure wonder of life recreating itself.

Two and a half years ago I'd looked at our baby, mine and Leo's, and I'd been happy. It had been a perfect moment. And now looking at this baby, for the first time it occurred to me that even though our happiness had ended, it didn't make that moment any less perfect. Hope and love and innocence could be ruined but they couldn't be destroyed. They would rebirth themselves, moment by moment, life by life.

On the screen, the baby suddenly kicked and Pippi jumped as if she could feel it and my family laughed. Me too.

'That all looks fine,' said the technician, moving the instrument to focus on one part and then another, adjusting her computer to find measurements. 'Do you want to know the sex?'

I noticed, suddenly, that I wasn't pressed up against Leo's leather jacket any more. I turned my head away from the screen and saw that he was leaning back against the wall. In the muted light, his hair was dark and his face completely white, an echo of the ultrasound. He was still holding liquorice laces in one hand.

'Leo, are you all right?' I said. He wiped his forehead with one hand and briefly shook his

418

head. He looked as if he were about to be sick.

'Let's get some air.' I put my hand on his elbow and opened the door. He came with me out into the waiting room, which seemed to have been taken over by two toddlers joyfully scattering magazines on the floor. We went out into the corridor instead.

'Are you all right? Are you going to be sick? I told you you should have given the coffee a miss.'

Leo's face was so pale that the veins under his eyes stood out like blue lines; there was a sheen of sweat on his forehead. He shook his head again and walked, quickly now, to the end of the corridor and out through the sliding glass doors of the exit. I went along with him, and he stood, gulping in air, next to a sign saying *NO SMOKING ON HOSPITAL PREMISES*. On the other side of the sign, a man in pyjamas and a wheelchair was rolling a cigarette on his lap. He glanced at us and wheeled himself away.

'Leo, what's the matter?'

'I hate hospitals.' He tried to rub his face with his hand, encountered the liquorice laces, and threw them into a nearby bin. 'My mother died in this hospital.'

'Oh.'

'Clara died in a hospital.'

'Yes.'

'I hate them. They make me feel sick and helpless and worthless.'

I didn't know what to say. I wasn't sure how I'd managed my 'yes' just now. I wanted to touch Leo, as you'd touch anybody who was hurting

419

and sick. But I couldn't.

Five minutes ago I'd been thinking about joy. And now, I knew that if I touched him I would have to feel what he was feeling, have to share the helplessness and worthlessness and the image of our child hooked up to tubes to help her breathe and eat.

'I know you hated me for not visiting her,' he said to me. 'You were at her bedside every day and I hated myself for not being there too. I just couldn't see her, Alice. It felt like — it felt like if I didn't see her, then it wasn't real. She wouldn't die. But I think I told myself that because I was too much of a coward to do what you did.'

'Why . . . ' I began, but my throat had closed itself up and I had to clear it and start again. 'Why didn't you tell me you felt like this?'

'How could I tell you that I was a coward? How could I do that and still live with myself? No. I told myself it was better if I stayed away.' He leaned against the hospital wall, shoving his hands in the pockets of his jacket. I could hear the rustle of more sweet packets. 'Why would you want me there anyway? I was a failure. I couldn't help. Do you know what I did while you were in the hospital with our daughter? Every one of those six days and nights?'

'Went to bars and parties, I assumed.'

He let out a bark of laughter that sounded nothing like the Leo I knew. 'The bars and the parties came later, when it was too late. While Clara was in the hospital, I walked. I walked all over Boston, all the places I'd ever been before and everywhere else, too. I brought along a can

420

to tag buildings. That's what I'd done when my mum was in hospital. I put my tag all over Brickham when she was dying, and I did the same thing in Boston. If I could claim the city, if I could make it mine by walking over it and seeing it all and putting my signature on it, then I'd have done something. Every night I made my tag bigger. I'd bring a backpack of paints with me and I found walls to cover with painting. But I knew it wouldn't help. It hadn't helped Mum and it wouldn't help Clara. I knew deep down that I was trying to run away from my own failure and I couldn't see you because every time I did, it reminded me of that. And then when it was finished, when she was gone, I wanted something back. Some happiness, some life. That's when the bars and parties started.'

'I didn't know.'

'Every day,' he said to me, though he wasn't looking at me, he was looking at the car park, the tops of the red and blue and silver cars, all of them empty. 'Every day since then I've hated myself for what I did to both of you. And to me, too.'

'You said it was because I pushed you away.'

'You did push me away. But I can't blame you for it.' He pulled out the bags of sweets from his pockets and began to toss them into the bin. 'I thought I could handle this, and now I've ruined an important day for your family.'

I caught a bag of wine gums mid-air. 'Hey, don't take it out on the treats.'

'Distractions. It's always about distractions with me. As if sweets were going to distract anybody. Fucking pathetic. And now I'm making you listen to my self-indulgent list of failures instead of letting you be with your sister.'

'It's okay. You didn't ruin it for us. Here, keep these — Pippi will probably want them when she comes out.' I gave him the bag of wine gums. For a second, before I let go of the bag, our eyes met.

That was the new thing in Leo's face, the way he'd changed. Sadness. It was in the leanness of his body, in the darkness of his eyes. I hadn't seen it before because I didn't want to.

And now that I'd seen it, it made me . . .

How did it make me feel? I felt sorry for him. And that made me angry. Why should I have to deal with his sadness when he'd never dealt with mine? Why should I understand him when he'd run away instead of trying to help me?

Or was I being a coward, as much as he had been?

This was what I'd wanted: for Leo to admit he'd been wrong. To admit he'd cared. I'd thought it would make me feel better.

It didn't.

I let him have the sweets and balled my hands up in my own jumper. 'I don't want to bring this all back,' I said. 'I want to move forward and be happy for my sister.'

'It's what I wanted to do too. But it's there, Alice. The more we push it away the more it's going to want to come out in the open. Our daughter died and we need to talk about it at some point.'

'It won't do any good. What's happened has happened.'

'That sounds like the same rationalisation I

gave myself for not being with Clara. It didn't work.'

Nothing works. I pulled my jumper closer around myself and looked at the cars, at the smoking bloke, at the sign, at the bicycles locked in the plastic shed. Anywhere but at Leo, because if we talked about this any more I was going to look like he did. Sick and sad and as if he'd made the biggest mistake of his life and knew he could never ever take it back.

Or I might be tempted to take him into my arms. And look where that had got us last time. Absolutely nowhere.

'And you know the funny thing?' he said, though his voice was raw and not laughing at all. 'Those paintings I did on the buildings, while Clara was in hospital, they're what started it all for me. They're what got me noticed. And I have to think of that. Every fucking time.'

I bit my lip. 'Leo . . . '

The glass hospital doors slid open and Pippi came out, peering around. 'Oh, there you are.' She skipped over to us, throwing an arm around my shoulders and Leo's waist. 'Oh my God, that was so amazing! Did you see? Did you see what I'm having?'

'The lady said she wasn't completely sure,' said Mum, following. 'She said unless she actually sees a penis, she can't be one hundred per cent.'

'So did she see a penis, or not?' I asked, my head whirling from the change of mood.

'No, she didn't see anything. I'm having a girl — isn't that cool?'

423

'Another Woodstock female,' said Mum. 'We've got strong X chromosomes in this family.'

'That's very cool,' I said to Pippi.

'And that means we can buy lots of pink clothes! She was so beautiful, wasn't she? Absolutely perfect. I can't wait to meet her. Are those wine gums for me? I'm starving.'

'Yes, they're for you,' said Leo, handing the bag to her. I dared to look at him; some of the colour had come back into his face, and he was smiling at Pippi. Probably nobody but me could see that he was having to force it.

'How are you feeling?' Mum asked him. 'You looked a little unwell back there.'

'It was stuffy. This jacket is quite warm. I'm fine.'

'Well, I'm *freezing*,' said Pippi through a mouthful of sweets. Leo took off his jacket and draped it over her shoulders. It hung off her slender frame and made her look even younger. She immediately stuck her hands in the pockets to hunt for more sweets.

'You should eat some proper food, Pippi,' Mum said.

'Can we go for pizza? I really fancy some.'

'Let's all go for pizza,' Dad said.

★ ★ ★

I didn't want to understand why Leo had stayed away from Clara in the hospital. I didn't want to think about the double pain he must have felt from the memory of his mother dying, too. I didn't want to remember how sick and sad he'd

424

looked outside the hospital doors.

If I understood him, I couldn't stay angry with him. I couldn't resent him. I couldn't blame him. I'd have no reason at all not to let him come close to me.

And if he came close to me, I'd have to talk with him about Clara. I'd have to understand all the depth of feeling he had, too, on top of everything I felt. I'd have to touch his grief. I'd have to relive it.

I didn't think I could deal with that. They weren't only his grief and his failures; they were mine, too. He blamed himself for not helping me, but I hadn't helped him, either. We'd both isolated ourselves in our own little bubbles of unhappiness. Maybe if we hadn't — maybe if we'd been able to open up, let each other in, we'd still be together now. Maybe we'd have begun to gather some new happiness.

Or maybe not. Maybe we'd been waiting to fall apart from the beginning.

I didn't want to have to make choices about Leo any more. I had a new life, now. It was one thing to pretend to be living in the past, and quite another to actually revisit it. You couldn't edit the real past, or change it.

But what would have been the point of all those moments of joy, if I never looked back at them? Wasn't it wrong never to think about Clara, to hide all traces of her away under my bed with my failed novel? You didn't do that to someone you loved.

I'd loved Clara. And I'd loved Leo, too.

When I was safe in my room, I got down on

my knees. I reached underneath my bed, past the dust bunnies, and took out the box.

It wasn't the cardboard box that held the pages of my unpublished, unfinished novel. It was a big round box, with flowers on it. It had originally held a teapot that Leo had bought me for our first anniversary. The top was dull with dust. I brushed it with my hand and then wiped my hand on my jeans. It left a grey smear, but the flowers on the box were brighter now. As bright as the day Leo had given it to me, in a Boston September when we'd been happy. I didn't know where the teapot was. I'd left it behind, as I'd left almost everything behind except for my favourite books and my clothes and this box. Leo had probably sold it, or given it away, or left it behind himself. Another thing, like his motorcycle, that used to mean something and was now gone.

We'd left Clara behind there too. Her ashes, scattered in the sea. It had been my mother's idea, and I hadn't had the energy to think of anything else to do.

This flowery box wasn't important. It was what was inside it. A nurse had given it to me, on the afternoon when I left the neonatal ICU. 'We find these things are sometimes useful to help to remember,' she'd said to me.

I don't need things to help me remember, I had thought at the time. I need something to help me forget.

But I took what she gave me and I brought it to our flat and I put it inside the prettiest box I could find, along with some other things I couldn't bear to look at or to throw away. Then when I came back to Brickham I put the box under my bed and I hadn't touched it since.

I sat on my bed and put my hand on the lid. I felt this box's presence, sometimes, when I was lying in bed. I could picture it with my eyes shut, even though I never looked at it. I'd even pictured the dust. It had sat there for two years. Did I want to open it up? Did I want to remember?

Faintly, downstairs, I could hear a radio playing. Leo was in the house. He said he'd come back to Brickham to make peace with the past. Whereas I'd always found it much easier to have the pain hidden under this bed.

But it hadn't been hidden, had it? I'd always known it was here.

'To help to remember,' I murmured, and I took off the lid.

The photographs were loose in a pile on top. First was the scan picture, black and white on curling paper. It didn't look the same as Pippi's picture, the one she'd carried around and shown to the waiter at the pizza place this afternoon. This picture was blurred in more places, as if Clara had moved while it was being taken. You could see a perfect foot and the curve of her shoulder. She was facing away, into the darkness of the womb.

I'd seen that as a good sign, I remembered. 'She's got a mind of her own,' I'd said to the technician; Leo hadn't been there. He'd had some kind of appointment, I couldn't remember what it was now, but I did remember being cheesed off with him for finding something more important than seeing his child for the first time.

Now I wondered if it was because he didn't trust himself at a hospital. If he was afraid he'd freak out. Or spoil the moment.

He'd pored over the photo when I'd brought it home. He'd asked me to point out every feature, and then stuck it on the wall over the derelict fireplace in our living room. I turned over the photo; it still had a trace of Blu-Tack on the back of it.

I put it down on the bed beside me and took out the next photograph. I was watering a Swiss-cheese plant. Being pregnant had made me feel like enough of an earth mother to buy a pot plant. You could see my slightly rounded belly, one shoulder and one arm, and my face looking back over my shoulder to grin at Leo, who held the camera.

The plant hadn't lasted. I remembered it as withered twigs. I turned quickly to the next photo. I was on the Common in Leo's overcoat, walking through the snow. I had unlaced boots and the winter light in my hair, which looked as bright as a flame. I was reaching out to the camera and saying something. I couldn't remember what. Probably something unimportant, something fleeting, some part of our life together.

Leo liked to catch me unaware with the camera, in the middle of doing something, in the middle of a conversation or deep in thought. Sometimes I didn't even know he'd taken a photo until I saw the print. 'It's how I see you,' he told me when I protested at his stealth methods. 'If I tell you I'm going to take it, you pose. If I just snap it, I get the real you.'

In this one everything was white and my hair looked like a beacon. I was beautiful.

I leafed through the other photos. Wedding photos, where Leo never let go of my hand. Pictures of us exploring our new city together, one of me typing on my Mac, back to the camera and a pen holding up my hair. A lot of them were of me in various states of pregnancy: in pants and bra, with belly barely swollen; in one of Leo's T-shirts, painting the kitchen shelves; back in time to me holding the pregnancy test, beaming and pointing at the little blue plus sign in the plastic window. The last one was one of the latest, taken of both of us by a friend in a restaurant where we'd had dinner one evening. Leo's beer and my orange juice rubbed shoulders on the table. Leo had his arm around me, his other hand on my belly. I remembered how, right before Abraham had pressed the button, Leo had leaned over and blown into my ear. I was laughing and his lips were pursed, in the act of kissing my cheek.

I could feel his lips on my face, the tingle of his breath in my ear; I could hear the conversation at the other tables, the buzz of traffic outside. I could taste the orange juice on my lips. Clara kicking her daddy's hand.

None of it posed. All of it real.

All of it months, or days, from ending.

The smaller box lay underneath the photographs. I put them on the bed with the scan, a series of glossy moments, to reveal the box. It was square, about the size of a shoe box, and covered with pictures of teddy bears. There was a pink ribbon around it.

I took it out of the bigger box and held it in my hand. It was light. I remembered it as being heavier, when the nurse had given it to me. Maybe everything had felt heavier then. But it seemed such a small thing, such a slight container for all that was left of my baby. I remembered I'd thought, How American, when I'd seen the teddy bears. As if noticing the cultural differences would make it more distant.

I swallowed.

What could there be in this box that I didn't know already? A lock of hair that I'd touched, the print of a foot that I'd held?

I didn't want to know what was in it. But there was someone who hadn't been there during her short life. Who hated himself for it.

I put the smaller box back inside the bigger one and laid the photographs on top of it before I put the top back on. Then I went downstairs to the first floor. Leo was in his bedroom; the door was slightly ajar, and I could hear the radio through it. It was playing Aerosmith, 'Walk This Way'.

I looked at the box, and then at the door. Maybe he'd left it open for me. I knocked.

I heard him get up from the bed. When he opened the door, he was running his hand through his hair where it had been flattened by the pillow. 'I was taking a nap,' he said, yawning. 'Are you all right, Mermaid?'

I held out the box.

'This has been under my bed for two years. I thought you might want to see it.'

I saw him recognise it as the box from the teapot. Then I saw him realise what might be in it. He reached out his hands and I put the box in them.

'I don't want to talk about her yet,' I told him. 'I'm not ready. But I love our daughter too much to pretend she didn't exist. She's too important to forget or to run away from. That's why I want you to have this.'

He held my gaze with his for a long moment. I saw the questions in his eyes. *Do you forgive me? Do you understand?*

I looked straight back. He must have found some answer there, because he nodded, and looked back down at the box, feeling its slight weight in his hands.

'Thank you,' he said.

'It all belongs to you too,' I said. And went back upstairs, leaving Leo with our memories.

New Clothes

'It's of blond lace embroidered with silver, over a salmon-pink petticoat. The body is silver, trimmed round the top with a quilling of blond, edged with silver. The sleeves are short and full, of blond lace secured by silver ornament, with silver cord and large tassels tied on the side in long loops and streamers.' Lady Fitzwilliam pronounced each word as if they were precious pearls. 'As described in *Ackermann's Repository* this month. The gown is upstairs, if you wish to see it.'

'I really do,' replied Valerie, the Fashion Editor. I knew it was Valerie because, to my astonishment, she'd actually rung me three days before to tell me that *Hot! Hot!* was planning a feature on Regency-revival fashion as a tie-in with my columns, and that she was turning up at Eversley Hall with a photographer on the Sunday morning. He'd been snapping away from the minute he'd entered the Drawing Room, taking in Lady Fitzwilliam's morning dress, Isabella's gown and Arthur's elaborately tied cravat. Lady Fitzwilliam was positively preening.

'It is truly wonderful to meet someone with an eye for fashion,' she said now.

'And what are *you* going to wear to the ball?' Valerie asked Selina, who was standing near the window.

'Oh. It's white silk, with a flower on the sash. It's very pretty.'

'Not that you deserve a new gown, after the way you've disappointed your family,' Lady Fitzwilliam said to her, with a smile that belied her words.

'Perhaps she's hoping to catch herself a better husband than my brother,' Isabella said archly.

'No,' said Selina. 'I just want to dance. I've been practising. It's fun.'

'You had better hope that someone will take pity upon you and ask you, then,' said Isabella. 'I am sure my brother will not.'

'You're wrong there,' said Arthur. 'Of course I'll dance with Selina. No reason not to. And I'll dance with you, I hope, and Miss Woodstock as well. Bound to be no one prettier in the room than the three of you.'

'I'll dance with her too,' said James. 'Merely because a young lady has flown in the face of her family's wishes for her, and persists in being headstrong and wilful, is no reason why she shouldn't enjoy a dance.'

'But you're engaged to dance with me, James,' Isabella reminded him.

'I have promised you the first dance, Isabella, but I will also dance with my sister and my cousin.'

'Miss Woodstock,' Isabella said to me in feigned surprise, 'I had no idea that you intended to dance. How delightful that you think it appropriate to join our party, despite your mourning.'

Valerie turned to me. 'Aren't you allowed to dance?'

'Alice promised me that she'll dance,' Selina

433

said quickly. 'If it isn't appropriate, it's my fault. I asked her specifically.'

'I had planned to dance, yes,' I said. 'I know I'm still in mourning, but I don't think my parents would have objected.'

'How very independent-minded of you, to flout convention,' murmured Isabella. 'And you have, no doubt, also had a new gown made for yourself?'

'I have not,' I said quietly. Isabella didn't bother to hide her triumphant smile.

'Black is very now,' Valerie said to me.

'Very 1814?'

'Actually, you sort of remind me of Kate Bush and Stevie Nicks — that whole Gothic-Romantic look? All that is coming back now.'

The photographer trained his lens on me for the first time. I resisted the impulse to toss my head back and start singing about *Wuthering Heights*. Instead I turned to James.

'I have a request of you, Cousin,' I said.

'Believe me, I haven't forgotten your last request,' he replied. 'I've invited no fewer than three bachelors who do not live in Grosvenor Square to the ball, as potential husbands. You may have your pick.'

'I'm very grateful. May I invite one more?'

'Whom do you want to invite?' asked Selina.

'On the lookout for new dance partners?' Isabella asked her sweetly.

'No,' said Selina. 'I'm curious. I didn't think Alice knew anyone.'

'I have one or two acquaintances up my sleeve.'

434

James looked interested. 'Please don't tell me that you've already found yourself a husband without my help. My feelings will be hurt.'

'Oh no, nothing like that. If I become engaged, you will be the first to know.'

'You are certainly welcome to invite anyone that you choose.'

'Is it perhaps the gardener's cousin? Or the kitchen maid's brother?' asked Isabella.

I resisted the urge to roll my eyes at her. Leave it to her to get all snobby about my friendship with the people playing servants.

'It is a gentleman of my acquaintance,' I said.

'He would be very welcome, if my stepmother doesn't mind.'

'Of course you should invite anyone you like, Alice,' Lady Fitzwilliam said. 'We shall be glad to meet him.'

'I'd like to take some shots outside,' said the photographer. 'Maybe of the gentlemen.'

'Certainly,' said James. 'We can go through the Saloon.' He and Arthur went out, accompanied by the photographer. And, of course, Isabella, who considered herself joined at the hip with James. The three of us were left with Valerie and a handful of tourists.

'May we give it to her now?' Selina asked Lady Fitzwilliam.

'I don't see why not.'

Selina did a little dance and clapped her hands.

'What are you talking about?' I asked.

Lady Fitzwilliam went to a cabinet on the far side of the room, underneath an oil painting of a lady eating grapes. She took out a large, flattish package wrapped in brown paper.

'Selina and I thought it was time for this,' she said, and gave it to me. Selina removed a large vase of flowers from a table, so that I could lay it down to open it.

'A gift?'

'It's something you need for the ball,' Selina said. 'Open it!'

I ripped the paper open. Inside was lilac silk and dove-grey lace. I pulled out the gown and it fell in a cascade from my hands.

'It's beautiful,' I said. The waist was trimmed with a purple satin ribbon, and small silver roses were embroidered on the bodice. I held it up to myself. Next to my black dress, it was a riot of quiet colour.

'I did the roses,' said Selina.

'And I chose the style,' said Lady Fitzwilliam. 'Do you like it?'

'I absolutely love it.'

'Lilac and grey are half-mourning,' Lady Fitzwilliam told Valerie. 'The stage before a bereaved person moves back into wearing their normal clothes and leading their normal lives.'

'We thought it was time,' said Selina.

'You're so bright and full of life, Alice,' said Lady F. 'It's easy to forget you've had some sadness. But you have, my dear, haven't you?' She touched my hand with her soft fingers, and looked into my face. I remembered that moment in the car on the way to dancing practice, when I felt she and I had known the same grief.

'I try to forget it here,' I said quietly.

'I think it's time to for some colour, don't you?'

I nodded. I threw my arms around her neck, still holding the dress, and hugged her tight. I hugged Selina, too.

'Thank you,' I told them.

Then I held the dress up to me and spun around, hearing the swish of silk, grinning from ear to ear.

'I can't wait to see how Isabella likes it,' I said.

★ ★ ★

I was singing 'Dancing Queen' to myself as I slipped the key into the door of my house. I pirouetted across the hardwood floors, waved at Mr Allingham, and jetéed into the kitchen.

The first thing I saw was Leo covered in pink.

He had it all over his hands, over his Flaming Lips T-shirt, spattered on his jeans and in his hair. There was a smudge of it on his chin.

'Oh my God,' I said. 'Have you just lost a fight with a fairy princess?'

'Worse. I've been helping Pippi paint the baby's room.' He reached into the fridge and took out two bottles of Orangina. He tossed one to me. Against all odds, I caught it.

'She's obsessed with pink. Light pink walls with dark pink flowers all over them. If it gets out that I did this, my artistic integrity is going to be ruined for ever.'

'It's a funny world where painting a baby's bedroom can ruin a reputation built on illegal vandalism.' I twisted open my bottle and took a long drink. Leo pulled out a chair at the table, but he didn't sit down.

'You're in a good mood,' he said.

'I had a good day.'

'This historical re-enactment stuff really floats your boat, doesn't it?'

'Yup.'

'Can I say something without it ruining your good mood?'

'Today, yes, you probably can.' I twirled the bottle top on the table, making it do a little dance.

'Thanks for giving me the box.'

'You're welcome.'

'Does it mean you've forgiven me?'

'Don't push your luck.'

He laughed. 'I'm getting Chinese food and a mindless action flick. Want some?'

'Yup.'

'Why are you so happy?'

'Because I'm not covered in pink. And I got a new dress today. And I'm getting better.'

He stopped, mid-lift of his Orangina to his mouth. 'Better?'

I hadn't meant to say that out loud. I hadn't even known I'd been thinking it. But now that I had, I might as well finish. 'For example, a few weeks ago, the idea of Pippi painting a nursery for a baby that hasn't even been born yet would probably have sent me over the edge.'

'It's like tempting fate,' Leo agreed. 'I've been thinking that. But — '

'But Pippi is Pippi, and she's different from us. There's absolutely no reason to think that anything is going to go wrong with her pregnancy. And it would be mean to want to spoil her anticipation. Even if something does go wrong, which it won't, and even if having a baby is harder than she thinks it will be, which it will be — why shouldn't she have this joy right now? You've got to take happiness where you can get it. I've lived too long without it to begrudge it to anyone else.'

'Or yourself?'

'Liv will tell you — she probably has told you already. I've been living like a hermit for the past two years. I've hardly been out of this house and I haven't dared write anything that would make me think or feel in any way. But I'm not like that any more. I feel as if . . . ' I thought of what Lady Fitzwilliam had said ' . . . as if I've been hiding away in mourning for too long, and now it's time to get out and actually live.'

'And this Regency stuff has done this for you,' Leo said. Quietly, and more sombrely than his pink decoration, and my announcement, would seem to warrant.

'Yeah. It has. I like the person I am in 1814. I sort of feel that I can start to be more like her in real life now. It's like the rebirth of Alice Woodstock.' I smiled at him.

'So you *have* forgiven me.'

'That depends.'

'On what?'

'On whether or not you're paying for the Chinese.' I jumped up and grabbed a menu from a drawer, and dropped it into his hand before I went, whistling, up the stairs to change.

The Ball

Faithful Readers, the Eversley Hall Ball is this weekend. This might not sound like such a big deal, when you compare it to mega-events of the summer like Wimbledon and the Notting Hill Carnival, but you have to remember that here in 1814 the world is smaller. You can't travel for miles to camp out in a field with thousands of other people, unless of course you're in the Army and your idea of fun is getting killed, and even that option is tricky now that Napoleon's been temporarily defeated. You live in a restricted circle of family, friends and acquaintances, all of whom have to be of the correct social class. A ball is one of the most exciting ways you can meet new people. It's also one of the few socially acceptable ways for single men and women to engage in physical contact.

Anything can happen. You could meet the person who will change your life for ever. A single dance, an overheard remark, could alter everything.

Plus, if you're lucky, you get to wear a really nice gown (see pages 67 to 73 of this week's Hot! Hot! magazine).

At Eversley Hall, things have been going crazy for weeks now. Samuel the gardener has been spending every spare minute, when he's not sneaking off with Lucy the kitchen maid, getting the garden ready for night-time visitors. Mrs

Collins and her team in the kitchen have been cooking up a storm to produce a feast of Regency food and drink. (Personally I'm looking forward to trying ratafia.) Out of tourist hours, they're being assisted by lots of modern-day people cooking and cleaning and setting up and planning and doing such un-1814 things as ensuring emergency access and Porta-loos and everything else that I, Miss Alice Woodstock, couldn't possibly be expected to know about or understand.

Me . . . I have an amazing gown. I've been practising my dancing at every available opportunity. For good measure, I've also been obsessively watching the Netherfield Ball scenes in the various versions of Pride and Prejudice. I'm engaged for one dance with Arthur Grantham, and one dance with James Fitzwilliam. I'm sure you know which one I'm looking forward to most.

My real-life family are also turning up, which might be a little bit weird. They won't be in Regency costume; the ball is open to members of the public. (Though I'm sorry — all the tickets are sold out already. Went faster than tickets to Glastonbury this year. Apparently ball gowns and the 'Duke of Kent's Waltz' are the new rock 'n' roll.) Of course we've always had people in modern dress in Eversley Hall, as visitors and support staff, but this is the first time I'll have to pretend not to know my own mother, father and sister. No anachronisms allowed, remember, and I'm supposed to be a lonely orphan.

Come to think of it, being allowed not to

441

know my family is one of my teenage dreams coming true.

There are also the proper guests, most of whom are members of various historical re-enactment societies, or Regency scholars and enthusiasts, who will be turning up in full regalia to be part of the show. We have specialist musicians to provide entertainment, military historians to talk about the Napoleonic Wars, trained livery-clad servants to ensure that everyone remains well fed and watered from the greeting glass of champagne to the elegant supper at the peak of the evening.

James Fitzwilliam has been working every hour God sends to make sure everything goes exactly according to plan, to fulfil his passionate dream. I'll leave you to decide whether I find that behaviour to be attractively heroic or not.

Personally, I don't think everything is going to go exactly to plan. Why not? Well, that's for me to know . . . and you to find out.

★　★　★

'It's like Fairyland,' sighed Selina, spinning around on the grass in her white dress. 'I can't believe how beautiful it is.'

'I can,' I said. Lanterns sparkled from tree branches, and every window of Eversley Hall was lit up. For health and safety reasons I knew that the lighting was all electric, but it had been selected to mimic candlelight, bathing everything in a warm yellow glow. In the dusk, the flowers growing in the garden were ethereal fogs of

442

colour. The splash of the fountain mingled with the murmur of conversation and the musicians tuning their instruments in the Saloon. 'It's exactly the way I pictured it.'

'Well, you have a better imagination than I do.' Selina linked arms with me and we started back to the house, where we were supposed to be, to greet guests. 'You look fantastic. I love your hair.'

'My sister Pippi did it. She'll be here tonight.'

'That's cool, I'd love to meet your family. Are they the mysterious people you said you invited?'

'No, they're not mysterious at all. You'll know them the minute you see them.'

'It's great they could come. I wish my parents could have — but it's too far for them, all the way from Cumbria.' She sighed. 'It's probably just as well. They don't want to see me tripping over my own feet and they would have a conniption fit if they knew I was acting all rebellious.'

'Have you talked with them about what you're going to do this autumn?'

'I don't know myself, to be honest. It's probably easiest if I go back and finish my course and work at the hotel.'

'If you wanted to do the easiest thing, you'd be on the verge of announcing your engagement to Arthur Grantham.'

She fiddled with the flowers in her hair. 'Are you looking forward to your dance with James?'

'Maybe a little.'

'Or is it the mysterious man who's making your cheeks so pink?'

'It's probably sunburn.' I put my hand on the

open French door into the Saloon.

'Alice! Yoo-hooo, Alice!'

'Speak of the devil,' I said, and turned to see my family making their way towards the house, cutting across the lawn from the car park. Mum was waving her hands at me, and Dad and Pippi followed close behind. Pippi was beginning to have the pregnant woman waddle; it was more pronounced from a distance. She wore my cream dress. Of course.

'Welcome to Eversley Hall, madam, sir, miss,' I said politely to them as they approached.

'Oh that's right, you're not supposed to know us, are you?' Pippi said.

'If you enter via the front door, Munson the butler will assist you, and you will meet your host and hostess. Do you dance, sir?' I asked my father.

He narrowed his eyes, as if trying to remember. 'I'm not sure.'

'Your dress is gorge,' said Pippi. 'And the hair's held up well.'

'Thank you, miss, I had some assistance from a talented coiffeuse. May I present Miss Selina Fitzwilliam, madam?'

Selina bowed.

'Oh, yes, it's lovely to meet you,' Mum said. 'Alice has said so much about you. Why are young girls so slender these days?' She turned to me. 'You sound just like someone out of a book. I knew you'd be good at this. And you look beautiful. Proud of you.' She kissed me on the cheek. 'Come on, you lot, let's get inside — and Pippi, no trying to sneak any champagne, missy.

444

I'm watching you.' She bustled my family into the Saloon.

'They seem really nice,' Selina said, sotto voce.

'You'll have to come round for dinner so my mother can stuff you full of food and talk your ears off. Next week?'

'Definitely.' We went into the Saloon together. It looked as stunning as the garden. The carpet and most of the furniture had been removed, to give space for the dancing; the emptiness made the room seem larger and even grander, and brought attention to the silk-covered walls and the elaborate plasterwork on the ceiling and around the doors. There were occasional chairs of the non-irreplaceable variety scattered against the walls, to give guests a place to sit out a dance. Huge flower arrangements filled the air with the scents of lilies and roses. The large mirror over the fireplace reflected the gowns and plumage of the Regency upper class, and the liveried waiters carrying around trays of glasses.

We crossed through into the Hall, where James stood greeting guests along with Lady Fitzwilliam. Munson was stationed nearby, issuing programmes for the evening. I allowed myself a moment of pure appreciation of James. He wore white satin knee-breeches and a blue long-tailed coat, with snow-white waistcoat, shirt and neck-cloth, spotless gloves, white stockings and glossy black shoes. It was simple, tasteful and perfect, and he'd never looked so handsome.

Too bad Isabella was hanging on to him for dear life. She was absolutely resplendent in a crimson and gold gown and what looked, from here, like real pearls in her hair and at her throat.

'Of course, she feels that as the future mistress of Eversley Hall, it's her duty to help greet the guests,' I said.

'She's dancing the first dance with James too.' Selina giggled suddenly. 'Do you want to go over and let him see you in your new dress? I can lure Isabella away if you want.'

'How? She doesn't look as if an earthquake could shift her.'

'Oh, I've got my ways. Watch and learn, Cousin Alice.' I stepped back a little into the doorway as Selina crossed the Saloon. She greeted everyone she met, exchanging civil words with several guests and re-enactors, and plucked a glass of champagne from a tray carried by Munson, with a charming smile for him.

That girl. When she came out of her shell, she did it right. That said, it was probably a good thing that we still had another three weeks of the season to go, before she went back home. Maybe the confidence she gained from being her own woman in 1814 and in Eversley Hall could help her stand up to her parents. But it was one thing to be brave when you were pretending to be someone else, and quite another to do it in real life.

As I watched, Selina reached her pretend family and joined them to welcome guests, on the other side of Isabella from James. Many people had made efforts towards Regency costume, especially the women. I suspected there were a lot of bridesmaid dresses getting a rare outing. I recognised Arthur's real-life parents, whom I'd met at dancing practice, greeted warmly by their friend Lady Fitzwilliam. His father wore the red coat and tall hat of a military re-enactor. There was a definite family resemblance.

Selina curtseyed and the glass of champagne in her hand tipped, spilling liquid over Isabella's glove.

I couldn't hear their conversation from here, but I could fill in the blanks by Isabella's sharp look and Selina's apologetic face. They spoke rapidly to each other for a moment and then Isabella swept past the guests and up the stairs, with Selina following her. Evidently Isabella was off to repair the damage quickly before she had to dance in wet gloves. Selina glanced back over her shoulder and winked at me.

And that was my chance. I immediately made my way over to the Fitzwilliams. James caught my eye as I approached and I saw him look at me from the crown of my head to the hem of my gown.

'Alice,' he greeted me, holding out his hand to guide me gently to his side, where Isabella had been standing. 'Allow me to present you to the Mayor of Brickham, Mrs Jan Morris, and her husband Mr Ian Morris. This is my cousin, Miss Alice Woodstock.'

'The writer,' said the Mayor, smiling at me. She was wearing the fur-trimmed red robe, heavy gold chain and tricorn hat of her office, and hardly looked out of place at all. 'Yes, I've enjoyed your pieces about Eversley Hall.'

I couldn't actually respond to that, as the Miss

Alice Woodstock I was being at the moment wasn't a writer, but I smiled, bowed my head and said, 'Lady Mayor.'

'Oh no, not Lady, just Jan is fine. We think you're doing wonderful work here, James, with attracting people to the local area. And Eversley Hall is so impressive.'

She said more, but I'd stopped listening because I saw the next person after her in the queue of people waiting to be greeted at the door: Reuben Rogers, the film director and my own personal guest. He was wearing velvet knee breeches and a green velvet cutaway coat over a gold satin waist-coat — flamboyant next to James's austere blue and white. His goatee wasn't quite period, either. But he looked rather dashing, and quite hand-some. Like an eccentric, insanely rich, intensely eligible Baron.

'Lord Fotheringay!' I said, reaching out my hands for his. He smiled at me and took my hands, kissing me on either cheek.

'Alice,' he said. 'This place certainly suits you. Thank you for inviting me.'

'I'm so glad you could come. Allow me to intro-duce you to my cousin, Mr James Fitzwilliam, and his stepmother, Lady Fitzwilliam. This is George, second Baron Fotheringay.'

James raised an eyebrow and bowed. 'It's an honour to meet a friend of my cousin's, Lord Fotheringay.'

'The honour is all mine. This is a wonderful house.'

'Lord Fotheringay has recently built a country house outside of Sonning,' I told James.

448

'Is that so,' he said, glancing between me and Reuben. The Mayor had paused and was looking at Reuben too.

'Aren't you — ' she began.

'George Fotheringay, at your service, madam.' He bowed low over her hand. He'd been watching a lot of movies, evidently, to get the manners right. Though it was his job, I supposed.

'Would you care to take a turn with me and see the house?' I asked him.

'I'd be delighted.'

I put my hand on Reuben's arm and we moved across the room together. I was thinking as we walked. We wouldn't be able to discuss anything in private indoors; the whole place was packed. We might get a chance outside though, if we were lucky. I led him through the Saloon and out of the French doors into the garden.

'Thank you so much for coming tonight,' I said to him, taking a flute of champagne for him from a passing waiter.

'Thanks for inviting me. This is incredible. I wish I'd brought a cameraman with me.'

'Shh!' I raised my finger to my lips. 'No anachronism allowed, sir.'

'Oh. Right. Of course. Where's the young lady you were telling me about?'

'She had an accident with her gloves and some champagne.'

'Oh my God, you look fabulous! Can I take a photo of you two?'

I paused, my hand on Reuben's arm and a smile on my face, while the large woman who'd accosted us clicked her digital camera. Then I nodded to her and we continued on our way.

'Does that happen to you all the time?' Reuben asked in an undertone.

'Yes, and you have to pretend that — oh crikey, quick — duck behind this statue, it's that Rosemary Phipps.'

We stood behind a plinth until the costume expert had wandered off.

'Does *that* happen to you all the time?' Reuben asked.

'Thank heavens, very rarely. Let's try over here.' We rounded the corner of the house, only to see a large group of people posing for a camera holding bottles of champagne and cheering. They wore T-shirts saying *Austen Kicks Ass!*.

'Some sort of appreciation society,' I said.

'There isn't a whole lot of privacy around here.'

'Tell me about it.'

'Ladies and gentlemen,' called Munson's voice from the house. 'If you will please take your places for the Grand March.'

'Do you have to go?'

'I'm supposed to — wait! You can dance with me. If we get to the bottom of the set, we should be able to talk for a few minutes.' Something else struck me. 'Can you dance?'

'Miss Woodstock, is that any question to ask a Baron?'

'Being a Baron doesn't have much to do with it, I'm afraid.'

Reuben merely smiled and held out his gloved

hand. 'Trust me,' he said.

I put mine into it, biting my lip, and we went into the Saloon, where couples were beginning to gather. It was quite a sight: there must have been thirty couples, all in satin and lace, brass and feathers. We slipped in next to Selina and Arthur.

'The Grand March is a few turns around the room,' I whispered to Reuben. 'It's to show off our finery, basically. Then there are two longways dances. They'll be called; all you have to do is listen to the person with the microphone.'

'Microphone? That's not very 1814.'

'You have to make some compromises with authenticity when there are guests here. In 1814 they might not have called the dances at all.'

The music began and the couples moved forward in procession. I craned my neck to see where Isabella and James were, near the front.

I hoped Reuben could dance, or at least follow instructions. If he made a spectacle of himself, Isabella wouldn't even deign to notice him. My plan could crash and burn within fifteen minutes of Reuben turning up at Eversley Hall.

'Sorry,' Selina said to me, 'Isabella had a spare pair of gloves. She was all hot to get back in time for the first dance.'

'It's fine,' I told her. 'You did a wonderful job. Lord Fotheringay, this is Miss Selina Fitzwilliam and Mr Arthur Grantham.'

'Charmed,' said Reuben.

'Nice waistcoat,' said Arthur.

'Likewise.'

'Good luck dancing,' I said to Selina.

451

'I'm going to need it.'

The music began and she quickly snapped to attention. The poor girl, dancing for the first time in front of an audience. At least she had Arthur, who knew what he was doing. But I couldn't spare another moment to see how she was coping because I had to begin to dance for the first time in front of an audience myself.

Fortunately, the Grand March was pretty easy. We began to walk through the centre of the room. I tried to do it gracefully.

'So who's the lady you want me to meet?' Reuben murmured.

'She's the blonde with James Fitzwilliam. They're going to pass us on the left on their way back around.'

Reuben glanced over. Isabella was talking to James as they marched; his gaze met mine for a moment, and he quirked an eyebrow as they passed.

'Not my type,' said Reuben.

'Really? She's gorgeous. She looks like a movie star.'

'That's the problem. I see enough movie stars on a daily basis. I like a woman who's a little bit more real.'

'It's just for tonight. Then I promise you never have to see her again, unless of course you want to. Maybe you'll get to like each other.'

'Stranger things have happened,' said Reuben. We reached the top of the room and branched off to the left to make a circuit. 'So basically you want me to dazzle her with my considerable charm. And all my . . . coal mines in Wales, was it?'

'Yes. And please dazzle her in full view of James Fitzwilliam, whenever possible. If you can manage to dance with her, all the better. She loves talking about art and architecture and history and pretentious stuff like that. I'll introduce you as soon as this dance is finished.'

'Agreed.'

'I really owe you one, Reuben.' We ducked under the hands of the lead couple, and went down the room to find our places in the long set for the next dance.

'If you can find me one of those *Austen Kicks Ass* T-shirts, I'll consider us even. And if you ever do write that novel about what's going on this summer, get Bryce to bung me a copy.'

I was going to reply, but I saw that the twists and turns of the Grand March had led us directly down the set from James and Isabella. If Reuben couldn't dance, there wouldn't be any hiding it. The musicians struck up the beginning of 'Captain MacIntosh's Fancy'. We bowed to each other, and then the dancing began.

Ten minutes later, I was laughing and breathing hard, having been enthusiastically partnered up and down the set. 'Told you so.' Reuben grinned as the music for the second longways dance began. 'Shall we do this one as well?'

I nodded. 'Did you learn it at school?'

'I have a choreographer for *Cherry Summer*. I might have spent a couple of afternoons with her.'

'It's fantastic.' We bowed to each other, and began again.

When the second dance finished everyone applauded, and we had a moment to talk and catch our breath as people changed partners. 'I see you found yourself a charming partner, sir,' said James to Reuben.

'I was about to say the same thing to you, sir.'

'Miss Isabella Grantham,' I said, 'this is Lord Fotheringay.'

Reuben bowed low to her. 'Very pleased to meet you, Miss Grantham.'

'Lord Fotheringay has recently built a house outside of Sonning,' I said. 'From the sounds of it, it's quite impressive.'

'I'm glad to learn I have such amiable neighbours,' said Reuben to Isabella. 'Tell me, Miss Grantham, have you ever been to Rome? For there is a marble in the Palazzo Nuovo to which you bear a quite striking resemblance. It is Hadrianic, a statue of Isis, with a contemplative expression. I was strongly reminded of it from the moment that I saw you in the Grand March.'

He captured Isabella's arm in his and led her off, still talking. James watched them go.

'Lord Fotheringay works fast,' he said.

'Isabella isn't putting up much of a fight.'

'He seems a man of considerable culture.'

'I believe he is also a man of considerable fortune.'

'He was certainly fortunate to obtain you as a partner for the first dance. You and I are dancing the cotillion, aren't we? May I fetch you a drink first?'

'Yes, please.'

James went off in the opposite direction to

Reuben and Isabella, and I stood in the Saloon, watching couples dancing. It was so pretty to watch, as an observer. You didn't get the full effect in the films, because they tended to focus on one couple. From the sidelines, it looked like a swirling of silk and sparkle, a mannered and delicate courtship between men and women.

In a way, I wished I hadn't agreed to dance the first cotillion with James; it seemed too early in the evening for the high point. I'd rather have looked forward to it for a little bit longer, especially as this was probably my only dance with him. You were only supposed to dance two dances with the same person, and the cotillion was a long dance so it usually counted for two. If Isabella were monopolised by Reuben, James might ask me to dance again, even though strictly we shouldn't. He might even ask me for the *second* cotillion.

I'd never actually danced with James. He hadn't come to our dancing practices, though from the looks of it, he knew exactly what he was doing. The cotillion with him was going to be absolutely —

'Fantastic,' said a voice at my elbow. A very familiar voice. I spun around.

He was wearing a black coat over a white shirt that accentuated the tan of his skin and the darkness of his hair and eyes. A cravat, carelessly tied, giving a glimpse of his neck between the points of his shirt. A plum-coloured waistcoat. Black leather boots, completely unsuitable for formal evening wear, and no gloves. And buckskins that fitted him like a second skin. His hair was pushed back from his forehead, rather more tidily than usual, but rakishly enough for 1814.

I looked at Leo Allingham, dressed like a romantic hero, and my mouth fell open.

'If I'd known this was going to be your reaction, I'd have dressed up like this years ago,' he said.

I tried to speak. Nothing came out. The clothes could have been made for him. They were what a Regency gentleman would have put on to ride a motorcycle.

He was looking at me as if he were hungry, as if he wanted to eat me up. It was not a look a Regency gentleman gave to a lady.

I couldn't breathe.

'You look stunning,' he told me.

You look beautiful.

I cleared my throat. I wasn't going to say that. 'What are you doing here?'

'I wanted to see what was so great about this place that you were spending all your time here.'

'Where'd you get those clothes?'

'I thought a lady didn't ask a gentleman a question like that, but if you've got to know, I can give you the address of my tailor.'

I bit my lip. I'd forgotten all about avoiding anachronism.

'I don't think you're quite dressed for a ball,' I said.

'My choices were rather limited.' He looked around the Saloon, at the costumes, the lights, the decoration. The mixing of 1814 and the present. 'So this is Eversley Hall. I see why you like it. It's right up your street.'

'So they tell me.'

'Where is he?' His stance was casual, his eyes were sharp.

'Where is who?' I said.

'You know who I mean. That's him, isn't it? The guy with the poker up his arse who's coming this way with a glass of punch.'

James was making his way towards us; he was taller than most people in the crowd. 'He hasn't got a poker up his arse.'

'You're right. A poker's far too common.'

'Leo, stop it.'

James stopped short of us, a few paces away. His expression didn't change from its usual good nature, and after a moment he came the rest of the way up to us.

'Your punch, Alice,' he said to me, handing me a cool glass, and then turned to Leo. 'I don't believe I've had the pleasure, sir.'

'Leo Allingham.' Leo held out his hand. To me, who knew him so well, it was obviously more of a challenge than a greeting.

'James Fitzwilliam.'

'Have we met before? You look familiar.'

'Maybe you passed the oil painting in the Hall on the way in,' I suggested.

'Welcome to my home,' said James. Surely I was imagining the slight emphasis on 'my'. But there was something going on between these two men; they didn't drop eye-contact for a moment.

'All of this is yours?'

'Yes.'

'Lucky you.'

'The cotillion is next,' I said to James. I wasn't sure what was happening here, but it wasn't part of the plan and I didn't like it very much. I'd never seen Leo hit anyone in his life, but he looked as if he was ready to. And James had gone all cold and correct.

'This dance is mine,' James said, and held out his arm. I put down my drink.

'Please, don't let me get in your way,' said Leo, folding his arms across his chest. I walked off with James, and we took our places for the dance.

It was a good thing that I'd practised dancing so much, because my mind was whirling. What the hell was Leo doing here? If he wanted to know what I got up to at Eversley Hall — though I couldn't think why he would be interested — he could have come any weekend, during the day. Why had he gone to the trouble of dressing up in costume and turning up at the biggest event of the summer? I glanced over my shoulder; he was still standing there, watching us begin the dance. Still looking . . . incredible.

He met my eyes for a moment, then turned away and walked out of the room.

It was one of his impulses. Something he thought would be fun, done on the spur of the moment. That was the only explanation. And when it came down to it, it wasn't my problem. He'd probably look around, get bored and go home. Or maybe he'd find my family and hang out with them for a little while. Eversley Hall wasn't his scene.

Though I couldn't stop thinking about how

perfect he looked in those clothes. If he'd been alive in 1814, he would have dressed exactly like that — casually, with no niceties of fashion, like a sexy rake.

I swallowed. And what he'd said when I'd been surprised to see him — *If I'd known this was going to be your reaction, I'd have dressed up like this years ago.* As if Regency clothes were some sort of sexual fetish with me. Well . . . maybe they were, come to think of it. But it was more than the clothes. It was the tradition, it was the romance.

James caught my hand to go forward with the other couple. 'The room appears to be full of your friends this evening,' he said.

'It's a pleasant surprise.'

'Perhaps I needn't find you a husband after all.' We stepped back.

'Oh, I think your choice would be just fine.'

He took both my hands to turn me round, and then we were caught up in the whirl of the dance again. Regency people must have been incredibly fit, to do this all night. It seemed so delicate, but it was hard work. Like putting on a show.

★ ★ ★

'Oh my God,' whispered Selina in my ear, 'have you seen the guy in the uniform?'

I fanned myself with the silk fan Lady Fitzwilliam had lent me. I could see why they were necessary at balls. Dozens of people dancing energetically in layers of clothing and gloves pro-duced a lot of heat, even when the doors to the

459

garden were open. And that cotillion had taken it out of me; I was glad to rest and have a chat.

'Which guy in uniform?' I asked, shielding my mouth with the fan. 'There are regiments of them. We've got all the Napoleonic re-enactors here.'

'The one standing sideways-on to us, in the dark green. Don't look!' She gripped my arm.

'How am I supposed to see him if I can't look?'

'Oh, okay, look now. I thought he was going to see us. Do you see him, the one with the spiky hair?'

I did. His hair had too much gel in it to be strictly 1814, but he was wearing a beautiful dark green and black velvet uniform, spangled with silver buttons and with a deep red silk sash around his waist. 95th Rifles. Everyone wanted to be Sharpe.

'What about him?'

'Isn't he lush?'

I noticed that several people were observing us. 'Selina Fitzwilliam,' I said with mock-strictness, 'do you mean to tell me that you rejected marriage with a very respectable gentleman only to fall for an Army officer?'

'Well, I wouldn't say that I've fallen for him exactly. I just, you know, like the look of him.' She frowned. 'What do you think I should do?'

'The proper course of action is to see if your brother thinks it's suitable to introduce him to you.'

She bit her lip. 'You don't think I should go up

and talk to him myself?'

'It's not generally seen as polite.'

'But I'm afraid that James won't think it's suitable to introduce us.'

'Then you have to make up your own mind.'

I saw Selina was pondering. Then something occurred to her, and her face got excited again. 'What about Henry Pelmet?'

'Did I introduce myself to Henry Pelmet?' I repeated, surprised that she was bringing up my fictional romantic past. 'Well, in a way. It's rather difficult not to become acquainted with someone when they rescue you from falling on your face in the middle of a crowded dance floor. You could try something similar, if you liked, but it's not easy to choreograph. You might end up in the arms of the wrong person.'

'No, I mean, you didn't tell me that Henry Pelmet was going to be here!'

'Pardon?'

'Your special guest — I had no idea that it was going to be Henry Pelmet. Your true love.' She sighed.

'Oh, no no, my guest isn't Henry Pelmet. It's Baron Fotheringay.' I pointed with my fan to the dance floor, where Reuben was dancing 'The Soldier's Joy' with Isabella. It was all seemingly going very well indeed.

'No, I'm not talking about Baron Fotheringay. Baron Fotheringay is dancing with Isabella, and after he met you Henry Pelmet would never dance with anybody else. I remember your story. And he turned up at a ball, again. That's so romantic.'

461

'I'm quite at a loss, Selina. I only invited one guest.'

'Alice, you don't have to be coy with me, silly. I saw you talking with him just now. Before you danced with James?'

'Oh no, that's not Henry Pelmet. That's Leo Allingham. He's a — a friend of the family.'

Selina shook her head. 'I don't care what his real name is. I saw the way the two of you looked at each other. That's Henry Pelmet. I can see why you changed his name in your story, to avoid gossip and everything. But anyone with eyes could see that the two of you are still head over heels in love with each other.'

For the first time, I wondered if I had created a monster in Selina. 'Henry Pel — I mean Leo Allingham — and I are not head over heels in love.'

She grabbed my arm again. 'Shh! He's coming over here now.'

Leo had, indeed, appeared out of nowhere and was making a beeline in our direction. I didn't have time to make an excuse and slip away before he reached us. 'Alice, we need to talk,' he said. 'Now.'

'Mr Allingham, I hope you are enjoying the evening,' I said, hoping to prompt him into remembering some semblance of manners. 'This is Miss Selina Fitzwilliam.'

'Nice to meet you,' Leo said, barely glancing at her before turning his attention back to me. 'Come on, let's get out of here for a minute. There are too many people around.'

'It's very nice to meet you too, Mr *Pelmet*,'

462

said Selina, with a giggle. I frowned at her.

'Thank you for your invitation, Mr Allingham,' I said, 'but I think it would be the height of impropriety for a single woman to disappear off with a single man. Perhaps you can confine your conversation to what may safely be said in public.'

Leo ran his hand through his hair, disarraying it further. 'This etiquette stuff is very convenient, isn't it?'

'Or maybe *in*convenient,' chipped in Selina. 'Do you need me to make a distraction with champagne again?'

'No, I do not.' I lowered my voice. 'Leo, I love this job. Please, please don't muck it up for me.'

'Miss Alice Woodstock!' trilled a honeyed voice, and Isabella appeared beside me, with Reuben in tow. What was this, Paddington station? How these people were managing to work their way through a crowded ballroom without tripping over themselves or anyone else, I did not know. Anyway, it looked as if 'The Soldier's Joy' had come to an end.

'You're a dark horse, Miss Woodstock,' she said. 'I had no idea you had such a wide acquaintance.' She took my arm cosily in hers, for the first time in my life, and I stared at her in surprise. She wasn't looking at me at all; her ice-blue eyes were focused straight on Leo. 'Aren't you going to introduce your friend?'

'Um — yes, oka — I mean, certainly. Miss Isabella Grantham, Lord Fotheringay, may I present Mr Leo Allingham.'

Isabella beamed at Leo so brightly I was

surprised he didn't blink. 'Mr Allingham, what a pleasure to meet you. I know you by reputation, of course.'

'The pleasure is all mine,' said Leo, and I said a silent thanks for the return of etiquette. Of course it would be impossible for Leo to resist being charming to a beautiful woman.

'I've seen your artwork,' Isabella continued. She'd let go of me now, in order to fully concentrate on Leo. 'I think it's astounding.'

'Thank you very much.'

'Are you enjoying the ball?' She sidled closer to him, tilting her head in a winning way, and Selina put an elbow in my side.

'Alice,' Selina hissed into my ear, '*do* something. You can't let Isabella get her hooks into Henry Pelmet, too. He's yours!'

'I — '

'The ball is very interesting,' said Leo.

'Isn't it?' Reuben seemed cheerful, despite Isabella's latching on to Leo. For a film director, he seemed to be remarkably ego-free. 'There're all sorts of dramas going on. It reminds me of a novel.'

'And have you seen any potential heroines?' I asked him, tilting my head towards Isabella and raising my eyebrows. *Get her back.*

'Lots of them,' said Reuben. 'After all, isn't every woman, from the greatest of queens to the lowliest of servants, the heroine of her own story?'

'Some are even the heroines of several stories,' Leo said. 'Isn't that right, Alice?'

Isabella laughed, a bell-like chime. 'What a

464

charming idea,' she said to Leo, regardless of the fact that Reuben had actually been the one to say it. 'Don't you think that holds true in art, as well? Take the *Mona Lisa* for example; part of her attraction must be because of the multiplicity of stories behind that smile. Does she have a secret? Or is she perhaps in love?' She fluttered her eyelashes.

'I never knew you had such a vivid imagination, Isabella,' I said.

'It doesn't take a great deal of imagination to construct stories about something that's meant to be enigmatic,' said Reuben. 'It's much more rewarding to find the story behind something that appears to be mundane. There's nothing so intriguing as a person who seems to have no secrets. The humble person, the shy person: you think you see their whole life in a glance, and yet if you dig deeper, there's often treasure.'

'Do you really think so?' Isabella said. 'How fascinating. There's a parallel here with your artwork, isn't there, Mr Allingham? How you take something so mundane as a building, and make it into something quite extraordinary.'

Selina elbowed me again. 'You must have some experience of transforming ordinary materials, Lord Fotheringay,' I said quickly, 'having recently built a new country house. Pray, tell us about Sonning End.'

'Oh well, it's just a little country retreat,' he said in an offhand manner, 'twenty bedrooms or so, for intimate friendly gatherings.'

'*This* is quite a friendly gathering,' interrupted yet another voice, this one smooth and warm and belonging to James Fitzwilliam. He was standing next to me, on the other side from Selina.

'James,' I said, not sure if what I was feeling was relief or panic. It was a good thing he'd appeared right now, wasn't it? It didn't matter who Isabella was making eyes at, as long as it was someone other than James. In fact, it was even better if she made eyes at Reuben *and* Leo. He couldn't possibly refrain from noticing that. And saying something.

'I've just introduced Mr Allingham to Isabella,' I said, in case he hadn't caught the signals Isabella was putting out. I felt another pang of something as I said it though. Spite at Isabella, probably. That wasn't so good. I wasn't doing this whole thing to get back at Isabella. I was doing it because I genuinely believed that James Fitzwilliam would be miserable married to Isabella Grantham, no matter what the historical records said. It was altruistic. Look at the way Isabella was gazing at Leo. Right in front of James. Shameless.

I noticed that my hands were clenched tightly enough to drive my fingernails into my palms.

James, of course, kept his pleasant face on. In fact, he didn't even seem to notice Isabella behaving like a hussy; he turned to Selina instead. 'I have a young man here who would like to meet you.'

Beside me, Selina had gone absolutely still, and I could see why: the young man who was standing beside James was the Rifles officer that she'd pointed out to me a few minutes ago. Up close, he looked even younger. He had a little pink flush on his cheeks, as if he were shy.

'This is Lieutenant Marcus Waltham,' James told her. 'Lieutenant, this is my sister, Miss Selina Fitzwilliam.'

Selina held out her hand. She was blushing too, with more ferocity than the young man, but it made her look even prettier. Their gaze met and I saw her, faintly, smile.

It was nothing, and everything. A meeting. But I could see, standing beside them, that the entire ballroom had vanished in their eyes. My heart gave a sympathetic thump.

The musicians made signs of starting up again. 'Dance with me?' murmured the young man in green, and Selina nodded, then seemed to remember herself. She looked at James in some confusion.

James smiled his permission. She practically floated with Lieutenant Waltham onto the dance floor.

Isabella was going to *flip*. I looked at her to see how she was taking this blow to the Grantham family honour, but she was still making doe-eyes at Leo. 'Of course,' I heard her saying, 'so much of this world is subjective. I think when you find one person who really appreciates what you're doing, who shares your vision for your art, that's worth more than what any critic could possibly say.'

'I couldn't agree more,' said Leo. 'But it's rare to find the one person who truly understands you. When you do, you have to hold on to them.'

'That's very true, Miss Grantham,' said

Reuben. 'I perceive that your heart is as fine as your intellect.'

I checked James; he wasn't watching the happy young couple any more, and had switched his attention back to the scene unfolding in front of him. Anyone else would think he was calm, but I could see a tension in the corners of his eyes and mouth. I bit my lip. This couldn't be easy for him, but it was for his own good in the end.

'Do you dance, Mr Allingham?' asked Isabella, oblivious to James's observation.

'Dancing,' said Leo, breaking into a wide grin. 'That's it. Thanks for reminding me.' Isabella smiled and began to extend her hand towards his, but Leo strode forward and grabbed my wrist.

'Come on, Alice,' he said. 'Dance with me.'

'But — '

'I went to a lot of trouble to get dressed up for this thing, so the least you can do is dance.' He tugged me away, towards where Selina and Lieutenant Waltham stood, still gazing starrily at each other.

'Leo, I'm right in the middle of something,' I whispered in dismay.

'It'll wait. It's dancing time.'

'But I've got a plan!'

'Of course you do. It's something to do with that blonde boaconstrictor, isn't it?'

'How'd you know?'

'Alice, sometimes you forget quite how well I know you. You're trying to set up the blonde with the Fotheringay bloke. He seems all right though. He deserves better than her. She should stick with Fitzwilliam.'

'No, she shouldn't, that's the thing. James is all keen for him and Isabella to get married because she was actually his great-great-great-great-grandmother. But they're not suited at all.'

'What on earth do you see in a man who wants to marry his own grandmother?'

'He doesn't actually want to . . . ' I saw the futility of trying to argue with Leo about this, especially when other people might hear us. 'Anyway, James is amazing. Did you see how he let Selina go off dancing with Lieutenant Waltham?'

'Wow, what a prince. He lets a young woman with her own brain and heart actually do what she likes.'

'This is 1814, Leo.'

'I don't care what year it is. Let's stop talking about the sainted James Fitzwilliam and dance.' He steered me into position beside a stout lady in white, and stood next to a man in an Army Captain's uniform.

'Do you even know how to do this dance? It's 'The Duke of Kent's Waltz'.'

'How hard can it be?'

Oh, God. I'd never seen Leo Allingham dance to any music older than the Supremes' 'Can't Hurry Love'.

'I don't think this is a good idea,' I said, as the music began.

'You can lead.'

'This is eighteen — '

' — fourteen, I know, and I also know you won't let a silly thing like historical sexism stop you from doing whatever you want to do.'

'But if I take the male place, it'll mess up the whole thing.'

'I'll pick it up as we go along, then. That person with the mic tells you what to do anyway, doesn't she? I'm a quick learner.'

I looked back at where we'd come from. James, Isabella and Reuben were all still standing there. James and Isabella were looking in our direction; Reuben was quite happily surveying the room.

This was a disaster. James and Isabella would probably end up dancing together again, which was pretty much tantamount to a betrothal. I had to shake Leo off and get back there and do . . . something. I didn't know what, but anything would be better than Isabella with James. 'I've got to — ' I started to say, at the moment that the dance began.

The dance floor was thronged with spectators. I couldn't escape without being extremely obvious. And if I didn't move, then the fat woman in white was going to trample me.

I moved. 'A star!' I stage-whispered to Leo. 'Put your right hand in the middle and walk round.'

'Got it.'

'Now left! No, left Leo, your left hand, and walk right!'

'Oh. Sorry,' he said to the second man, with whom he'd nearly collided. The star finished and I grabbed his hand to lead him down the set.

'Why was that woman calling me Mr Pelmet?' he asked.

'Oh. That's Selina's little joke. She thinks you're a fictional person.'

'Isn't everyone around here a fictional person?'

'No, just me. Everyone else is an actual person who was alive in 1814.'

'But they're still fictional.'

'No, it's all as real as they can make it.'

'Except for Mr Pelmet? And what kind of name is that, by the way?'

'It was sort of a joke.'

'Right. I'm sort of a joke. Do we turn here?'

'It wasn't you.'

'Okay. I'm being mistaken for a sort of a joke. And why are you fictional?'

'There wasn't really an Alice Woodstock in the house in 1814. I've been brought in to provide interest.'

'And gossip? And matchmaking?'

'Well, yes, I suppose so.'

'Because you're so damn good at that sort of thing. You love it, don't you? All the intrigue and the romance. But none of it is real.'

'That's what I've been trying to tell you — it *is* real. All of it except for me. Go around the other man's back into the second place.'

'Right.' We parted, then reunited facing each other. 'What's the deal with Fitzwilliam's kid sister? Why shouldn't she dance with whoever she wants to?'

'Right hand, step forward. She was meant to marry Isabella Grantham's brother, Arthur. Now back. They're old family friends, have pretty much been engaged since birth, though she didn't know about it. Turn me under your arm. No, under! But Selina isn't in love with him, so she refused to marry him and there was a huge uproar. Isabella blames me for filling Selina's head with romantic notions. Now left hand, do the same thing.'

'Wow. You really have been living in a novel.'

'It's better than a novel, because it's real. Ouch!'

Leo stumbled. 'What? Was that you I just trod on?'

'It was my foot! Be careful, Leo. These dancing slippers aren't exactly steel-toed.'

'Sorry.' He took another step, and squashed another toe on the other foot.

'Ouch!! Back, and turn me under! Then dance with the opposite lady, to the right.'

I turned with the opposite gentleman, and then met Leo for the left-hand turn.

'I'm sorry, Alice,' he said. 'I can't help but think that all of this is my fault.'

'It's definitely your fault! It was your idea to dance this blasted waltz when you didn't have the slightest idea how,' I hissed. 'Now we're at the end, and we don't do anything for a minute. Thank God.'

'I don't mean treading on your toes,' Leo said as the other couple led down the set. 'I mean that it's my fault that you've been driven to live in a fictional world.'

'Driven to live!'

'Yeah. I've turned up, out of the blue, and taken over your space. When I got back here, I didn't expect you to still be so angry at me. I thought maybe time might have smoothed things down. But then when you were still furious, and you kept on sparring with me . . . I couldn't leave then, Alice. I'd promised myself I wasn't going to run away any more. And besides, I actually enjoy arguing with you.'

'That's why you're so persistently annoying? Because you enjoy arguing with me?'

'Even if it's anger and frustration, it's genuine emotion. Even if it's sadness.'

'And what exactly does this have to do with my job here at Eversley Hall? Which you are probably putting in jeopardy even at this moment, Leo.' I glanced up the set, to see who was watching. We were safe for right now, but for how long?

'Because I know you. Because we're both the same. When something makes us uncomfortable, we run away from it. I made you uncomfortable, so you retreated here, into your nice little safe fictional past.'

'How many times do I have to tell you — it's *not* fictional, Leo! It's a re-creation. We're not even allowed to wear knickers.'

'You're not?' he said, looking interested. Then he shook his head. 'Never mind about the knickers. It's obvious that for you, all this is real. And it's not only a job, either. It's become more than that. You're even dating the guy who's pretending to own Eversley Hall.'

'You're wrong about that, too. James *is* the owner of the house. It's been in his family for generations. He's restored it all.'

'No. The land might belong to him, the

building might belong to him. Everything in it might belong to him. But he doesn't own Eversley Hall. He owns a theatre.'

'I keep on telling you — this isn't a play, it's a re-creation.'

'Then he owns a history book. He doesn't have a home. Nobody lives here. You all come in every weekend and pretend. You, probably more than anyone else. And it's because you're running away from me.'

'You're completely full of yourself, aren't you? Okay, we're in again. Right-hand star again now, then left.'

He managed that, at least, this time. Then we were facing each other again in the second position, waiting for the first couple to lead down and up and cast.

'Don't get me wrong,' he said. 'I think you've done extraordinary work. Your writing about this place is wonderful, and if it's got you unstuck, there couldn't be anything better. But when you're here, you're not dealing with what the real issues are. The real issues are me, and your family, and our past.'

'The real issue,' I said furiously, 'is why you've come here to mess everything up. This is a really important night for me, Leo. It's not the time to discuss what you think I should be doing with my life. Right hand, forward then back.'

Leo took my hand in his and pulled me to him. Up close, I could smell the shampoo in his hair, the odd scent of rented clothing. In this warm space, it was warmer next to him. 'I haven't come here to mess everything up,' he said, close to me. 'I came to see what you've been doing, because I care about it. I care about you.'

I stepped back, and turned myself under. Left hand to Leo, forward. 'Okay. So now you've seen it. You've even danced it. You've been a Regency tourist, you've learned about what I've been doing for the past two months, you've even got to wear some great clothes for a couple of hours. Let's finish this dance so you can go.'

Leo was supposed to let me go back and spin me under his arm. He didn't. He stayed close to me, not moving, ignoring the next steps and the people around him.

'That's the thing, Alice,' he said. 'That's what you don't understand. I'm not going anywhere. Even when I knew you didn't want me here, even when you pushed me away after we'd slept together. I'm not going to leave you. These two years without you have been the most miserable of my life. And I know that's my fault too, and that's why I've come back. That's why I haven't left Brickham and why I came here dressed up in these clothes and why I'm dancing a dance I don't know how to do. Because I still love you.'

Real Life

'Move,' I told Leo, pulling at his hand, which still held mine.

'Did you hear me? I just told you — '

'I heard you. But I'm not dancing with you any more, and if we don't get off the floor, we'll be going down like dance-floor dominoes.' I tugged again, and this time he came. We dodged through dancing couples towards the French doors, my head ringing with what he'd said.

Leo still loved me? How could he still love me? And why? We'd spent the last two years running away from each other. You didn't do that if you loved someone. If you loved someone, you wanted to be near them.

But he'd come back. He'd refused to leave again.

I pushed the thought away. Leo was impulsive, he was irresponsible, he was reckless. He had an enormous ego. He was quite capable of convincing himself that he loved me, because he'd seen that I was interested in James. He'd had any number of chances to declare his love, if it was real . . . significant how he chose the moment after he'd seen me dancing with an attractive man.

It wasn't love. He might feel something, but it wasn't love. It was possessiveness, it was jealousy, it was some twisted desire to shake me up, when everything was going right for me at last.

We were out of the door, and he was pulling

me now. Round the side of the house. For the moment, we were alone, and there was enough noise coming from the open windows to mask our conversation. I removed my hand from his grip.

'You don't believe me,' he said, before I could open my mouth.

'No, I don't. Of course I don't. You can't just tell me you love me out of the blue and have me believe you.'

'The first time I told you I loved you it was out of the blue. You believed me then.'

'Things were different then. We were different people.'

'No, we were the same people. But we were younger, and we didn't know how to handle loss and sorrow and disappointment. We didn't expect them. But now we do.'

'So you're saying that we belong together because we suffered together? Because we lost Clara and split up with each other? That's insane, Leo.'

'You gave me Clara's box. That must have meant something. It must have meant you forgive me.'

I sighed. Inside the house, someone laughed. 'I do forgive you,' I said, and I knew it was true. 'But that doesn't mean I want to get back together. You should want to be with someone because they make you happy.'

'You make me happy.'

'You must like arguing a lot more than I do, then.'

'Does that James Fitzwilliam character make you happy?'

'Yes. He's a new start for me. A new life. You

say none of this is real, but it is to me, Leo. I'm better here. I feel better, and I'm a better person. It's time to move on.'

'This isn't moving on. It's pretending. We belong together, Alice. We always have. You need to stay in the real world long enough to see it.'

'It isn't me who has the problem with understanding the real world, Leo,' I said, and at that exact moment two things happened: the music stopped, and James, Isabella and Reuben walked out of the Saloon doors onto the terrace, not five feet away from us. My words echoed in the suddenly quiet air.

'I — I mean, thank you for the very pleasant dance, Mr Allingham. I'm afraid I'm engaged for the rest of the evening.'

He bowed, his expression stormy — and sad, with the sadness I'd only just learned how to see. 'Mermaid,' he said.

Something turned over in my chest. I opened my mouth.

'Mr Allingham,' trilled Isabella, hurrying over. 'You simply must allow me to give you a tour of the *objets d'art* in Eversley Hall.' Isabella had obviously been waiting for the dance to finish, so she could pounce. She smiled up at Leo.

'I believe Miss Grantham knows more about the paintings here than I do myself,' said James from where he stood beside her. 'Miss Woodstock, you seem weary. Would you like to sit down and rest?'

'I — I'm fine,' I managed.

'Oh yes, James, you are so considerate and kind. Your face is pale, Miss Woodstock — do allow your cousin to escort you to a chair. I believe they are announcing supper. Mr Allingham, would you care to take me in, and we can discuss the paintings in the dining room?'

Leo cast one last long glance in my direction. 'Might as well,' he said at last, and the two of them went off together.

'That was an interesting waltz to observe,' James commented.

'It was an interesting waltz to participate in,' I said, watching Leo's back.

'Alice? Isabella was right — you do look pale.'

I looked up into James's concerned face and said, 'I'm fine. Thank you.'

'Did Mr Allingham say something to upset you?'

'No.' I forced my lips into a smile. 'Thank you.'

'May I take you in to supper?' Reuben asked me.

'Thank you,' said James to Reuben. 'I would take you in myself, Alice, but as the host I'm expected to escort Lady Ramsay.'

'Of course.' I put my gloved hand in Reuben's. 'I should love to go in to supper with you, Lord Fotheringay.'

This evening was so not going the way I had planned. To say nothing of my life.

★　★　★

The big mahogany dining-table and matching chairs had been removed, replaced by several round tables which allowed more guests to fit

479

into the room. Additional tables were set up in the Hall. James, Lady Fitzwilliam and the more distinguished guests sat at the top table between the screen of marble-effect columns. I sat between Reuben and my father, with Selina and Lieutenant Waltham on Reuben's other side. Another 95th Rifleman was sandwiched between Pippi and my mum.

I looked around for Leo. He was at a table on the other side of the room, under the pair of Batoni paintings depicting saints. Why you would want saints in your dining room, I did not know, but he and Isabella seemed to be discussing them in great detail.

I poked at my main course. I'd been told what it was, but I didn't really care at the moment. The last thing I felt like doing was eating.

Leo had said none of this was real.

'I'm sorry,' Reuben whispered to me. 'I really did try with Miss Grantham, but she zeroed in on your friend like a heat-seeking missile.'

'It's all right,' I said. 'I think she likes artists.'

'Still, your purpose is accomplished anyway, I think.'

'Yes. Probably. Thank you.' I lapsed into silence.

'So, what do you do, Mr Woodstock?' Reuben asked my father, pouring out wine for me and Selina sitting on either side of him. Selina didn't even notice. She was deep in conversation with Lieutenant Waltham. They were speaking low enough so that I couldn't tell what they were saying, and she was facing away from me, but I could see the movement of her hands, the tilt of her neck.

Over on the top table, I heard Lady Fitzwilliam laugh, and I saw James nodding, talking politely with his neighbour. Arthur was three tables away, on the far side of the room with his back to us, sitting with his parents and some other re-enactors.

These people were real. Even if I didn't call them by their real names, I knew them. I knew Lady Fitzwilliam had a flowered sofa and a television in her sewing room, for evenings when her husband wanted to watch football and she wanted to watch a chick flick. I knew she'd made her niece a 1950s-style frock for her wedding and I knew that she'd become interested in clothes when she used to watch her own mother getting dressed up to go out. I knew that she'd always wanted to teach her own daughter to sew, if she'd had one. That she was teaching Selina.

I knew that Arthur had a talent for comedy and that despite his clownish act, beneath it he was sensitive and vulnerable. I knew so much about Selina, more of the details of her life than I knew about Pippi's. I'd laughed and talked with all of these people, and they were my friends, in real life. Well, not Isabella. But aside from her, I was pretty sure that even after the summer, we'd all stay in touch. With Kayleigh and Samuel and Mrs Collins, too. We'd all keep seeing each other.

Everything we did in the house was for show. But that didn't mean it wasn't real too.

'Hey. Aren't you Reuben Rogers?' Pippi asked across the table.

'Me? No, Miss Woodstock, I'm Baron

Fotheringay.' Reuben winked at her, and addressed my father across me. 'Handley Page, did you say? I did a V/1500 last year.'

'Maybe you'd like me to change places for dessert,' I suggested. 'I think you two have a lot in common.' I stood up and let Reuben exchange seats with me. Of course that left me near Selina, who was wrapped up in her own bubble. But that was okay. I had plenty to think about.

Mermaid.

The waiter took away my untouched plate.

And James — how real was he? Our dates had meant something, surely. Those heated glances, the flirtations . . . And Eversley Hall was real to him. It wasn't a history book. It represented the future as well as the past.

A waiter placed a dessert plate in front of me. I didn't look at it.

'Yes, that's me,' said Mum to the smiling 95th Rifleman beside her. 'It's one of the proudest achievements of my life, except of course for my daughters.'

'Can you show me?' he asked.

'Well, of course. Do you happen to have a spare banana?'

The Rifleman looked around. 'You could use the hilt of my sword.'

Pippi laughed, suddenly and loudly. 'Oh my God, you are so predictable,' she said to my mother.

'There's nothing wrong with being predictable,' said Mum, holding out her hand calmly for the man's sword. 'Predictable is quite comforting.'

'But there seems to be a lot of down angle on

the prop shaft, something like three to five degrees,' said Reuben. 'Do you think more thrust would cause it to pitch down?'

'Well,' said my father slowly, 'theoretically the answer is clear. It . . . '

Across the room, Arthur was leaving through the door to the Saloon. He walked quite close to Leo and Isabella, who were still deep in discussion.

Leo wouldn't do anything stupid like getting off with Isabella because I'd rejected him — would he?

As I watched, the two of them stood, leaving their desserts behind, and followed Arthur into the Saloon.

'No, no, Mum, you've got that wrong. Jeez, no wonder I got pregnant. Here, let me try.'

I stood up. 'Excuse me,' I said, and I made my way across the dining room, past Arthur's table where his parents were laughing, past Leo and Isabella's table filled with people I didn't know, and into the Saloon.

It was deserted. The floor that had been so full of dancers was empty, filled only with the scent of flowers. The French doors to the garden were open, and I hesitated, wondering whether to go outside. But there wasn't any art outside. And maybe they were just looking at art. I crossed the Saloon instead, to the door to the Green Drawing Room.

This room had been set up for gaming, with square tables scattered with cards and dice, abandoned now for supper. Except for one table in the middle, where Arthur sat sprawled in a

483

chair, turning over cards.

'Hello,' I said, and he looked up, startled, before he smiled.

'Hello yourself,' he said. 'Didn't care for your sweet?'

'It seemed like there were more important things.' I came over to his table. 'Have you seen Isabella?'

'No.'

'Oh.' I pulled out a chair and sat down. This was silly. I wasn't going to go chasing after Leo all over the house. He'd said he loved me, and I hadn't believed him. He could go off with every woman in the world, as far as I was concerned.

But what if I did decide to believe him?

I took the pile of cards Arthur had discarded, tidied them up, and began flipping them over. It was slow, quiet and calming, like a jigsaw puzzle. The muted snap of Arthur's cards on the table felt companionable, as if for a moment, neither one of us had to try.

Some guests came into the room, chatting, and we both instinctively sat up straighter. For the audience. But they installed themselves around the whist-table, without coming over to talk with us. Still, we were on duty now.

Arthur cleared his throat. 'It looks as though Miss Fitzwilliam has made a new friend,' he said.

'James introduced them,' I explained.

'Good show. Sensible man.'

'You don't mind?'

'I wish Miss Selina Fitzwilliam every happiness in her life.' He toyed with a card: the queen of hearts, I saw. 'Did James also fulfil his promise

484

of finding an eligible husband for you? I still think old Bertie would suit, if you can't find anything better. I'll mention it in the club next time I'm in London.'

'Arthur,' I said, 'can you answer me something?'

More people were filing into the room. Dessert must be over.

'Anything, my dear Miss Woodstock. Unless it is who I fancy to win at Cheltenham. I could not condone tempting a young lady into betting at horses.'

I picked up my own card. Knave of diamonds. 'If — if, say, Selina suddenly changed her mind again, and she wanted you back — I mean, she consented to the engagement — what would you do?'

'I don't fancy the odds of that happening, do you? I make it a habit never to cross a man who knows how to shoot a rifle.'

'And you were never in love with Selina anyway.'

'I have the utmost esteem and respect for the amiable Miss Fitzwilliam.'

'But what if someone you used to love, someone who broke your heart — what if that person wanted to come back into your life? Would you even consider trusting them again?'

Arthur's smile vanished. 'Would you like some coffee? I could do with some. Or port. I wonder if there's any port. Please excuse me, Miss Woodstock.' He stood and left the room.

I was kicking myself as he went. In my preoccupation, I'd forgotten that Arthur had had his own heart broken. He wouldn't want to discuss that here, in front of an audience. I'd inadvertently turned his own confession against him.

I sighed and resolved to apologise whole-heartedly, and surreptitiously, to Arthur once he reappeared with our coffee, or port, or whatever.

Meanwhile, I was in a room surrounded by people I was supposed to be entertaining. If I stayed here, someone was going to ask me to play cards. And I couldn't play anything except for Snap. I got up hurriedly and went back into the Saloon, where the music had begun again.

And there were Selina and Lieutenant Waltham, dancing.

I watched them. They were beautiful together. Her white dress, her gleaming hair, his shining buttons and broad shoulders. They looked every inch the hero and heroine of a novel or a fairy tale. They smiled at each other, smiles of attraction, bone-deep. The way you smile when you're wrapped up in something you've never experienced before, and when you know the other person is feeling the exact same way. They touched hands. They whispered.

They were in love. It had only been two hours, maybe a little bit more, but they were in love with each other. Maybe Selina had listened too hard to my stories, but the unavoidable truth was that it had happened to her exactly as I'd described it. She'd met someone's eyes across a crowded ballroom, and she'd known.

With Leo and me it had been a summer picnic with fifteen years of knowing each other beforehand, and no crowds at all. But it had been the same thing.

It wasn't like that any more between us. There were Selina and Marcus, the two of them, innocent and smiling. In step together, moving as one. He didn't tread on her feet. She didn't get angry at him. There were no whispered accusations or apologies. No winding each other up, no betrayals or grief. They were young love, pure and simple.

Not something damaged and worn, compromised and forgiven. Something stitched together from tatters.

I bit my lip and watched them, yearning in my chest below my silk half-mourning gown. Was it too much to ask for, that I could have again what they had now?

Someone tapped me on the shoulder. Pippi was standing beside me, her hand in the small of her back in the characteristic posture of a pregnant woman. 'Oh my fucking God,' she said. 'Are you really friends with Reuben Rogers? *Reuben Rogers?* And is he really totally BFFs with *Dad?*'

'They seem to have a lot in common.'

'Do you think this means that Dad is cool? Do we have to, like, re-evaluate our entire lives to see that he really does have a clue somewhere in there? Because Reuben Rogers is *so* cool. He said that plenty of actresses have babies and that I could — '

Pippi stopped talking abruptly, a circumstance that was so unlikely that I tore my attention away from the young lovers and looked at my sister.

She was wide-eyed, wide-mouthed, and staring across the Saloon at Arthur, who had entered via the Hall and was staring right back at her.

'What's the matter?' I asked, but in that instant my sister flushed the brightest red I'd ever seen her and put both her hands on her belly, and I knew. 'Oh my God, Arthur . . . '

Pippi turned around and ran.

In Which I Win

'Pippi!' I called after her, but for someone who thought she looked like a whale, she moved remarkably quickly and had disappeared out of the room within seconds. Arthur, on the other hand, was still standing at the spot where he'd seen her, the wine in danger of falling out of his hands. I hurried over to him, took the glasses of port and put them down on a cloth-covered table.

'Your sister is pregnant,' he said in his normal voice, in a daze.

I glanced around. Of course everyone in the vicinity was watching us, and we were going to gather even more of a crowd in a minute. 'Mr Grantham, I must show you something,' I said, grasping his sleeve and tugging him back into the Hall. The Library and the upstairs weren't open and there were likely to be people on the lawn, so the only option was the small servants' door. We dodged inside the tiny corridor and I snapped on the lights.

'Is Pippi the girl who broke your heart?' I whispered urgently.

'I didn't know she was expecting a baby. She never told me.' He looked at me for the first time. 'Who's the father?'

'If she's the girl you've been talking about, the one you were in love with, then I think *you* might be the father.'

He shook his head. 'She'd have told me.'

'If you know Pippi, then you also know she's incredibly stubborn when she wants to be.'

'She must have met someone else, that's why she broke up with me. Who did she tell you the father was?'

'She won't tell anyone. She says she broke up with the father as soon as she found out, because he has too much ahead of him to be shackled down with a baby.'

Arthur didn't say anything. From in here, we could vaguely hear the music from the Saloon and the chatter from the Hall. The air was cooler and the whitewashed walls were stark.

'We met at theatre camp last summer,' he said at last, 'but we didn't get together properly until this Easter when we were in *Much Ado* together.' He paused. 'How far along is she?'

I told him.

'She split up with me right after I'd got the comedy club gig — the first week in June. She was really weird beforehand — went all quiet. Pippi's not usually quiet.'

'Why didn't you say anything to me?' I asked. 'You must've suspected she was my sister.'

He leaned back against the wall. 'I knew you were Pippi's sister as soon as I saw you, and then when I found out your name. I thought maybe you knew but you were trying to be nice to me by not bringing it up. And I didn't want to talk about it. It hurt too much. She wouldn't even return any of my calls or my texts — it was total silence. I thought she really hated me.' He bit his lip. 'She must hate me. She's been going through

490

all of this by herself.'

'She's a bloody-minded fool, if you don't mind me slandering your formerly beloved.'

'I can't believe it. I can't believe she's — that we're — what should I do?'

A great burst of laughter came from the other side of the door. I didn't think we could be heard, talking in low voices behind the wall, but I led him a few steps up the narrow twisting staircase before I spoke again.

'Do you want to be involved?' I asked him.

'If it's my baby, of course I do. I do anyway. I want to be there for her. I still — I still care about her a lot. But she broke up with me. As soon as she saw me, she ran away.'

'Pippi might be a fool but she does love this baby, and she's got to see that having the father in the picture is the best thing.'

'But what if she doesn't want me to be involved?'

'Then you've got to convince her. It's the right thing to do, Arthur.'

'I don't think I can.'

He looked up at me, on the step above him. He'd never seemed so young to me before, his face a picture of confusion, hurt, surprise, longing.

'This is your moment of truth,' I said to him. 'It's the moment where you make the big decision about what kind of person you're going to be. Are you going to keep on being a boy, or are you going to become a man? Are you going to let your fear rule you, or are you going to do what's right and go after what you want? You're lucky, Arthur. So many people don't get this moment, and here it is for you. Right now is where you get to decide whether you're going to be someone ordinary, or if you're going to be a hero.'

He looked at me, really looked at me. I could see tears being held back in his eyes.

'I want to be a hero,' he said.

'Then go after her. Go and find her. Right now.'

He turned around and went straight out of the door. I stood in the empty servants' corridor, my heart beating hard.

★   ★   ★

Thinking it would be wisest if I didn't emerge from the same door as Arthur, I went up the stairs and came out on the upper landing. When I walked down the grand staircase, my parents were practically in front of me. Reuben and my dad were still talking intently, and Mum was standing with a group of young women who were gazing up at the portrait of James Fitzwilliam.

I caught their eyes. 'Madam, sir, might I have a word in private?' They followed me to the far corner, near the entrance, where there were no crowds for the moment.

'He's a very good-looking man, isn't he?' Mum said, indicating the painting. 'Very noble.'

'Yes. Yes, he is. Listen, Mum, something has happened.'

'What's wrong?' asked my mother instantly. 'Are you all right? Is Pippi all right? Oh God,

492

what's wrong with Pippi?'

I had to give her credit, at least, for getting the correct daughter to freak out about. 'I've found out who the father is,' I told them.

'Where is he? I'll kill him,' said my father. I stared at him. He appeared to mean it.

'What?'

'Gavin,' said my mother reprovingly. 'Where is he?' she asked me. 'Who is he?'

'I'd love to tell you, but I think Pippi should do that herself. He really cares about her, he was heartbroken when she split up with him, and he had no idea she was pregnant.'

'That's what *he* says,' said my father, still in his unexpected Neanderthal vein.

'No, Dad, I believe him. I — I know him already, you see. He's a nice guy. A really nice guy.'

Mum was twisting her hands together. 'What are we going to do? What's happening?'

'Well, she ran off as soon as she saw he was here. And he's gone to find her, to convince her that he wants to help.'

My father looked a bit less ferocious. A part of my brain thought how odd it was to see him, the consummate geek, that way. I supposed it was some primal paternal instinct that hadn't been damped down even by years of reading and rational research. I wondered, fleetingly, if Leo would have been the same way had Clara grown into a young woman.

'So what do we do?' Mum asked.

'We just wait, I suppose. Let them try to sort it out.'

Mum checked her watch. 'There isn't much left of this evening.'

'They've got a few months yet.'

'Well, he'd best sort it out sooner rather than later,' Dad said dangerously.

'*Gavin.*'

'And I'd better get back to work,' I said. 'I'm not supposed to be out of character.'

'Where's Leo?' Mum asked. 'I saw him come through here on some sort of art tour with one of your friends, but they went through a door that's closed to the public and I haven't seen them since.'

Typical that Isabella would have an 'access all areas' pass-key, to get into the parts of the house that weren't open tonight. Such as the bedrooms. A swift picture seared into my mind, of Leo and Isabella lying on one of the beds, tearing at each other's clothes. My stomach turned over.

No. He wouldn't do that. And if he did, it wouldn't matter.

So why did I feel jealous?

'She's just showing him some art,' I said emphatically. 'Listen, if I find Pippi, I'll let you know. But I've got to get back to work.' I put my hand on my father's arm. 'Please don't worry, Dad. He wants to do the right thing. It's whether Pippi lets him.'

I left them in the Hall, talking anxiously with each other, while I tried to concentrate on doing my duty: talking with guests, answering questions about Eversley Hall and 1814, pretending never to have heard of *Hot! Hot!* magazine. I'd been so caught up in my own story that I'd pretty much forgotten everything else. And I would have felt guilty, except I was too busy feeling jealous and anxious.

Damn Leo for making me feel this way. At least I'd done the right thing with Arthur and Pippi. Hopefully.

The clock in the Saloon said it was nearly eleven; the next dance would be the last one of the ball. I kept my eyes open for Leo and Isabella, or for Pippi and Arthur, but I didn't see them anywhere. Reuben was back in evidence, charming Lady Fitzwilliam from the looks of it. I caught a glance of Selina and Lieutenant Waltham, from a distance, strolling in the moonlight with eyes only for each other. Finally I spotted James and hurried to his side.

'Alice,' he said with a warm smile. 'You're alone. I am afraid I haven't found you a husband this evening, after all.' A few bystanders, probably the ones who'd heard about this part of the story, laughed.

'One never knows,' I said. 'Perhaps this evening will bear fruit in other, more unexpected directions.'

'Are you engaged for the final dance?'

'No.'

'I had planned to ask Isabella, but she's nowhere to be found. Have you seen her?'

'No.'

'Then perhaps you'd dance with me instead?'

'Of course,' I said, making myself smile delightedly. This was exactly what I'd wanted, after all: to shove Isabella off onto another man so that I'd have James for myself. It was still what I wanted. I was going to dance with the most beautiful and amazing man in this world. And he wasn't even going to step on my feet.

The penultimate dance was still in full swing, so James and I strolled around the rooms, smiling and nodding, exchanging pleasantries with guests. Like the master and the mistress of the house.

'You're a very clever woman, Alice Woodstock,' he said to me.

'Why would you say that, James Fitzwilliam?'

James smiled down at me. 'Here you were, asking me to find you a husband, when all the time you were arranging things to your own satisfaction.'

'What do you mean?'

'You do play the innocent very well, don't you? It hasn't escaped my attention that your two guests, Baron Fotheringay and Mr Allingham, are precisely the sort of men that Isabella Grantham would find irresistible.'

I glanced around; we were in full hearing of several people. 'It's certainly a happy coincidence.'

'It's no coincidence. You've made a blunder though, Miss Woodstock.'

'How so?'

'You've over-egged the pudding. If there were only one guest to capture Miss Grantham's attention, I would have thought that it was a coincidence. But two is one too many. Didn't you trust Mr Allingham's attractions? Were you holding Baron Fotheringay in reserve, in case

Isabella didn't take the bait?'

'I do not understand you, Cousin,' I said coolly.

'Oh, I think you do.' He smiled at me again. We stepped outside the front door into the columned portico. The stars were out, and the moon. The estate stretched out in all directions around us.

'It's very flattering,' he said in an undertone to me. 'But why would you do it? I've already told you that Fitzwilliam and Isabella married. You can't change history.'

'You are,' I pointed out. 'You introduced Selina to that guy she fancied.'

'There was a Lieutenant Waltham at the real ball. I didn't know they would get on so well together, but I'm willing to improvise at times.'

'But she can't marry Arthur if you've set her up to be in love with someone else. She won't do it.'

James shrugged. In the dark, in his black clothes, he was a gleam of white waistcoat and a glitter of eyes. 'We're not talking about Selina here. We're talking about your devising an elaborate plot to get Isabella to spurn me in public. What did you tell them to do? Were you hoping that Leo Allingham could persuade Isabella to compromise herself?'

The two of them, in a bedroom. I closed my eyes momentarily, and then opened them to look into James's handsome face.

'No,' I said. 'I thought that she'd go for money and fame. I thought that if you saw her true colours, if everyone saw her true colours, you would have to end the engagement.'

'Everyone's seen her true colours, all right. And yours, as well. One could say that this was a very manipulative and calculating thing for you to do.'

I stepped backwards, colliding with the balustrade. 'Do you think so?'

He took my hand. He was warm even through two layers of gloves. 'No. I think it's rather sweet. And I was expecting something like this, after reading your columns. I think lots of people here tonight expected it too. You would have let us all down if you hadn't come up with some novel plan.'

'I was really hoping my plan could involve dashing highwaymen, but it was too hard,' I admitted.

James laughed. 'You're incredible,' he said. 'You couldn't get highwaymen, so you got two men to flirt with you and Isabella. The net effect of which was to make me wildly jealous. I think I might have preferred to be held up at pistol-point.'

'Oh no. Have I ruined your night?'

'I don't think it's been quite as much fun as yours and Isabella's. But the house is the important thing.'

Fun. That was one thing this evening had *not* been. Nerve-racking, yes. Frantic, definitely. Toe-crunching, even. Not fun.

Even this moment that should be a triumph, when I should be enjoying this intimate tête à tête with James and looking forward to our last dance, when I should be revelling in sexual tension . . . even this moment wasn't fun. I was on edge, biting my lip, curling my fingers in my free hand. I glanced around; there was no sign of Leo and Isabella, nor of Pippi and Arthur.

This was ridiculous. I'd won.

Inside, the music stopped. The next dance was ours. James led me back into the house, my hand on his.

'So you're not angry with me?' I asked.

'I can't be. You've gone to so much trouble to prove that you're the best woman. I can honestly say it's one of the most romantic things that anyone's ever done for me.'

I couldn't help smiling at that. 'Really?'

'Really.' He looked down at me. 'You're an extraordinary woman, you know.'

'Extraordinary does have its good bits, I suppose.'

'Definitely. I will admit, though, that Allingham did have me worried for a little while. He seemed rather keen on you.'

I focused on winding our way through the Saloon. 'Did he?'

'He appeared to have you flustered. If he hadn't gone off with Isabella, I would have been tempted to have a word.'

'Oh, that wouldn't have been necessary. We had a little . . . disagreement, that's all.'

Smoothly, James took me to the top of the dance figure, at the head of the room.

'You know, Selina thinks he's the legendary Henry Pelmet. Isn't that funny?'

'Hilarious.' I managed a laugh.

'I didn't tell her the truth.'

'What's the truth?'

'That the only eyes I want you to meet tonight across a crowded ballroom are mine.' We were in place for dancing, but the music hadn't begun yet, and he hadn't dropped my hand. 'I'm glad we have this last dance together. You've made this summer magical, Alice.'

He was looking right into my eyes, and his were blue and beautiful. If you took this moment out of time, you couldn't write it any more perfectly.

'You've made it magical for me, too,' I said.

He squeezed my hand and glanced over my shoulder. 'Look who's turned up,' he whispered.

I turned my neck and saw Leo and Isabella coming into the Saloon. Neither one of them looked as if their clothing was in disarray; they weren't flushed or breathing heavily or exchanging secret looks. Actually, Leo was frowning and looking around, not appearing to listen to what Isabella was saying to him. He caught my eye and I saw his frown deepen.

'They've seen us,' James murmured. 'It's my turn to join in the game.'

The music began, but James didn't let me go, or start to dance. Instead, he pulled me closer and kissed me full on the lips.

Whirling music, a blur of colour and light and shadow. I felt James's lips on mine, felt his strong hands at my waist holding me to him, the starch and rustle of his clothing, and I remembered another kiss, in a sunny field with only the whisper of the breeze.

I heard applause. Growing, spreading. And

whistles. The music continued its jaunty course. James finished kissing me and spun me round and round.

Out of the corner of my eye, as the room spun about me, I saw Leo's back as he left the Saloon alone.

Happily Ever Afters

That night I slept in my old room at my parents' house. It was my mother's sewing room now; she had a trestle table crammed into one side with her 1970s sewing machine on it, and plastic boxes full of scraps of cloth. She'd made some sort of abstract sculpture with spools of thread.

Although 'slept' is a loose term for what I did. By the time I climbed into my old, lumpy bed it was significantly past two o'clock in the morning. Arthur and Pippi had emerged as the ball was ending, with twigs in their hair and grass clippings on their shoes, looking very much as if they'd spent the past hour hiding in the bushes talking, which was exactly what they had done. As they had appeared not a metre from where my parents were standing, they weren't able to make a discreet exit. Coincidentally, my mother had been talking to Arthur's mother at the time, not knowing who she was.

Dad had been all mouth and no trousers and he'd failed to murder Arthur on sight. Instead, my mother had rounded on both of them and told Arthur in no uncertain terms that he was coming back to our house for a cup of tea, and his parents were coming too. Also fortunately, this had taken place out of sight of James Fitzwilliam (and me; I found it all out later), so Arthur didn't get in trouble for hanging out with the modern-day teenage girl he had impregnated instead of pretending it was 1814.

As they were leaving, my parents had found me and told me that Pippi's 'young man' was coming back with them, and I immediately decided that the best thing to do was to go back to theirs and help sort out the situation I had pretty much brought about. In case Arthur needed any more pep talks, or Pippi needed any sisterly advice.

Plus, I didn't want to go back to my house. Not tonight, when Leo was there, and there was the probability of having to talk about the feelings he'd confessed to me and my very public kiss with James. Somehow it seemed much easier to stick with my sister's life.

My sister's life, however, didn't need too much immediate sorting. During their time in the shrubbery, Arthur (or rather, Nick) had persuaded Pippi to confess that the baby was actually his, and to agree that she should at least let him find out about what was happening. Both of them were still too shocked to come to any definite conclusions, and Arthur/Nick's parents were nearly speechless. His mother was still in pale blue silk with an ostrich feather nodding from her turban, and his father wore military red and gold. They were quite an incongruous sight on the worn sofa, surrounded by clutter, holding mugs my father had been given at the 1998 Molecular Quantum Mechanics conference in California.

But Nick sat in an armchair, his neckcloth loosened and his waistcoat and coat off, and submitted himself to the Celia Woodstock

Inquisition, which was the barrage of questions our mother launched at any person who happened to fancy getting romantically involved with one of her children. It was a bit terrifying. I couldn't help but think now that I'd got off easily, in that department at least, by marrying a boy about whom she already knew almost everything.

I watched how Pippi and Nick looked at each other. Their hesitancy that melted away at sudden moments, when he made her laugh, or when she acted almost shy with him. The way he watched her touch her belly, wonder already growing in his face. How he pored over the photograph of the scan.

He was scared shitless, I could see. But he should be scared shitless; it was the only reasonable emotion to have. The remarkable thing was that there were other emotions there too. Maybe even enough emotions to mean that they could make it.

His parents went home about half past midnight, leaving Nick behind to talk with Pippi. They shook hands with all of us, still looking bewildered, and my parents and I went to bed.

I lay upstairs listening to the murmur of talking downstairs, looking at the wedge of light coming through my door from the staircase. I used to do the same thing when I was a kid and my parents were talking downstairs. I'd found it comforting, I remembered. Before I'd had to make any of my own decisions, I'd lain here and trusted in the infallibility of adults, their omnipotence, the power of their love to protect.

I pulled the duvet up to my chin. My body instinctively curled round to avoid the place where the mattress sagged and the other place where the spring poked through. Funny how your body never forgot things like that, no matter how long it had been.

The last time I'd slept here was the night before I'd married Leo. He was sleeping in Wendy's old room down the landing. I hadn't slept then, either; my mind was too full of him. He'd sneaked in here after everyone else was asleep.

I curled and uncurled myself in the bed, and then went back to how I'd been before. I couldn't stop thinking about what he'd said tonight. Even when I'd been downstairs with Pippi and Nick and our parents, I'd been thinking about him.

I came here dressed up in these clothes and I'm dancing a dance I don't know how to do. Because I still love you.

I hadn't believed him then. But something in the intervening hours had changed my mind. Maybe it was the way I'd felt when he went off with Isabella. Or when he'd come back from being with Isabella, and I'd known without even looking closely that he hadn't touched her. I'd known all along that he wouldn't. All the jealousy wasn't because I thought he would run off; it was my guts' own way of telling me that I cared enough not to want him to.

Maybe it was the way he walked off when he'd seen me kissing James. He hadn't fought for me, like one kind of hero. Instead he'd walked off, leaving me with my choice, like a wholly other kind of hero.

Maybe it was the memory of how he'd looked at me last night. And every minute since he'd returned.

He loved me. It was the only explanation that made sense. He loved me enough to stick around in Brickham and try to sort things out. And he loved me enough to walk away and let me choose the life that would make me more happy.

Mostly though, it was my heart that told me. Literally, I could feel Leo's love there in my chest, burning. I'd felt it on my wedding night, all mixed up with anticipation and excitement. This was heavier. Sadder. More complicated.

It was still there.

I turned over in bed again and heard the springs creak. 'Damn parents never replace anything until it totally falls apart,' I muttered, but it was only a failing distraction. I was thinking of Leo with Pippi when she was afraid. I was thinking of Mr Allingham painted on the wall of the living room. I was thinking of a thousand times of him running his hand through his hair, of the rock music in the house, of the flash of his dark eyes and the way he made the house buzz with his presence. His bitter laughter when I'd rejected him at Liv's wedding, the surprised understanding when I'd handed him Clara's box. Those fast, frantic moments in his bed when I wanted someone to turn to.

Leo still loved me. And I still loved him, too.

I stopped pretending to sleep and sat up. Yes, I loved him. The knowledge gave me no joy.

Instead, I felt my insides sinking into dread.

If I loved him, we had another long road to tread together. All the history and grief and all the forgiving.

Maybe if I hadn't shut him out after Clara died, we'd still be together. Maybe if I'd tried to understand him and accept him, we could have helped each other. Our love could have grown stronger.

But it was too late. I'd already made my mistakes, and Leo had made his.

I thought of Selina and Lieutenant Waltham. How, the moment they met, their world had exploded into quiet joy. Even the new couple downstairs, the young people who were about to become parents. They had their challenges ahead of them. Maybe they wouldn't stay together as a couple. But they had something that Leo and I didn't have any more. Maybe it was optimism. Maybe it was the hope of beginning something new. Maybe it was bloody naïveté.

Whatever it was, whatever would happen to them, they had their now.

It all came down to that moment in the scan room, when I'd watched Pippi's baby come into focus, and I'd realised that you couldn't let the future steal the wonder from the present. You had to live every moment as it happened.

I'd had enough of history and grief. Beds I had to twist myself around to accommodate their failings. Wasn't it time for me to have something new?

★ ★ ★

507

I woke up with my head on the bottom of the bed, my feet on the pillow and the light streaming through the 1980s bamboo blinds. I blinked sleepily, my first thought to wonder what lessons I had first thing this morning at school, and then I sat up and quickly reached for my handbag. It was stashed underneath the chair of my mother's sewing desk, with my ballgown draped over the back.

My mobile phone showed one unread text message from Selina, sent this morning, and a time of 10.16 a.m. Shit. Eversley Hall opened at 10.00 a.m. on Sundays. Even the morning after the ball.

I jumped out of bed and pulled off Pippi's borrowed pyjamas. Nobody else seemed to be stirring as I hurried to the bathroom and wrestled a brush through my hair before pinning it up the best I could. Oh God, did Regency gentlewomen never have bedhead, even after a ball? I was nearly done when I noticed a long lock at the back of my neck that I hadn't tucked away with the others. To do it properly, I'd have to take down everything I'd already done. Or I could pin it up. But I didn't have any more pins. I opened the bathroom drawers, looking for a contraband twenty-first-century hair grip, but couldn't find anything apart from a small red, pink and white Hello Kitty hair-slide.

It would have to do. I twisted the lock up and stuffed it underneath the weight of my hair at the back, secured it with the slide, and then re-arranged my hair quickly to cover up the wide-eyed kitty. Then I splashed water on my face, brushed my teeth with my finger, collected my Regency clothes, and ran down the stairs.

The kitchen sink was full of last night's unwashed tea mugs. I wished for a cup of tea and had a glass of water instead, dumped some food into the cats' bowl to make Maggie, Tim and Fuzzicat stop winding around my legs, and stuck my head through to the living room.

Arthur was asleep on the sofa. My mother's multi-coloured crocheted throw was pulled up over him. I went in and shook his shoulder.

'Arth — Nick. We're supposed to be at the house.'

He screwed up his eyes, and then looked around and sat up, rubbing his chin where a slight unshaven roughness had appeared. He'd gone to sleep in his linen shirt and looked an odd combination of old-fashioned and totally present-day young man.

'What time is it?'

'It's nearly half past ten.'

His eyes widened. 'Oh. Shit. Okay. Um . . . I'm not wearing trousers.'

'Okay.' I retreated to the kitchen, where I turned on the kettle. If I had to wait for him anyway, I might as well see if I had enough time for a quick cuppa.

I checked the text from Selina; it had been sent at about nine o'clock. *Am ok, talk later. Xx*

Of course she was okay. She was in love.

It was already a beautiful day outside; I saw blue sky and fluffy clouds through the window. The kind of day for new beginnings.

I'd made my decision at some point last night,

while tossing and turning in my childhood bed. I was going to start again, with James. I was going to see where that public, romantic, storybook kiss took us.

I loved Leo. But the truth was, he reminded me of grief and heartbreak. I'd been angry when he'd turned up because he'd hurt me two years ago, yes — but I'd also been angry because he'd forced me to remember. And remembering hurt.

It was what I'd said to Nick last night: there were moments when you got to be a hero — or in my case, a heroine. Moments when you made the choices that would lead to the rest of your life. I wanted to be happy right now.

So I was choosing James.

The kettle was erupting steam when Nick appeared in the kitchen, buttoning his waistcoat over his breeches. 'Blimey, we're really late, aren't we?'

'I'm making tea to go,' I said, reaching for my dad's flask. 'We can drink it in the car. Want some?'

He nodded. 'I'm going to go upstairs and say goodbye to Pippi. Er . . . which room is hers?'

He was so sweet and awkward, asking where Pippi slept when the two of them were going to have a baby together. I smiled at him. 'It's the first right at the top of the stairs. The best bedroom in the house. Of course.'

I poured water on tea bags while he loped up the stairs. This morning, it looked like that was going to be another happy ending. For all of Nick's joking and Pippi's dramatics, there was some deep feeling there. It wasn't going to be easy. But they were young, and still courageous.

I paused, mashing tea bags. Here I was, thinking of myself as ancient. That was another reason that James was the right choice. There wasn't the weight of history there. I wouldn't have to be afraid that memory or grief would ambush me when I was least expecting it. I could stop hiding.

'Okay,' said Nick, coming back into the kitchen. 'Let's go.'

I poured milk into the flask and grabbed an extra plastic mug. 'How are you today?' I asked him as we headed out of the door and to the 2CV.

'I'm all right. Actually, I'm pretty good. The whole baby thing doesn't seem so shocking any more.'

'That's because you're *still* in shock.' I started the car, and he laughed.

'Yeah, maybe.' He sighed. 'I don't think I've ever had so many emotions at once. I have no idea how I'm going to do Arthur today.'

'Maybe do Arthur with a hangover.'

'Good idea. Tea?'

'Yes, please.'

'I really care about your sister, you know, Alice. Thank you for making me talk with her. I think if you hadn't said anything, I'd have run in the opposite direction. And that would've been easier in the short term, but in the end it would have just made everything even harder. I believe I made the right decision.'

I accepted my tea and drank it with one hand while keeping my eyes on the road. We were

511

going through the ugliest part of Brickham, all the smashed bus stops and scruffy retail estates, the modern detritus before we reached the rolling hills and calm river on the way to Eversley Hall.

I wasn't running away from anything. I was running *to* something, to a new life. I'd made the right decision, too. I felt lighter this morning for having made it. That meant it was the right one, didn't it?

The right decision didn't always have to be the more dangerous one. It didn't always require courage.

I wasn't as brave as Nick. But maybe I didn't need to be.

We lapsed into silence as I drove. I put my foot down as soon as it was safe, and Nick looked out of the window at the passing houses and trees, lost in his own thoughts. When we got to Eversley Hall the visitor car park was already half-full.

'We're going to be in so much trouble,' Nick said. 'I'm glad I'm with the boss's favourite.'

'We'll have to make up some kind of story for cover,' I said, pulling into the staff car park.

'Like what?'

'I'll think of something. Just go, run to the staff room now while there's no one around to see you getting out of a car in your costume.'

He looked both ways, then leaped out of the 2CV and ran, head down, like a character under fire in an action film. I laughed, and folded up my gown carefully before I followed him in a more normal manner.

The staff room was deserted, though the chairs were still in their circle from the morning's briefing. Highwaymen, I mused as I tightened my own stays and slipped into my black day dress. Could we have been ambushed by highwaymen between the shrubbery and the Drawing Room? Or footpads, at least, who tied us up and stole Arthur's non-existent signet ring and my non-existent jewels, before I managed to use a pin from my hair to free Arthur's hands so he could seize the lead robber, making him drop his pistol where I could snatch it up, having freed my own hands, causing the other villains to drop our valuables and flee into the woods?

James would laugh. I'd have to remember not to use the Hello Kitty hair slide as evidence. I fastened the final buttons, tied the final ribbons, and emerged from the female dressing room to find Nick awaiting me, back in his non-ball Arthur clothes. His cravat was perhaps less elaborately tied than normal, and his hair was still dishevelled, but if you didn't know he'd spent the night on the sofa belonging to the family of the mother-to-be of his child, you could believe he was a young Regency gentleman who'd got rather too foxed at the ball the night before. And then was waylaid by footpads. Maybe.

'I don't dare go in there without you,' he said. 'Have you thought up a good story?'

'Sort of. It's implausible. I think I'll have to play it by ear. Just agree with everything I say, okay?'

He nodded and together we rushed across the

courtyard from the west pavilion and up through the front door.

The Hall was deserted. The house was quiet.

'Where is everyone?' Nick asked.

'Maybe one of us was supposed to be in this room and there's no one to take care of it.'

'Where are the visitors though?'

We stood still and listened. Nothing. No murmur of guests, no Isabella's ringing voice in the next room. I put my head into James's Library; it was deserted too. 'Do you think everyone's outside?'

'Let's check the Drawing Room. Maybe James had something planned.'

Nick's footsteps echoed on the marble floor of the Hall; my feet, in slippers with leather soles, made only a whisper. The silence, the empty house, reminded me of a time I'd had to read and read, fill my head with words, to drown out the silence.

I felt dread growing, dark and shadowy, inside my chest.

I could hear something now from the direction of the Drawing Room: muted low voices, and something louder, something that sounded like a sob. My heart sank further and despite themselves, my feet hurried.

There were lots of people in the Drawing Room. Not as many as there had been last night, but nearly. The normal furniture had been reinstated and the visitors lined the walls, forming a circle around the people in Regency dress. The candlelight was gone and sunlight streamed through the windows, bright enough to

514

illuminate the tiny motes of dust and pollen that danced in the air. The room still smelled of lilies.

Mrs Smudge, Mrs Collins and all the people in servant dress stood in a semi-circle that was nearly a huddle. The sobs were coming from Lady Fitzwilliam, who sat on the sofa, a lace-edged handkerchief pressed to her face. Isabella held her other hand.

Aside from the dancing dust and Lady Fitzwilliam's shaking shoulders, nothing moved when we came into the room. It was like stepping into an odd painting, a mixture of period and anachronism. All that was missing was the caption on the bottom, to explain the meaning.

James was the only person who reacted to our entrance. He turned his head and said in a quiet voice, 'Ah. Here you are.'

The lilies, and the crying, and the quiet. 'James? What has happened?' I asked, my voice made choked and small.

He crossed the room and took me into his arms. For a confused moment I thought maybe he'd told everyone he'd broken off his engagement with Isabella. But that wouldn't make everything so quiet, would it? Isabella wouldn't just be sitting there, her face pale, holding on to Lady Fitzwilliam's hand? Past the circle of James's arms I could see another person in period costume — Lieutenant Waltham, still in his dress uniform, sitting in an armchair as if he'd been knocked into it. Next to him was a little thin man I didn't recognise, in a dark coat and black waistcoat.

Who was he? What was Waltham doing here? I pulled back from James's embrace and looked around. 'Where's Selina?' I asked.

James's arms tightened around me. 'Alice. Arthur. You haven't heard.'

'Heard what?' I tilted my head back and looked into his face, into the grave blue eyes. 'What's happened, James?'

'Our dear Selina is no longer with us.'

'What? Where did she go? She didn't run off with someone, did she? Lieutenant Waltham is right here, and she's not the type to elope, is she?'

'I wish that she had eloped with Lieutenant Waltham. You sleep so soundly, dear Alice, you must have missed everything.' I felt him draw in a long breath. 'Selina was taken ill last night after the ball was over. Her mother has been nursing her all night, and Lieutenant Waltham has been standing vigil. I rode for Doctor Jillings.'

He took in another breath as dread sank into my body, deep into my bones. 'Doctor Jillings said it was a burst appendix,' he said. 'He gave her laudanum for the pain, but he could do nothing else. The infection was too rapid. This morning, in her mother's arms, Selina died.'

Goodbye

I stiffened and grabbed James's arms. Lady Fitzwilliam wailed. It sounded real. Not like a fictional mother mourning a daughter who didn't really exist.

'She what?' I said.

'We've lost Selina,' James said gently. 'She died this morning.'

'But she can't have done. She — she was in love. She was going to be happy.'

'I know. Lieutenant Waltham was the one who first saw that she was unwell. He's been pacing Eversley Hall with us all night.'

I looked from James to Lieutenant Waltham, to Lady Fitzwilliam. To Arthur, who was standing with his hand on his heart, stricken.

'Is this real, or not?' I said.

'Alice. This is a shock to you. Please, sit down, and Mrs Collins will bring you a glass of water.'

'No, I don't want to sit down. I want to know what you're talking about. Is Selina really dead? She's not, is she? This is all part of the historical act?'

The historical act. My perfect world. My happy ending. I began to shake.

'Alice,' said James again, stroking my shoulder. I heard a slight warning in his voice.

'She can't be dead,' I said. 'That's not right. People don't die of appendicitis.'

'It is an acute and deadly infection,' said the

517

thin man in black, who I assumed was pretending to be this Doctor Jillings person. I hated him. 'People do indeed die of it, even in these modern times. Surgery can in some instances save them, but in Miss Fitzwilliam's case, it was too late.'

'It's a stupid thing to die of. She can't be dead. She shouldn't be dead. James, how did you let her?'

'I tried everything I could to save her,' he said gently. 'Everyone did.'

'No, you didn't.'

James frowned, and I pulled myself out of his arms, anger surging through me, replacing the dread. I welcomed it.

'You could have saved her,' I said passionately, 'but you didn't. You're in charge of this whole thing. She was happy, James, she was coming out of herself for the first time. And now you've killed her, you've let her die. You've sent her away and we'll never see her again.'

'Alice, you're becoming hysterical. Please, sit down.'

'I won't sit down! You can't do this, James! It's — it's wrong. This was supposed to be the happy ending. What's the point in all this — this dressing up and playacting if you're going to ruin it all?'

Everyone was utterly still, even Lady Fitzwilliam. James grasped my wrist. 'You are upset. You don't know what you're saying. Come with me, my dear.' He escorted me firmly through the silent room, out of the door and into the Hall, where he opened the secret servants' door and

518

propelled me upstairs and into his office.

'What on earth are you playing at?' he demanded, his blue eyes snapping, his voice low, but full of anger. 'I can see how this news would be a shock to you, but you know that the one rule, the *only* rule here, is that we maintain the illusion that this is 1814! What are you doing, talking about playacting in front of visitors?'

'Is that all this is to you?' I didn't bother to keep my voice low. 'Is it playacting? Is it a game? How could you kill her, James?'

'I didn't kill her. Selina Fitzwilliam really did die. Exactly as I told you it happened. Her appendix burst after the ball in August and she died the next morning, a Sunday. I have her death certificate signed by a Doctor Jillings.'

'You've known this from the beginning?'

'Of course I have.'

My mouth dropped open and for a split second, I was speechless. Then the words came bursting out.

'You knew? You've known all this time that Selina was going to die? And you never told her? You never told anyone?'

'I've explained before that sometimes it's best to withhold information so that it can cause a genuine reaction in the house. Do you think Lady Fitzwilliam is a good enough actress to fake tears like that? Do you think Selina could have played her part as she did if she'd known she was going to die? She'd have worried about it. She'd have given up. Instead, look at the blaze of glory she went out in.'

'That's what you're thinking of — a blaze of

glory? Creating real tears? Where is Selina now?'

'She's on her way back home. I bought her a first-class ticket. Calm down, Alice. You love this illusion as much as anyone — more than anyone. But Selina isn't really dead.'

'Yes, she is.' I sank into a chair. 'You're the one who made her real to me. You're the one who made all of this real to me. And now you've destroyed it.'

'Alice,' he said. He put his hand on my shoulder. 'I love how you're so immersed in the world of Eversley Hall, but you've got to pull yourself together. Selina Fitzwilliam died. It's an historical fact. I haven't destroyed anything: I'm keeping it accurate.'

'The accuracy isn't what's important! It's the feelings. It's my feelings, and Lady Fitzwilliam's feelings. She never had a daughter, you know. Selina didn't even want to go back to Cumbria. She was happy here.'

'She didn't have to go if she didn't want to.'

'She really was falling in love with Marcus. She wasn't acting.'

'I'm not keeping her from him,' James said, his voice reasonable. 'She had no more reason to stay, now that her part is over.'

'Now that you killed her, you mean.'

'I didn't kill her,' he said, and now he did sound testy again. 'You keep on saying that, and it's not true. Appendicitis killed the real Selina Fitzwilliam, and my cousin Sarah, who was pretending to be her, is alive and well in a first-class carriage to Penrith.'

'But you could have made it all happy,' I said.

'I thought that was what you were doing last night when you introduced her to Lieutenant Waltham. I thought you'd decided to let go of the whole historical accuracy thing and let her have her happy ending. But instead, you — you knew she was going to die, and so it didn't matter.'

'It could have happened that way,' James said. 'History doesn't document everything. There's nothing to prove that Selina Fitzwilliam didn't fall in love the night before she died. That's where the interest lies, where the imagination can help. That's what you've been doing so well, up till now.'

'And what about you and me? Why did you kiss me, if all you care about is historical accuracy?'

'I wanted to.'

'No, you didn't. You did it for the house.'

The silence before he replied was just a beat too long.

'I really do like you, Alice. A lot.'

'But the house is more important.'

'And that's what I've always said, isn't it? It's not fair to throw it in my face now, at this point.'

'You care more about Eversley Hall than how real people feel.' I felt tears burning in the back of my throat, and I swallowed them down. I'd rather have the anger. Anger made you full. Tears made you empty.

'I can't believe you killed her. I can't believe you told Lady Fitzwilliam, just like that, in front of everybody, because it made the tears more real. You've got a child, James. You've got a son.

How would you feel if someone told you he'd died, just like that?'

'Calm down, please, Alice. Look at this rationally.'

'There is no rationally about it. You let her die. Somebody's child.' A single tear escaped and slid down my cheek. I wiped it away.

'Everyone dies, Alice. In fact everyone in Eversley Hall is playing the role of someone who died. Someone who's dead already. All of us are dead — the Fitzwilliams, the Granthams, all of the servants. They're dead, and their children are dead, long ago. The only person who's playing someone alive is you, and that's because Alice Woodstock isn't real.'

'I'm real,' I said. 'The feelings are real. It's what I keep on telling you, and you don't get it. You've been manipulating people's feelings so that you can get a better reaction, so that you can put on a better show for the public, so that you can get more people in here — and what for? For your son? You don't even *see* him, James. He's alive right now and you're spending all your time in this house instead of watching him grow up.'

James flushed with anger. 'Charles has nothing to do with — '

'He has *everything* to do with it. But you can't see it because you think Eversley Hall is more important than the people you're supposed to care about.' I took a deep, shuddery breath. 'I don't want to be a part of it any more. I'm leaving.'

'Alice — '

'No.' I strode to the door and wrenched it open. 'I'm finished. I'm sick of putting on a show for you. Goodbye.'

I ran through the passage, back into the Hall, pulling the pins from my hair as I went. Some visitors had wandered into the Hall; I couldn't tell whether they were the ones who'd witnessed my outburst, or new ones who'd recently arrived at the house and didn't know the latest developments yet. I didn't care. I wasn't going to do my job and repeat James's news about Selina's death over and over for them, in between talking about the furniture and the architecture. I'd come to Eversley Hall to escape talking about death and failure.

I dropped pins in a trail on the marble floor. They made small pings as my hair fell down around my shoulders, into my eyes. The last one was the Hello Kitty slide, the one 200 years out of date. I dropped it with the others. And then I walked out of Eversley Hall.

Little Mermaid

I drove from 1814 to the twenty-first century without seeing anything except for the road, with my hands tight on the wheel and my dry eyes staring straight ahead of me. I was still wearing my gown, pulled impatiently up over my knees so I could work the brake, clutch and accelerator.

My heart was hammering like crazy in my chest when I pulled up in front of my house and walked to the door, staring straight ahead, not to the left or to the right, because if I started looking around too much, if I started thinking about what I'd done and what I felt, I would realise I'd just thrown away everything I'd wanted. I would remember the Selina I knew dancing, remember Selina giggling, think of the real Selina Fitzwilliam cold in her bed of a burst appendix, think of everyone at Eversley Hall dead. I would remember, again, the silent, empty apartment in Boston. The empty life I thought I'd left behind, filled with dead books and false stories.

I put my hand on the doorknob, focusing on the doorknob only. It turned under my hand, seemingly by itself, and then the door opened and Leo was standing on the other side of it.

'Alice?' he said. 'What are you doing back?'

I stared at Leo. He was wearing jeans and a Stealers Wheel T-shirt. He held a garment bag marked *Madhouse Costume Supplies*. Behind him, in the house, the radio was playing.

'Mermaid? Are you all right? Tell me what's the matter.'

I stepped forward. I knew his T-shirt would be warm and soft from many washings before I touched it. I put my hands on his chest where his heart was beating. I looked into his eyes, his dark sad eyes.

'She died,' I said.

His brow creased slightly with feeling, but his eyes stayed on mine.

'I know,' he said.

I didn't think of how Leo would know that Selina was dead. I didn't think of anything. Just Leo's eyes, and his T-shirt, and his heart. I stepped closer and he folded his arms around me. I put my cheek on his chest, which rose and fell with his breathing. I wrapped my arms around his waist.

I closed my eyes and that's when the tears came. Like a release. Like a wave washing through me. They rose hot in my blinded eyes and coursed down my cheeks and I sobbed in breaths full of Leo and let them out.

Let them out.

He murmured down into my hair. I didn't hear the words, but I felt the warmth from his lips and felt him holding me. I clung to him and cried, like I hadn't for two years. Not in Brickham, not in Boston. Not even in the hospital when the nurse had given me a box. I cried because my child had died and my friend had been sent away and my illusions had all been untrue. I cried because Leo and I had had a love that was beautiful and I wasn't brave enough to snatch it back. I cried for the perfect rooms in Eversley Hall, a living museum of the dead.

I don't know how long I cried; the tears had a momentum of their own, and they had been building up inside me. I was vaguely aware that Leo was lifting me, taking me out of the doorway and carrying me upstairs, with his arms looped around my back and around my knees, like he'd carried me across the threshold of our first home as a married couple. He put me down on my single bed in my room and I clung to him until he lay down beside me and held me, stroking my hair.

'I know,' he was saying, again and again, in a soft voice. I put my hand to his cheek and it was wet, too. Blinking away drops and smears, I looked at his face for the first time since I'd started crying.

'I miss her too,' he said to me.

And I saw he'd been crying for Clara. I'd never seen him cry before, not in all those years.

'I — I'm not even . . . ' I sniffed. 'I didn't mean Clara. I meant — I meant Selina.'

He wiped his eyes, and then he wiped my cheek. It didn't seem to be doing any good, especially since the tears were still leaking out of my eyes. 'Who's Selina?'

'You met her last night. She's my friend.'

'She died?'

'She . . . ' I took a long shaky breath, and incredibly, I laughed. 'No. It's a long story, she . . . ' I wiped my own eyes, and my nose, with my hand, which came away wet and slimy. 'Oh God, I really need a tissue, this is gross.'

Leo raised his head. 'Do you have any in here?'

'No.' I reached for my pillowcase, but Leo's shoulder was on it. There wasn't actually that much room on this bed.

'Here. Use this, it's already covered.' He sat up and pulled off his Stealers Wheel T-shirt. I buried my face in it.

'Sorry,' I said, my voice muffled by his shirt.

I felt him touch my shoulder. 'You're worth a little extra laundry. You're going to need to wash that dress now, too.'

I wiped my nose and eyes. The sobs were still coming, small and hiccupy. 'I don't think I need the dress any more.' I held out his T-shirt for him. 'Thanks.'

'You can leave it on the floor, I think,' he said, smiling gently and stroking my hair back from my face. I caught a glimpse of his bare arm and the tattoo on it I'd noticed weeks ago. I hiccuped in surprise and propped myself up on my elbow to see it more clearly.

It was small. A baby mermaid, with perfect hands and face and a delicate green tail. It was drawn in Leo's style. Underneath it, in tiny letters, the name CLARA.

'Leo,' I said.

I touched the tattoo with my finger. Leo's skin, our daughter's name. Mermaid, his name for me.

'When did you do this?' It wasn't recent. It had settled into his skin and blood, lived with him, tanned in the sun in a foreign country.

'A year ago. A year and a half. After you left, the time blurs together.'

I traced it. She had such tiny hands, so tiny you could hardly believe they were real, with wrinkles that seemed wrong on somebody so young. They would curl around my finger and you could see the papery fingernails. She had dark eyes and the faintest fuzz of red hair.

'You've carried her with you all this time,' I whispered.

'I've carried both of you,' Leo said to me.

And the tears came again. This time, I was crying purely for Clara and Leo, and I did it with my eyes open, looking at that tiny fragile figure with the child's body and the fish's tail. It wasn't real. And yet I cried because she was more real than anything, or anyone, else. Except for the person who'd drawn her and helped create her, who held me, whom I'd carried with me all this time, too.

★ ★ ★

When I woke up it was still light outside. I felt shaken and empty, but it wasn't a bad empty. I felt washed clean.

I sat up. Leo wasn't lying next to me, though I knew he'd held me while I slept. I put my hand on the pillow where his head had lain, and it was still warm. His crumpled T-shirt lay on the floor.

For years, I hadn't cried because I'd been too afraid. I thought if I cried that I'd be admitting something was wrong. If I cried then I would

528

never stop. But I'd done it now. And the sun was still shining. The world was still going on.

I got up off the bed and took off my black mourning gown. I found modern underwear and jeans and a T-shirt. Then I twisted a pencil in my hair and went downstairs.

He wasn't in his room or in the bathroom either, though I washed my face while I was there. I looked pale with blue shadows under my eyes. I had no idea how long I'd slept. I did know that I'd felt safe, beside Leo. I'd felt at home in a way I hadn't felt since we'd been apart.

I'd been right when I'd thought he was a different kind of hero. Not the kind who'd fight dragons for me; not the kind who'd promise me a happily ever after. He was the kind that happened after the happily ever after. The kind who'd stand beside me and argue with me and suffer with me and fail and try harder, and make me try harder, too.

He was the real kind.

'I love you,' I practised saying to the mirror. 'I still love you, too.'

It sounded okay. It sounded right.

'Leo?' I called from the top of the stairs. I didn't hear him answer. I hoped that meant he was in the kitchen, making coffee and tea. I walked down the stairs, smiling.

This morning seemed a century ago. I'd woken up for the first time today determined to start a new life with James, and now I'd woken up again and I knew I had to renew my life with Leo. If James hadn't let Selina die, I would still be with him now, still plotting to overthrow

Isabella. Still playing at feeling.

Selina. I suddenly remembered the message on my phone, and her text message which had a completely different meaning from what I'd thought. I found my bag where I'd dropped it by the front door, and located my phone.

There were two of them now. I reread the first one, which had probably been sent from the train and was meant to be a reassurance that she was, in fact, alive.

The second message was also from Selina. It had a distinctly triumphant tone. *Got off train in Birmingham, coming back. C u in pub after work? Unless u r with Mr P?* ☺ *Sarah xx*

I held the phone, grinning like Selina's smiley. Or rather, Sarah's. 'Leo!' I called. 'Selina's coming back to Brickham!'

There wasn't any answer. For the first time since I'd arrived in the house, I looked around.

It was neat. All of it was very neat, as neat as it had been when Liv was still here. No jumpers thrown on the sofa, no paperbacks or magazines, no coffee cups or sketchbooks. The radio wasn't on, and the air hung with the clean, start-over smell of fresh emulsion.

Something was missing, something more than Leo's clutter. I turned around, scanning the room, until I realised two things at the same time. Two suitcases sat near the sofa. And the picture of Mr Allingham was gone. Painted over with fresh, blank white.

I stood, phone in hand, as if I'd been quick-frozen right there on the hardwood floor. Leo was packed. Leo was leaving.

Had the suitcases been there when I'd got home? Or had he packed just now? What about the painting — surely he hadn't done all that while I was sleeping? Or had he? I racked my brain to remember, but all I could recall was walking straight into his arms and crying my heart out.

'Leo!' Unstuck, I threw my phone on the sofa and ran into the kitchen. He wasn't there. It was clean and tidy. The coffee pot was back in the cabinet. Even the tea towels were perfectly aligned.

He couldn't leave. Not now, not again. He said he'd stopped running away.

But what if I'd driven him away, by choosing James? By not believing him when he'd said he loved me?

His suitcases were still here. He couldn't have gone far, not yet. Maybe he was hailing a taxi. I raced to the front door and wrenched it open and ran out into the sunshine, under the chestnut trees. 'Leo!' I yelled.

I didn't know what I was going to do. A heroine would find him. She'd track him to the ends of the earth, or at the very least turn up at Heathrow as he was going through security and shout that she loved him in front of a thousand people who would all burst into applause as he vaulted the X-ray machine and swept her into his arms.

Get a grip, Alice. This wasn't a romcom. This was real life, and Leo wouldn't go anywhere without his bags. But it was hard to think past the pure panic in my stomach, the gnawing fear that this was it, he was gone, that I'd realised that I loved him too late.

'Alice? What are you doing?'

I whirled around and he was there on the pavement, wearing a clean T-shirt, holding two takeaway drinks cups in his hands.

'I thought you'd left,' I gasped.

'I did leave, to get chocolate milkshakes. You need fluids and sugar, and Spiros is some sort of genius.'

'No, I thought you'd left. For good.'

'Ah. You saw the suitcases. Yeah.'

'Where are you going?'

'London, at first. Then probably San Francisco. I made some phone calls last night.'

'But why? You said you were done with running away.'

He put the milkshakes down on the front step, then sat down beside them. 'I don't want to run away, but I don't know what else to do. I can't stay here if you're with another man. I learned that last night. I'll just do something stupid that I'll regret. It's better to go.'

'I'm not with James.'

'I saw you kissing him last night, in front of everyone. That was a pretty definitive sign.'

'I thought I wanted him. But I don't.'

Leo sighed. He leaned his elbows on his knees. 'You're saying this because something's happened to upset you at Eversley Hall. But it *is* what you want, Alice. I saw it last night, though I didn't want to. It's changed you, it's made you happy. And what have I done? Fucked around the States making art that didn't change a damn

532

thing. I never even rang you. You're right to choose him. He hasn't let you down, and I did.' He picked up the cups and held one of them out to me. 'We might as well have a milkshake together before I catch my train.'

'No,' I said. 'I don't love James. I loved the image of what I thought he was. I loved the oil painting. But you're a person, Leo, with faults and mistakes. You're real, and that's why I love you.'

He didn't move. He kept sitting there with two chocolate milkshakes in his hands.

'What did you just say?' he said.

'I love you. I knew that last night, and I know it even more now. I didn't let myself choose you because I knew if I faced you, if I really talked with you, I'd have to face my own pain, because it's your pain too. I'd have to cry. And I was afraid of crying because I thought I'd never stop. It seemed less dangerous to keep on going, keep on reading, keep on making up stories.'

I took a long, shaky breath. 'But I've cried now and it wasn't as scary as I thought it was. It was good. It felt right. I need to feel that pain so I can move through it. Not to forget Clara, but to start living again.'

Leo nodded. He nodded again. Then he put down the cups, carefully, on the steps, as if the next few minutes of his life depended entirely on him not spilling a single drop of chocolate.

'I get the pain part,' he said. 'But can we maybe get back to the love part again for a minute?'

'I love you,' I told him.

'Really?'

'How can I not love a man who gives me his favourite T-shirt to use as a tissue?'

'Second favourite. Come here.'

He grabbed my hand and pulled me down into his lap, right there on the steps in the front of the house. I wrapped my arms around his neck and we kissed.

Not out of desperation or anger or sadness. A proper kiss, with his body as warm as sunshine, a kiss full of the past and possibilities, sadness and joy, and more than anything, the truth.

We kissed and kissed and kissed again and he pulled me tight against him.

'Actually,' he murmured, 'I think that T-shirt is my favourite one now.'

Welcome To Now

'Coming to the Duke of Wellington?' I called to the room of people changing back into modern life.

'Definitely,' answered Nick, tossing a Hessian boot in the air and catching it by its heel. 'I like good old Arthur Grantham, but I want to celebrate not being him any more.'

'Sarah and Marcus will be there,' Lady Fitzwilliam said. Her real name was Pamela. She smoothed her black gown on the hanger, letting her fingers linger on the chenille trim. 'You know, I'm tired of wearing black, but I'm almost going to miss this dress.'

'Almost.' I hung my own black dress on the rack next to hers. 'I'm more excited to see what you've made for the Hampshire ball next month.'

'Oh! I found the most delectable watered silk in a sort of buttery yellow, and gold brocade for the pelisse.'

'I still owe you that drink,' Kayleigh said to me, from her perch on Samuel the gardener's lap. 'Do you have any money?' she asked him. He smiled, tightened his arms around her and nodded.

Isabella zipped up a heavy garment bag. 'Well,' she said, 'I'll wish you all adieu. It's been an interesting summer.'

'Aren't you coming to the pub, sis?' Nick asked.

'No, I've got to prepare for tomorrow; I'm starting as Anne Boleyn. Here's my card, if you hear of anyone looking for a professional.' She put a small stack of white cards on the table next to a discarded tea mug, and nodded to all of us before she left.

'There's a happily betrothed woman if I ever saw one,' said Mrs Collins. 'From being engaged to James Fitzwilliam to Henry the Eighth in half a day.'

'She's moving up in the world, though I hear it doesn't end happily.' I packed all the bits and bobs from the summer into my bag. Hairpins, mostly, and my own spare shawls. The house got chilly now that autumn was creeping in.

'Is James coming to the Duke of Wellington, do you know?' Pamela asked, giving Lady Fitzwilliam's mourning dress one last stroke.

'I think he has something important to take care of first. He said he might come later to see Sarah.'

'I'll come,' said Mrs Smudge, heaving her bag onto her shoulder. It looked as if it had rocks in it. 'I can't pass up the chance to finally say goodbye to you lot.' She went heavily out of the door. Fiona followed her, texting or tweeting or something like that.

'Want a lift?' Samuel asked me. 'I noticed your car wasn't in the car park.'

'It's getting a new clutch. Thanks for the offer, but I'm being picked up. We'll see you there.'

I gathered my stuff, pulled on my leather jacket and stepped out of the staff room into the courtyard of the west pavilion. We'd had a beautiful last day of the season at Eversley Hall. I hummed as I walked round the building, my boots crunching on the gravel. The leaves of the great trees in the front of the building were beginning to turn yellow, echoing the golden stone of the house.

'Goodbye,' I said to it. I let the autumn sun kiss my face.

I was glad I'd decided to finish off the season here. It felt right, though it had been different from the earlier part of the summer. No dramas, no intrigues. Just a quiet interaction with visitors and other interpreters, a calm discussion of history. What really happened.

Well, most of the time.

James had invited me to come back next year. As myself, or as Isabella Grantham, who would become Mrs Fitzwilliam in August 1815. He'd also asked me out to dinner again. I'd said no, on both counts, but suggested someone he might like to be a daily part of Eversley Hall instead.

I breathed in a long, deep breath. The air here at Eversley Hall was different. It felt older, grander. I'd probably miss it occasionally. But I could always come back to visit.

I heard the low rumble of a motorcycle engine and I turned and ran for the staff car park. I got there as Leo drove up on his Triumph. He pulled off his helmet. 'Hey, gorgeous. Going my way?'

I kissed him on the lips. 'You taste like spray paint.'

'Working. I interrupted an important piece of art to take you to the pub to celebrate your last day with your friends. You'll have to do something especially nice for me in return.'

'Clean your brushes?'

'I was thinking something a little more exciting.'

'Maybe we could get married again.'

He gripped my hand. We exchanged a long look. And then he smiled.

I pulled on my own helmet, stuffing my hair up into it, and swung myself onto the back of the motorcycle. I wrapped my arms around Leo and rested my cheek on his shoulder, warmed by the sun.

'Come on,' I murmured. 'Let's live dangerously.'

He hit the throttle, kicking gravel behind us. Leaves fluttered around us as we drove under the trees. On the lawn, three figures leaped and ran. James had thrown his jacket on the grass and his hands were up, while Nelson bounded at his feet. A tow-headed boy in breeches and linen shirt pointed a stick of wood at him as if it were a gun. I couldn't hear what they were saying, or their laughter above the engine, but the game was familiar enough. *Stand and deliver*. Charles Fitzwilliam was practising his future career as a highwayman.

I waved to them as we passed, and then Leo and I were going out through the iron gates into the modern world. I didn't look back once.

Acknowledgements

Thanks to my agent, Georgette Heyer *nonpareil* Teresa Chris; and to my editor, Sherise Hobbs, both of whom worked to make this book the best it can be. Thanks too to all the team at Headline, especially Maura Brickell, Vicky Cowell, Lucy Foley and Joan Deitch.

I owe a great deal to my knowledgeable friends in the Romantic Novelists' Association who helped me fake a knowledge of Regency England, especially historical novelist Louise Allen, and also Joanna Maitland, Beth Elliott, Susanna Kearsley, Janet Mullany and Jan Jones. John S. White of Select Society told me about the secret life of being a costumed interpreter; Lisa Stanhope and Adrian Philpott of the 95th Rifles Living History Society told me about seams and historical re-enactment over a pewter mug of tea in the grounds of Kingston Maurward in Dorset. They have the most beautiful clothes you can imagine, and they spend weekends blowing up fields. Excellent. Elaine Faulkener took me under her wing at my first Regency Ball. For period fashion advice, I also relied on costume historian Gillian Stapleton; corset-maker Charlotte Raine allowed me to experiment with stays.

The Hampshire Regency Dancers were generous and fun-loving, and showed me how to do 'The

Duke of Kent's Waltz'. I quite literally went up to two of them at Chawton House and asked if they were wearing underwear, and they not only took it in their stride but also invited me to a ball, so you have to admire their aplomb. Valerie Webster welcomed me to her Regency dance workshop, and Ruth Ng took her life in her hands and accompanied me as a fellow novice.

Thanks to Donald Ramsay of the National Trust for allowing me a behind-the-scenes look at Basildon Park, Berkshire, interviewing volunteers and workers and spending some quiet alone time with a stately home. Steward Neil Shaw was extremely helpful as well — as were all the National Trust guides and volunteers I spoke with while researching this book and visiting various properties. Lucy Inglis gave invaluable advice about restoring a Georgian house.

Fellow Heyer and Austen fans Brigid Coady, Anna Louise Lucia and Kate Walker showed me how to be a heroine in very trying circumstances. Lee Weatherly and India Grey listened to me babbling about the various difficulties of trying to write a novel in two different time frames, one of them entirely fictional. Helen Corner and the participants in the 2010 Cornerstones Writing Women's Commercial Fiction course were also quite patient with me — as were all of my friends.

I'd like to thank the staff of the Royal Berkshire Hospital for their sensitivity to the grieving parents in their care.

Finally, as always, thanks to Dave and Nathaniel and Mom and Dad, without whom this book wouldn't have been written.

We do hope that you have enjoyed reading this large print book.

Did you know that all of our titles are available for purchase?

We publish a wide range of high quality large print books including:
Romances, Mysteries, Classics
General Fiction
Non Fiction and Westerns

Special interest titles available in large print are:
The Little Oxford Dictionary
Music Book
Song Book
Hymn Book
Service Book

Also available from us courtesy of Oxford University Press:
Young Readers' Dictionary
(large print edition)
Young Readers' Thesaurus
(large print edition)

For further information or a free brochure, please contact us at:
Ulverscroft Large Print Books Ltd.,
The Green, Bradgate Road, Anstey,
Leicester, LE7 7FU, England.
Tel: (00 44) 0116 236 4325
Fax: (00 44) 0116 234 0205

Other titles published by
The House of Ulverscroft:

SPIRIT WILLING, FLESH WEAK

Julie Cohen

Rosie Fox is a really good liar. But when you're a stage psychic who's not actually psychic, you have to be. One night, while pretending to commune with the dead relatives of her audience, Rosie makes a startling prediction — which tragically comes true. Suddenly she's trapped in a media frenzy, spearheaded by the handsome journalist Harry Blake, a man intent on kick-starting his stalled career by exposing Rosie as a fraud. Yet when his interest in her goes from professional to personal, she thinks she can trust him not to blow her cover — but maybe she's making a huge mistake.

DESTINY

Louise Bagshawe

Kate Fox is determined to make her mark in the world. Life hasn't been easy and when she attracts the attention of media mogul Marcus Broder — sophisticated, powerful and wealthy beyond measure — it seems as though all of Kate's dreams have come true. But marriage to Marcus isn't everything she imagined. A closet filled with designer clothes, and nothing to do with her time but shop, lunch and be beautiful, does not bring happiness. Before long, Kate wants out of her marriage, a career of her own, and a chance at love. But Marcus has other ideas, and he will stop at nothing in his attempts to destroy her . . .